I0708584
THE
SAVED
AND THE
SORRY
T. MARIE ALEXANDER

The Saved and the Sorry
Copyright © 2020 by T. Marie Alexander

Copy Editing and proofreading by www.amyjacksonediting.com

Paperback 2nd Edition

Please visit my website at www.tmariealexander.com

ISBN. 978-1-7352320-7-2

WARNING

Although this novel features a young adult main character in high school, it is a dark contemporary romance and is not suitable for younger teens due to mature content and language. The recommended age is eighteen+. Some scenes in this book may be triggering.

PROLOGUE

WRAN

A thunderous crackling erupts around the room as the gun in my hold jerks once, then twice. The middle-aged man standing before me peers down at the budding pool of red soaking his button-down, spreading outwards like creepy inky veins. As if in slow motion, he brings a finger to his chest and touches the torn fabric where my pellets entered him. He groans, but it's so low that it comes out more like a wheeze. He drops to the floor, eyes glossy and wide. My stare shifts to Rox, lying unconscious behind her quaking bastard father, before I really take in what I've done.

The gun drops from my hand, and I take a few steps to get to James Raine. My feet are like lead and the atmosphere smells of copper. I want to back away from this; it isn't me. I don't do things like this. I don't kill without any reverence for life. It's despicable. It's evil.

I'm despicable.

I'm evil.

James shifts to glare up at me. His grip lessens on the shirt. He offers me a lazy smile. "She found," he attempts to say, but a whooping cough chokes him off. He wipes at his lips, blood smearing on the back of his hand. I can see the alarm in his wavering eyes for a split second before he collapses back on the floor. "Someone like me," he manages to choke out before going completely silent and still.

I fall to my knees and shake my head, the weight too heavy. No, I'm nothing like James fuckin' Raine. Crying has me glancing around the room, but I spot no one. My eyes focus back on Rox's lifeless form. She will never love me now. She can't. I'm a murderer. I just murdered someone. I just murdered her fucking father.

Fucking fuck, fuck!

I murdered someone . . .

Crying and footsteps catch my attention, and I force myself to turn around. Cade stands in the doorway, eyes wide and trained on the bloody scene in front of me with a crying little girl in his arms. His shirt is ripped. My gaze drifts over to the crying child. She has long, curly dark hair and doe eyes the color of my own. Tears stream nonstop down her delicate face. I look her up and down, noticing the fabric wound around her tiny leg. She is hurt. This fuck–turd injured my . . . I can't even bring myself to think the word. She deserves better than me too.

Turning back around, I dart across the floor on my knees and grab James. I shake him once, then twice.

"Wake up, you fucker!" I scream into his void face. "Wake up and fight me like a man!"

The wailing behind me grows louder, spurring me on. I pound my fist into James's chest over and over. He needs to wake up. He can't be dead. I didn't kill him. I didn't kill anyone.

"Mommy!" the little girl cries, her youthful voice coming out like broken bells. "Mommy, Mommy, Mommy!"

She sounds like Rox.

I fall on my ass and stare at the red coloring my hands. I did this. I really killed someone. I have taken a life. A hand comes down on my shoulder and I glance behind it to see a worried Cade staring at me.

Ha!

When the rich prick starts looking at me like I'm in deep shit, you know things are screwed beyond fixing. This can't be fixed. I can't fix this.

"We have to get this place cleaned up before the police arrive. Josh is on his way."

I shake my head up at Cade. "This can never be rinsed away. I'm fucked."

I jerk awake in the dark and just lie there, heart hammering and breath coming out in huffs. Lying against the damp sheets, I peer up at nothing. It was just a nightmare. Except it wasn't. I really did kill James Raine, and no matter what, my dreams keep reminding me that I'm just as bad as he. I didn't think twice about shooting him—pointing the gun at his chest and letting it go. I didn't think twice about corrupting evidence to make him look even more guilty.

I cover my eyes with my arm and let out a grunt.

Does that make me the villain?

A movement to my side pulls my attention away from the memory. I can barely make out Rox's silhouette in the dark, but I'd know her in a crowded room with fifty feet between us. She rolls over toward me in her sleep and drapes an arm across my bare chest. She lets out a soft whimper and subconsciously brings her knees up into the fetal position. I stare down at her, even though I can barely see her, and let myself relax to her breathing. At least she's breathing. That's more than James Raine is doing.

I take in a deep breath and then exhale. I repeat that motion until my eyelids are heavy, and the only thing my brain is focusing on is the constant rhythm of both Rox's and my breathing.

We're the ones that are alive.

We survived the nightmare.

And I got my girl back in my arms.

It can only go up from here, right?

My mind briefly flickers back to the glazed-over, lifeless eyes that now seems to haunt my dreams.

It was just a dream.

It was just a dream . . .

It was just a dream!
I am not a murderer.

CHAPTER 1

ROX

5 days ago

I watch the fresh snow in silence as Josh drives us to the Aspen police station. Everyone gave their statements the day I was brought to the hospital, but apparently being drugged by my father doesn't exempt me from being questioned. I don't want to do this. I don't want to sit in a room with people I don't know and relive things that my father did. They couldn't even give me a day after being discharged from the hospital to question me. My father is dead. An evil man is off the streets. Can't they just be happy with that?

I scoff to myself. Of course not.

"Are you paying attention, Roxanna?" Josh's voice with an annoyed tone.

I roll my eyes at his use of my full name. He knows I hate being called Roxanna. Most people just call me Rox or

Roxy. Those are a thousand times better than my full name; that only makes me want to cringe. My father called me that when he was angry and drunk and took it out on me. Up until recently, I didn't remember much of my past. I knew unspeakable things had happened to me. My nightmares of the day I ran away from home reminded me, but I didn't have an exact reason for wanting to be called something other than Roxanna. With my memories resurfacing, I suppose I now have a true reason. A name used in animosity is a name I don't want.

Turning my vision away from the powdery snow and toward the front of the car, I give Josh my full attention. In all honesty, I'm grateful for Josh. According to what Cade told me earlier, Josh helped them get out of a very gruesome situation. He didn't give me too many details as to what happened after I blacked out, but I can guess. Wran loathed my father with a passion no sane person can possess. I was unconscious. Wran most certainly went ballistic. Still, Josh-along with Wran-has been telling me the same thing over and over and over since I was discharged from the hospital: don't mention anything about the letters and don't mention anything about a premeditated plan.

According to them, we were spending spring break in Aspen. My father just happened to show up. I'd pointed out that that didn't make any sense, considering that Lynn also had to give a statement about Harley being taken and that the stories didn't add up. Josh assured me that the stories wouldn't clash. Lynn had no clue where I was prior to the events of this past weekend. She couldn't make a statement on my or the guys' whereabouts.

I don't know why mentioning the letters would make any difference where we are concerned. If anything, it would only make my father look like the psycho he is . . . was. He's dead. Past tense. He can't do anything now. Nothing at all.

"Roxy!" Josh raises his voice when I don't answer him.

"If you yell at her one more time—" Wran starts to threaten but Josh cuts him off.

"I don't mean to yell." He looks at me in the mirror.

I pull my eyes away from Josh's stormy gray ones and glance over at Cade. He gives me a gentle smile and I relax a little. I'm glad he's still here. Cade's the only one that hasn't been nagging and coaching me about what I should and shouldn't say when we get to the precinct.

"I understand," I tell Josh. "I'm not going to tell them anything that would get you all in trouble. You know that."

"I know you wouldn't on purpose, but you have to remember that I'm a cop. If they believe you know more than you are sharing, they will twist your own words to get more information out of you. You have to be careful with your word choice."

"She's not stupid," Wran huffs out.

Josh pulls his gaze from the road and glares over at Wran. "I never said she was, but hey, if you're okay with a miscommunication that could lead them to believe your actions were anything other than self-defense, I won't say more."

I roll my eyes at their bickering. They really need to get over their issues. While I haven't forgiven Josh for his part in this nightmare—let's face it, I suffered the most—I can at least understand the reasoning behind his actions. He is Wran's older brother, after all. He should want to protect Wran from things that could ultimately ruin him. That's what older brothers are supposed to do. I'm sure mine would have done the same thing if he was alive. Josh didn't have to threaten to have Wran imprisoned for being with me three years ago and force him away, but I do get it.

"I understand," I say again before Wran can escalate this. The fact I'm just getting out of the hospital isn't going to rein in his temper. And I really don't want to listen to them argue again over what I should and shouldn't say. "I will be careful with my words, Josh. I will do my best not to say anything to put either of you in a compromising position."

Wran snorts but says nothing further. Neither does Josh. I turn my attention back to the passing scene out my window. Aspen is so beautiful. I don't particularly like snow or the cold—not after being found buried in it as a child—but the snow here makes everything look whimsical. Not to mention the pine trees, which seem to be everywhere here, are a lot more appealing than the leafless trees back home that look like sharp talons.

My phone pings in my coat pocket and I pull it out. There's a text from Cade and I glance over at him, brow arched. Why in the world is he texting me while we're in the same car? He points to my phone and then tilts his head toward the front of the car. Ah, he doesn't want the Belmonts to hear. I input my code into the phone and the message opens.

CADE: U do know u don't have 2 listen 2 them, right?

I glance over at him and nod before replying to his message.

ME: It's easier not 2 argue.

CADE: I get that. But u do have ur own mind. If u don't want 2 lie, don't.

ME: I get that, but I will not get u all in trouble bcuz of me.

CADE: U still have options. No one made us do wat we did.

I stare at his message for a long moment. I know I don't have to do what they say, but they are only in this situation because of me. I went to my father. I strayed from the plan. Sure, they had planned on killing him before that, but I don't think they would have. None of them are bad men. They would have come up with some other way to deal with my father. I believe that wholeheartedly. Wran may argue otherwise, but a guy that is willing to give up his childhood and teen years for someone he claims to hate is not capable of murder without feeling bad about it. He would have maybe beaten my father until he wished he were dead, but Wran wouldn't have gone that far if it wasn't a dire situation. Pressing the power button, I lock the phone and don't reply to Cade's final message. There are no options. I will not betray my family for a man that hurt me. That hurt my Harley.

It takes us another half hour to make it to the police department. When we come to a stop outside of a massive red brick building with huge windows, I gulp. I really have to do this. I really have to talk to them. I look over at Cade and he nods. He unbuckles his seat belt and I mimic his actions. The sooner I get out this car, the sooner I will be inside the building and can get this over with. Cade slides across the seat to me and takes hold of my hand. He squeezes it gently and I open the door and get out.

Wran gets out of the front passenger seat and turns to me. His eyes immediately zero in on Cade's and my joined hands, and he frowns. I tug my hand away from Cade; I don't need Wran getting all territorial over something so simple. Not outside of a freaking police station. He takes hold of my now free hand and pulls me to his front. Wran only lets my hand go to wrap his arms around my waist. His mouth moves to the back of my neck and I freeze for a second. I have no reason to; he's my boyfriend, after all. My father said some things about him I need answers for as well. We haven't had a chance to talk about any of what happened or the things my father said to me; it's mainly been them telling me what to say once we got here. James Raine, though, was many things, but he was never a liar. If he was able to keep tabs on me, then he undoubtedly kept tabs on the people that were surrounding me.

I need to know if what he said has any truth to it.

I need to know if Wran is the reason for so much torment in my life.

Sure, Wran has had his moments of cruelty. I can name so many occasions that I've questioned my thought process when it comes to him. Then I think about all the good things he's done and all the great times. Every time he has done something wrong, he has made up for it. I don't want to believe he loathed me to the point that he had my classmates bully me. That he made Claire hate me.

I glance back at him, taking in his chocolate brown eyes with specks of gold and amber and his dark hair that has grown immensely since he first arrived back in Kingston. He smirks down at me and gives me a swift peck on the lips. My cheeks heat from the small gesture, and I turn away from him.

Nope. I don't believe he's the man my father accused him of being. James just wanted to get under my skin. And apparently it worked if a kiss on the neck has me on edge.

A cool breeze zips past, and I shiver even though Wran bought me a wool coat. Taking that as my indicator to get moving, I walk the snow–cleared path to a set of black steel doors with glass centers, bypassing a black-and-white "Aspen Police" sign. I stare through the glass at all the cops sitting at desks. From what I can see, there are about four setups holding two computers on opposite sides. There are chairs next to each desk. A female cop looks up from whatever she's doing and catches my watchful gaze. She starts to rise from her seat, but I open the door and go inside.

All right, I guess I really am doing this.

A few more people look up and take me in but quickly return to their tasks. I begin to head in the direction of the female cop but stop when a man intercepts my route. He's wearing a pair of crisp black dress slacks and a white button-down shirt with a paisley printed tie. His leather shoulder holster carries a gun, and his badge is on display at his waist. I finally bring myself to look at his face, only to see a kind smile on it. I wasn't really expecting a cop to be smiling at me. His eyes flit to the three guys flanking me and his demeanor shifts. The smile disappears.

"Sheriff Belmont, thank you for coming," he says to Josh.

"I told you we would be here as soon as she was discharged. I never go back on my word," Josh tells the man as I finish taking in the officer's receding hairline, peppered goatee, and green eyes.

The man shifts his attention back to me and holds out his hand. "You must be Roxanna Raine. I'm Detective Williams."

Biting down on the inside of my cheek, I hesitate to give the man my hand. When I finally do, he grins down at me. I don't return the gesture. All I want is to get this questioning over with so I can go back to the cabin and sleep. I took some pain meds before leaving the hospital, and the nurse that checked on me said the meds could make me drowsy. They are supposed to help some with the pain in my shoulder from where my father stabbed me. Right now it's manageable, but I'm tired as all crap.

"I suppose these gentlemen told you the reasoning behind this summoning?" Detective Williams asks.

I nod.

"Right, then." He looks over my shoulder at the guys. "You all can take a seat, and I'll take Miss Raine back. It shouldn't take too long."

Turning a little, I watch as all the guys nod in understanding. I thought they would be coming back with me, like in the movies when actors stand outside the door, looking inside through a one-way mirror. Cade and Josh make their way over to some metal chairs and sit. Wran must see my confusion because he turns me around toward him and cups my face. He lowers his forehead to mine and looks me in the eyes.

"Don't be nervous. We're all right out here, including your dickwad of a friend." Wran kisses my forehead and pulls away, going over to where his brother and Cade sit.

I turn back around to the cop and inhale. I guess there's no time like the present to do this. Not that I really have a choice in the situation. It's not like I could just skip out on the questioning. The man walks past the desk and I follow him. He opens a metal door that leads to a narrow corridor. I take one more peek over my shoulder at the guys before following the detective. This is all going to go fine. I know what to say; I know what not to say. Besides, there isn't much I can really tell them. I was unconscious for the actual crime. I didn't see anything.

Detective Williams comes to a stop outside a metal door with windows on each side of it. He opens the door and motions me inside. I take in the dark gray concrete wall and the single table that's bolted to the floor, along with the chairs that have chains on them. Blinds are drawn on the windows, and the only source of light is coming from a pendant fixture that's hanging above the table. I gulp and look back at the detective.

"Why are there chains on the chair?" I ask him.

"Don't worry about that." He motions to one of the chairs. "Please take a seat. Can I get you anything? Water? Coffee?"

"Coffee would be great. Thanks."

"I'll go get that and my partner, and then we can begin."

I nod and watch him leave the room, closing the door behind him.

Biting down on my bottom lip, I take in the concrete room once more. If this room is meant as an intimidation tactic, the goal is accomplished. I don't know how anyone could sit in this dark, gloomy room and not be pressured to spill their guts. There is literally a spotlight on me. I peek up at the hanging light and gulp before turning my eyes back to the door.

Moments later Detective Williams reenters the stone chamber with a white paper cup in hand and a tall lanky man holding a folder on his tail. They make their way over to the table and sit opposite me. The tall guy pulls out a small black recorder and presses a button. Detective Williams hands me the cup, and I examine the brown liquid that is my obsession. Bringing the steaming substance to my lips, I gulp a hefty amount of it back, ignoring the burn and watching the men over the thin rim. I set the cup down just as the second cop flips through the folder that's overflowing with papers. I stare at them both, not sure how to start this interrogation.

"Thank you for coming in today, Miss Raine. I'm Officer Neilson, and we will be recording this session," the tall guy says, and points to the recorder.

"Okay," is all I say. It's not like I can say anything else. Pretty sure I would have been arrested if I'd refused to come in.

"Fifty-six hours ago we received a distress call," Detective Williams starts. "When we arrived at the location, we found a body on the floor." Neilson hands Williams a piece of paper and he sets it down in front of me. "Can you identify the person in this photo?"

A gasp leaves my lips as I stare at my father's wide, dead eyes. Scrapes, bruises, and blood mar his face. Cade told me in the hospital that Wran shot my father. The purpling underneath his eyes doesn't look like a simple gunshot. This looks like my father decided to play with a bull, got trampled, got back up and played some more. There's no way Wran only shot him.

"Miss Raine, please answer the question," Neilson demands.

I nod my head. "Yes, I know the person."

"Can you inform us how you know the deceased?"

I just stare at Neilson. Is this a trick question? They already know who he is to me. "H–he is my father."

Was, I remind myself again. He was my father.

And now he's dead.

Both policemen nod in acknowledgment. Detective Williams takes the folder from Neilson and goes through it. He watches me for a second before he asks his next question. "Are you aware that James Raine kidnapped a two–year–old toddler that goes by the name of Harley Raine from her social service home?"

"Yes," I answer.

"What is your relation to Harley Raine?"

I stare at Detective Williams for a long time. Other than Cade, no one outside of the family services and the Belmonts knows about Harley. I've tried so hard to keep her a secret, and yet these men are asking me to blow the door off that. I don't understand why they are asking me these questions. They know who I am. They know the answer to these already. Why must I give them information they don't need?

"She's my daughter," I say so low that I'm sure the recorder didn't pick it up.

"Please answer a bit clearer," Neilson tells me as he shifts in his chair.

Looking over at the recorder, I inhale and do as ordered. "Harley Raine is my daughter."

"Where were you during the time when James Raine took Harley Raine from her home?"

I look Neilson square in the eyes and answer him the way Josh and Wran told me to answer. "I was in the back seat of a car headed here to Aspen."

Williams searches through the folder that I take holds all their notes for this case. My eyes move over to the door and then around the room—anywhere to keep me from focusing on the two cops in front of me. I don't like deceiving the authorities. I don't like lying, especially when I know it can backfire. I bet Josh regrets giving Wran that ultimatum now. If Wran wouldn't have been forced to leave, none of this would be happening. Josh wouldn't be putting his integrity and career on the line. And none of us would be going through these interrogations.

"Why were you and your friends coming to Aspen? According to a May Fields, that we contacted back in Kingston, you were scheduled to work the Friday prior to the events."

Crap!

I stare wide-eyed at Williams, not sure how to answer. Josh and Wran didn't think of that question. I don't think anyone thought these cops would contact anyone back in Kingston. And I can't tell him that I wasn't at work that day due to a dispute Wran and I had that ended in me passing out in a closet.

Taking a long sip of the bitter coffee, I try to think of something to tell them that might in the least sound believable. When I finally come up with a lie that sounds good enough, I set the coffee back down on the table.

"Cade invited me to go on spring break with him—even said I could bring Wran. Since it was so sudden, I thought it would be best to just go and deal with the consequences at a later date. I had planned on telling May I was sick." My voice trails off in hope of selling the lie.

It sounded decent, and part of it is true.

What teenager hasn't lied to their boss to get out of work? I'm positive I am not the first.

Detective Williams narrows his eyes at me, but he doesn't call me out on my fib. Either he can't tell it is a lie or he's going to try to trap me in a lie. Josh said they do that sometimes. He leans over to his partner and whispers something to him. My eyes go back and forth between the men. Is he allowed to do that? I thought everything had to be recorded.

"Okay, Miss Raine, can you please tell us how you were able to locate James and Harley when the officers in your town couldn't do it?"

Easy. "He sent me a text message with a photo of her. I recognized the room."

Williams nods. "Has he contacted you prior to that?"

I uncross my legs under the steel table and then cross them again. Shaking my head, I tell the officer, "No."

"A Lynn Adams with social services informed us of a letter that was left in Harley's bed indicating that you were aware of a potential threat. Did you receive any letters from your father?"

I shake my head again, biting down on my inner cheek and attempting to remember exactly what Lynn told me last Saturday night on the phone when I called. I don't remember. The only thing I recall is freaking out when she told me Harley was missing. Everything else was a non-issue. I really hope Lynn doesn't suspect that I was aware of the threat and didn't say anything. That's a surefire way to assure I never see my daughter again. Maybe I should have told someone about the letters. Maybe I should have confided in Josh. He is the sheriff, after all. He could have done something. Ohmygod, what if I ruined my chances of getting Harley back? Surely that can't be held against me. I am the one that found her. Not them. Ohmygod, I'm screwed!

I run my hand through my hair and shake my head again. Calm down, Rox. Calm down. If they catch me in a lie, I really am out of luck. "No, sir. I didn't receive anything from my father before the message he sent at the cabin."

I'm going to hell.

"Are you sure about that?" Neilson asks in an accusatory tone. "Lynn handed over the letter for evidence and it said he warned you. The only way he could do that is if he had previous contact. Now, would you like to answer the question again?"

Uh oh.

My eyes flick between the men setting in front of me, their eyes never wavering from me. Neilson raises a brow and his hands ball on top of the table. Hives spread over my arms and I shake my head again, sticking with my answer. I will not say anything that will cause a messy situation for Cade, Josh, or Wran. They did what they did to help me. To save me. Detective Neilson starts to lean forward, but Williams stops him from moving. He lays the folder on the table and rests his hands on it.

"Roxanna," Detective Williams starts, "you do understand that withholding information is a crime, right? You don't have to be afraid of us. If you had any type of communication prior to the message you received, we need to know."

Williams gives me a kind smile that doesn't reach his eyes. He sounds sincere, unlike Neilson, who just seems to want to bag this case. Sighing, I relent a little. I can tell them something without outing my guys.

I nod. "I got one letter. I wasn't sure it was from my father. It happened at school and I thought one of the other girls had put it in my locker. I thought it was a cruel prank since the news had been talking about my father. It wasn't until I got the text message with the picture of Harley that I even let myself believe it was him."

"That wasn't so hard, was it?" Neilson's comment comes out like a sneer and I ignore him. He can play bad cop all he wants, but he's not going to break me. I have too much to lose.

Williams sits back in his chair, cracks his knuckles, and proceeds. "In your own words, can you tell us exactly what happened leading up to the death of James Raine?"

I nod and begin retelling the events of that day. "I had just arrived in Aspen with Cade; Wran took a plane, so he arrived a day earlier. I was excited to see him, and we sort of started making out—"

"Let me get this straight," Neilson cuts in. "You arrived in a car a day later with a boy that is not Mr. Belmont and then proceeded to make out with Mr. Belmont?"

"Yes." I tilt my head down so he won't see the heat rising to my cheeks. When he states it like that, it makes me sound like some floozy.

"Seems odd that you would rather ride in a car with a guy that isn't your boyfriend for such a long period of time."

"I never said Wran was my boyfriend," I protest, even though it sounds halfhearted.

"I just assumed since you were making out with him and he's Harley's father."

"Who told you that?"

"Doesn't matter. Please continue, Miss Raine."

I stare at Officer Neilson for a long moment. These two obviously know more than they are saying, but oh well. Neilson can try to get under my skin all he wants, but I'm not going to budge. Not on this. Turning slightly, I give Williams my full attention. At least he's not being an uber dick.

"Anyways, I told Wran we had to stop. Cade was downstairs, and I didn't want to make him uncomfortable in his own cabin. He invited us, after all, and he didn't have to do that. We went downstairs and I got the message then. It was a picture of my daughter in a yellow dress, in a pink room, playing. We called my father and he wanted me to come to him. Cade and Wran disagreed, so I snuck out of the cabin. When I made it to my grandmother's abandoned house, my father was there waiting for me. He had Harley and was talking about how we were going to be a family. When I disagreed, he took me from the pink room and down the hall to the green room. He drugged me and I don't remember anything after that. He was very much alive when I passed out."

Both of the police nod.

"That's pretty much what Cade and Wran told us," Williams confirms.

Biting down on my lip, I scoot to the edge of the chair. "Is that all?"

"Just a couple more questions and then you're free to go," Williams tells me.

Neilson lets out a humph, and I glare at him. What is this man's problem? I understand that as a cop his job is to get to the bottom of things, but he's just being rude. He levels his murky brown eyes with mine, a grimace on his face. I don't know what's up with the whole good cop/bad cop these two are playing at, but I wish they would just let me go. I obviously didn't kill my own father. I have medical records to prove it.

Williams shoves his partner and Neilson's hard eyes pull away from me.

"Is there any evidence to prove your story? Maybe your phone?" Williams asks.

I shake my head. "No. Wran sort of threw it against the wall when my father contacted me. But you can get my call list from the store."

At least that's the only time my father contacted me via phone. That's a saving grace.

"Have you spoken to anyone about this incident?" Williams continues to question me.

"Only Cade when he told me my father was dead at the hospital. I haven't really wanted to talk about it. I don't know how to take it."

"That's understandable," Williams tells me. He rises from the chair and reaches a hand to me. "Thank you for coming in today. We really appreciate your cooperation."

I rise from my chair and take his hand. Thank God this is over. Williams motions to the door and walks ahead of me. "If we have anymore questions, we will call. You are free to leave."

I bolt from the room before he has time to change his mind. When I get back to the lobby, all three of the guys rise from their chairs. Wran comes over to me and takes my hand, bringing it up to his lips. He presses a kiss into my palm.

"Now, let's get the fuck out of here," he mumbles into my hand.

CHAPTER 2

WRAN

1 day ago

We left Aspen right after the cops were done interrogating Rox. Josh thought it would be a bad idea to stick around. I kind of wanted to hit the slopes, but Rox had the few things we brought packed in under fifteen minutes. She forced us into the car and threatened a particular body part that I deem essential, and not just for pissing. We arrived back in Kingston faster than we were supposed to.

I take a swig of my whiskey just as Rox prances into the living room of our small apartment in a short black dress with long sleeves. Her blue hair is hanging loose around her shoulders, and the hem of the dress flutters around her lean legs, making them seem to go on forever. Not to mention she's wearing thigh-high black boots. Fuck, she's hot. Rox

frowns at me when I take another sip of the contents in the glass.

If dreaming about killing the fucker wasn't enough, now I have to attend his funeral. Rox thought giving the bastard a proper burial was the decent thing to do. Ha! I would have burned his body and flushed the ashes down the toilet. James fucking Raine doesn't deserve a proper burial. He doesn't deserve the amount of time Rox put into this funeral. Granted, she didn't have to do much; he had a will that laid out exactly how he wanted to be buried. Can you believe that? What a pretentious fucker!

Rox takes a step toward me, eyes on the glass in my hand. I set it down on the small island, but her gaze doesn't leave the tumbler. She goes to grab it but I slide it away from her. No way is she making me go to a funeral for that man—the man who took every damn thing from me and nearly took her—without something to keep me in my right mind.

"Why are you drinking?" she asks me in a low voice. Her eyes pull away from the glass and she finally takes me in. "Why aren't you dressed? We're supposed to meet Cade and Josh at the gravesite in forty minutes."

I look down at my clothes, a simple white T-shirt and blue jeans. There is no way I'm dressing up for that man. She can parade around in dresses and heels like the man didn't ruin her life all she wants, but I won't pretend to care about James Raine.

"I'm dressed," I tell her, and gulp down the rest of the whiskey.

"Wran!" She says my name like a slap, and I smirk at her. "Please put on something else. You have a nice suit."

I rise and step closer to Rox, my eyes raking over her slim form. Reaching up, I finger a piece of her hair. "Nope! You want me to go, then I'm wearing this. Not like I give a fuck about him. I don't even see why we are having a funeral. He doesn't deserve one. Besides, no one is coming. This is a waste of money and time. He didn't even put you in the will."

Rox takes a step away from me as if my words physically hurt her. It makes no sense why she cares so much. She should be the main one drinking and celebrating her father's death. After everything he put her through, I don't see why she is pretending to mourn him. Sure, it's the proper thing to do. No one here in Kingston expects her to care about the bastard, though.

Grabbing the hem of her dress, I tug her back to me and wrap an arm around her waist. I lean down and kiss the side of her neck, loving whatever soap she used to bathe this morning. "How about we ditch this thing and go have a celebratory fuck. We can fuck James Raine out of our systems."

Her eyebrows go up and a tiny gasp leaves her pink lips. She shoves me away. The next thing I know, a loud smack sounds throughout the room. I bring my hand to my cheek and rub, grinning at her. She's hot when she's angry. Her face gets all red and her cheeks puff out. It's cute and hot.

"Don't be a prick!" she yells at me and rounds the island to the apartment-sized refrigerator that came with this place. She pulls out a bottle of water and downs it in one go. Bet she could use something stronger. "Go get dressed."

"No," I protest. I'm not dressing up for that man.

Rox whirls around to face me, clutching the plastic bottle in her hands. "Why are you acting like this? You've known about this funeral for the past four days."

I pull a flask from the pocket of my jacket lying on the stool next to me, unscrew it, and take a drink. Usually I'm not a huge drinker. The last time I drank this much, I ended up hurting Rox, which I haven't forgiven myself for. But when she mentioned giving this man a celebratory home-going service, I sorta flipped. And today, well today I don't want to remember standing at a graveside listening to meaningless talk about a man that everyone loathes.

"Maybe I'm acting like this because a blue-haired freak thought it would be a good idea for me to go to a funeral for a man I hate."

Rox looks away from me and at the floor. "He was my father, Wran."

"Yeah, and it was Josh and I that raised you. He was too busy being in prison for murdering your nanny. You have no reason to want to do this."

"You know what? Screw you!" she shouts at me. "You have no right to say that! Sure, you and Josh took me in, but he gave me life. That man that you hate so much is the reason I am here and the reason you have a child. That's never going to change. He was my father, even if he was a murdering bastard. You can't really judge him, now, can you?"

Before I know what I'm doing, I grab the tumbler off the island and throw it. Rox ducks and the glass shatters against the wall behind her. She peeps up at me from her crouched position on the floor, shaking and eyes wide. I take a step towards her and stop.

Fuck!

I can't believe I just did that.

Closing my eyes, I throw my head back and groan. See what this bastard makes me do? This is all his fault.

"I'm sorry. I didn't mean to do that. I'm just tired."

"You're drunk." She says it like a fact.

I'm not drunk though. I promised myself I wouldn't get drunk again after I hurt her.

"Let's just go to this service and get it over with. I'll be fine."

Rox creeps back up with a wary expression painting her face. Her hand goes to the spot on her shoulder where she got stitches and rubs it. Her eyes turn to slits, and I suppose I deserve that. She inches around the island and over to the wicker chair I took from my pops' townhome a few weeks back. She gives me one last scathing look before she heads out the door. I really messed up this time. Putting the flask back in my pocket, I follow her. The sooner we get the memorial done with, the sooner we can forget about James Raine.

Ha!

I thought when we killed him it would be the end of this mess, but he's still ruining our lives. Shaking my head, I head out of the apartment and down the rusting staircase. At least it's not cold today. Rox and I really would be having a problem if she were trying to get me to stand in the freezing cold for that man.

As I make my way over to my car, I notice Rox sitting on the driver's side. I shake my head at her, but she doesn't slide across the seat. Opening the door, I arch a brow at her. It's very rare that I let anyone drive my car. And the only time she has driven it was that one time it was raining and she had to work at Aunt May's diner. Don't get me wrong, I love Aunt May—she's the sweetest woman I know—but waitressing isn't a job I see for my Rox.

"What do you think you're doing?" I ask her. "Scoot over."

She shakes her head almost violently. She really needs to stop defying me. "No, you've been drinking and I'm not letting you drive while drunk."

I'm not drunk.

I can drive just fine.

I don't tell her that though. She would just argue against me, and I don't want to argue with her again. "Fine."

I round the car and get inside. This is ridiculous. I can drive my own car.

"Put your seat belt on," she tells me.

Turning in the seat, I stare her down. When has she ever known me to wear a seatbelt? She points to the belt, and I mutter gibberish under my breath to keep from lashing out at her again. I don't know what's wrong with me today. Scratch that. I know exactly why I'm off the rails: James Raine. I can't escape him.

I fasten the belt and Rox reaches her hand out. I take the keys from my pocket and drop them in her hold.

"Thank you," she mutters and pulls away from the red brick buildings.

We come to a stop on side of the road behind a red pickup truck with black stripes. Of course Cade would be here early. Hell, I'm pretty sure that rich prick would do just about anything to get closer to Rox. The driver's door to the truck opens and the prick steps out in a black suit and nice, glossy black shoes. I bet they're Italian or some shit. I slump back against the seat and pull my eyes away from him.

I focus on the black gate with lettering that reads "Dixie County Cemetery" and the rows upon rows of tombstones laid into the ground. Farther back, behind the flat ones, are giant ones that look like monuments. I bet that's where James will be buried. Where everyone can see just how noteworthy he thought he was. I pull out the flask again and take a couple huge gulps. Here goes nothing. I get out of the car and push through the gates.

"Wran!" Rox hollers after me, but I ignore her and walk the gravel path until I see Josh standing with an older man in head-to-toe black. His suit looks hot—the overcoat coming down to his feet. He has on a black hat that's overkill, and a beard that looks to have not seen a razor in years. Where did Rox find this guy?

I come to a stop next to Josh. He turns from the priest and looks at me, eyeing the open container in my hand. Taking another mouthful, I grin at the asshole. Just because he helped in Aspen doesn't mean he's off the hook. He still lied to me. My daughter is still not with me.

"This isn't an Irish funeral. Put it away," Josh commands.

"Yeah, well, y'all should have thought of that before making me attend this thing." I tip the bottle back, but nothing comes out. Damn. I should have brought the whiskey bottle. I'm nowhere near ready to stand here and listen to pleasantries about this man.

The crunching of gravel behind me has me turning around to see Rox and Cade strolling up to us side by side. I grunt at the sight of them—well, him with her. As much as I hate to admit, his black suit complements her dress well. Maybe I should have worn the damn suit. Them looking like they belong together doesn't sit well with me. I reach for Rox and she recoils a little. If it weren't for the fact that I'm ogling her like a piece of filet mignon, I wouldn't have noticed. From the way Cade steps forward and clutches her hand in his, I'd say he noticed too. He pulls her around me and goes to stand next to Josh.

Just great.

Just fucking great.

That's going to get nipped in the bud fast. I might have played nice in Aspen when Rox was in danger, but I'll be damned if I let this dickwad believe he's her knight in shining armor. That spot is already filled, and she isn't looking for a replacement.

At least I hope not.

After what happened, she might be.

I . . . I killed someone. I took someone's life. I played God, and now I'm damned. James Raine made me become the very thing I never wanted to be. If Rox can still love me after that, then she's more damaged than I am. Not to mention I threw a glass at her an hour ago. Rox has no reason to not go searching for someone better. I should set her free from my nightmare of a reality, but I can't.

My lost girl needs me.

Me. Not Cade.

And I need her. She's the only one that can tame the beast clawing at my mind and being. Without her, I just might break and there will be no redeeming me.

Why did I have to pull that trigger?

I reach in my pocket for the bottle, before remembering that I already guzzled it down. Shit, I can't believe I drank all that. Glancing up, I look over at Rox. Her eyes are on the big open hole in front of us, and for the first time since coming over here, I look down at the grave. The casket is black and gold—too luxurious to house a murderer. It's also closed. I don't even want to think about what his face looks like after what I did. Pretty sure a mortician couldn't have fixed it. Pulling my attention away from the closed casket, I glance over the hole at Rox. I frown when I see Cade's hand planted on her lower back.

And he says he's okay with being friends.

I go over to their side of the grave just as the priest starts to talk, and relieve Cade's hand from Rox's back, tugging her over to me in the process. She glares at me for a second before coming over. That's my girl. I pull her into me and lean down to her ear.

"I'm sorry. I'm not going to hurt you." I whisper so no one else can hear.

No one here needs to know what goes on in my place. And Josh certainly doesn't need to get any more ideas that will lead him to threaten me again. It's been three years since he sent me away for being with Rox, and I'm still highly pissed at him for taking the one thing that means the world to me. I should be over it by now, but I'm not. And I'm not giving him more ammo to use against me where she is concerned.

Rox tilts her head up to me. "You're drunk at my father's funeral," she hisses at me, venom leaving her lips like a bullet aiming straight for my heart. "I've never asked much from you, Wran, but this is too far."

"I'm not drunk. I haven't had nearly enough to drink," I mumble back to her. "But you know I never wanted to be here. I didn't like the idea when you first voiced it, and I hate it even more now. I killed this man, Rox. A murderer shouldn't be attending his victim's funeral. It's sick."

It makes me sick.

And not just because I hate the man. This is all so wrong.

"I didn't think of it that way." Her voice sounds regretful and I wish I hadn't said anything. I don't want her to feel bad. If I'm sadistic, then Rox is the definition of altruistic. Not in a good way. She'll put others first even if it pains her. I should know; I've used that against her many times.

Rox turns her head forward just as the priest starts to recite a scripture. "You know I don't see you that way, right? As a murderer, I mean. You did it for me. To save me."

She might not see me that way, but I am a killer.

If anyone other than the four of us around this grave knew what I did, they would see me that way too. As the sick, barbaric bastard I am. Only an animal could do what I did and stand at this funeral.

I don't say anything else to her, just hold her while she listens. She knows how I feel now. She might not know the exact extent, but she gets it. I don't know how people live with themselves after doing something like this. It's been a week since it happened, and the fucker won't leave my mind. Am I destined to regret this forever? Hell, the man deserved it. I mean, I could have shot him anywhere. I could have spared his life. I could have done so many things differently. I could have fought like a man instead of a person possessed.

Shaking my head, I mentally scold myself.

Stop!

Stop thinking about James Raine!

He didn't think about harming Rox or Harley, and they are his blood. If he felt no guilt over his actions, neither should I. I did the world a justice. He would have only been sent back to prison if I hadn't done it. Back to prison with a chance he would be set free again. A chance he would come after Rox again. I did the right thing; I will not be sorry for this. I won't let him make me the villain. My daughter is now safe. Fuck, daughter. That still sounds strange. Rox is safe too.

I'm a good man.

I'm a decent man.

Someone elbows me in the side, and I turn to look at Cade. He has a handful of dirt and he tilts his head downward to the ground. I glance around the small group and sure enough, everyone has a handful of soil. Rox also has a yellow rose in her grasp. Where the hell did she get a yellow rose? I didn't even feel her leave. She smiles at me, but it is not the usual smile she gives me. It's void, alone. It doesn't reach her eyes, and the pink that usually tints her cheeks when we're in the same vicinity is absent. I did that to her. I've lost her just after getting her back. Bending down, I grab a handful of the dirt and turn back to the open grave.

"Would either of you like to say a few words to the departed?" the priest asks us.

We shake our heads. Anything that came out of our mouths wouldn't be suitable for a man of God. He would probably flee in terror and renounce his oath after listening to the words we would speak.

"None?" the priest makes sure. When we nod again, he continues. "All right, then. Dust to dust, ashes to ashes, may this soul return home and rest in peace."

May this soul burn in hell for all eternity.

Josh, Cade, and I take turns tossing our dirt onto the casket. When it's Rox's turn, she just stares down at the casket. Silent. I place a hand on her shoulder and she winces. Right, the stitches.

"It's okay," I whisper into her ear. "You were right. He was your father. It's okay to grieve him."

I don't know why she would. The man was a terrible father, but whatever Rox is experiencing, I want her to know that it's okay. The fact that I hated her because of him was something she never held against me, and I shouldn't hold her emotions against her. Besides, I'm pretty sure if my pops died, I would mourn him too. My pops isn't the best father either, but he is still my pops.

Exhaling, Rox tosses the dirt onto the casket, followed by the yellow rose. I wrap my arms around her shoulders and hug her gently to me, inhaling the sweet scent of her hair. Cade reaches for her hand and I frown. I want so badly to tell him to keep his hands off what's mine, but I don't.

I'm not going to let him get under my skin. She takes his hand, their fingers winding together, and I don't know how to feel about that. The priest says a few more words before dismissing us. Josh turns and leave, but the three of us stay in place.

"Someone will bring the memorial statue your father picked out later today. You can come back tomorrow to see it if you like," the priest tells Rox, and he comes over to us. "If you ever need to talk to someone, the church is always open."

Rox nods, and the priest gives her a small smile before leaving. We all turn in unison and watch him go. When we can no longer see him, we all relax. Being here felt like being a puppet—a string on my sanity being tugged to its breaking point. I glance down at the casket and the single yellow rose on the pile of dirt. I'm positive yellow roses aren't the norm for homegoing services.

"Why the yellow rose?" I ask Rox as we make our way back toward the graveyard's gates.

"Because I'm free now," is all she says as she rounds my car and gets in the driver's seat.

CHAPTER 3

ROX

Present

Bringing my hand up and fingering my new blonde locks, I stare at myself in the small mirror and sigh. Today is going to be hard. The news has been running stories on my father and me ever since we arrived back here in Kingston. I seriously started to second-guess going back to school today, but I must face everyone. I don't even want to know what Claire is going to say on the matter. She's probably going to gloat about how she was right three years ago when she started the rumor that I was pregnant. She told people that was my reason for leaving school for the remainder of freshman year and part of sophomore. Of course she was right, but there was no proof then. I could deny it. With the news reporting about Harley, it's a little impossible to do so now. Ugh, I hate this!

Breathing in and out a few times, I turn away from my reflection and grab the door handle leading out to the hallway. I open it a little and peek out, listening for any life in the house. I don't really want to run into Wran before school. We haven't talked since the burial ceremony yesterday, and I kind of don't want to. He acted like a jerk all day. I thought once the funeral was over he would stop being so on edge and cranky and mean, but nope. He took a nap yesterday evening and woke up even worse. He stormed out of the apartment and didn't come back until late last night.

When I don't hear him, I walk out of the bathroom, tugging the hem of my skirt down a little. The smell of fresh ground coffee tells me that my beverage of choice is done brewing and I head to the kitchen. Entering our open-concept kitchen/living room area, I come to a stop. Wran is sitting at the island with a newspaper in his hand, sipping from a mug. I really didn't want to deal with him before school.

I ignore his presence and go over to the makeshift coffee bar and pour some into my favorite pink mug. I take a sip and the bitter taste of plain coffee sends a rejuvenating burst throughout me. It's not Starbucks, but it's still just as good. Ever since Cade started picking me up for school, I've been brewing more of my own coffee at home. There's not much time to stop at the cafe and wait in a line—not with Cade picking me up so close to the first bell.

Turning around, I bump into Wran, who's now standing right behind me. His eyes roam up and down my body. I can tell that he's clenching his teeth from how tense his face is and how hard his eyes are on me. His hands ball into fists and his frown turns into a downright scowl.

"What happened to your hair? What the fuck are you wearing?" he asks, eyes flickering back and forth between my head and my body. His question comes out strained as if he's trying to keep himself from yelling at me.

I bring the mug up to my mouth and take another sip of the coffee before looking down at my outfit. Yesterday, after he stormed off, I called Cade and told him I wanted a makeover. We drove to Arlington and got my hair dyed blonde. Platinum blonde. The way Cade's eyes bugged out and he choked on his energy drink was the funniest thing I've seen in a long time. At first, he said he liked my natural hair color better, that blonde made me look like every other fake girl at our school. But I didn't want natural. My father always loved my long sable locks, and I wanted to get as far away from that as possible. After a while, though, Cade took a liking to it, even saying that I look like Marilyn Monroe and should buy a short white dress. We spent the whole evening at the Arlington Mall after that.

This is the first Wran is seeing of my new hair and pur-chases from yesterday. I don't think the leather miniskirt and cropped black graphic tee are too bad. It's a departure from my usual cutesy, girl-next-door attire, but I like it. It's perfect.

"Clothes," I finally answer him, and sidestep him, going to the other side of the island and taking a seat.

"Clothes?" He turns around, eyes wide as if shocked by my statement. "Really, Rox? You went from fucking Pollyanna to Mary Magdalene overnight. Every guy at Kingston High is going to come apart in their pants if you walk in like that. No. Go change!"

I shake my head at him. I'm not changing. It's not my fault if guys can't control themselves when they see a girl in a short skirt. It's also not my problem. "I like this outfit. I look hot."

Wran comes over to my side of the island, and he takes me in again. He licks his bottom lip and trails his hands up the outside of my thighs. "I never said you weren't hot. The sight of you alone could give Aphrodite a run for her money. That being said, I don't want any guy gawking at what's mine."

I'm not sure what to say to that, so I just gulp down the rest of my coffee. His sweet words don't change the fact that yesterday when I needed him to act like a boyfriend, to be there for me as I buried my father, he acted like a petulant child instead. No, he acted worse. Not even Harley acts like that, and she's only two.

A knock on the door pulls my attention away from Wran, and I set my mug on the island. I guess it's time to face my peers. I step aside Wran and head to the door. He grabs my wrist and pulls me back to him.

"Please change," he says again as he rubs circles on the underside of my wrist.

"No," I state and pry myself away from him. I go over to the door and open it. Cade stands in the doorway with a Starbucks cup in his hand. He hands it over to me as he looks me up and down, pretty much like Wran did when he saw my look. Cade might have been with me when I picked everything out, but I didn't try them on. I don't like trying on clothes in public places.

"Wow," he says, and I smile.

Why couldn't that have been Wran's first reaction?

"It looks okay?" I ask him and tug on the hem of the skirt again. I haven't worn anything this short in a really long time. "I'm a bit nervous."

He nods and removes my hand from the skirt. "You look better than okay."

"Thank you. I need to grab my backpack and we can go."

He nods again, and I rush down the hall to my room. I grab my backpack off the floor at the foot of the bed and quickly go through it, making sure I have my sketchbook and pens. I'm not sure why, but for some reason the brushes are calling my name. I haven't wanted to paint in such a long time.

I go back out to the living room only to find Cade and Wran at a standoff. After what happened in Aspen, I assumed they would be on better terms. While neither of them has given me any details as to what happened after I ventured away from them at the cabin, I know they had to put their differences aside to find me and Harley. Cade was the only hope Wran had in tracking me down.

"What's going on?" I ask them as I shift on my feet. This doesn't look good.

"Nothing," they both say, and Cade backs up.

It's still quite mind-boggling to me that Cade is actually Caden, my childhood friend. Times like this, though, when he's plainly lying to me, I remember that the Caden from my childhood would have never done that. He would have just stayed quiet and apologized later for upsetting me. This version of him doesn't care about lying and hiding truths.

"Then I guess we can go. I don't want to be late."

Cade turns to me and takes my backpack, leaving the apartment. I stay back for a moment and glare at Wran. I'm done with all the lying. He's going to tell me what that was about.

"Wran, what were you guys talking about? And don't say nothing," I demand of him.

He leans into me, giving me that stupid cocky smirk that always makes me weak. I bat away the fluster growing in my stomach and cross my arms over my chest. Wran trails a finger up the side of my right thigh, ignoring my gesture. His finger keeps going up and up and up until his hand teases at the lace of my bralette, leaving a fiery trail behind his touch. I shove his hand away from me, even though it felt nice, and stomp my feet at him. Yeah, I know I'm too old to do that.

"I was reminding your other boyfriend that I'm the one you come home to every day, and that I will always be the one you run to," he tells me and then turns away.

I gawk at his back as he goes back over to the bar and picks up the newspaper. "You know it's not like that with Cade. He's—"

"Just a friend," Wran glances over his shoulder at me and finishes my sentence. "So you keep saying. Go to school, Rox."

I frown at him. Cade is just a friend. I don't understand why he thinks we're more than that. I surely haven't given him any reason to think I'm the disloyal one. If anything, the way he's been acting should make me want to be. I just can't. I let out a sigh and leave for school. There's no use talking to him about this. He's going to believe what he wants.

When I get in Cade's truck, he bumps the music up a few notches and swerves out of the parking lot. He's been trying to improve my taste in music, so he says, ever since I told him his favorite song was sexist. Admittedly, some of his music is great. I'll never tell him that though; he's already too confident.

When we make it to the school, Cade pulls around the side to senior parking. Neither one of us move. Walking through those double doors is going to change how everyone has perceived me over the last few years. Claire is going to be proven right, and the teachers. . . I can already imagine the pity that's going to be painted on every single one of my teacher's faces. Especially my art teacher. Not to mention Tasha. Josh's whole cover-up for that got blown out the window the moment the news started reporting on me.

I lean back against the seat, my breathing coming out in sharp gasps. I can't do this. I can't walk through those doors.

"Hey, hey." Cade reaches over and unbuckles my belt. "Calm down. I promise you everything will be okay. Ignore them. I'll be by your side all day."

My eyes cut to him. "Last I checked, we don't have the same classes."

He grins and runs his hands through his tousled golden hair. "That may be, but no one is going to talk smack to you in front of the teachers. You're safe. And if someone does say anything, just let me know."

I roll my eyes at him and take in a deep breath. Sitting in this truck isn't going to change anything. Even if I did go home, everyone would still know. It's not like I can just not come back here or never leave my apartment. Kingston is a small town—too small, if you ask me. I would have to become a hermit in order to get out of what is coming my way.

Cade opens his door first and gets out. He comes to my side of the truck and opens it. Taking my hand, he pulls me out and I stumble a little on my landing, causing me to fall into him. He tightens his hold on me and smirks.

"You know, if you wanted in my arms so badly, all you had to do was ask. I'm more than willing to make you mine if Belmont isn't up for the task."

I straighten myself and frown at him. Shaking my head, I grab my backpack from him and head around the building. Cade shouldn't say stuff like that. And he shouldn't ogle me in front of Wran either. While I admit it was a nice welcome compared to how Wran greeted me, I still should have told him not to look at me like that—at least in front of Wran. Maybe that's why they were at each other's throats. Seriously, I can't believe Cade just said something so . . . so . . . ugh! Cade catches up to me just as I'm about to pull open one of the glass double doors to the school. He grabs my upper arm and pulls me back, allowing a few students to bypass us and go inside.

"I'm sorry. That was inappropriate," he murmurs to me, and lets go of my arm. "I know you said you don't feel that way about me."

I sigh and dip my head a little, letting my new hair shield me from by-passers. "It's not that. I thought after everything that happened, you and Wran would get along better. You're both still taunting each other though. What was that back at the apartment?"

"It was him reminding me that I can't look or touch. And it really sucks, Roxy. He's the one that doesn't deserve you."

"You don't know all the parts of him that I do. If you did, I think you two might actually get along," I tell him, knowing it's the furthest from the truth. If Aspen didn't have them forming a bromance, nothing will.

"Roxanna," Cade says as he takes my hand and opens the school's door, "I don't want to know every part of Belmont. I don't swing that way."

I glance up at him and giggle. I would hope not. It would be a shame for someone like Cade not to make some lucky girl smile.

We head inside the building only to stop in our tracks. The hall is flooded with people and there's a rowdy group near my locker. Cade's hand tightens on mine as people start turning around and pointing at us. Or more accurately, me. Cade drops my hand, only to drape his arm around my shoulders. The stitches in my shoulder tingle, but they are becoming bearable. Cade guides me closer to him and whispers "ignore them" in my ear. I do my best to do that as I force my feet to move. The crowd parts and Cade steps in front of me like a shield as we make our way to my locker. Snickering invades my ears, but I don't search for the culprits behind them. I keep my eyes on the black-and-white checkered floor.

Cade's feet stop moving and I glance up to see what halted him. He turns around and begins dragging me away from the locker. I stop and yank my hand from his. I need my books.

"Don't turn around." His words come out clipped; they only make me curious. He's never been snappish before. Disobeying him, I cautiously rotate back toward my locker, still ignoring the ever-growing crowd. My eyes grow wide at the sight of the threatening red words on my locker. *Murdering slut.* The kids around me burst into laughter and I step back, right into Cade. His hand goes to the small of my back, but that does little to comfort me. My gaze flicks from one student to another to another to another until they all start to blend in with each other. Why would anyone paint that on my locker? The crowd parts again across from me and Cade, and Claire steps forward, flanked with her two bandits. She's applying red lipstick in the same shade as those words.

"What the hell, Claire? I thought we had an understanding," Cade yells at her over my head. His hold on me becomes tighter as I start to tremble in his arms.

How could Claire write that? What did I ever do to her?

My father's words about Wran come to the forefront of my mind, but I shove them back down. Wran wouldn't do something so awful that would turn Claire into this cruel being. He wouldn't.

"That was before you vacationed in Aspen with this baby momma whore."

"You don't know what you're talking about," he hisses at her.

Her eyes drop to mine. "I kinda feel bad for hooking up with Wran a few weeks ago now that I know he knocked you up, but then again, he was so good."

I gasp and shake my head. She is lying. I know she's lying. Wran wouldn't . . . even if he joked about it. Claire's only seventeen, and he wouldn't. I know it. "Y–your making that up." I manage to get the words out, but with the stutter they sound pathetic, even to my ear.

Claire twirls a piece of her long hair around her finger and smiles. She holds out one of her perfectly manicured hands and one of her friends places a phone in it. Claire presses a button on the device and something begins to play.

"There is no me and Roxy," Wran's voice sounds from the phone.

I scrunch my nose up at the recording. He sounds upset, but that's nothing new. Pretty sure his fuck you tone is his normal tone.

"Then this really shouldn't matter." Claire's response on the phone comes out breathy and flirty. There's some shuffling in the recording and then, as clear as day, I hear lips smacking and a moan. A pleasurable moan.

I bite down on my shaky lip to keep Claire from seeing any type of reaction on my part. She doesn't get to see me hurt. With as much strength as possible, I square my shoulders and face her head on. So what? Technically, Wran and I weren't back together. He could have fucked whoever he wanted. I didn't think he would actually go for Claire; he's never liked her, but I guess he did what he had to do to break me. Wran did admit to hating me, after all. There was no reason for him not to stoop this low.

"So what?" I ask Claire. "You think fucking Wran Belmont makes you so special? Newsflash, I'm sure he's banged half of Kingston. You're not special."

"I took him from you. In your own apartment. We laid on your couch and fucked like wild animals."

She's lying. I know she's lying. She has to be. Wran wouldn't do that to me.

Cade's hands tighten on my shoulders and I do my best not to wince. "You're forgetting awfully fast that he's my baby daddy. I know how well he fucks."

I turn away from her and push my way through the crowd with Cade right on my heels. I need to get out of here and fast. I run down the hall, the laughter still echoing in my head. I whizz around the end corner and head out the set of glass doors to the common area. I dart across it to the tiny gym I took PE in my freshman year. It's empty, thank God. Cade comes in behind me and closes the door, flipping the latch so no one else can enter.

The tears finally fall, and I let myself go down with them, my knees hitting the rubbery floor. Cade kneels in front of me and pulls me into him. He lifts my face and swipes at the tears. It doesn't help. They just keep coming. I can't believe I ever thought Wran would be faithful to me. I mean, we're talking about Wran Belmont. He brought girls to the apartment just to taunt me. Of course he wouldn't want to be with me and only me. I don't know why I ever thought that he would. But Claire? How could he? He made it sound so bad that he was with me. That I was fifteen. That I was a minor. But Claire?

I look up at Cade and he peppers my forehead with kisses. "Don't cry over him. He's not worth it."

"What did you mean by an understanding back there? D–did you know?"

Cade drops his head and sits down the rest of the way on the floor. He nods. "She let me listen to the recording and said she would play it for the entire school. I told her I would take her to prom if she didn't do that to you."

"Why would you do that?" I ask him through sobs. "You didn't have to do that. I knew she would try to get back at me. I was waiting for it."

"You love him, Rox. You love Belmont more than I have seen anyone our age love anyone. I didn't want such a beautiful heart to break."

I shake my head at his words. "He slept with her, Cade. Since he's been home. How do I let that go? I haven't even . . . it only happened once."

He cups my cheeks and brings my forehead to his. "As much as I hate the dude, I think you should talk to him about this. I'm not the right person, and we are talking about Claire. Do you really believe that recording is real?"

I opt to ignore the end of his statement. I don't care if it's real. Wran put himself in a situation with Claire where she could manipulate things. That alone is betrayal. He shouldn't have been with her in the first place.

"Why?" I ask him instead. Cade is my friend; I should be able to talk to him about anything. I know he will give it to me straight.

"Because I'm biased. I'd tell you to dump him. That you can do better."

Right . . .

My head falls to his shoulder and the tears stop. Maybe I need him to hammer that fact into my head. For the life of me, I can't get Wran out of it. I know he's cruel. I know

I could do better. I know all the things Cade wants to tell me to be true. But I also know that Wran can be sweet. I know deep in my soul that he is not a bad man. If I let the way he acts when his life is hard push me away, what kind of partner would that make me? I'm supposed to be able to handle him at his worst. I'm supposed to be able to forgive and move on.

But this?

What if I can't forgive him for being with Claire? If he even was with Claire. We haven't even been together in that way since the first time. My first time. And I haven't been with anyone since.

"How about we blow this popsicle stand and go stargazing?" Cade suggests. "I know how much you love them."

"The observatory?"

He nods.

"Okay." I guess that would be better than hiding out in a gym all day.

CHAPTER 4

ROX

Cade pulls to the side of the road outside my apartment complex and my eyes immediately zoom in on the green car Wran restored three years ago. He's home. Grabbing my things, I get out of the truck. I'm going to have to see him sooner or later. By now he's probably heard what happened. Kingston is a small town, after all, and nothing in this town goes unheard, even if it is happening inside a high school.

"I have football practice, but if you need anything, call me," Cade yells after me.

I turn around and give him a nod before heading up the stairs. Opening the door, I take in a deep breath and go inside. The living room and kitchen are empty. The mug I had this morning is still sitting on the island with the paper Wran was reading beside it. I drop my backpack onto the wooden chair and head down the hallway, skipping my

room entirely. I crack open the door to Wran's room to find him passed out on top of the navy comforter, shoes on.

Shaking my head at the scene, I take a step inside the room but stop myself and revert that step. What am I doing? I am not his mother. The fact that all I want to do is tuck him in and take off his shoes tells me how screwed up I really am. He might have cheated on me. He might have cheated on me with Claire, of all people, and I still want to take off his shoes and tuck him in bed. To touch him.

I'm pathetic.

It's as simple as that.

Closing the door as gently as possible, I go to my room and set the bags in my hand down on the bed. After the observatory, Cade and I went to this little craft store I love and picked me up a few canvases. Art was always my way of expressing myself, but when Wran left I didn't really know how to do it anymore. Scurrying over to my closet, I pull out one of my easels and the package of charcoals that Josh bought me for my fifteenth birthday. They have been in here for three years, untouched. Hopefully they are still some good.

I set everything up and start sketching the first thing that comes to mind. Since the "Aspen Accident," the news has been showing images of my mom. I don't remember much of her, but the pieces that have been coming together in my head since the "Wran Accident" have been pleasant. She used to laugh a lot. I remember that. She had the most awkward laugh that sounded like a honking. If what I am remembering serves me correctly, it was awful, but at least she was able to do it.

I wish she was here.

I wish I had someone other than Wran and Josh and Cade.

They're guys. They don't see things the way I do. It's hard talking to them. They're all subjective when it comes to me.

Thirty minutes later and I have a pretty good outline of my mother's face. I'm sure it's not accurate, seeing as I'm doing this from a five-year-old's memory and flashes of an image from TV, but it's the best I've got. It's decent, but this is nowhere near my best work. There's a knock on my door, and I turn to see Wran standing at the entrance. His eyes are partially open, his hair is messy and matted, and he looks tired. Too tired. Maybe that wasn't an excuse yesterday. The beard growing in shows plenty of evidence that he hasn't been keeping himself up. Then again, I could blame that on the drinking. He's been drinking heavily since we made it back to Kingston. I don't know why. He's just been mean and cruel since then. Not just to me, but everyone. Josh came over the day before the funeral to discuss Harley, and Wran literally punched him. Josh hasn't been back since, and I don't know how I'm supposed to get to Lynn this weekend.

"You're painting again," Wran exclaims through a yawn as he makes his way over to me.

I roll my eyes at his small talk. I guess that's what we are now: two people who can't have a normal conversation and resort to meaningless chatter to prevent the awkward tension that has been blooming since this morning. I'm sure it has been building for longer than that, but now it is obvious.

I finish smudging the under-eyes of the portrait before responding to him. Eyes have always been my weakness, so I generally start with those. "It's actually charcoals, but yeah."

"When did this come about?" He inches closer to me. "I know I've been out of it for a minute, but I would have remembered you painting again."

I go to clean my grubby hands but stop at the sight of the leather skirt. Yeah, I'm not ruining this. "Today is the first day I've felt the need to put an image on paper."

"It's beautiful." Wran moves in closer to me. So close his body heat is seeping into me. "You did her justice."

I frown at his comment and turn around to face him. Wran doesn't give me compliments on my work. He never has in the past. More than likely he would tell me something that could be fixed or just flat-out degrade it. He has always wanted me to be something more than this town, and to him, criticism was the best way for me to improve.

"What's that look for?" He studies my expression.

I shake my head at him. "You've never said my work was good. Is it really that bad?"

He shakes his head. "I've never thought any of your work was bad. This just seems raw. Maybe it's the . . . charcoals you called them?" I nod. "It's good."

I go to turn back around, but Wran stops me. He grabs hold of my hands and leads me over to the bed. I let him. He sits down in front of me and lets out a long, drawn-out breath. When his eyes finally meet mine again, I'm tempted to ask him why it looks like he hasn't slept in a week. I want to ask so badly, but I don't. I don't want to be the girl he's made me to be, the one that cares about him even though I know I shouldn't. I don't want to be his stepping stone.

"I'm sorry about this morning," he apologizes and wraps his arms around my bare legs. "I could blame it on a number of things, but that was me being a dick. I don't like the idea of others being able to see the beauty that's only meant for me."

I snort at that. Is he for real right now? Taking hold of his arms, I pry them from my legs and turn away from him. He doesn't get to treat me like a possession when he's out fucking other girls. If I don't have that same right, then neither does he. No matter if it does make me sick.

Wran looks up at me, his brows drawn and eyes searching my face. Easing up from the bed, he steps to me, leaving some space between us.

"What's going on, Rox?" he demands. "What did I do now?"

I shake my head at him but stay quiet. If I voice it, I have to face the facts. I don't think I can hear Wran admit to being with Claire—or anyone, for that matter. I know he's a guy and it's been three years since we've been together the way that guys need. I'm not dumb enough to think he was as loyal as me during that time, or when I told him no when he first came home. He made me understand that before I even understood what my feelings for him were.

"Rox?" He takes my wrists in his hands. "Talk to me, baby."

Studying his fatigued chocolate eyes, I let myself voice one of my worst nightmares. "Claire?"

He blinks at me a few times. "What about Claire?"

"Did you . . . Was she in the apartment?" I force myself to ask him.

Please say no.

Please say no.

Please say—

"Who told you that?" He cuts off my internal begging. "Did she tell you that?"

"Was she, Wran?"

He drops my wrists and takes a step back. "It's not what you think, Roxanna. I swear."

"She was here!" I yell at him. "How could you?"

He raises his hands up in defense. "Just stop. Let me explain."

I stalk forward and shove him. His sturdy form doesn't budge an inch. He slept with her. He freaking slept with her. I shove at him again, but this time he takes hold of me and pulls me to him, caging me against his body so I can't move.

"Stop," he hisses in my ear. "She came here, but it's not like that."

I elbow him in the stomach, and he lets me go as he hunches over. My hand goes flying across his face before I can rein in my rage. There's no other way it can be. He can't explain this away. He could have told me before I found out like this. He could have admitted to it while I was spilling my guts to him at Cade's place. Better yet when we were in Aspen and I thought I might die. He's had plenty of time to explain this. I slap him again, the sound of flesh against flesh echoing off my four walls.

Heart racing and hair sticking to my face, I glare down at him. He peeks up at me through narrowed eyes, a scratch on his upper right cheek. He starts to say more, but I shake my head at him. I'm done listening to him. I'm done being the loyal one when I receive nothing in return. I'm done being his lost girl. I don't have to be anymore. My dad's dead. And as much as he likes to remind me that he and Josh raised me, they aren't my dad and I'm free to do whatever I want.

Hitting the hammer on the nail, I sneer at him and say, "You really are the pathetic pedophile Josh says you are."

Wran jerks upright, eyes wide. I step away from him. Wran stalks forward, and before I can react, his fist meets my cheek. A burst of sharp pain spreads across my face as I crash into the easel. I attempt to catch myself on the canvas, but it slides off the stand and I go down. I turn around on the floor to see Wran frozen in place, mouth agape and staring at his fist in horror. His face has gone a ghostly white.

Slowly, oh so very slowly, his eyes move from his hand to me on the floor. He drops down to the furry pink rug and scoots until his back is against my bed. He buries his face in his hands and I can hear his horrified sobs.

I ignore them and get to my feet. Going over to him, I glare down at his shaking form. "We're done," I tell him. "Get out of my room."

Wran yanks his head up and shakes it. "No."

"Yes," I correct him. "We are so done."

"What about Harley?" he asks me.

"You will never see my daughter. Now. Get. Out."

He gets to his feet and stares down at me with reddening eyes. "I didn't mean to do that. You know I would never hit you."

Yeah, I do know. "But you did. You obviously have something going on in your head you can't control. I won't stick around while you deal with that."

"You can't leave me."

"Wran, please go."

"We can—" He starts.

"Go!" I scream at him. "I don't want you!"

Wran stares at me for a long time before his shoulders drop. "Fine."

He walks out of my room, slamming the door behind him. I go over to my door and head to the living room, retrieving my phone and backpack. Once back in my room,

I climb onto my bed and unlock my phone. I stare at Cade's number for a long time before pressing the message button. I send him a quick message asking him to come get me. When he doesn't respond right away, I lie back on the bed and let the tears of Wran's betrayal fall. I can't believe he slept with her.

I don't know how long I lie there, gazing out my window, but when my phone finally pings with a message the sky has turned a midnight shade and a crescent moon is illuminating my room. I bring my phone up to read the message and sigh. Cade's here. He came.

I get off the bed with my backpack and go to my closet. I grab clothes, not bothering to pull them off the hangers, and shove them in my bag. When I can stuff no more inside, I leave and go to the living room, heading straight for the bookcase that holds my old, stuffed, one-eyed rabbit and Peter Pan book. I would have never thought I would need to leave my Neverland, but something is not right here. We're too dependent on one another and Wran is too angry at the world. He'll never get his crap together if I'm a factor.

"Where are you going?" I hear his voice behind me.

I whirl around and Wran's eyes dart from my stuffed bag to the book and rabbit in my hold. "I'm leaving."

"What?" he asks, walking into the living room. "Because of Claire? Nothing happened with that girl. I would never lay a hand on her!"

"That doesn't matter, Wran." I go over to the door. "I couldn't care less about Claire, but I do care about you. You need to work through whatever is making you so . . . so angry all the time. And I can't be around you when you do it."

"We're supposed to be a team, Rox. You can't just leave when things get fucking hard!" His voice rises. "I–I'm sorry about hitting you. Please don't go. I need you."

"I can't stay."

"Why not?" His question comes out pleading.

"Because I have Harley to think about. And I have myself to think about. I had to deal with being my father's target; I'm not going to be your punching bag too."

"Do not compare me to him. I'm nothing like that bastard."

I don't respond to his statement. As much as I hate it, Wran has become a lot like my father, and some part of me thinks it's my fault. I've been the constant in his life. I'm the one that has always picked up the pieces when he broke them. Maybe I never let him learn to fix them himself. It's time he does.

"I'm sorry. Get some help and we'll talk."

"Fine," he chokes out. "You can run but know that I will always chase you."

I leave the apartment before he has time to say more. A loud yell comes from inside, followed by the sound of something breaking. I close my eyes and bite down on my lip to keep from going back in there. Exhaling, I rush down the stairs to Cade's waiting truck and get inside. I hear his intake of breath as I drop my bag on the floor. In my periphery, I see his hands flex tightly against the steering wheel, but I make no move to look at him. I don't want to see his expression, and I don't want to know how bad my face looks.

"What the hell happened after I left?" Cade asks as his hands open and close around the steering wheel. "He hit you."

I shake my head and I don't know why. My face says it all. "I provoked him."

"Don't you dare do that! Don't you make excuses for that trash."

I flinch at Cade's harsh words. Never have I heard him speak like that, with such venom and loathing. Maybe I really am the problem in everyone's life. Maybe I am toxic. Cade's hand jerks from the wheel and to the door. I rotate in the seat and take hold of his arm, keeping him from moving.

"Don't," I tell him. "I'm fine. Just get me out of here. Please."

Cade glances over his tense shoulder at me. At first I think he's going to ignore my wants, but then his shoulders slump and he lets out a string of curses. When he's gotten it off his chest, he looks me straight on. "I'm only dropping it because you asked. But if he comes around you one more time, I won't hold back. He doesn't get away with hurting you."

I nod. There's not much I can say to change Cade's mind. Not about this. Cade pulls away from the curb just as the door to my apartment opens and Wran comes out.

I watch him grow smaller and smaller as the truck gets farther and farther away from him.

CHAPTER 5

WRAN

I watch as Cade's truck pulls away from the curb, taking my Rox with him. I should have known she'd call him. He's the only one stupid enough to try to take something of mine. A low growl leaves my lips just as a door to my left opens. A guy in a ribbed white shirt comes out, a cigarette in hand. He tilts his head in acknowledgment as he let out a long string of smoke and sighs.

"You sounded like you need a smoke." He offers me one.

I shake my head at the guy. "Those things cause fucking cancer."

"Gotta go somehow," he replies and takes another drag of the cig. He drops it on the concrete path and stomps it out.

I've lived here for almost five years now and I still don't know my neighbors. I scan the street again as if searching is going to bring Rox back here tonight. My eyes travel up to the night sky and I curse at the stars above. These things would be out in full force on the one night they shouldn't. I don't need Rox looking up at these and remembering tonight.

With a groan, I turn around and stomp back into my apartment, slamming the door so hard the frame of the building seems to rattle. Stepping over the pieces of pink ceramic, I head over to the couch and slump down. I can't believe she's gone. I can't believe she had the balls to leave me. Fuck. I run my hands over my face and groan into them. Rox is gone. Like really gone. I should have known she would leave me. Everyone fucking leaves. Mom left. Pops checked out. And now Rox. I don't know why I expected any different from her. She runs. That's what Roxanna fucking Raine does. She runs when life gets too complicated.

Jumping up from the sofa, I stalk off to my room. No, she's not leaving this time around. She's not taking the only thing I have left in this world from me. Grabbing my phone and keys off my bedside table, I hurry out of the apartment. I won't let her go that easily. Her or Harley. I jump in my car and floor it as soon as the engine roars to life. I hear a horn blaring at me as I zip past the only stoplight in our small town and head over the tracks to where that wealthy fucker dwells.

It's still hard to believe that I used to be one of these privileged pricks before my father became a no-good waste of space. He was one of the best lawyers in the state, working for Rox's father. Now being on this side of town sends a violent tremor up my spine. And Rox . . . She knows my thoughts on *them*, yet she ran off with one. With Cade.

I slam my hands down on the steering wheel and push the car to go faster. I glance at the gauge and ease up a little. After Aspen, it would be really ironic to get arrested for going sixty over the limit. I keep heading straight until the houses grow farther and farther apart and they get more and more outrageous. In another town, houses like this—houses that look like they came off the pages of some magazine—would be guarded by a gate or some crap. But not in Kingston. Everyone here knows everyone. Meaning no one can get away with anything. I don't think Dixie County even knew what a crime was before James Raine decided he was the law. As soon as I see the red truck that looks out of place with the white exterior of the Southern house, I jump out of the car, not bothering to cut the engine. I don't make it halfway up the stairs before I hear Rox's sweet voice yelling "don't" and Cade comes busting out of the door.

He should have known I would come for what's mine. No one is taking her from me. Not again. Not that I now have her back where she belongs. Rox runs out of the house after Cade and stops when she sees me. She grabs his hand and pulls him back before the bastard can make it over.

"Leave!" he roars at me, but I ignore him and march over to where Rox has him restrained. And that's exactly why Rox will never love him. Not like she loves me. She needs a real man. One that can take care of her. One that can love her. One that is not living off Daddy's money. One that can't be restrained. My eyes drop to where her flesh meets his, and I glare over at her. She shakes her head at me, begging, but she made her decision when she decided to run with this prick.

"Wran, please, just go home," she begs me, pulling Cade back with her.

"How the hell can you even suggest that?" I yell at her. "You're supposed to be mine, yet you run because of some slutty-ass girl. No, I'm not going anywhere, unless you're with me."

She shakes her head again. "I told you. It's better this way."

"Like hell it is!" I reach for my girl, but my fingers never meet her supple flesh. The next thing I know, I'm being tossed back. I land with a hard thump on my back, an almost animalistic snarl leaving my mouth. Cade stands over me, a wide-eyed Rox standing behind him with her mouth wide open. She bites down on her lip and I can see the need to come to me in her darting eyes. I rise up on my elbow, but Cade's boot meets my chin.

There's a gasp, and I groan. Fuck, that hurt.

"You stay away from her," Cade seethes. "You lay one more hand on her and I will show you just how much of a rich prick I can be. You'll be in handcuffs so damn fast—"

Rox grabs hold of him, stopping his words.

Cade can spit a thousand threats, but at the end of the day, Rox will always love me.

"You said you loved me," I mumble to her.

She takes a step forward, but the douche pulls her back. She yanks her arm away from him and bends down to me.

The soft skin of her hand finds my cheek and I nuzzle into her hand.

My eyes droop close for a second before they snap back to her. "Why are you doing this?"

"I do love you, Wran. I will probably always love you, but you need help I can't provide. It's not safe for me to be with you right now."

"I would never hurt you," I mutter to her.

"You hurt me today, and if there's even a slight chance of me getting Harley back or forgiving you, I'm going to have to prove that I can take care of myself first. Go talk to someone, and then we'll see what happens. I promise."

Cade lets out a humph behind her, but we both ignore him.

I rise to my feet, pulling her up with me. I lean my forehead against hers and let out a long breath. "I will do whatever it takes to make you feel safe again."

She smiles at me, but it's not her happy smile. I know that smile all too well. Dropping her hand, I step away from her and move back to my car. I give my girl one last look before I'm inside and driving away. She wants me to get help, then I will get help. I will talk to whoever I need to in order to get her back.

My car doesn't come to a stop again until my old childhood home is in view. Josh's motorcycle is in the drive, along with his police cruiser and the old car he uses whenever his motorcycle isn't an option. I get out of the car and go up the path to the door. I breathe in and out, trying to calm my racing heart. I'm probably the last person my brother wants to deal with. Honestly, I don't even know why I came here, of all places. Maybe because out of everyone in my life, Josh has stayed. Even if he has made my life a living hell. I knock on the door, and moments later it opens. Josh stands there with his cop uniform half open. There's a purplish bruise on his face from where I hit him. He steps aside and I walk in, heading straight to the tan sofa my mother picked out when she was alive. Sitting down on the edge of the couch, I let my face fall into my hands. My brother's feet come into my downward vision and I lift my head up to meet him. He sits on the coffee table.

"What happened?" he asks, eyes raking over me. That fucker probably left a bruise when he kicked me. "Are you all right?"

I shake my head at him. I don't think I've been all right in such a long time. And now . . . How do I live without Rox? "She left." My voice comes out in a whisper. "She walked out on me."

"Just tell me what happened." He gets up and moves to the leather chair. "Does this have to do with you being drunk at her father's memorial?"

I shake my head at him. If anything, it has more to do with me. Rox would have never left over something so miniscule. "I hit her."

I don't even believe my own words. I. Hit. Her. Never would I have done something like this before. James's words from before he died come back to me in a flash. Maybe I am just like him. Maybe we are cut from the same cloth. I killed him. I killed a man, and it wasn't in self-defense. It was because I hated him. It was because he ruined my life. Because I . . . I'm just like him.

"You hit her? What the hell, Wran?"

"I didn't mean to," I defend myself. "I just got so angry and she started saying things. I didn't mean to. I need her back." I drop from the sofa and to my knees in front of Josh. "You have to help me. Please. I–I can't be without her."

Josh rises from the chair and my eyes travel up to meet his. He doesn't say a word as he watches me. Yeah, I know I'm pathetic, pining after a girl that wouldn't even let me explain, but I need her. Not once in the twelve years we've known each other have I thought I was anywhere near as dependent on her as much as she was dependent on me. I was wrong. Rox left and I'm falling apart. My heart hurts. Everything hurts.

"She told me to get help. To talk to someone. But I'm not fucking broken," I tell my brother.

He drops down to the floor in front of me and pulls my head to his shoulder. I want so badly to yank away from him. I'm not a child that needs consoling. I'm not some emotional chick, but I can't bring myself to pull away. I need Josh. I need someone that isn't going to run away when things get a little tough.

"Have you thought that her leaving is a good thing?" he asks me. "I believe she may be right. You do need to get some help."

I simply nod into his shoulder. "What do I do?"

"How about you sleep this off and we will discuss it more tomorrow when you're not so manic and can think clearly? Do you know where Rox is right now? Is she safe?"

I nod again. "Yeah, she's with Cade."

"I see," is all Josh says as he gets up from the floor.

I get up as well and look in the direction of my old room. I haven't been back there since I left this place. Rising, I push past my brother and head down the hall. I come to a stop at the sight of all the trophies and posters still on the wall. It's exactly like I left it before I took Rox and moved. The bed even still has the same red covering. I go over to the bed and sit down. My eyes find the photo of Rox and I that I left on my bedside table. She is about nine in the photo and we're at the fair that we loved to go to. She has cotton candy in her hands, and she seems so happy. I'm smiling in the photo. I haven't smiled like that in such a long time. Maybe I do need more help. Maybe figuring out why I am the way I am will get us back to the place we were in this image. With a heavy sigh, I lean back on the bed and look up at the starless ceiling. It's wrong; there should be stars. I turn away from the empty ceiling and toward the door, only to see Josh standing in the doorway with his arms crossed over his chest.

He takes a step inside, and I sit up. He comes over to the bed and sits down. "Do you remember when you were seventeen and I tried to get you to talk to a therapist about all the anger you were bottling up?"

I shrug my shoulders. My focus wasn't on Josh at that time. Rox was twelve, in middle school, and friends with Claire. I was too busy trying to ward off one girl's advances and trying not to fall for the other. I did a lot of stupid stuff at that age just to keep my mind from thinking of Rox as anything other than the girl whose father ruined my pops. The only conversation I truly remember having with Josh back then was when he kept telling me Rox wasn't family. That was one of the main reasons I left this side of town. I didn't want Rox to hear Josh, the man who practically raised her with me, saying shit like that. I mean, she was twelve. No twelve-year-old should have to listen to that. I should know; I heard that type of talk enough from my pops at that age.

Boy, can't you get a job?

Boy, you're no good.

Boy. Boy. Boy.

Rox didn't need to be around that.

"I remember questioning if you had a thing for Rox. You always looked at her like you did," I respond, deflecting from the fact that no, I don't remember him even voicing the topic. The first time I even had to deal with an anger management coach was a year after I left Rox, and my commanding officer said I had to talk to someone or get court-martialed. I took the therapy. There was no telling what the hell would happen if I was court-martialed. I heard stories of dishonorable discharge, confinement for more than a month, and so much more. I couldn't risk being discharged and coming back home. Not with Rox still being a minor and with Josh's threat looming over my head. Besides, I needed the money after quitting the car garage.

"I never looked at that girl like that. You are just too possessive. If anything, I felt bad for her. The girl has had an impossible life." Josh shifts on the bed. "Anyways, when I was in high school I had this counselor named Thomas. You might remember him. He's been working in a rehabilitation center for behavioral health for quite some time. I think you would benefit from going there for a while."

I turn around on the bed and face my brother. First, he sends me away. Then he keeps the fact that I have a daughter from me, and now he's trying to get me put into some insane asylum. He has got to be fucking kidding me. I start to tell him what I think about his idea when he raises a hand to stop me from saying anything.

"Before you say anything, know that it's not permanent. You do get visitations, and it's only a four week program to see if it's a right fit. Afterwards, it's by appointment only. You should really consider this, Wran, especially if you want Rox back. I don't think you two are good together, but you are my brother. I will do what I can for you. Even if sometimes you dislike my methods."

I run my hand through my hair. Four weeks isn't that long. Hell, I went three years without Rox. If I can endure that, then a month should be nothing. I start to tell him all right but stop myself. That would be a month without seeing Harley as well.

"Harley?" I ask him. I'm not sure how this whole thing with her works, but I'm pretty sure the state isn't going to give custody to someone with anger problems. I don't want that on my record.

"What about her?"

"Isn't there a meeting this Saturday with Lynn? I don't want to miss that." I've already missed enough time with my daughter.

"I'm pretty sure it's canceled now." My brother mur- murs.

"Why?"

He turns to face me. I want to see my daughter. "You hit Roxy. I know firsthand that your hits leave a bruise. She can't go see Harley with a purple blotch on her face. Too many questions and no answers that wouldn't be a blatant lie."

Shit!

I close my eyes and fall backward on the bed. I didn't even think about that. Hell, she's probably more than pissed at me.

"Yeah," Josh mutters. "Just think about this center and we'll—"

"I don't have to think about it," I cut his words off. If going to this center will help me with Rox, I'll do it. I need her in my life. And like I told her, if she wants me to talk to someone, I will. "I'll do whatever it takes. I love her, man."

Josh nods in understanding, but his face tells it all. He only wishes I was doing this for myself and not for a girl.

"All right. We'll pack you a bag in the morning and head out. I'll email Thomas and let him know we'll be coming."

Josh leaves the room and I lie back on the bed, looking up at the starless ceiling again. Maybe he's right. Maybe this will be good for me. Maybe this will get my girl back. I let out a deep breath again and close my eyes. Rox is gone. She really left, and she has taken the part of me that believed in Neverland. The part of me that believed in all her dreams of happily ever after and peace. I know she may be upset right now, and rightfully so, but I also know without a doubt that she is mine. She is the only one for me, and I am the only one for her. If going to a mental institute will save my relationship, I guess there's no second-guessing what I'm doing.

CHAPTER 6

ROX

"It's not that bad," Cade tells me. I snort at his assessment. It might not hurt that bad, but it looks like I stepped into a boxing ring and let them practice on my face. I grab the one-dollar concealer I've been using and dab more on my face. When caking the stuff doesn't help hide the ugly black bruise, I toss the concealer back on the bed. There's no way I can go to school with my face like this. I'll be the talk of the freaking town. There's no way I will be able to go see Harley Saturday if this isn't gone.

How could Wran be so thoughtless?

Cade pulls me from the mirror and turns me around in his hold. "If you want, I can get someone to come and do your makeup. I know a few girls that are really good at this stuff." He motions to the spilled bottle of concealer on the bed. Crap! I didn't mean to do that. It's bad enough he has me living here without his father knowing, I don't need to ruin his furniture too. Going over to the bed, I pick up the bottle and screw the top back on.

I shake my head at him. "That's okay. I'll just stay here for the day, and if the concealer isn't working by tomorrow evening, I'll call Lynn and let her know I can't make it this Saturday."

"Won't that be a point against you where getting custody of Harley is concerned?"

I look up at Cade from under long lashes and fake a smile for his sake. It's cute that he's worrying about that, but he should not be. Harley is my daughter. She is mine to worry about. I will handle it on my own. Knowing the system, not showing will affect me, but there's nothing else I can do. Accepting every offer Cade throws my way will only give him false hope. He might not think I can see it, but the moment I told Wran to leave, the glow that left in Aspen reemerged. Wran being gone doesn't change that I'm not ready to move on. I don't know if I can. I won't hurt Cade by using his affections and taking advantage of his generosity.

"I'm sure Lynn will understand," I tell him. "It's not the first time I would have had to cancel."

"No, but it's probably the first time with no legitimate excuse."

I roll my eyes at him and dismiss the truth of his statement.

"C'mon, Rox, let me help. I have resources. You're my friend. Let me help you."

My eyes stay trained on him for a good moment. As much as what he's saying makes sense, I don't want to go down that path. I don't want to hurt him when he starts to think more of me accepting things. "Cade, you're just a friend. You know that, right?"

Cade steps closer to me. "Of course. You just broke up with Belmont, and you guys have been an item for years. I can wait my turn until you're over him."

"That's not what I meant."

He smirks at me. "Calm down. I know what you meant. Doesn't mean I'm not going to try with you again now that Belmont's out of the picture. Let me help you. I'm going to keep bugging you until you agree that my help doesn't mean anything."

But it does; it so, so does.

Ugh!

I let out a humph and walk past him. Cade has the annoying habit of being persistent when he wants something. "Fine. Call whoever you must to fix this." I point to my face. "I really do need to go to school. Missing a few days after the Aspen Accident was one thing; I don't really want to miss because of Wran."

He beams over at me. "See! Was it really that hard?"

I sigh and arch a brow at him.

His help is going to bite me in the butt.

Cade grabs hold of my hand and pulls me out of the room and down the staircase. I frown at his hold on me. Ever since last night when Wran showed up, Cade has found every opportunity imaginable to touch me. If I was in his shoes, I would probably be the same way. I mean, I was him a few years ago when all I wanted in the world was for Wran to see me as more than the lost girl he found. I would use every chance I got to touch him too. At the same time, I knew I had a chance with Wran. Small things he did—like washing my hair and breathing in the scent of my shampoo, or when he took me shopping and let it slip that I would look amazing in some dress he would normally call slutty—told me that I had a chance. I don't think Wran even realized he was doing those things. With Cade, though, he has no chance. My heart isn't in this the way he wants it to be, and he's not getting that. Even if he claims he does.

"I got us breakfast from Aunt May. She's worried about you," Cade announces as we hit the last step and round it, moving toward his dining room.

I frown at his comment. Aunt May has been like a family member to me since she moved to Kingston. I haven't spoken to her about anything that has happened since returning from Aspen. With the news blurting out information, there's so much for her to take in and none of it is coming from me. I should have given her some information when she texted I had the week off following my father's memorial.

"Can you take me to see her after school?" I ask Cade as we come to a stop in the dining room. There's a china cabinet holding a lot of shiny plates that I'm sure cost more than everything in my shared apartment. There are no deer heads on the wall, which I'm relieved with. Don't think I would be able to eat anything with an animal's glossy eyes staring at me, practically screaming "you killed me, you killed me, you killed me." Honestly, I don't get the fascination with hunting for sport. Then again, that may be because Wran has always had an aversion to killing anything.

My body goes stiff at that realization.

Oh.

My.

God.

I pull a chair from under the dining table and sit down. I run my hand through my thick hair. I can't believe I didn't put two and two together. Wran killed someone. He literally took a life. A flipping life. Granted it was my father, and he loathed my father with every part of his being, but he still snuffed out a life.

The way he's been going off the rails since we got back. The drinking. The tired eyes. How did I not put this together? I shake my head, disgusted with myself. He. Killed. Someone. I can't even begin to think what that would do to a person that already has issues—never mind, someone that hates the idea of killing even an animal.

Wran has always been cruel on the surface. There's no denying that. I know who I love. That's how he wants the world to see him; he believes that is what Kingston deserves after they shunned him and Josh. But a boy that would take me in—clothe me, bathe me, love me, even though he said he hated me—can't be a bad guy.

I will never believe Wran is a bad guy.

"All right," Cade says as he sits down at the table, grabbing a blueberry scone from a platter and pouring himself a glass of orange juice. "I texted her; just don't freak out when she gets here."

My eyes immediately snap to his. "Why would I freak out? Who did you text?"

He shakes his head and takes a bite of the breakfast dessert. He motions to the spread in front of me and I take it in. I don't even know if I can eat now. Wran's been going through this crap for a week, and I haven't even noticed the toll it has taken on him. I didn't see the turmoil bubbling on the freaking surface. I'm the one person that should have seen it. On top of that, I left him. I. Left. Him. And came to Cade.

Crap on a stick!

I need to talk to him.

I need to see him.

"What's wrong?" Cade asks as he sets his glass down and turns to face me. "Do you not like any of this? Aunt May said you love pancakes."

My eyes roam over to the platter of chocolate pancakes, and I grin. My stomach roars to life at the sight of them. I do love pancakes. "Everything looks good. You didn't have to do this. I would have been fine with just coffee."

"I know your whole motto is 'coffee, books, repeat,' but you can't survive off merely coffee. That's why you're too skinny now."

I glance down at my body. No one has ever called me too skinny. The only time I thought I was too skinny was when I first ran away from home when I was six. My dad had just murdered my nanny and finding food was hard. Whenever I did, someone would recognize me and I would run. It went that way for almost three months before Wran found me. In no way, shape, or form am I too skinny now. Not after having Harley. I have boobs. Like real boobs. I never thought I would have those. While many of the girls I knew were wearing B-cups by eighth grade, I was still in training bras. It sucked. Claire had told me once that if I played with them, they would grow. It felt awkward and didn't start to be pleasurable until Wran began teasing me.

Grabbing a few of the pancakes, I drench them in maple syrup since there's no chocolate sauce on the table. I might as well eat since he went out of the way to get me breakfast.

We sit in silence for a good twenty minutes, eating, until a bell chimes throughout the house. I glance around to find where the chime came from when Cade gets up from his seat. I watch as he goes, hearing a door open moments later. There're hushed whispers that I can't make out—not that I should be trying to in someone else's house. It's rude. Turning back around to the spread in front of me, I pour myself another cup of coffee from a canister. When I hear two pairs of footsteps, one in clacking heels, I turn around in the dining chair to see who has joined us. My eyes go wide at the sight of Claire standing next to Cade in a red, long-sleeved dress. She has her arms crossed over her chest and she looks just as unpleased to be here as I am to see her.

Really?

This is who Cade called to help me.

As I turn to glare at Cade full on, a small gasp leaves Claire. I glance at her, her eyes on my face. Quickly, I drop my head and allow my hair to secure me from her view. I don't need her pity or help. I just won't go to school today.

"Bye." I get up from the chair and start to walk past them.

Cade grabs my arm. "Rox, please be reasonable."

I yank my arm from him. This is reasonable. If I wanted to be unreasonable, I would grab her by those fake extensions and drag her out of the house. And yes, I know they are fake; she's been wearing the same ones since I picked them out with her in seventh grade. Seeing as this isn't my house, though, I'm just going to exit the room.

"Let her go. Doesn't bother me any if she has to go to school looking like she's just been in a boxing match and lost," Claire taunts.

I whirl around on her, shoving Cade aside. "This is your fault!"

"Mine?" she shrieks. "I'm not the one that smacked you upside your head, but trust me, I would love to have that honor."

"No, you're just the one that slept with my boyfriend!"

Her eyes widen and she doesn't say anything else for a second. "Wran did this?" She turns to Cade. "You said she had an accident. I'm not going to help her hide something like that. She should be calling the police."

I roll my eyes at her. "It was an accident. Wran didn't mean to do this. Now, are you going to help or are you just going to be a pain in my butt?"

She arches a brow at me. "Why in the world should I even help you? It's not like you've done anything for me besides steal guys that I like and ruin my life."

"I do not—"

"How about you help her because you two used to be best friends?" Cade cuts in. "How about you two get over your shit with Belmont, because he's a crappy guy and doesn't deserve either of your attention."

Claire examines my face and shrugs. "I've been over him and thank God if he's hitting on her."

"Then why did you sleep with him? I have never done anything like that to you."

Claire tosses her hands up in a sigh. "For crying out loud, it was a freaking joke! I wanted to get back at you for going out with Cade."

"I'm not going out with him. Besides, he's taking you to prom," I shout back at her. "You slept with my boyfriend because of him." I point to Cade.

"I didn't sleep with Wran! I went over there and he turned me down. And I know you're not with Cade, but everyone sees the way he looks at you. He's only taking me to prom because your too stuck up to see a good guy."

My hands clench at my side. I went off on my boyfriend because she's a jealous bitch. I pushed Wran away all because she can't control the little green monster on her shoulder. I start to inch forward, ready to yank those extensions free, but Cade steps in between us. How dare he? He brings this . . . this witch over here and now he doesn't want to deal with the ramifications? He was there at school yesterday. He saw what she put on my locker. He knows what type of person she is. Yet he's trying to get us to play nice. He's out of his mind. I turn away from them both and run for the room, the door to my temporary dwellling slamming shut behind me.

I can't believe he thought this was a good idea. Nowhere do the words "Claire" and "help" and "me" belong together. I go over to the side table and yank up the bottle of concealer. I can do this on my own. Going back over to the mirror, I dab an absurd amount of the white liquid on my face. This has to work.

The door to the room opens and I hear the clacking of stilettos before I smell the god-awful scent of her overpowering perfume. The clacking gets faster and faster until Claire is across the room and yanking the makeup from my hold. I whirl on her, lips pursed and ready for this fight. My life is crap right now. She doesn't want to get in the middle of that.

"Why do you always have to play the freaking victim?" she spits and then laughs. "It's funny if something doesn't go

Roxanna Raine—oh wait, Roxanna Belmont's way, she gets all pissy and temperamental. It's not always about you."

My brows knit together at her analysis of me. "Me, temperamental? That's funny coming from the queen of mean."

"Yeah, well, I learned early in life not to put all my trust in a so-called best friend. Thanks for that, by the way."

Huh?

I take a step away from her and examine her fuming face. What is she talking about?

"Doesn't feel too good when someone calls you out on your shit, does it, Roxy? I didn't have to come over here at all, but I did."

I turn away from her as my father's words slam into me full force. Wran did something to her. My father wasn't lying. That's impossible. Wran wouldn't . . . Claire's just talking out of her butt, trying to turn everything around on me. It's what she does.

But then again . . .

With my shoulders square, I turn to her furious face. "I don't know what you're talking about."

"Ha!" She takes a step closer to me, and my eyes dart anywhere but at her. "You can't even admit to the things you did."

My eyes snap back to her. I've had to admit to everything I did; I've had to live with every single choice I've ever made in my life. Her being a spoiled, self-entitled brat isn't one of them.

"Don't." I jab a finger into her chest. "You. Dare. Think for one second you know me. I did nothing to you. Nothing! One day you were my friend, and the next you were tossing mashed potatoes in my hair. All because I told you Wran was mine. If either of us is temperamental, it's you. You knew how I felt about him."

"You think this has to do with Wran?" she shrieks at me. "Unbelievable! This has everything to do with the fact that you're nothing more than a homewrecking bitch. You're the reason my parents got divorced!"

There are no words for what she just claimed. All I can do is watch her, panting, rage rolling off her in endless waves. Her fury is so palpable. I knew her parents got a divorce. The whole town of Kingston knew. Claire's father left her mom with nothing. Well, I wouldn't say nothing. Her parents' marriage was a marriage of convenience, of sorts—or at least that's how I saw it when Claire explained it to me in seventh grade. Her mother's family was well endowed. She went into the arrangement with a trust fund. Came out of it with that same fund and now lives in a nice house not far from here, actually. Their divorce had nothing to do with me.

"I have no clue what you're talking about," I tell her. I really don't. I've only ever met her father a handful of times, and neither of those times was pleasant.

"Stop lying or I will march right down to that station and report Wran for that!" She motions to my face, and my hand immediately go up to hide the bruise.

"You forget, his brother is the sheriff."

"That may be, but not even he can go above the mayor."

Crap. Stupid rich people and their connections. "You can't."

"And why not?" she taunts.

"Because I will lose all rights to see my daughter!" I slap my hands over my mouth as soon as the words leave my lips. I close my eyes and move back to the bed. I can't believe I just blurted that out. And to Claire, of all people. The one thing that could ruin me, she now knows. If any of this got back to Lynn, she would have all the proof she needs to take Harley from me. She would claim that living with Wran isn't a safe home. That I'm incapable of protecting Harley and myself. God, I can't believe I just gave this information to Claire.

Claire takes painstakingly slow steps over to me. I glance up at her, arms still crossed over her chest. "Maybe I should have Daddy contact the mayor then. Let you face what it's like to lose someone. Do you have any idea what I had to go through when my mother left?"

"I promise you, Claire, I had no hand in that. Why would you believe I did?" I ask her.

"Because I saw you!" She glares down at me. "We were preparing for a sleepover and you went into the hall. Said you had to go to the bathroom. You were taking so long that I went to check on you, and there you were. With my father. In the hallway. His hands on you. You not pulling away. You stood there and flirted with him, knowing my mother was down the fucking hall!"

I shake my head at her. "Claire—"

"Don't 'Claire' me. I saw it all! When my father turned you down, you must have told your precious Belmonts something. The next morning my dad was beaten to a flipping pulp, and my parents were arguing. It must make you glad to know you ruined a family."

"Shut up!" I yell at her the same time the door to the room comes open. We both snap our heads to peer at Cade.

"Just wanted to let you know that we're all going to be late for school."

"Get the fuck out!" we both scream at him, and Cade backs out of the room.

We turn back to each other, and I rise from the bed. She's hated me for years because of this stupid misunderstanding. "I did not come on to your father," I announce, giving it to her straight. I never told her about this, mainly because her parents got the divorce almost right afterward and she had given up being my friend. I didn't see a point in adding more to her stressful life, even if she couldn't care less about the things I was going through.

"I didn't come on to your father," I state once more, so she'll get this. "I would have never done something like that. That night, I went to the bathroom and he stopped me in the hall. Told me how much of a good influence I was on you. Told me that I could come over whenever I wanted. I smiled and thanked him; I didn't know what else to say to that.

Then he asked if I wanted a drink. I told him no, and he said I might as well have one if you were going to sneak booze into your sleepover. I told him you wouldn't do that, but he said he knew his child. I defended you, and he said some snide remarks about me and you and things I don't really want to recall. Yes, I told Wran and Josh. And yes, they got upset. I didn't know about them hurting your father, and I certainly didn't cause your family's mishap. I'm sorry that you think I did."

"You're lying," she whispers. "I saw his hand on you."

"His hand on me. Not the other way around. I'm not lying and you know that. You know what your father is like. You know how strict and callous and, well, you know."

She lets out a sigh and sits down on the bed. "Everything was fine before that night. Every time I tried to make sense of what happened, you were always the solution. You were the only one there. You were the only one that talked to him before he came home the next day and my life went to hell."

"I'm sorry, Claire. Truly, I am. If I knew Wran and Josh would have done that, I wouldn't have said anything to them."

Claire swipes at her face and squares her shoulders. She flips her blond hair back and turns to me. "Doesn't matter. I still don't like you. Why in the world would you want to be with Wran if he's hitting you?"

I notice her deflective mannerism right away. She used to do it a lot. Instead of calling her on it, I let her change the subject. "Because I love him. I know it makes me stupid, but I truly believe he didn't mean to do this. This month has just been tough."

"I'm sorry your father kidnapped your daughter. I'm sorry I wrote that on your locker. It really was meant to be a joke. You take things way too seriously. Always have."

"Well, I sort of have to, with my life. Besides, you made my life hell. Do you know how hard it is to keep bullying from a social worker?"

Claire cringes. "Sorry. Do you want me to do your makeup?" She points to the bottle on the dresser by the mirror. "That cheap crap is definitely not going to work, and your face looks like it belongs on a prostitute."

"Geez, why don't you tell me how you really feel?"

There's a knock on the door, and I look to see Cade sticking his head inside. "Is it safe? I hear no more yelling."

I glance at Claire, not sure how to take this confrontation. Trusting her is not going to be easy. Scratch that, I'm pretty sure it is impossible, but at least we are sitting in the same room again. And neither of us have a scratch on our face. I nod to Cade and he walks into the room, coming over and taking a seat on the bed in between Claire and me.

"See? I knew you two just needed to get over your shit."

"Shut up," we both say at the same time.

Claire leans forward and glances at me. "Let's get started. My father will blow a gasket if he gets a call from the school about me being tardy."

CHAPTER 7

WRAN

I stare up at the massive red brick building and lush green courtyards that remind me of a refurbished monastery. I read the sign once again before turning around to face Josh. There has got to be another way. Who in their right mind would voluntarily check in to a place called Pleasure House? If I'm being technical, the sign reads Pleasure House Rehabilitation Center: Where we turn frowns upside down. Seriously, is this place for toddlers throwing temper tantrums? I shake my head to myself, answering my own question. This place looks like one of those communes in horror films that seem nice and dandy on the outside but threaten unforetold pain on the inside. I look past Josh and to the gate that's going to cage me inside for the next month. There's nothing but green fields and trees for miles outside the gate. No one to hear anyone's cry for help. I'm pretty sure there are going to be plenty.

"You have any better ideas?" I ask my brother. Right now I'm considering getting back in Josh's crappy police cruiser and heading back to Kingston to Rox. If she can't handle me this way, then she can't handle me at all.

"Do you want your girl back?" is all my brother asks me.

I let out a huff and walk up the steps. It's the beginning of April and their lawn looks like it's midsummer. Something sinister has to be happening in this place. It's not normal. I push open the glass door and a few people—inpatients, I guess—step out. A girl with mousy brown hair and sunken cheeks nods her head in thanks. She takes the hand of the guy behind her and they walk out. I step inside the building and come to a complete stop. I reverse my step.

Hell. No.

Josh is out of his ever-fucking mind if he thinks I'm staying at a place where nuns are walking around dressed in dark red robes and there are crosses all over fake wood paneled walls. This isn't an episode of American Horror Story. Nope. I'm leaving.

Josh places a hand on my back to keep me in place. One of the nuns comes over and bows her head.

"May I help you gentlemen?" she asks.

"Yeah, I'm looking for the nearest exit that's not being guarded by my brother."

The woman's eyes flicker between us. "Excuse me?"

"He's joking." Josh takes the lead. "We're here for Dr. Thomas Harding. I emailed him last night and he should be expecting us. I'm Josh Belmont."

The nun beams up at my brother. "Ah, of course. Counselor Thomas did mention you this morning. I'm Sister Helena, by the way. If you'll follow me, I'll show you to his office."

Her eyes skim over to me and her smile wavers a little. She turns around and leads us down a hall. I look back at the door and then around at the lobby area. There're not many people sitting around. Just the nuns. I accidentally meet one of their eyes, and he—yes, I said he—gives me a gentle smile and bows his head. I arch a brow at the man. If only he knew how ridiculous he looks in that red robe, he wouldn't be smiling like all is well in the world. With a groan and one last look at the exit of this place, I take off after my brother and the woman.

I'm doing this for Rox.

I'm doing this for Harley.

They'd better be grateful.

When I catch up with my brother, he sends a scathing glare to me over his shoulder. I shrug. What does he expect? When he told me about Dr. Thomas last night, in no way, shape, or form did he mention that I would have to sell my soul to the devil. He didn't mention that Dr. Thomas worked in a convent in the middle of nowhere and that I would be trapped inside a building with nuns and monks or whatever. If he had given me all the details, I wouldn't be here. I would have found a decent therapist that didn't look like he was going to try to exorcise my issues out of me.

Sister Helena pushes open a set of double doors that lead outside. We head down a long skyway covered with mosaics and stained-glass windows. I glance to the open side, out to the courtyard. There's now a group of people stationed around the fountain. A few of them look our way but turn back to their session. So group therapy is a thing here. I don't know how that will play out, but I told Josh I would try anything. If group therapy will help me get my temper under control, if it will help me not lash out at Rox and everyone around me, then I am willing to try anything.

I still can't believe I hit her. Talking down to her is one thing, but hitting her . . . I really hope I didn't leave a bruise. Fuck! How hard did I hit Rox? I must have just made a sound because both Josh and Sister Helena turn around to look at me. She makes the cross symbol over her chest and I frown at her.

"I'm not a fucking demon you need to ward off, lady," I chastise her.

She turns back around as we make it to the end of the hall, opening another door. We enter a room opposite of the one in the lobby. The walls are white and blue and absent of any crosses. No nuns are walking around, which I take as a good sign. Maybe they are just in that part of the building.

"This is the mental behavioral unit," Helena states as she turns to the right and points to some blue and yellow chairs. "If you'll please have a seat, I will go get Dr. Harding for you."

The woman doesn't wait before she's scurrying away from us. If this is where they "turn frowns upside down," then the mission board really needs to work on their welcoming committee. I go over to one of the hard plastic chairs and take a seat. Josh follows, sitting down right beside me. He crosses his arms and glares at me like I'm some juvenile delinquent that needs to be put in his place.

"What is your problem?" he hisses at me.

I shrug. "She's the one that acted like I was Satan incarnate. Why the hell didn't you tell me you were carting me off to some monastery?"

"Because you wouldn't have come. And this isn't a monastery. The nuns just work here from time to time."

I cross my arms, slouching in the chair. "I don't want to be here."

"We have to do things we don't want to sometimes, Wran. Grow up."

My hands clench into fists, but I hide them. I'm getting really sick of people telling me I need to grow up. I had to grow up much faster than most people my age. For fuck's sake, I'm only twenty-two. I should be out partying every night, living up my early years. Yet I'm not. I'm protecting a girl that doesn't seem to get just how much I love her. I'm putting up with a rich prick that's probably trying to get in my girl's pants right this moment. I gave up the right to be a kid, but somehow I still need to grow up. I scoff to myself.

Maybe everyone else just needs to leave me alone and let me handle things my way.

"Look." My brother exhales. "I know this isn't what you were expecting, but this is a good place. Thomas is a decent man. I wouldn't have brought you here if I didn't think it would help with your anger problems."

My hands unclench at Josh's sincere tone. I stare at him, not knowing if I can truly trust his words. While he's the only person I could have gone to with this, he's still the same brother that sent me away from Rox. He's still the same brother that neglected to tell me about my daughter. I run a hand over the stubble that has begun forming on my face. I know Josh believes what he does is for the best for everyone. If my flaw is anger issues, then Josh's flaw is believing he knows best for everyone. I get it, I do. Josh had to take on the role of father at a young age, and he's been acting as such ever since. But he needs to learn that I'm not the eleven-year-old boy that lost all his friends.

"So, you said you used to see Thomas?" I ask my brother. "I can't picture the perfect Josh Belmont needing to speak to a therapist."

He snorts and tilts his head back against the white wall. "There's a lot you don't know about me."

"Care to share?"

"I didn't realize we were on sharing terms." He points to the bandage across his nose from where I hit him the other day. "I'm pretty sure your exact words to me before Aspen were that you were done with me."

I roll my eyes at him. "Don't be such a chick. I was angry, and I had every right to be. You should have told me about Harley."

"I wanted to, but Rox didn't think it was a good idea. And I sorta agree with her, after seeing how you reacted. The situation with Harley is complicated; we didn't need you coming in and ruining anything."

Really? Why does everyone seem to think I would have gone off? Sure, I would have been upset, but I know how serious my daughter being with social services is.

"I was only with her once," I mutter to Josh. "You never let me explain that before you shipped me off."

"Once was enough. She was fifteen."

Running my hand through my hair, I don't say more about that situation. He'll never get it. I know how old Rox was. And yeah, we had been messing around, but I never intended on being with Rox that way before she was old enough. I was perfectly happy with the make-out sessions and the taunting. Seeing her smile had turned into my greatest joy, even if it felt like I was betraying myself to put the smile there.

"I know you don't believe it when I say I love that girl, but I do. She owns every part of me." I glance at him.

He opens his eyes and looks at me. "After last night, I believe you, but that doesn't mean I'm going to change my mind about this situation. You two are no good for each other. You're too dependent on one another. That type of relationship isn't healthy."

"And you would know what's a healthy relationship? You go around telling a girl that you practically raised that you don't care about her."

Josh sits up and turns to me full on. "I have never said that I don't care about Roxanna. I love her like she's a damn sister, but when it comes to you and her, I draw the line. I don't want to watch as the only family I have pull themselves apart. And that's exactly what's going to happen if you are together. Neither one of you know how to handle your emotions."

"Rox seems perfectly fine to me," I mutter.

"The girl started using sleeping drugs so she wouldn't have to feel when you left. That's not normal."

I don't say anything to that, just lean back in the chair and rest my head against the cool wall. I suppose he has a point. Rox shouldn't have turned to those. I can't believe she turned to drugs. All because of me.

A shadow looms over me and I sit up just as Josh does. He gets up from his chair and greets the man that's standing in front of us. He has sandy hair and gentle brown eyes that demand respect. I get up from my chair as he turns to me. He's younger than I would have thought for a therapist—or at least one that was helping Josh in high school with who knows what. He holds out his hand to me and I shake it.

"Thomas, thanks for seeing us on such short notice," my brother greets the doctor.

Thomas looks at my brother with a wide grin and they bump shoulders. This man was a high school counselor? "Good to see you, Josh. How have you been?"

"As good as I can be with this knucklehead." Josh points to me.

"Wran, right?" The doctor turns to me. "Good to meet you. Josh mentioned in his email that you've been a bit on edge lately and could use someone to talk to."

I laugh at his assessment. On edge. That's stating it lightly. I'm pretty sure this man doesn't really want to know what has me on edge. "How about you tell me about your time with Josh? What could my brother possibly need help with?"

For some reason, I really want to know the answer to this. Josh has always seemed to have his shit together. Never have I once thought that he was the type of person that would need a psychotherapist to help him with anything. It's just not how he is.

Thomas glances to Josh and Josh nods. "Do you honestly think your brother has no issues of his own after dealing with the way your lives have gone? He's had to care for you and Roxanna since he was fourteen."

My brows shoot up at the mention of Rox's name. So he knows about her. I wonder how much info my dear brother shared about her. I look at Josh and he shrugs his shoulders. Some part of me already knew that Josh couldn't have been okay with all the crap we've had to go through. He was just a kid too. But he seemed so put together all the time. He was the opposite of me in every way. So calm and collected. Most days it was like he didn't even care that Pops was a drunken bastard, and he was the only reason we went unhungry. He went through his days as if it was all normal.

Shaking my head at Thomas, I don't give him an answer to his question. From the sound of it, Josh didn't handle things as well as I assumed. I really am a crappy brother for not seeing it. Hell, I'm sure I didn't want to see it. One of us needed to have our head screwed on right, and since he was the oldest, I suppose I let him take that job. My only focus was the purple-eyed beauty that taunted my days, nights, and dreams.

"Let's head to my office and I'll give you some information about my program," Thomas states and begins walking down a short hall. His office is the last door on the right. It's a decent size with a big wooden desk in front of a window. Outside of it, the only thing that can be seen are trees, which has me second-guessing this place again. Pulling my gaze from the reminder that I've agreed to seclude myself in this place, I take in the rest of the room. There are two nicely cushioned chairs in front of the desk, along with a Buddha statue in the corner. On the wall adjacent to the window are two frames displaying his degrees. Other than that, the walls are bare.

Josh takes one of the chairs, and I follow his lead. Thomas turns on his computer and then turns to us both. "I'm guessing that you already know that my program is a four-week inpatient program. During this time, you will be required to attend independent sessions along with daily group sessions. You will be attending those sessions with others that have behavioral problems. I strongly believe that you all can benefit from each other's stories and learn from tactics that have worked for others."

"And what if I don't want to share with others?" I ask him.

This may be a place for people with issues, but I doubt anyone here has ever slaughtered a man. Unless Thomas has done something as heinous as that, he can't possibly understand me. I hardly understand half the things going on in my head. I hated James Raine, yet I can't seem to get the man to leave my dreams alone. Every night, every time I close my eyes, his limp form and glossy eyes are there to remind me that I took his life.

"Participating isn't necessarily required in the group sessions, but you must attend. I recommend participating. You might not think so right now, but talking with a group of people with similar issues can be very gratifying. It can help you feel less alone in some sense."

"Does everyone here have anger management problems?"

"No. Some are sex addicts. Some are hyper-manic. But your group session will only include those dealing with their anger."

I nod at him.

"Does this sound like something you will be willing to try, Wran?"

I glance at my brother and then back at Thomas. "My girlfriend told me to get some help. And I'm tired of hurting her, so yeah. I guess this is something I'm willing to try."

He smiles and turns to his computer. He types something out before standing and leaving the room.

Josh places a hand on my shoulder. "I'm proud of you," he says. "I really thought you would bolt."

I shake my head. "No. Not this time. I need her, Josh. She's everything good in my life."

The doctor comes back into the room, holding some papers. He sits back down in his black chair and shuffles the papers. "All right, Mr. Belmont, all I need is for you to sign yourself in and then we can begin the evaluation and get you settled into a room."

Gulping back, I stare at the papers and then out the window again. I'm doing this for Rox. I'm doing this for Harley. I'm doing this for myself. I will be a better person, hopefully, after coming out of this. Picking up the pen, I sign the forms by the X and slide them back across the desk. Josh squeezes my shoulder and I inhale. Fuck, I can't believe I just signed those papers.

CHAPTER 8

WRAN

I've been at Pleasure House for two days now, and I can't say I hate it as much as I thought I would. It's actually been . . . pleasant. After Josh left the other day, Thomas started asking me a shit-ton of questions about my life as part of his evaluation. He said he needed to know my triggers. I only got upset with him twice: when he brought up my pops and Rox. I don't know why Rox is a trigger, but apparently she is. Fucking great for me, right? The one thing that doesn't need to be a trigger sets me off. Yesterday he let me get comfortable. I didn't leave the room they assigned me except for lunch and dinner. The food was pretty good, not going to lie.

With all that being said, it has been a long two days so far. They took my phone and I haven't been able to contact anyone. Thomas said after the first two weeks I'll be allowed visitations but going two weeks without hearing from Rox sounds like torture. Even when I was in the military, I had her voicemails that I could listen to every day. Now I have nothing.

Today is the first day that I have to participate in anything. I'm a little worried. I don't do good with people—especially people that are going to be talking about how I should and shouldn't act. Glancing at the clock on the wall, I frown when I see the time: 9:45 am. Group therapy starts in fifteen minutes. I've avoided getting to meet any of the other residents here. I have nothing against them, but I'm screwed up enough; I don't want to get to know more people like me. We would clash hard. My blunt disregard of them hasn't stopped them from knocking on my door and introducing themselves to me though.

There was a guy, Steven, that stopped by last night and invited me to play pool. Apparently we get free time after dinner until ten, which is lights out. That part sucks. I haven't slept in these two days. I don't want strangers hearing me jerk awake because I'm having dreams about James Raine. I don't want them in my business.

Clicking off the thirty-two-inch TV mounted to the wall, I head out of the room and down to the courtyard. Thomas is already sitting there with a couple of other patients. Mats are arranged in a circular formation, so everyone can see everyone. It's a nice day, which is still odd to me. This time of year in Kingston, we would be wearing light jackets and long sleeves. The sky would be getting ready to open and drench us in spring rain. Not here. Everything is so bright and cheerful. The grass is green. Birds are chirping. And the sky is blue. Last night as I watched the stars, hoping Rox was watching them too, it seemed so fake. This place seems so wrong, even though it's mere hours away from Kingston.

I take a seat on one of the mats as more people make their way over to where we are. After all the mats are filled, Thomas finally stands and starts the session. He greets everyone and then turns to me. I narrow my eyes at the man, shaking my head. This isn't my first day at a damn new school, and if he makes me introduce myself like so, I swear I'm walking away from this.

He doesn't though.

Thomas simply motions to me and then addresses the rest of the group. "As you can see, we have a new member joining us today. He's a bit . . . shy, I'll say, and I would like you all to introduce yourselves to him. I want him to feel comfortable here with you all. We're all family here."

I arch a brow at him. Family? I search the small group, but none of them make a move. I bet none of them feel like we're all family. I certainly don't. The only family I have is Rox and Josh, and they're both miles and miles away from Pleasure House.

The guy from yesterday, Steven, stands and looks at me. "Hey, man. I'm Steven, in case you don't remember. You know, the dude that invited you to play pool? Yeah, well, I'm Steven. I've been here for the past two months. Court-appointed. I sorta have an issue with my aggression."

Really?

He has an issue with his aggression?

I would have never guessed, considering this is an anger management group.

"Sup," is the only response he gets from me.

After Steven's bravado, everyone else gets up and introduces themselves. It's a mess. Some of them only say hi and give a name while others give me their whole back story. There's a woman by the name of Teri who tells me all about how she ended up here. Apparently she was a stripper and some dude pinched her ass while she was on the pole. She threw her heel at him, and then proceeded to jump off the stage and smash him in the head with said shoe. I didn't need or want to know all that. Quite honestly, I don't think my anger is anywhere near as bad as half these people. Some of them don't even have reasons for why they act the way they act. At least I do. And now he's dead.

After everyone has gone, Thomas turns to me again. "Would you like to tell the group a little about yourself?"

I stare at him point blank. Does it look like I want to share anything with these idiots? When his eyes don't leave me, I look around the group at all the expectant eyes and let out a sigh. Damn. He knew this was going to happen.

Standing, I glare at them all. This should be illegal. No one, and I mean no one, truly gives a damn about what is going on in other people's lives. Not unless those people happen to actually be real family.

I give a lazy wave to the group. "Name's Wran Belmont. I'm not here to make friends." My eyes cut to Thomas. "I only want to learn how to manage my anger so I can get my girl back. Nothing more. Nothing less."

The other ten pairs of eyes never leave me. As soon as I'm back down on the mat, they begin clapping. What. The. Fuck? Thomas smiles at me like I just won the Nobel Prize or something, and then he too joins in with the clapping. Why the hell are they clapping?

"You did good, Wran," Thomas states. "Most people don't say anything in their first session. You just showed me that you do want to get better."

Really?

He got all that by me basically telling him to back off?

I shake my head and lean back on the mat on my elbows, soaking up the sun. These people are crazy, but I suppose this could be worse. I could be back in the army with General Townsend barking at me. Telling me what I'm doing wrong, how my attitude better change, and that I'm a no-good piece of dirt that's never going to advance in rank. This is a whole lot better than that.

The rest of this group session goes by without me saying another word. Thomas asks everyone how their night and morning went, if anyone felt a substantial amount of rage. Not many people did. Only Teri had an issue within the last twenty-four hours. Apparently she was out during free time and saw a patient from another wing with her boyfriend. The boyfriend said or did something to the girl and Teri said she threatened to gut him with her nails. Pretty sure Teri has an issue with men and affection and shit. I'll make sure not to bring up Rox in these little meetings if I ever decide to talk.

I'm about to leave and head back to my room when Steven comes up to me, cheerful as can be. At least this therapy seems to be working on someone. "Hey, man! Where you heading?"

I stare at him for a long minute. Did he really not get the hint last night or an hour ago? I'm not here for friends. "My room."

"Why don't you come hang out with us in the theatre room? They're showing Wizard of Oz."

I furrow my brow at him. Dude has to be in his thirties and he's watching a movie meant for little girls under the age of ten.

"I know, I know," he defends himself before I tell him to get lost. "It's no Avengers, but it's better than the four basic channels we get in our room. Plus, they only show us non-violent films here. Think it will help soothe us out."

Soothe us out? "Didn't a house fall on a woman in The Wizard of Oz?"

"Yeah, but it's PG."

With reluctance, I give in to Steven. Doesn't look like he's going to quit trying anytime soon anyways. Besides, he has a point. After two days in a row, Family Feud does get old. "Fine. I guess I can watch it."

"You won't regret it. Everyone's pretty rocking."

I arch a brow at him. Rocking?

"Is that not the right word nowadays?"

I shake my head at him. "Rocking is fine."

He grins and leads us to the theatre room.

It's after dinner when I get back to my room. After Dorothy, Steven finally talked me into a game of pool. One game turned into two and two turned into three. I hate to admit that I had fun with the nutjob. It was nothing like hanging out with Rox. While I love doing things with her, I kinda forgot what it felt like to hang with guys and someone I'm not striving to make cry. We talked about dumbass shit and it didn't end in an argument. I didn't have to guess what anyone was talking about. Not even Teri. She's the most straightforward woman I have ever met. Well, besides Janice. I have an inkling those two would hit it off.

I go over to the small desk in front of the window and take a seat, looking out at the stars. Today wasn't bad. Not even the one on one meeting I had with Thomas after the movie. I didn't say anything, but I'm sure he expected that after this morning. I don't know why this is so hard. No one else seems to have a problem spilling their guts about the stuff they've done. I've learned more about these people in one day than I have anyone.

With great force and a yawn, I pull myself away from the window. Rox is probably at work right now. She's not watching the stars with me. I climb on the extra-long twin bed that you only see in college dorm rooms and fold an arm over my eyes. I wish I could talk to her, hear her. I miss her. I need to apologize again.

Groaning, I turn over on the bed and bury my face in the oddly comfortable pillow. Why can't I get her off my mind? Rox definitely didn't have any second thoughts about walking out on me. She had no second thoughts about calling that prick Cade when things got a little out of hand. I'm here for her, trying to better myself for her, yet she probably hasn't even thought about me today. Bet she doesn't even know I'm not in Kingston anymore.

I grab the first thing I see, the remote to the TV, and heave it against the wall. With a pop, it breaks into pieces. Fuck! I get up from the bed and go pick up the pieces. Great. Just great! I set the parts on the desk and get back in bed. Just as I reach for the small lamp, a knock sounds on my door. My eyes dart to the clock and I roll my eyes. For the past two days, nurses have been coming around to do nightly check-ins on us as if we're babies. It's stupid; we're all adults here.

Getting up from the bed, I march over to the door and yank it open. I expect the shy little nurse that has been coming to my room. She was so nervous the first time she came by, and I couldn't help but give her a hard time. It was funny watching her squirm when I gave her that cocky smile that I know gets Rox every time. She didn't stay long. Just looked in my room, blushed, and ran off. She didn't even stay long enough to give me the little pill Thomas prescribed for my little sleeping problem. Apparently my brother has a big mouth and informed Thomas that I didn't sleep the night I stayed in my childhood home. I haven't been taking the little pills. I refuse to be one of those people that results to drugs just to sleep. Besides, Rox lost my daughter taking those damn things. They won't be entering my mouth. If I can't sleep the old-fashioned way, I won't sleep at all. Well, not until my body decides it's going to give in to those damn dreams. Sooner or later I will have to sleep. It's inevitable.

The little nurse isn't at the door, though. Standing there in a long blue robe and navy boxers with rabbits on them is Steven, his hairy stomach slightly protruding. I ready myself to close the door in his face but second-guess it. I did have fun with the nutjob today, and if I'm going to be in here for another twenty-eight days, I might as well make at least one acquaintance. Besides, he's not all bad. Just a little too pushy for my liking.

"Hey, dude, I was in the area and heard a bang. Everything okay?" he asks, peering inside my room and looking around.

I nod and pull my door in a little closer to keep him out of my space. Dealing with Dorothy and playing pool is one thing. Him being a nosy fucker is a whole 'nother. He doesn't need to be gazing inside my room.

"Everything is fine. Just got a little frustrated. You know how it is."

"What made you upset? Sometimes I get that way, you know. Need to let off a li'l steam." He pulls the strings of the robe together and ties them before leaning against the wall, waiting for me to answer him.

I look down the hall, begging for the little nurse to make her way down here, and fast. Steven is starting to get on my ever-loving nerves. He asks way too many questions. He did the same thing during our pool game, but I let that slide since playing with him and a few others was a thousand times better than sitting in this room, but now he's pushing it.

"It was nothing," I tell him, easing back a little into the room. Hopefully he'll get the hint and leave before I go off on him. I don't need to find out what these people will do to me if I injure another inmate. He doesn't get the hint though and pushes inside the room. I bite down on my lip and stare at the blue wall across from me, fist clenching against the door. He really needs to get the hell out of my space. Slowly turning around to him, I see him sitting on my bed. On. My. Fucking. Bed.

"Get. The fuck. Out," I say in what I consider to be my calm voice.

His eyes widen and he gets up off the bed. "Oh, dude, I'm sorry. I didn't mean to crash your vibe. Just wanted to check on you."

I let out a deep breath and unclench my fist. "You can't barge into people's rooms. Are they not teaching you shit?"

The jovial expression that I've seen on his face for the past two days fall, and his eyes seem to darken in an instant, almost like a switch has been flipped. Then he closes his eyes and starts counting. Out loud. Like a true nutjob. Steven's hands clench and unclench, and by the time he reopens his eyes, he's counted all the way to one hundred.

I guess this is one of those techniques Thomas said I'd start learning tomorrow.

I hope not.

That's weird as fuck.

Steven exhales and then walks out of the room. He turns back to me. "Sorry, dude," he says for a second time. "People tell me that I have boundary issues. I'm still learning that there is a thing as a bubble. If you ever need to talk to someone about your anger, I'm here to help. Being here alone can do a number on a person. Especially at night when your brain runs free."

I nod at him. "I was thinking about my girlfriend. She sort of dumped my ass. I don't even know if 'dumped' is the right word."

"Is she your trigger?"

"Thomas thinks she is. I don't know."

He rubs the back of his neck and then scratches at his chin. "Do you love her?"

I lift a brow at him. What kind of question is that?

He raises his hands up in defense and I stop myself from darkening his eyes. I'm getting real sick of everyone questioning my frame of mind about Rox. If I didn't love her, I wouldn't be in this mental ward. I wouldn't have taken care of her for all of these damn years. And I most certainly wouldn't have killed for her. If I could separate my thoughts of Rox from her father, I would have a long time ago. Steven doesn't know this though. He doesn't know a thing about me and my relationship with Rox. I have to tell myself that his question is just a question.

"I can see that you do," he answers for me. "My advice is to have her come to a session when you are allowed visitors and talk out your frustrations with her. Thomas is really good at coupling. He helped my wife understand a lot of crap about me and my rage. You won't see the results overnight, but the more you talk to her, let her in on your thoughts, the less she'll be a trigger for you."

That doesn't make much sense to me, but whatever. "Thanks." I hear a door to my left close and I lean out the door to see. The nurse is making her way down to me. I smirk to myself.

"You know fooling around with the staff is against the policy, right?"

I turn my attention back to him. "I'm not gonna fool around with her. She's not my type. And even if she was, I would never think about hurting my girl in that way."

"All right. I'll see you tomorrow. Just keep your cool for the rest of the night and try not to break anything else. Every item you break they add to your bill."

"How did you know—"

"I saw the remote on the desk when I entered your room. Take deep breaths and everything will be rocking."

I nod. If he's going to be hanging around, I really need to update him on the language. I don't think I can handle him saying everything is rocking.

"Thanks for the advice."

Steven turns and leaves just as the nurse comes to a stop in front of me. I lean against the door and smirk at her. The smile that was planted on her face seconds ago vanishes and she takes a step away. She makes this so easy.

"Mr. Belmont," she states in her childlike voice, hands on her hips, giving me her most stern face.

"Nurse."

CHAPTER 9

ROX

I wrap my light cardigan around me as I stand on the porch and wait for Josh to show up. He's been dodging my calls for three days now and I don't know why. He managed to get whatever stick was shoved up his butt out last night to send me a single text to let me know he wasn't bailing on our Saturdays with Harley. That was only one of the things I wanted to discuss, considering I have no clue how today is going to go. I wanted to ask him about his brother too.

Wran made it clear he was going to fight for me, yet I haven't seen him once in three days. He's not answering calls or text or anything, and it's really starting to feel like three years ago again. I know I left him, but I can't go without him. The fact that I've been blind to the way he's been feeling has kept me awake at night. If he would only answer his phone or something, let me know he's okay, I'd be fine. I'd be completely fine.

I pull my phone from my skirt pocket and look at the time. Josh is late. He is never late for our Saturdays with Harley. I press the call key next to his name and wait for the ringing. It doesn't ring, just goes straight to voicemail. I glance up and down the street for his old beat-up car, but only see the black SUV that's been sitting down the road for a few days. Kingston is probably the safest town anyone can live in—nothing really happens here—but I can't imagine why someone would leave their vehicle, a nice vehicle, on the side of the road. I would have at least called the garage to tow it. We do have one of those. It's small, but we have one. Wran used to work there before he decided to up and leave three years ago, like he's doing now.

"He's still not here?" I turn around to Claire's voice.

I shake my head. She came over again this morning to do my makeup. The bruise is nowhere near as black and bad as it was before, but it is still far too noticeable on my face. Claire worked a miracle once again.

"Is he ever late?" she questions and leans against one of the columns. I shake my head again. "I could always take you. I need to go shopping anyways."

"I'll give him another ten minutes," I tell her. As much help as Claire's been over the last three days, I don't want my daughter anywhere near her. I still don't trust her. I'll let her do my makeup, but when it comes to Harley, I draw the line. I will not put my daughter in any more crosshairs. Besides, Harley knows Josh. She expects Josh. I don't know how she or Lynn would react to me bringing new people around her.

It could be unhealthy, introducing her to so many new faces only for them to vanish from her life if I don't get custody. After the Aspen Accident and Lynn finally finding out that one of the Belmonts did indeed father my baby, I don't know what my chances truly are. Lynn made it very clear at the hospital that knowing Wran was her father was not a good thing.

I really don't want to lose my baby just because of who fathered her.

There should be a law against that.

I should investigate it. It's not like I put Wran as the daddy on the birth certificate. She could just look like him. People look like people they're not related to all the time.

"Hey, what are you thinking so hard about?" Claire asks me as a swift wind swoosh past us.

Pulling my cardigan a little tighter, I tell her, "My daughter. I don't know how I'm going to get her back."

"How did she end up with family services?"

I turn and look at Claire. We aren't friends. I don't think her doing my makeup twice warrants her that kind of information, but as I search her usually snotty face, I don't detect any malice. Still, I don't know if telling her is wise. She could easily use it against me.

"I get it," she states. "I haven't been the nicest person."

"No, you haven't," I mutter—more so to myself, but I know she still heard me.

"I deserve that. But you could at least—"

Claire stops talking just as Josh pulls up to the house. I let out a breath and rush down the steps. He gets out of the car and comes to a stop in front of me. He looks me up and down and I arch a brow at him. Josh pulls me to him, hugging me so tightly I can barely breathe. He takes my face in his hold and turns it to the side. He lets out a sigh and drops my face, going back over to the car and getting inside. That was flipping weird.

I turn around to Claire to respectfully decline her offer to drive me to Arlington, only to find her head tilted to the side and glaring at Josh. Guess she's not over the Belmont brothers putting her father in his place. Although I do find it incredibly weird that she's not like that with Wran. I'm pretty sure he would have done most of the attacking in that situation. Yet when he came to my school, she had goo–goo eyes for him. Maybe her libido overrides her anger. Ignoring her, I go over to the car and get inside. Josh looks at my face again and then starts up the car. He pulls away without uttering a word to me.

When we are on the interstate and the silence is finally too awkward, I turn around in my seat to face him. "So you didn't answer any of my calls. What's with that?"

He looks my way for only a second before giving the road his full attention. "I've been busy. Sorry that Wran hit you."

"Why isn't he taking my calls?" I question. They've been ultra–evasive and I need to know why. "I haven't seen him in three days, Josh. I'm worried."

Josh bats his hand at me. "Didn't you dump him for the pretty rich boy?"

Is that what Wran told him? "No. I'm not with Cade. I told Wran we would talk if he got some help. Would you prefer I stayed with him and be his punching bag? You wouldn't be able to see Harley that way."

"Of course not!" He jerks around to me and the car swerves a little. I steady myself against the dash as Josh straightens back in the lane. I glance behind us but there are no cars. "I'm glad you had the decency to leave, but why didn't you come to me? Why go to the one person you knew Wran would go crazy over?"

I sit back against the seat. "Because he's my friend. Wran can't choose my friends."

"The boy is in love with you, Rox. You know that."

I roll my eyes at him, even though he can't see me. So what if Cade is in love with me? I can't change it. I've done my part in informing him that we are never going to happen. I haven't given him any reason to doubt my word. If Wran can't handle the fact that other guys might find me a little bit attractive, then that's on him. I can't control Wran's actions any more than I can control Cade's moods.

"Last I looked, you and Wran weren't on good terms either," I huff out. "What makes you think he wouldn't have gone crazy on you too?"

"We're on better terms than him and Cade, and you know it."

I don't say anything to that because I have no clue what terms the brothers are on. They are apparently talking, if Wran had time to tell Josh that he hit me. Just not enough time to pick up the phone and answer one of the fifty calls of mine. I cross my arms over my chest and stare out the window. Maybe I made a mistake. Maybe I should have just accepted his apology. I know Wran has never done anything like that before. He's never hit me. I'm not going to count the incident before Aspen. He was drunk, and even then, he didn't hit me. Maybe I should have given him the benefit of the doubt. I shake my head to myself. No, I did the right thing. If I would have let that go, how many more times would he blame his anger? How long before he would realize he does have a problem that needs to be fixed?

"Sorry I was late today," Josh says, changing the subject. "There was a bit of an issue at the station."

"What kind of issue? Did someone steal a cookie from the diner again?" I laugh at myself. Nothing but nothing happens here. The last time Josh had an issue, it was because someone TPed a house during Halloween last year.

Josh side-eyes me and I stop laughing. "You could take my job a little more serious. It did put food in your stomach and clothes on your back."

All traces of amusement leave me at his words. "I know. I'm sorry. Being a cop is a noble career. It's just that nothing happens in Kingston. I didn't mean to belittle your career choice."

He runs a hand over his hair like his brother always does, and nods. "I know."

The rest of the car ride passes by achingly slow. Neither Josh nor I say anything to each other. The silence does make riding with him a little awkward, but I've learned to deal with it. Josh isn't the type of person that likes a lot of noise when he's driving. When we pull into the parking lot outside of the social service department, I glance at the clock. We're ten minutes late. Not once in three years have we been late to see Harley. Without waiting on Josh to turn the car off, I jump out of it and sprint inside the building. The same guard that's here every Saturday opens the door and allows me to step inside the x-ray machine. It beeps once and I groan. Forgot to take out my phone. I set the phone in the bucket on the conveyer belt and step inside the machine again. It turns green and lets me through. Josh follows close behind.

As I turn the corner to the check-in desk, I notice the old lady that's normally here. She smiles at me and open the doors that lead to a waiting room. Lynn and Harley are not sitting out for us like they usually are, which causes me to pause for a second. I know we're a little late, but ten minutes is not that much. I pull my eyes away from the empty chair and multi-colored blocks and head down the hall to Lynn's office. I knock on the wooden door once.

"Come in," Lynn calls out.

I peek over my shoulder at Josh, and he tilts his head toward the door. Lynn is always hanging around in the waiting room for me. Coming straight to this office is not right. When I make no means to push forward, Josh pulls me back and steps through the door. I gulp and go in after him. I come to a stop next to Josh and my eyes widen at the sight of the judge that granted me Saturday visitations with Harley. I glance at Ms. Adams and then around the room. There's no Harley. This is not good.

"Where's Harley?" Josh asks, voice sounding of steel.

The judge motions to the two chairs in front of Lynn's desk and I make my way over to one of them. Josh doesn't move for a minute or two, but then he does. He sits down beside me and tenses. He knows nothing good can come of the judge being here and not Harley.

Lynn straightens in her chair and plants a smile on her face. It wavers a little as her eyes look back and forth between us and the judge, and then she's letting out a sigh. Her shoulders slouch a little, but not much. If I wasn't watching her so intently, I wouldn't have even noticed the slight movement. But I am. Watching her. She needs to tell me where my daughter is.

"Where's Harley?" I repeat Josh's question but in a much calmer tone.

"She is in another room. Don't worry," Lynn reassures me, but it does nothing to calm my nerves. How can she tell me not to worry when the judge is here? Her very presence means I have something to worry about. "We only wanted to speak with you prior to your outing—without Harley in the room."

"What's this about?" Josh leans forward in the chair, his eyes never leaving my social worker.

The judge moves around the desk to stand behind Lynn, letting us know they are a united front on whatever she is about to say. I bite down on my bottom lip, my fingers toying with the hem of my skirt. The judge's eyes move between Josh and me but settle on Josh. Guess she thinks Josh is more equipped to handle whatever she's about to spit out.

"Lynn informed us all that your brother fathered Harley," she says, and I suck in a huge breath. I didn't want them to find out.

Flicking my eyes up to Lynn, I find she doesn't meet my gaze. Of course she doesn't. She knows she could have kept that to herself if she wanted. The fact that she didn't only proves that she doesn't really care if I get my child back or not. Then again, she has told me that. Her main concern has and always will be the little girl with dark bouncy waves and chocolate eyes. Not me.

"We would like to set up a meeting to talk with him. As you well know, Roxanna Raine was a minor when the affair started, and we are aware that she is cohabiting with him now."

"They were both teenagers. Besides, she's no minor anymore. She's allowed to live with whoever she wants."

"Not if she wants custody of Harley," the judge threatens. "And even so, your brother broke the law. We can't exactly go on Lynn's words, but we do require Wran Belmont to submit to a paternity test."

"No!" I blurt out. "You can't do that. He's not listed as her father. You can't just do blood tests on people."

"Actually, we can." Lynn voices. "Under these circumstances, we can. We can't grant custody to you if he's the father and you are living with him."

I shake my head at her. This isn't happening. They can't do this. "That's not fair."

Lynn's eyes dip. "Roxanna, I've told you before that life isn't always fair."

"You shouldn't have taken her in the first place. I'm not a horrible mother. I'm not hurting her."

"You were doing drugs," the judge states, pulling my glare away from Lynn. "If that doesn't make you unfit to be a parent, then I don't know what does. A jury would agree with us."

"I didn't do drugs. I told you that before. My doctor said the sleeping pills were fine. I needed help sleeping; that's all." My voice comes out broken and like a plea, but I don't care. They are basically using whatever they can to take her from me.

"Cocaine," is all the judge says.

I shake my head at her. I've told them over and over that I have no clue how that stuff got in my system. Never have I even wanted to do that drug. Never have I even had the inkling to participate in those types of recreational activities. I didn't take it. I didn't take it. I didn't take it!

"She didn't take that. We've told you that a million times," Josh defends me.

"That doesn't change the fact that it was in her system and neither of you did anything to find out how it got there. Not to mention her alcohol level was well above the limit, and she was a minor."

"I know this is hard, Roxanna," Lynn says. "You've done everything we've asked of you, but with the newfound information on hand, plus your past with narcotics, the judge thinks it would be best not to award you custody. Of course, we can't do anything right now without confirming that Wran Belmont is the father."

I turn away from Lynn and get up from the chair. I glare at the judge, hatred for the woman seeping to the surface. "You can't do this to me. I've gone through hell for that little girl. She is mine! You can't take her!"

"I suggest you lower your voice, Ms. Raine, before we take your visitation rights away as well." The judge looks past me and at Josh, who's now standing behind me. "Make sure your brother comes in for a screening. Monday."

"That's going to be a problem," Josh utters.

"Why is that?"

"He's not in town."

I gasp and look up at Josh. His eyebrows pull together as if telling me sorry. So it's true. Wran really did leave me like three years ago. He would much rather have his anger control him than get some help. He would much rather leave me, even after finding out all he found out. Ohmygod. I ease back down to the chair, biting my bottom lip even harder.

He left.

He. Left. Me.

Ohmygod.

"Do you know where he is?" the judge asks.

"No. He called me a few days ago and said he had to handle something and that he would be gone for a while. I haven't seen or talked to him since."

"Roxanna?" I look up at Ms. Adams holding a tissue to me, a contrite expression gracing her strong, sharp face. "You still get to take Harley today, if that makes this any better. An official ruling hasn't been made. We just wanted to inform you what was going on."

I nod and take the tissue. I'm losing Harley. I've lost Wran. What more is this world going to take from me? I can't handle anymore.

Lynn rises from her desk and walks around to our side. "If you'll follow me, I'll take you to Harley."

"Just hold up one second!" the judge yells. "I don't think she deserves this outing. Did you not hear how she talked to us?"

"That really isn't for you to decide, Judge Thomlison. Without the ruling, she still has every right to see her daughter." Lynn turns back to us. "Now, if you will follow me."

CHAPTER 10

ROX

Lynn leads us down a hallway that turns from the normal beige to a bright blue with an ocean mural painted on it. There are a ton of different sea creatures, and the scene makes me smile. At least this is a little bit of color after the nightmare Lynn subjected me to. I can't believe she informed them about Wran. Not after he was the one who got Harley back when she was taken from under Lynn's nose. I guess that really does go to show that I can't trust anyone. Not with my child and most certainly not with my heart.

We come to a stop outside a door with a starfish painted on it. Lynn pushes open the door and we all walk in. Harley looks up from where she's seated on the floor with the stuffed bear I bought her the last time we went to the mall. At least she's going to have something of me when they take her.

"Poshy!" Harley jumps up from the floor and runs over to Josh. He bends down to pick her up and she throws her arms around his lean neck, her arms not completely circling him. When she's done hugging him, she looks over at me. "Mommy!"

I smile at her use of Mommy. It took Harley what seemed like forever to even call me that. She took a liking to Josh right away, though. She reaches her short arms back to me and I immediately take her out of Josh's hold before she changes her mind and decides she wants to stay with her Poshy. Harley wraps her arms around me the same way she did Josh and hugs me. I hug her back, placing a gentle kiss into her soft curls. This might be the last time I get to hold her . . . kiss her.

My gaze moves to the girl that gets up from the floor. She's beaming and doesn't look much older than me. Maybe early twenties.

"Hi," she greets me. "You must be Roxanna. I'm Lauren. I've heard so much about you. I'm so sorry about your father."

I frown at the girl and then turn to look at Lynn. Why would anyone be sorry about that man? He's better off six feet under. He did nothing but cause problems for everyone. I'm glad he's dead. I know I should be remorseful, but I'm not. I am free now. That man will never again hurt me or mine.

"This is my daughter." Lynn motions to the girl. "She's been like a sister to Harley. A huge help around the house."

"She's not her sister," I snap at Lynn. She will never be her sister.

Harley pulls my face away from my social worker and grins at me. She points behind me at the girl. "Sissy!"

I shake my head at my daughter. "No." My eyes cut to Lynn again. "You've been telling my daughter that's her sister?"

"Roxanna, Harley lives with us. It's only normal that she sees us as family. I know it hurts, but we've been taking care of her since she was born. This is normal."

This is not normal. "Next thing I know she'll be calling you Mommy. I gave birth to her. Not you. I suffered that pain. She's mine, Lynn."

Lynn nods but doesn't say anything to that. I shift Harley in my arms and grab Josh's arm, pulling him past Lynn and out of the room. I need to get out of here before I say something that will get me in trouble. Once outside the room, Josh grabs Harley from my hold and heads toward the building's exit. I follow him all the way to his car and watch as he straps Harley in her car seat. When he closes the back door, I lean against it and let the tears shed. They are going to take my baby away from me. Josh pulls me away from the car and into him. He hugs me tightly and runs a hand up and down my back.

"I can't," I mumble into his chest. "I can't. I can't. I can't."

"It's okay," he soothes me. "They won't be taking her. I won't allow it."

"How can you stop them?"

He pulls my face away from him and swipes at my tears. "Do you trust me?"

I nod. Josh might have been a jerk recently, but I trust him with my life. With Harley's life. He might not see me as family, but I have always seen him as my family. He's been here for me since I was six years old.

"Then trust me to fix this. Now, let's go before they see you like this."

I nod and go around to the passenger side of the car.

As Josh pulls away from the building, I notice that he's not headed back toward the zoo or mall or any of the places we go with Harley. Instead, he heads toward the interstate. Out of Arlington.

"Where are we going?" I ask him as my blood begins to pump faster in my veins. We've never taken Harley out of the city. Lynn told us not to. "We can't. Lynn—"

"What Lynn doesn't know won't hurt her." Josh cuts me off before I can begin ranting. "I know a family lawyer that works here in Arlington, but since it's Saturday, I'm going to his house. Hopefully he's home."

"Do I know him?"

"You might. He was around the house a few times, but you were young. I went to high school with him. Bennett Tanner?"

I shake my head at him. I don't remember anyone hanging around the house with that name.

"Then I guess you're meeting someone new today. Hopefully."

I turn around in the seat and look at Harley. She's asleep in her seat with a tiny smile on her face. She has the tendency to fall asleep when she's in the car. Turning back around, I nod. I'll meet whoever I must in order to keep my little girl.

After driving forty-five minutes, we come to a stop in front of a sky-blue plantation-style home with a wraparound porch on the outskirts of Arlington. There's a black Lexus sitting off to the side. For as far as I can see, there's nothing but greenery and white fencing. There are a few horses in the field to the side of the house. It's cute. I could see myself living here with Harley and the horses, away from society. I bet that's why this lawyer lives here. He doesn't have to put up with nosy neighbors and people gossiping, like in Kingston. Must be nice.

The screen door opens and out steps a tall man in khaki shorts and a peachy tank. He has blond hair that is almost brown but not quite. His skin looks like he bathes in sunlight. It's so golden and tan and glowy. I have never seen a man with a tan like this. I turn around in the seat to check on Harley, only to see her looking at the porch in fascination as well. Josh gets out of the car and heads up the gravel drive to the man. They one-arm hug before the man turns back to the car and points at me. Josh nods and beckons for me to come.

I get out and go around the vehicle to Harley. I undo the belt keeping her confined to the seat and then head up the path to the porch. As I approach, the man smiles down at us. Harley touches my cheek and then points to the man. I grab her hand and pull it away.

"Don't point, sweetie. It's rude," I whisper to her.

She wiggles in my arms and shimmies down to the ground. Harley slowly crawls up the steps and then stops beside Josh, completely ignoring him and looking up at the man. She points up at him again.

"Yellow boy," she says, and the guy's grin grows greater. Josh bends down to pick up Harley, but she shakes her head. My eyes widen at that; she has never turned down Josh. "Yellow boy."

The man—Bennett, I believe Josh said his name is—bends down to my daughter. She touches her hand to his face and smiles. Bennett lifts his arm up and looks at his skin. "I guess I do look yellow, huh?"

Harley nods as if she completely understands what he just said. She reaches up to him, and I turn to Josh. He looks just as shocked by Harley's interactions with the stranger as I do. This is too weird. I bend down and take hold of her, pulling her away from the man. She shouldn't have reached for him like that. Harley's waterworks are instant, and she pulls away from me and toward the man. Josh takes her from my hold and she quiets some, but she's still fixated on Bennett.

"Shh," Josh coos in her ear as he begins rocking her. She stops all the fussing and lies against Josh, her eyes closing a little. After about ten minutes of Josh just rocking her, Harley's out cold. Maybe she was just sleepy.

Josh turns back to Bennett. "Sorry 'bout that. Harley's never like this with people."

"You don't have to apologize. She is sweet. Plus, I tend to have that effect on kids. You remember how my sister's kids were." His eyes move from Josh to me and back to Josh. "Is she yours?"

Josh shakes his head. "No. She's actually Roxy's and Wran's."

The dude's eyes snap to me and look me over. "Roxy? As in little Roxy?"

I shift on my feet. So he knows me. "Hi," I greet him.

"Wow! You've grown up. Last time I saw you, you had long pigtails and were carrying around a Peter Pan book."

"As much as I wish this was a social visit," Josh starts, "it's not. We need your help. We need a lawyer."

Bennett motions toward the door and leads us inside. I come to a stop just inside the door and take in the modern décor that is completely at odds with the Southern charm of the exterior. Everything in here is of shades of white, black, or gray. I wasn't expecting this after seeing the horses. Then again, he owns a Lexus.

Bennett leads us through the house, and we pass an all-white kitchen with stainless steel appliances. I linger a moment by the kitchen before catching up with the guys. I want this house.

We finally come to a stop in front of a gray brick fireplace. I glance around the area as the guys sit down, and inhale. It's white. So, so white. I kind of don't want to sit on anything. The guys look at me, waiting, so I finally sit down. Cautiously. I really hope the black of my skirt doesn't rub off on this couch. My skirt was inexpensive, which means there will probably be some transfer. Crap. I scoot closer to the edge of the sofa, barely sitting on it, and turn to the guys. Bennett's lips pull up, but he doesn't say anything about my vigilant movements.

"So, what brings you all the way out here?" Bennett asks Josh as he leans on the couch with no worry at all.

Josh hands Harley over to me, and I sort of don't want to risk moving her. She is asleep right now, and I don't think it would be polite to have her waking up and throwing a tantrum in this man's home.

"As I mentioned, Harley here is Rox and Wran's daughter. Their nearly three-year-old daughter." He emphasizes Harley's age.

Bennett examines me but then turns back to Josh. "I am not understanding."

"Rox just turned eighteen, and Wran will be twenty-three in a few weeks."

Bennett's brows shoot up at that and then he's rotating on the couch to look at me. "You were a minor when you had her."

I nod.

"Wran was not."

I nod again.

"Yeah," I mutter out. I hate when people say it like that—like just because I was a minor and Wran was not that our being together is some unthinkable thing. Our age gap isn't that insane. It's barely an age gap at all. Besides, we grew up together. It's not that weird that our affections would develop into more.

"Did he—"

"No." I cut him off before he can even finish that question. I'm sick of that question. "It was very much wanted. He's not some creep. Geez!"

I don't know why I'm defending him now. He left. He. Left. Me. Again. I shouldn't be defending him at all. He should be here defending himself.

"It was consensual," Josh confirms. "But the thing is, Wran went into the military before he even found out about Harley and was gone for some time. During that time, Rox was drugged and now social services have Harley. Rox only gets Saturday visitation since she's still in high school."

Bennett nods.

"We need help," I voice since Josh is taking the round-about way of asking. "They just found out that Wran is Harley's father and are threatening to take full custody away from me. I can't lose her. I won't lose her. Is there anything we can do? Josh said you were a family lawyer."

"This sounds complicated," he tells us. "What exactly are you wanting to accomplish?"

"She wants custody of Harley. But they are against it. They think Wran raped her and that she's unfit to be a parent. They also think she's some druggie even though we've told them over and over that someone must have drugged her. They don't seem to want to negotiate."

Bennett turns to me. "Do you know who drugged you?"

I shake my head.

"Are you aware that no lawyer would touch this with a ten-foot pole? You are talking about fighting a system that has been in place for decades. They always win, and for good reason."

"I don't care. She's my daughter. I did nothing wrong." I glance down at Harley and place a peck in her hair. "I will fight for her."

Sitting up and leaning his elbows on his knees, Bennett lets out a huff and shakes his head. "Why was she taken in the first place?"

"Someone drugged her." Josh runs a hand over his head. "I found her passed out at a bar while going into labor. We have no clue how she got there. After she gave birth, I was informed that there was coke in her system. Social services were called."

Bennett rises from the couch and stretches, his eyes roaming from Harley to me. "As I said, this sounds like a messy case. I honestly don't know if you would even have a chance."

"Please. I'll pay you anything if you'll just try. I have money saved up." I have never wanted to use those checks that Wran sent home as much as I want to shove them at this man now. If using that is the cost I must pay to get my daughter back, to have her home with me and not have to drive to Arlington every Saturday, I will gladly part with them.

"I don't want your money, Little Rox. I will gladly do this pro bono. If I can win this case, I'll be the best damn lawyer there is. Can you imagine how my client list will expand? Nah, you have me for free."

"Really?" Josh and I both ask.

He nods. "Yeah, and besides, I owe Josh a favor. He kept all the seniors from beating on me when I was in high school. I was a bit nerdy. If it weren't for this guy, I probably would have dropped out of school."

I leap from the couch and throw my arms around the man. He tenses against me and awkwardly eases his way out of my grip. I step away from him. Yeah, that was probably way too much. I just can't believe it though. I can't believe he's willing to do this. I can't believe that I might have a fighting chance to get my daughter back. I have never wanted anything as much as I want Harley with me. Living with me. Celebrating the holidays with me. Spoiling her.

"Thank you, thank you, thank you," I chant to him.

"Don't thank me yet. This is going to be ugly. We still have Wran to consider. He did have sex with a minor, and this could blow up in his face. I would need to talk to him before proceeding."

Josh rises and Harley turns in his arms. He pats her on the back and she settles once more. "That might be a problem. He's currently away at a mental health retreat."

"What?" I shriek and turn toward Josh. "He's where?"

Josh looks down at me. "You told him to get better, Roxanna. He's doing it for you."

I suck in a breath. He's really getting the help he needs. He didn't leave me after all. It's not like three years ago. I feel the tears sliding down my cheeks before I even realize I'm crying. Wran is doing this for me. He does care. He cares about me. I swipe the tears away.

"How long will he be away?" Bennett inquires. "The sooner I talk to him, the sooner I can work on something where he is concerned."

"His program is a month long. So three and a half weeks more."

"Okay, umm, we'll work with Rox. I need to know everything that happened the night you were drugged."

I shake my head at him. "I don't know. I don't remember anything of that night."

"Okay, wow! This really is messy." He glances to Harley in Josh's arms. "How about you go lay her down and we'll talk some more. We're going to have to get you to remember something. Anything I can start with. This might take a while."

"We're going to have to get her back to my social worker before three."

He nods and starts leading us away from the sitting area. I really hope this man can help us. I know fighting social services is a long shot, but I will do anything for Harley.

CHAPTER II

WRAN

"Okay, Wran. Today I would like to focus on your mother and the relationship you had with her. I know a little bit about her through Josh, but I want to hear your thoughts."

I sit up on the couch, a little bewildered by the sudden change of topic. For the last week and a half, Thomas has only talked to me about Rox and my pops. While I'm not op-posed to talking about my mom, I don't get how talking about her will help this whole anger management whatever. She was the best woman I knew. Kind, smart, and an incredible cook. She was everything I want Rox to be.

"How does my mom fit into this whole cognitive behav-ioral mumbo jumbo? I thought the purpose of it was to help deal with my triggers and cope with shit."

"It is," Thomas states, and crosses his legs. "But some-times we must visit the past in order to move forward in our

lives. Things that don't seem to have mattered are some-times the things that count the most."

"You're starting to sound like an actual fucking doc, Doc," I tell him as I slouch down in the chair. These chairs are seriously comfortable. I think that's why I come here—to these one-on-one sessions. I could sleep on this piece of furniture.

"Tell me about her."

I stare up at the popcorn ceiling and try to think of something to tell him. Mom died when I was so young, and it's hard to remember a whole lot about her. The way she died, though, has never left me: lying next to me, humming. At the time, I thought she had simply fallen asleep. I should have known not. Mom had been diagnosed with cancer and she refused to live out her days in the Arlington Hospital. She had said it was too many miles away from her boys and that she would rather go in peace rather than hooked up to the machines. No one argued with her. Hell, I barely knew what was really happening.

"My mom was the most beautiful woman I had known. She had a love for life that rivaled any hippie from the seventies. She was the opposite of my pops. She lived to put smiles on people's faces."

"How did she make you feel?" Thomas leans forward and sets his notepad aside. I don't see why he takes notes on what I say when he records every session. A little redundant if you ask me.

"Important. Invincible. Happy, I guess," I tell him honestly. As a kid, I always had friends. That was never my problem. Josh, however, was older. Cooler. Smart. Pops loved him more because he was someone that could be just like pops. According to my dad, I was too much of a fucking wuss to be anything like him. Hence why I was boy and Josh was Josh. Mom gave me the extra attention that Pops didn't provide.

"And when she died?"

I sit up again, giving the doc a pointed look. How the hell does any child feel when their parent dies? That's a stupid question. "Like I lost a part of me. She was my mom, fucker."

"Does Roxanna make you feel the same way your mom did?"

Laughing, I shake my head. "Rox makes me feel like a man. A horny man. She's like the moon on a starry night. She brightens up my life. But then I think about her father, and all I want to do is cause her pain. I don't want to cause her pain. It's just something I can't control."

"A few days ago, you told me that Rox was everything you thought a good woman was supposed to be. Would you not describe your mother the same way?"

"Of course, but what does that have to do with anything?" I ask him. So what if I raised Rox in my mother's image? My mom was a great woman. Rox is a great woman. There is nothing I would change about either of them.

"How did you handle your mother dying? Did you mourn her? Cry for her?"

I let out a deep breath. Here he goes asking obvious questions again. Of course I mourned my mom. Of course I cried. She was my mom. If I didn't, that would have made me a sucky son. I like to think I wasn't. Sure, I wasn't the best. Pops yelled at me a lot, and I'm sure that caused my mom more stress, but I did try. Instead of saying anything to Thomas, I nod to give him my answer.

Why the hell do we have to talk about this? My mom is dead. It's not like anything about that is going to help me with my current situation. Discussing her isn't going to get me Rox back or keep my anger at bay. If anything, it's only going to piss me off. My mom is not a trigger, but I know what he's doing; Thomas is trying to forge some connection between my mom and Rox where there is none. The only thing they have in common is what I taught Rox to be. Nothing more.

"Next subject," I demand, and turn away from him.

"Just one more question on the topic and then we'll move on to some exercises."

"Fine," I grumble and relax back in the chair.

"Have you ever thought that Roxanna's father isn't the only reason you crave to cause her pain? Have you ever considered that you made her so much like your mother and the hurt you felt when she died is somehow seeping into your emotions for Roxanna?"

"What?" I shoot up and clench my fists into the material of the chair. Thomas takes a quick look down at my hands and then back at me.

"From what I know, not only from you but from what I remember of Josh telling me as well, your father didn't take well to her death. He didn't really allow you to mourn like a little boy who seemingly loved his mother should have. How long after she died did you get over her?"

Grinding my teeth, I glare at him. How dare this fucker even think for one minute that I'm not over my mother's death? "I'm going to say this once and only once, Doc: my issues with Rox have nothing to do with my mom. Got it?"

Thomas gives me a gentle nod and then glances at my hands again. I unclench them from the arms and sit back. My anger problems have nothing to do with my mom. They can't. She did nothing wrong. I'm not mad at her. I can't be.

We don't speak of my mom or Rox for the remainder of the session. Thomas focuses on breathing techniques for when I need to calm myself and suggesting situations that may send me off the rail. According to him, if I'm prepared for anything and aware of my mindset in the moment, then the anger will be easy to control. He always makes it sound so simple—like all I have to do is choose not to be upset. If it was that easy, I wouldn't be here. I wouldn't be torturing myself with these sessions. And I wouldn't be away from Rox. I would be home in Kingston, fighting that fucker Cade for my girl.

When the timer goes off, ending my session, my stomach growls. It's been four hours since the snack they provide in between lunch and dinner, and I'm hungry. Getting to my feet, I start to head for the door. Thomas gets up and steps in front of me. He reaches inside his blazer pocket and pulls out a small rectangular device in a green case with a cord wrapped around it: my phone. He hands it to me and I cock a brow at him.

"Monday will be two weeks that you've been here. You'll be allowed to have visitation. I think it would be a good idea for you to have a session with Rox and Josh."

I shake my head at him. "Rox doesn't even know I'm here. I can't face her."

"Because you hit her?"

I haven't told him about that. "What else did Josh tell you when he emailed you?"

Thomas's mouth quirks up at me. "That's for me to know. Just know that your secrets are safe with me."

Tensing at his words, I take the phone from him. What the hell did my brother tell him? I know for a fact that he didn't mention Aspen. Josh wouldn't incriminate himself by mentioning anything that happened there in an email. Yeah, the news has been reporting things in our favor, but it only takes a seed of info before we look like the criminals we are. Only a seed before I'm the one carted off in handcuffs.

"I'll call her, but she's probably not going to answer. Rox and I didn't leave things so good. Hell, I hit her. She had every right to run off with Cade."

"Cade?"

"Another time, Doc."

I turn and leave, heading straight for my room and forgetting about my growling stomach. As much as the burger on the menu sounds like heaven right now, hearing Rox's voice sounds even better, even if it's just her voicemail. Those are better than nothing. Keeping her voicemails from three years ago after coming home must make me the most pathetic man out there, but I don't care. As long as I keep them, I will forever have a piece of her. That's how I see it.

As I make it to my room, I close the door behind me and go over to the TV and turn it on. They didn't provide me with a replacement remote after breaking the other, so now if I want to watch anything I have to get up and press the button. To say it's annoying is an understatement. My sleeping habits haven't improved much since being here, and more times than not I find myself waking up after reliving killing someone. Mindless noise is the only way I can seem to get myself back to sleep without falling prey to those dreams. A shudder runs up my spine just thinking about the void, open eyes of James Raine in those dreams. Him telling me that I'm just like him. That I will hurt Rox. That she will run from me just as she ran from him. His words shouldn't haunt me—they are just words of a cynical man—but they do. Maybe 'cause I know I'm just as sardonic as he, and Rox has every right to fear me.

Sitting down on the bed, I plug my phone into the outlet. It chimes and displays a battery at zero percent. Should have known after almost two weeks that the thing would be dead. Now, at least, I have some time to think about how to apologize to Rox. If she even answers the phone.

Lying back on the bed, I stare up at the ceiling. I don't know how long I stay like that before someone is knocking on my door. It's probably my nurse; she's the only one that comes over this time of evening. The knock comes again and I get up from the bed. Yanking it open, I let out a frustrated groan at the sight of Steven standing there with a to-go container from the cafeteria. Most of the people here have learned that when I lock myself in this room, it means I don't want to deal with shit. Steven, though, hasn't learned. Yeah, I'm cool with the dude, and I haven't punched him yet, but I still prefer people not to come to my room.

"Hey, dude!" he greets me. "Didn't see you in the lunch-room. Thought you might get hungry."

He hands over the box, hands a little shaky. Guess I would be too if I was him. Steven never gets my good side when he comes to my room. Man has terrible timing. I take the container from him and open it. There's a burger that looks nowhere as good as the ones I get at Aunt May's Diner, and the fries are limp. There's no room to complain. I could have had fresh food if I would have gone to dinner. At least the man thought of me.

Scratching at the back of my neck, I give him the most genuine head nod someone like me can give. "Thanks. I could use this."

"Yeah, those veggie trays don't fill anyone," he says, reminding my stomach that the last thing I'd eaten was carrot sticks and hummus. "Jodi and I was gonna challenge the newbie to a round of doubles since he was talking crap earlier. Care to join?"

"Nah, man, I can't." I look back to where my phone is charging. "I'm about to make a call."

"Ah, right. Two-week mark. Giving your li'l lady a call?"

I lean against the inside of the door and pop open the container. Plopping a fry into my mouth, I nod. "Yeah. I'm hoping she'll answer. If not, I'll be blowing her phone up till she does."

"You ever gonna open up in group and tell us about the little lass?"

Two weeks of group therapy and I still haven't shared anything with these people. I don't think this program is working quite like Josh thought it would. Sure, I can talk to Thomas one on one, but telling a whole fuckin' group about myself is a no-go. Good thing Thomas is just okay with me doing the little activities and keeping my trap shut.

"Her name's Roxanna. She's a senior in high school. That's all I'm sharing." I give him something to tide him over. As crappy as I treat him, I'm surprised he sticks around. I'm glad he does. Steven is no doubt batshit crazy and clingier than a chick on her period, but he's the only person here besides Thomas that seems to give a fuck about the patients that come in and out of this place. He's tried to involve me in part of something here, along with the kid, Tevin, that showed up here a week ago. My treatment toward him has nothing to do with him personally; I'm just not into sharing. Been like that my whole life.

"All right, then, I'll see you at breakfast."

I nod and eat another fry. He heads off toward the game room and I close my door. Now I only have to find the courage to actually call Rox. I go over to my bed and sit the to-go box on the side table. Picking up my phone, I see the charge is at thirty percent—enough for me to turn my phone on and man up. When I do so, every message and call for the past week and a half comes in—most of them from Rox. I smirk at her name on the messages. I knew she couldn't just forget about me.

Instead of listening to the voicemails or reading the messages, I call her. The phone rings once. Halfway through the second ring, she answers. I can hear her breathing, but she doesn't say a word. Neither do I. What the hell do I tell her? How do I apologize for being an enraged dumbass and hurting her? How do I tell her that she's my world and that the moment my hand met her face it felt like my world had come crashing down?

She inhales. "Wran?"

I close my eyes and savor the sound of her sweet voice. God, it's like an eternity has passed since her musical voice invaded my head and left me reeling for more. I've missed hearing her. I've missed her. After this program is over, I am never leaving her side again. I will show her exactly why she fell in love with me to begin with, and if I have to win her back from that fucker Cade, I will. And I will do it the right way.

"Wran?" she asks a second time when I don't answer her.

"Rox." I breathe out her name like it's a prayer. "I'm so, so sorry."

The apology slips from my lips even though that's not how I wanted to say it. I could have come up with something better than that, but apparently my fucked-up brain had that in mind. She deserves to hear me beg. She deserves to hear me wallow. What I did deserves no less.

"I'm sorry too," she tells me just as I hear rustling on her end of the call, followed by a door closing.

"What do you have to be sorry for?" She did nothing wrong. Nothing at all. I might hate it, but I'm proud of her for standing up to me. I would want no less from Rox. It also means Josh and I did a damn good job in raising her.

"I didn't have all the facts before I went off on you about Claire. And I didn't see how much pain you were in following my father's death. I shouldn't have made you go to that funeral."

"Don't apologize, sweetheart. Never for that. It was my job to be there for you, and I let you down. I'm the one that's sorry. Sorrier than you will ever know. I never wanted to hurt you."

"Can you FaceTime?" she asks me.

I look around the room to make sure it's presentable. "Yes."

I pull the phone from my ear as the call turn into a video. I suck in a deep breath as she comes into view. If I thought the blue hair was crazy a couple of months ago, the blond is even crazier. It's going to take me a while to get used to seeing her as a blonde. It looks amazing though. Her purple eyes pop even more with the pale skin and platinum hair. Rox smiles into the camera and steals my breath. Fuck. She's gorgeous. I tilt my lips up into the smirk that I know she adores, and her cheeks turn pink. I love when that happens.

"I'm glad you're getting help. Josh told me where you were." She readjusts the phone and sits back on the bed that I got a little too familiar with when I hurt Rox the last time. She's at Cade's place still. While I wish she was at our place, at least I know she hasn't been alone. From the angle she's sitting, I can see the long shirt she's wearing and the tiny boxer shorts. The shirt is one of mine. At least she's wearing my clothes in that fucker's bed. Must kill him to see that.

"I see you're still blond." It's the only thing I can think to say.

"I see you're still too into my hair," she counters. "What's with you and my hair?"

"I guess I just love your natural hair."

I sit back on the bed and watch as she bites down on her lip, wrapping an arm across her chest. "When are you coming home?"

"Two weeks, but I get visitation rights starting Monday. Maybe you and Josh can work something out. My therapist thinks having you both attend a session will be good for me. I want you here."

She smiles and nods her head. "Of course." She leans forward and grabs the phone, going in and out of focus until she settles. "How long do you get your phone?"

"Thomas didn't say."

She lies down on the bed, head propped on a mountain of pillows. "Well, at least we have tonight."

I lift a brow at her. "You going to give me a show or something?"

Her cheeks heat again. "Is that something you want? A show?"

I shake my head at her as I ease down on the bed, forgetting about the burger that Steven brought me. "No. I only want the real thing. If I can't have you in person, in my arms, then I will wait. It'll be worth it."

Her head falls, her new hair shielding her flaming cheeks from me. When she looks to have her emotions under control, she lifts her head again. "I think that may be the only sweet thing you have ever said to me."

"You'll have cavities by the time I'm done with you." Maybe then I'll be less of the fucker I am and my "sorries" won't be worthless to me, even though they are genuine. I will make everything up to her.

"Stay on the phone with me tonight?" she asks, her eyes sparkling like a thousand stars.

"I wouldn't dream of hanging up this phone."

Rox smiles again, and for the first time in a while, I return it with the same ferocity. I don't give her a half smile or a smirk or any of the other gestures I'm known for. I give my girl a real, sincere smile.

We stay on the phone until she falls asleep, and even then I don't end the call. I watch her beautiful face all night and into the next morning.

CHAPTER 12

ROX

"We're going to a party tonight," Cade announces as we get out of his truck and head around the building to the school's entrance.

I quirk a brow at him. He knows my Friday nights only consist of waitressing at Aunt May's and doing homework. I need to be well rested and presentable for Saturday. After talking with Wran all last night though, I'm in a good mood. He seemed different. I don't know anything about anger management, but I wasn't expecting a completely different Wran when he called me last night. At first it seemed fake, but then we talked all night, and the act didn't falter. I know he's not better better, but at least it's a start.

"Okay, but it'll have to be after my shift at the diner," I tell him.

He drapes an arm over my shoulder and pulls the door open with his other hand. "Awesome! It's about time you do something with me."

"I do plenty of things with you, Caden." I shrug his arm off my shoulder and shift my backpack over. The stitches in my shoulder have dissolved, and even though there's hardly any pain, I still don't like my bag on that shoulder.

Opening my locker, I grab the books I need for my first couple of classes along with the sketchbook I keep here. I close the locker and turn around to find Cade's face barely an inch from mine. He places his hands on the lockers on both sides of me, caging me in, and I gulp. I glance down at the checkered floor, avoiding those dazzling blues like the plague. One of Cade's hands gently takes hold of my face and pulls it up to his.

"I forgot to tell you that you look beautiful today."

I try to pull my face away from his. Away from his peppermint breath on my lips. "You tell me that every morning."

"I mean it." He twirls a strand of my blond hair around his finger. "I think Kiellan would be happy that we're together."

I snap my head up at the mention of my brother's name. "We're not together."

"Not yet."

"Not ever."

"I have high hopes." He tilts his head so that it's resting against mine.

"Don't."

A locker slamming jerks me back and out of the close proximity of Cade. My head slams against my locker and I wince. Rubbing my head, I glance down the hall to where the locker slammed to see Claire fuming. I gulp. Crap. I pull my eyes from her and take a quick look around me. A few students are watching me and Cade. Some of them to my right make fanning gestures. Double crap.

Cade takes my hand and leads me down the hall and past Claire. Besides the few times she did my makeup, we haven't really talked. I didn't expect things to suddenly be gung-ho, but I didn't expect her to still be upset with Cade being my friend. Guess I shouldn't have expected. One girl-talk wasn't going to fix us. Nothing can fix all the things she's done to me over the years, and nothing can fix that her life became hell after Wran and Josh gave her father a pounding.

When we bypass my first classroom, I pull my hand free of Cade's and come to a stop. The bell for first period will be ringing soon and we don't have time to do whatever it is he has in mind. If he would have left the house earlier like I wanted, then maybe he could drag me off. He's the one that doesn't like to leave at a suitable time.

"Where are you taking me? Class is about to start," I tell him, peeking over my shoulder at the clock above the double doors that lead to the common area.

"Come with me to the library. I can get you a tardy slip." He takes hold of my hand and starts pulling me again.

"How?" I question him.

"Did you forget that I won this school the championship last semester? The principal loves me."

"I don't go to games, remember? And you don't talk about that stuff with me."

We round a corner and take the few steps to the wooden doors of the library. "You don't like sports. Figure I wouldn't waste my breath."

"I never said I didn't like sports. Wran played."

Cade tenses at the mention of Wran's name and he lets my hand go. He goes down the few steps that lead to the main sitting area, his body tense. I wish he would get over his crap with Wran. Maybe I should shove them both in a room and let them go at it. Hey, if it can get Claire and me talking after years of lethal glares, I'm sure it can do miracles on those two. Rolling my eyes, I take a step after Cade. My foot slips, and then my books are falling from my arms. I tumble down the steps, but Cade turns around just in time and catches me, easing us both down.

"Thanks." I straighten myself in his hold.

He gives me a toothy grin. "I'll always catch you if you fall. You never have to worry about that with me. I will always be your anchor."

My cheeks heat at his words, and my pulse beats a little faster. Flutters spring to life in my chest, and I gasp at the onslaught of feelings I know I shouldn't be experiencing. I start to pull away from him, but he tightens his hold on my waist. He tilts his head forward and his lips graze my forehead. My eyes widen for a split second as a heat I haven't felt in a really long time encompasses my body. I shake my head and yank away from him.

No.

No.

No!

"Don't say stuff like that!" I shout at him in a whisper. I glance around me at no one. There's no one in the library. Figures there would be no one around when I direly need them to be. I need someone to break this up. I need someone to hit me over the head and tell me I did not feel what I just felt. Nope. I didn't. I refuse to believe it.

"Don't deny your attraction. I saw your blush."

"I'm with Wran. W–R–A–N. Get that through your head."

"That may be so," he says down to me, "but that doesn't mean you have no feelings for me. That doesn't mean I don't make your blood rush or that I don't ignite a fire in you that you can't quench. It's normal, Rox. You've been living with me for almost two weeks. We sit together and watch movies. We laugh. I take you to work. You tell me about Harley. You might not have felt anything as strong before these two weeks, but like I said, I'm going to fight for you. I'm going to give you every reason to go weak in the knees."

I get up from the steps and grab my books, stomping away from him. I hear him get up as well and come after me. He grabs hold of my forearm and pulls me to a stop. Before I can pull away from him, his mouth is pressed against mine and I can taste the peppermint of his toothpaste. I shove him back and he breaks away from me.

"I told you before, and I'm telling you again, I'm in love with Wran. We're nothing more than friends."

"And I'm calling bullshit," he hisses.

"Cade, don't do this." I step away from him.

His eyes fall and he shakes his head at me. "Haven't any of the things I've done mattered to you? I'd do anything. Will Belmont?"

Just as I'm about to answer, the bell rings. We stare at each other until the door behind us opens and more students start to file in. Cade pulls his eyes from me first and I'm relieved. He holds out his hand to me and I give him mine.

"C'mon, let's go get you that tardy slip," he says, but his voice sounds all dejected once again.

I hate making him like that.

And I hate I just lied to him for the first time.

People's heartbeats don't sputter and pick up for no reason. Girls don't blush at guys' corny pickup lines if they don't feel anything. I should have felt nothing. But he was right. All the time we've been spending together has been nice. It's been great talking to someone that doesn't go off on me because I want to be my own person. It's been nice watching girly movies without someone criticizing them. If I'm honest, it's just been nice being with someone. For the past three years, I've been alone. And when Wran came home, it was like he was still gone. Spending time with Cade has been nice, but I'm with Wran. I love Wran, and no amount of time with Cade is going to change that. We're just friends. F-R-I-E-N-D-S. I let out a groan. Then why does it sound like I'm trying to convince myself?

I don't see Cade again until lunch, which I hate. Ever since I broke down in the hallway after getting that first letter from my dad, he's been walking me to and from classes. Guess I messed things up big time this morning.

With a sigh, I search the cafeteria for him and pause when I see him sitting at a table with some of the football and basketball players. There are a few girls hanging around, one of them sitting on his lap. Cade has a grin on his face as he watches the girl, one of his fingers twirling in her red hair much like he did with my hair this morning. Pulling my lingering gaze from that table, I look for one that I could possibly join. I haven't really eaten in here much. The common area is my go-to, but with the rain today, that's a no go. I glance down at my bowl of chicken alfredo and apple and turn around. I'm not that hungry anyways.

"Roxy?"

Someone calls me and I peek over my shoulder to see who called. I turn around when a girl with long braids, green eyes, and a nose ring gets up from a table. She's dressed in a black shirt and skirt set. She has on fishnet stockings and combat boots. She smiles, and it brightens up her otherwise darkly adorned face.

"You can sit with us if you want." She motions to the empty seat in between a guy with a guitar wearing a band tee and another girl with bright pink hair. I like her hair. I nod at her and take the seat. They all greet me, and it's a little strange. Not even when I hung out with Claire in the seventh grade did people take the time out to introduce themselves to me. They all just expected me to know who they were.

"You probably don't remember me, but we had science class together in middle school. We did a project together," says the girl who invited me to sit.

I look her over and try to remember her. Nothing about her stands out. "I'm sorry. I don't remember."

"Understandable. It was only like one project and you had cooler friends back then. I'm Raven."

I smile at her. "Thanks for letting me sit here."

"No problem."

The guy next to me, Charlie, stops strumming his guitar and looks over to the table Cade is sitting at. Without me. "You sorta looked like you needed a place to sit."

I pull my gaze from Cade. "I guess I did."

I take a bite of my lunch and the rest of them go back to doing whatever they were doing before I sat down. Charlie starts back strumming his guitar, making notes every so often in a notebook. The girl with pink hair takes selfies of herself and then of everyone else around her. I just sit here and eat my lunch. Occasionally my eyes drift back over to the table with Cade and the redhead. I can't believe he's that mad at me. It's not like that was the first time I've told him that we were only friends.

"So did your dad really, like, kidnap your daughter?" the pink-haired girl asks after going through the pictures.

I pull my head up from my lunch and stare at her. It's all over the news. Why ask me that? I shrug my shoulders, not really wanting to talk about the Aspen Accident. It's over. My dad is dead. I don't want to remember anything that happened. I guess it's too much to ask that I lose those memories too. If my brain can block out crap that happened to me as a kid, I don't get why it won't block out that event too. So much for the brain being its own freaking safety net.

"Really, Lex, really? I'm sure she doesn't want to talk about stuff like that," Raven hisses at her.

I shake my head at Raven. I don't want her jumping down her friend's throat because of something like that. "It's okay. It's not like it's not all over the news." I look at Lex. "Yeah, my dad kidnapped her. It sucked, and I wish I could forget."

Lex sets her phone on the table and leans forward, resting her chin on her hands that are propped on the table. "Why did he kidnap her? The news didn't give a why."

"You don't have to answer her." Charlie stops strumming his guitar. "Lexi thinks of herself as a journalist and she likes asking questions. Ignore her and she will stop asking them."

I grin at him and look at Lex. "It's okay. My father is crazy. *Was,* I mean. No one knows why he did what he did."

"So you have a daughter? I bet she's cute. You're pretty cute. Way hotter than the redhead." Lexi glances over at Cade and I follow her gaze. Cade is watching us, but he pulls his lingering gaze away when he meets my eyes.

"You don't have to say that. Cade and I are just friends. We're just having a bit of a disagreement right now."

"Friends? Have you seen the way that boy looks at you? I swear the halls were on fire last week when Claire put that on your locker." She shoves her pink hair out of her face. "You guys are so not friends."

I shake my head. Apparently I haven't made my stance clear to anyone. We really are just friends.

The bell rings and I let out a breath, giving me a reason not to comment on Lexi's observation. Getting up, I grab my tray and dump it in the trash. I head out of the cafeteria and down to my locker. Raven comes up next to me and holds up my backpack. My skin pales. She probably thinks there's something wrong with me for bolting like that.

"You forgot this." She hands it over. "Sorry about Lexi. She really is harmless."

"No, it's fine. I understand people's curiosity. It just sucks that no matter what, I'm going to be the town's gossip for a while."

"Yeah, that does suck." Raven turns and looks down the hall. "You want to walk to study hall together?"

I close my locker and turn to her. "You're in my study period?"

She nods. "Don't worry. I'm sure you don't know half the people in any of your classes. You don't look like you've really engaged with our peers in recent years. I actually haven't seen you hang with anyone after the queen bee herself."

I start making my way down the hall with Raven right beside me. "Am I that obvious?"

"Don't worry. It must be hard to do anything with a toddler. Not your fault."

I shove a blond strand of hair behind my ear. It is my fault. I let Wran's disappearance rule my life. I stopped living. I stopped socializing. After Harley was born, she became my main priority. Lynn never told me I couldn't have a life. She never told me I couldn't be a teenager. I just needed to make sure to keep my grades up and go to the AA meetings. Everything else was my choice. I could have had friends. I could have lived.

"It sort of is my fault." My voice comes out in a whisper. "After Wran, I guess I didn't think people would like me. Claire was really only around because of him."

"Well, you have a friend now!" Raven loops her arm through mine and pulls me into the study class. She drags me to my usual seat and plops down in the desk in front of me. "Are you going to the party tonight? It's not usually my scene, but Charlie and the band are playing a set. It could be fun."

"Cade invited me, but I don't know. I really shouldn't."

"Forget Cade. Come with me!" Her cheery tone has me giggling. I wouldn't picture someone that wears eyeliner as thick as a paint stroke and clothes just as edgy would be as cheery as her. It's odd.

"Okay," I agree, and her grin grows.

"Give me your phone. I'll put my number in."

I reach into my backpack and pull out my phone. When I hand it over to her, she starts pressing buttons and then her phone pings. She pulls out her phone, which is in a bright bubble gum pink case. I look the girl over again. From the fishnets to the chunky combat boots, nothing about her screams pink. Yet she has a pink phone. Something tells me that getting to know Raven is going to be interesting.

She hands my phone back to me. "There. I sent myself a text. That way I have your number too."

I look down at my phone and a laugh slips from my lips. She put herself in it as "the psycho pixie." Funny, considering I had a fascination with pixies. Okay, well, Tinkerbell. I roll my eyes and put my phone away.

"I'll text you tonight before the party. Wear something hot."

The second bell rings and Raven turns around. She doesn't even give me time to tell her that I'm supposed to be riding with Cade after my shift at the diner. Tearing out a piece of paper, I write it out in a note and pass it to her. She scribbles something and then tosses it back to me just as the teacher in charge of study hall prances into class.

Fuck Cade is all she wrote back. I roll my eyes and sit back in my chair. I look out the window and freeze when I see the same SUV that's been sitting outside of Cade's house for the last two weeks sitting on side of the road here. Narrowing my eyes, I try to see if anyone's inside, but it's useless. The vehicle is too far away and the windows are too dark. Maybe it's nothing. Maybe a student here owns it. Turning away from the window, I pull out my sketchbook and start mindlessly doodling. By the end of the period I have another portrait of my mother drawn. It looks even farther from what the one of her on the TV looks like. More like me. And I don't like it. I ball up the drawing and toss it in my backpack. I don't know why I'm drawing her anyways. She's dead too. Everyone in my family is dead.

By the end of the day, I'm ready to go home. My art teacher was glad to see me painting again and suggested that I put the painting I'm working on in some competition. I declined. As much as competing again sounds fun, I don't think my work is anywhere as good as it used to be. It still needs improvement. And I will only get that by doing more painting. And with the way things have been going with me, I probably won't even stick with it.

Cade finally comes out the building and around to the truck. He looks at me leaning against the passenger side and unlocks the door. When we get inside, he cranks up the truck and pulls away from the school without saying a word. Guess we're not on speaking terms again. Guess I'll have to get used to him being mad at me.

With a sigh I sink into the seat. What a freaking great day.

CHAPTER 13

ROX

I stare at my outfit in the diner's bathroom mirror. I had to bring a change of clothes since Raven insisted on picking me up instead of meeting me at the party. People finding out that I'm currently living with Cade is something I'm not entirely comfortable with. It's bad enough that Claire is aware of my living conditions. She hasn't said anything about it to anyone so far, but I'm not stupid enough to think that her doing my makeup is going to fix anything between us. Not after she saw Cade with me this morning at school. If anything, that little stunt he pulled ensured that the entire school, teachers included, will be asking questions come next week. I suppose I can always go back to the apartment. Wran's not there, and it is my home. And there's technically nothing keeping me at Cade's place.

A knock sounds on the door and I pull away from my reflection. I glance down at the hooker-heel boots and skintight black dress and let out a sigh. I look okay. I look like all the other girls my age. I look ready to party. I can definitely pull this off. Raven said dress sexy. This is the sexiest thing I own. Even if the dress is four years old.

Opening the door, I watch Mercedes's mouth fall open. She shifts on her feet and then pulls me out of the single-stall bathroom. "You look hot, but I got to like pee."

She slams the door in my face, and I head to the front of the house. It's ten at night and the diner cleared out around nine, probably due to the party. A lot of the students were here tonight. That wasn't so great for tips, but at least they cleared out early. I go over to the cash register where Aunt May is counting down the drawer. She looks at me and then does a double take.

Setting the money down, she walks around the counter and stops next to me. She props her hands on her waist and looks me up and down.

"Do I even want ta know, darlin'?" She gestures to my outfit.

My cheeks heat and I shrug. "I got invited to a party."

"Ya goin' to a party? Dressed like that?" She looks me up and down again. I really don't understand what's wrong with the look. I like the boots, and the dress isn't that revealing. I'm sure other people will be dressed way worse than me. "Good. You're gonna kill 'em, darlin'. Make Belmont work for ya."

I giggle at her. "He's not in town. He won't see this."

"Dat's probably for da best. We don't need another world war. Boy would kill somebody he sees you dressed like that."

"It's not too much?"

Aunt May bats a hand at me and goes back around the counter to finish counting the money. "It's 'bout time you act ya age again."

The bell to the diner dings and I turn to see who has entered the place. My eyes pop when I see Cade standing in the door in a fitted black polo and dark wash jeans. We look like we coordinated. He comes over to me and looks me up and down. His Adam's apple bobs and then he takes a step away from me. I wasn't expecting him to come pick me up. I know I told him I would go with him, but I figured after he gave me the silent treatment all day, he would just ignore me and go to the party with the redhead.

Geez! Why am I even thinking about him with the redhead?

Cade smirks at me. "You look good."

I glance over at Aunt May and the old lady has a grin on her face. Her eyes go back and forth between Cade and me. She's seen Cade with me plenty of times since she put me back on the schedule. I don't know why she's acting like we haven't had lunch and dinner here at the diner on multiple occasions in the last week.

I move back and take a seat on one of the stools at the bar. Cade takes a seat too.

"Thanks."

"I've never seen you in something like that." He motions to me. "You look . . . gorgeous."

My cheeks heat at his words. The last time he complimented me like this was the day after he took me shopping and I dyed my hair. I'm not used to compliments from people. Wran doesn't really do compliments. He would most likely be telling me to take this dress off or saying something that would have me wanting to take the dress off. I can imagine exactly what he would say. You look like shit. You look like you're trying too hard. A girl like you shouldn't wear a dress like that. A dress like that isn't meant for a girl that doesn't know how to work it. I could go on and on and on.

"Why are you here?" I finally ask Cade, breaking our staring competition.

"You said you would go to the party with me."

"I thought after this morning you would have changed your mind. You haven't really been talking to me today."

Cade turns on his stool as if uncomfortable, and then scratches the back of his neck. "I just needed time. It's hard getting rejected over and over."

I frown at him. Yeah, I guess I can understand that. I hated when Wran would do that. And I hate that I'm doing that. I don't want to hurt him or reject him, but we can't possibly be anything other than what we are. No matter what. I could never betray Wran.

The door to the diner opens again and Raven, along with all her friends, comes walking in. She takes a look at

Cade and then at me before she makes it across to the bar. The disappointment is clear on her face, but she hides it well with a giggly smile.

"Wow!" She bounces on one of the stools. "When I said hot, I didn't think you would go full-on Kylie Jenner."

I look down at my dress again. Maybe this is too much for a high school party. "Umm. . . I can change."

"No!" both her and Cade yell at me at the same time.

"You have a banging body. Keep it on, girlie," Raven tells me. She looks over my shoulder and then I turn to Cade, who's still observing me.

"Cade, this is Raven. Raven, Cade."

Cade looks past me and tilts his head in acknowledgment. "I think we have Physics together, right?"

Raven nods. "Yeah, I wasn't aware that the small people were on your radar."

Cade frowns. "Why would you think that?"

Raven shrugs her shoulders and leaps off the stool. She turns toward me and disregards Cade altogether. Okay then. She doesn't like him. "Are you still coming with us?" She points to her friends at the door, who haven't moved since they walked in. Lexi stands with her arms crossed over her chest, eyes in slits. I pull my stare from the group of people that befriended me and look at Cade. Technically I accepted his invitation first, but he has been acting like a douchebag all day. And I do want to get to know Raven and her friends. I think I deserve friends. Now that I don't have to worry about anything, I think I should live my life a little.

In order to do that, I need friends. Friends outside of Cade and Josh and Wran. God, I'm surrounded by way too much testosterone all the time.

"You can go with her if you want. I'll catch up with you at the party." Cade makes the decision for me.

"Are you sure?" I ask him.

He nods. "I'm not Belmont. You don't need my permission to do anything."

He slips off the stool and heads out the diner, bypassing Raven's friends without a word.

I turn back to Raven. "I didn't know he had still planned on picking me up."

"Darlin'," Aunt May says, and I peer over my shoulder at her. "Dat boy is hot. And he got it bad. If I was forty years younger . . ." She trails off and smacks her lips.

"It's not like that and you know it."

"But he wishes it was," Raven says, and drags me off the stool. She pulls me over to her friends and we file out the door. I hear Aunt May shouting for us to have fun before the door closes. Raven leads me over to a green, beaten-up van that looks like it belongs in a seventies cartoon. Raven, Lexi, and I get in as Charlie goes around to the driver's side. He pulls off, and out the window I can vaguely make out the black SUV that was at the school and Cade's place. Okay, so that van is working and following me.

No one else in the van seems to notice anything, but I don't expect them to. They haven't seen the van in three different locations. Pulling my phone from my crossbody bag, I pull up Josh's name and send him a quick message.

ME: What are u doing?

He doesn't answer right away, but I expect that. He's been having a lot more work at the station. He's most likely not off yet, and seeing as it's a Friday night and there's a party, he's probably planning on breaking it up. Every underage party here gets broken up. That's Kingston for you.

JOSH: Out. What's up?

ME: Out?

He doesn't go out. If anything, he sits at home and watches reruns of Law and Order. The only time I have ever known Josh to go out on a Friday is when he was dating that one girl. He never brought her to the house though, and I only know about her due to Wran. He had told me his brother was messing around with some girl when I had asked why Josh wasn't home one night. I must have been eight at the time, and I was mad at Josh. He hadn't brought me the ice cream he always brought me after he got out of school.

JOSH: Do you need something?

I stare at his question for a long time. This isn't that important. It's just a vehicle. It was probably someone having dinner at the diner. Aunt May's is the only place in Kingston to eat. Unless anyone wants day-old breakfast sandwiches from Starbucks, they will be driving to Arlington for something fancier than diner food.

ME: No. Just making sure ur going 2 be on time tomorrow.

JOSH: Yeah. See you in the morning.

I put my phone away and try to relax. The black vehicle isn't following me. I'm just a little paranoid after the whole Aspen thing. Nothing ever happens here in Kingston.

Tuning back into everything that's going on around me, I look up front at Charlie singing along to some rock song. The ride to the lake, where the party is apparently being held, is short. Charlie parks the car and gets out. We all get out, and when I see the girls going around back, I follow them. They each grab an instrument and walk off. Charlie hands me a purple guitar. I take it and follow them to wherever they're setting up.

In front of the lake, a small stage is laid out. I put the guitar down and look around. There's a bonfire and people are walking around with red plastic cups. They're drinking. Gulp. I should so not be here. If this gets back to Lynn and that judge, I can kiss custody of Harley goodbye. I should have never told them I would come. This was a bad idea. Someone taps me on the shoulder, and I turn to see Lexi holding two cups. We just made it here. When did she have time to grab drinks? I shake my head. Nope. I'm not going anywhere near the stuff. I don't even want to smell it.

"C'mon! We're at a party!" she screams over the loud music. "It's just one drink."

I take the cup from her, still not planning on drinking the stuff. She turns away from me and goes back to setting up the drums. I pour the drink onto the ground. Nope. Not drinking here. I don't care how many drinks they shove at me. I won't do anything that will risk me not getting my daughter back. Scanning the crowd, I see Claire and her friends. She doesn't notice me, and I'm grateful. Don't really want to put up with her out of school. I continue scanning the sea of vibrating bodies until I see Cade. He has a cup in his hand and he's grinning with a bunch of guys. The redhead from school is with them. He must sense me staring at him, because he starts looking around as well. When he sees me staring at him, he grins and leans into the redhead.

I inhale and turn away.

I don't care.

I'm with Wran.

Okay, technically, I'm not with Wran, but I'm still with Wran.

I'm loyal to Wran.

Cade and I are just friends.

I'm in love with Wran.

Getting up from the stage, I make my way through the crowd until I'm away from everyone. I don't want to be here. I just want to go home. I walk down the road until the music from the party is nothing but a buzzing in the background. Maybe I'm just not the type of girl who parties anymore. This whole scene was something I would have reveled in before Wran left and before I had Harley. Now it just seems like I'm letting my daughter down. No one would be proud of me if they knew I was here. Josh would probably yell at me. Being at a party with underage drinking does nothing for me. If anything, it makes me feel like that wrecked, lost girl that went completely off the rails because of a guy. I'm not that girl anymore. And I don't want to be reminded of that girl.

I keep walking until my feet hurt and I must take off the heels. I stop next to a tree and gaze up at the sky. Sometimes I forget just how beautiful the night sky can be. I smile and lean my back against the tree, taking in all the stars. I wonder if Wran can see the stars where he's at. All I know is that he's at a place called Pleasure House. I can't picture a place called that letting its patients out at night to stargaze. Pulling my eyes from the night sky, I'm momentarily blinded by bright lights. Shielding my eyes, I squint at the brightness. The car starts pulling away from the curb just as I hear my name being screamed. I turn around to see Cade.

"Roxy!" he screams at me and then takes off into a run toward me.

The screeching of tires has me whirling back around. My eyes widen and I see bright lights speeding toward me. Dropping my shoes, I race off the side of the road and down the little dirt path that leads to a trail in the woods. The car screeches and I look behind me. It makes a sharp turn and speeds down the trail. My breathing comes out in pants and I push harder to get to the woods. The vehicle won't be able to chase me in there. Just as I make it to the edge of the woods, something jabs into my foot and I stumble down. I hiss at the stabbing pain that's like a thousand pin-prickles in my foot, but my eyes never leave the vehicle as it gets closer and closer and closer.

Suddenly I'm being picked up and pushed into the trees. I land on my side and hiss. The headlights stop at the edge of the trees. Squinting, I try to peer through the window of the SUV, but I see nothing. It's completely blacked out.

"Rox?" Cade yells. "Are you okay?"

I don't pull my eyes away from the SUV until it starts backing away. I watch until it disappears down the dirt road and out of sight. My heart starts beating rapidly and I suck in a large breath. I inhale again and again, but it appears no oxygen is entering my lungs. Someone just tried to run me over. Ohmygod, someone tried to run me over!

"Rox, breathe. In. Out. In Out."

I do as Cade says, but it's not working. My vision starts to spot, but then I'm yanked up. Cade wraps his arms around me, crushing me to his body. A second later his mouth is on mine, and then I'm breathing. I'm getting air. I relax in his arms and my heart starts beating normal.

Cade's hand moves up my back, snapping me out of whatever trance I'm in. I shove him away from me. Before I'm aware of my actions, my hand lands across his face. The smack reverberates throughout the woods, causing it to sound worse than it probably is. Cade rubs his cheek and then he laughs. Laughs! I shove him back, accidentally putting weight on my hurt foot, and let out a string of curse words. Cade grabs me back and pulls me against him. He eases us down on the damp ground and runs a hand over my hair and down to my cheek.

"Are you okay?" he asks again.

"Yeah. I'm fine." I look over to where the vehicle was and then turn back to him, my eyes narrowing. "What the hell was that? Why did you kiss me?"

"It got you to stop freaking out." He leans back against a tree and pulls me with him. "Besides, you relaxed into it. You liked it."

I roll my eyes at him even though he can't see me. He will never hear me admit that I liked that kiss. "Someone tried to run me over, Cade."

He takes in a deep breath. "Yeah, I saw. We need to get back to the house and call Josh. We have to report this."

I shake my head at him. Josh is out; I don't want to bother him. And besides, it's not like I have much to tell him. All we saw was a black vehicle. We didn't get a license plate number. We didn't see a person. We got nothing. For all intents and purposes, it's like no one tried to run me over. I don't even know why someone would even want to run me over. I haven't done anything to anyone.

Turning me around in his hold, Cade leans his forehead against mine. "You are a death magnet. I didn't think you were going to be fast enough. That truck was right on your tail."

A shiver runs through me at the mere thought of actually getting run over. That really was close. My eyes drift back to the edge of the trees, and my body starts to shake all over again. Someone wants me dead. Someone really wants me dead.

"Hey!" Cade pulls my gaze away from the outskirts of the woods. "Don't think about it. I'm here. I have you. You never have to worry about anything when I'm with you."

I smile at his kind words. I know I don't have to worry with him. I wrap my arms around his neck and exhale into him. He wraps his arms around my waist and pulls me even closer to him. We stay like that for a while—me wrapped in his arms, saying nothing. When I do finally pull back, he hesitates to let me go. Using his shoulders, I ease myself up from the ground. He gets up as well and then scoops me up into his arms.

He smiles down at me. "Let's go get your foot looked at, my little death magnet."

I groan at him. "Do not call me that."

"I can't help it if you attract the reaper like a cat attracts fleas."

Punching him in the shoulder, I roll my eyes at him again. "Take me home."

CHAPTER 14

WRAN

Watching the old decrepit houses pass by, I feel my heart beat faster. We have been circling each street in search of that yellow house from the picture, but apparently Cade's memory isn't as fresh as he thought.

My hands slam down on the dash and I turn to scowl at him again. I know overreacting isn't going to get us to Rox any faster, but I can't help it. She's alone with that fucker. As much as I don't want to believe her father can't harm a hair on her head, I know he will. The fucker was capable of harming her as a child—a cute little kid that he should have loved above all else. He won't second-guess hurting Rox now.

"Calm down!" Cade hollers. "You freaking out isn't going to get us to the house any faster. Besides, where is your faith in your girlfriend? Roxy can take care of herself. She's a survivor, after all."

I sneer at him. This is me calm. And I know very well just how much of a survivor my girl is. That doesn't change the fact that I don't trust James fucking Raine. I don't trust him as far as I can throw him, and if he so much as touches Rox or my daughter, I'm going to go ballistic.

"Shut up and get us to the house. You said you knew where it was."

"I was five the last time I was here. Give me a break!"

Even with that being said, Cade picks up the speed, and we pass by three more houses. I sit back in the seat and try to calm down. Cade's right. Rox is a fighter; she will be okay until we get there. I repeat that over and over, scoffing at myself. I can't believe I let her walk out that door. I should have dragged her scrawny ass back inside and tied her to the fucking bed with those zip ties. I should have done some-thing. I run my fingers through my hair as Cade makes a right at a stop sign. A blue kid's bike comes into view, and I swear we've been this way before. I remember seeing that bike. I turn to him and I can see a nervous gleam in his eyes. Yup, he knows the same thing. We've been this way.

"If he so much as hurt—" I start.

"Do you think I don't care about her as well? I'm doing my best!" Cade snaps at me. "You're not the only one that would be losing someone, you know."

"They're my family. Not yours," I tell him for what seems like the hundredth time. He might think he cares about my Rox, but he has no clue who she is. He cares for the

girl she was before all the crap she was dealt. I turn away from him and he continues driving.

We go down each street, each house getting more and more rickety. I'm just about to tell him to let me take over when he slams on the brakes and I slide forward in the passenger seat. My hands shoot out against the dash to keep me from crashing into it. I grimace at the fucker and there's a smirk on his face. He points out my window and I turn to see a house that looks more black than yellow, covered in snow and moss and whatever the fuck else. The not-so-white picket fence surrounding it appears to have seen better days.

Without waiting on him to put the car in park, I jump out, heading up the snow–covered path. My girls are in there, and I'm getting them out if it's the last thing I do. I hear crunching snow behind me, and I peek behind to see Cade. I quirk a brow at him when I see the gun in his hold. No, if anyone is going to kill the fucker it's going to be me. I stop and hold out my hand for the gun. He's probably never even fired one of those things. Now is certainly not the time for him to practice. Not while Rox and my daughter are inside this house.

Cade shakes his head, refusing to hand over the device.

"Have you ever used a gun before?" I question him.

His face pales a little, but that could be the cold chipping away at him. "No, but there's a first time for everything. I'm not going in that house without protection."

"Rox and my daughter are in there." I reach down and pull out a knife from my boot. "I'm not letting an untrained rich prick with a gun anywhere near my family."

I hold out the knife to him. I might not like the guy—he's trying to steal my girl—but I wouldn't ask him to go in there with a crazy man unarmed. At least a knife is tamer than a gun. Cade bares his teeth at me in a snarl, but he knows it's the truth. He takes the knife from me and replaces it with the handheld. Turning back toward the house, I take the steps leading up to the battered door and go inside. The floor screeches under the weight of my shoes and I stop in my tracks. Dammit! I hope he didn't hear that. Cade comes inside as well and we look around the dark, musty house.

Soft cries echo throughout the house, and we head toward the back and down a hall off an outdated kitchen. We come to a stop at a pink door, but a loud scream erupts and my head snaps away from the pink door and farther down the hall. I shove past Cade without as much as a look inside, even though I know there's a possibility that my child is in there, and make my way down the hall to a green door. Geez, Rox's grandma must have been crazy. Who in the hell paints a house like this? I kick the door open and charge inside. I freeze as I come face to face with James Raine holding a barely conscious Rox. He looks just as I thought he would. Just like they showed him on TV.

My eyes move from him to an unconscious Rox. My vision goes red just as Cade comes running into the room.

James grins at us and then looks down at Rox. He drops her to the floor, and she lands with a thump and a whimper.

"Well if it isn't Thing One and Thing Two to the rescue," he taunts us.

A growl leaves me and I take a step toward him. Cade places a hand on my shoulder and I knock it away from me. I don't need him trying to control me. I'm controlled. James laughs at us and my hand flinches around the gun in my hold. I won't kill him. I won't give him the satisfaction of a peaceful death. He deserves so much worse.

"Go check on my daughter," I hiss at Cade without taking my gaze off James. No way will I be stupid enough to do that.

Cade's retreating footsteps are the only indication that he listened to me. James looks me over and I inch closer to him. His eyes drop to the gun in my hold, but he disregards it like he knows I'm not willing to kill him. I'm not a killer. And I won't become one for this bastard. That doesn't mean I can't make him pay.

He laughs again and bends down to Rox. He runs a hand over her blue hair.

"Don't you dare touch her."

James looks up at me from his crouched position, his hand still sliding over Rox. "You know I've done a lot worse than touch her. She's my daughter, after all. I have every right to every part of her. And I will discipline her as I wish."

"Discipline her? That what you call abusing her?" My eyes move to Rox's body. Flashes of all the bruises she had

when I found her flicker through my mind as if I'm watching a fucking slideshow.

"She shouldn't have been a troublesome little girl. Daddy knows best, after all."

"You sick fuck!" I yell at him, and he rises.

"Don't pretend you're nothing like me, Wran Belmont," he taunts again. "I know all about you. I know all the things you've done to my daughter. Someone you claim to love."

He chuckles, and the sound has me taking a step away from him. I might have done some crazy shit to Rox, but I have never hurt her. Well, not intentionally. Not like him. And I'm nothing like him. Not at all.

"Don't compare me to you. I might not be a saint, but I'm also not you."

"You honestly think that?" He takes a step in my direction. "You fucked a kid. A fifteen-year-old kid. I would say that's worse than a little beating. Don't you think? If you can fuck and leave Roxanna, what will you do to little Harley? No, they're better off with me."

"You're a murderer!"

"And you're a child molester."

I look at Rox lying on the floor unconscious and then back at the aging man, and before I know what I'm doing, the gun in my hand goes off, sending a jarring sound throughout the small green room. James's eyes widen as he looks down at where the pellet entered his chest, and I look at the dark splatters on the back wall behind him. I shake my head.

No.

No.

No!

The gun drops from my hand, and I take the few steps to get to James Raine. His hand comes up to his chest and he fingers the hole there. He chokes out a laugh and falls to the floor. I shake my head at the scene before me. This is not who I am. I can admit that I'm not the best person, but this isn't me. I don't kill. I'm not a killer.

James choke out another grin. "See? You're just like me. She found someone just like me."

I shake my head again as I watch the pool of blood grow larger around James and Rox. The life fades from his eyes and I fall to my knees. No. No. NO!

Crying and footsteps sound behind me. I pull my gaze from the lifeless form and look over my shoulder at Cade and a little girl. His eyes widen at the scene and he visibly shivers.

I did this. I–I killed someone. I k–killed Rox's dad.

My gaze moves from Cade and his torn shirt to the little girl in his arms. She has long dark hair and eyes like mine. There's cloth bound around her tiny leg. She glances around the room, and when she sees Rox lying on the floor, her cries grow. She starts crying "Mommy" over and over and over. My daughter. I pull my gaze from the little girl that shouldn't be seeing this and back over to James Raine. I scurry across the floor on my hands and knees and grab him. Shake him. He's not dead. I didn't kill him. I didn't!

"Wake up and fight me like a man. Wake up!" I scream at him as I pound my fist into his face over and over and over. He has to wake up. He has to! I didn't kill him. I'm not a murderer. I'm not a fuckin' murderer. He is. He did this to himself.

Cade grabs my fist before I can do more damage, and I stop. A sob breaks from me, and I fall to my ass.

I'm not a killer.

I'm not James Raine.

I'm not.

I'm not.

I'm NOT!

I jerk awake, my heart pounding in my chest like a freight train. I roll over on the bed and reach for Rox, but she's not here. Glancing around the room, I close my eyes and remember where I am: Pleasure House. I drop my head into my hands and groan. That damn dream. I look over to the nightstand and grab my phone off the charger. Thomas didn't take it back after I made my call to Rox. Thank God, 'cause I need to hear her voice. She's the only person that makes the dreams better. Seeing her. Knowing she's alive.

I press the key for her and wait for her to pick up. The phone rings and rings and rings. She doesn't answer.

I stare at the device in my hand, waiting for her to call me back. She always calls back. After five minutes of waiting with no ringing, I dial her number again. No answer. My hand tightens around the phone and my vision tents red. Why the fuck isn't she answering my call? Before I have time to stop myself, I throw the phone at the door, my breathing coming out in pants.

She'd better not be with Cade.

Not after last night.

I thought we were good.

But if she's not answering her phone . . .

"Fuck!" I shout out into the dark room.

There's a knock on my bedroom door and I turn my rage toward it. I stomp over to it and yank it open. The nurse that's on duty stands there with wide eyes. She takes a step away from me and I laugh at her. This place isn't helping me whatsoever. They can't even hire fucking help that can manage a person like me. This woman looks shit-scared out of her mind.

"If you know what's best for you, you will back the fuck away from me," I growl at her.

She takes another step away and then she sprints down the hall. I slam the door and it echoes around the small room. I sink down to the carpeted floor, my back against the door. I shake my head, trying to get the images of James Raine out of my head. I slam my head back against the door over and over and over, not hard enough to do any real harm. I bring my knees up and let my head fall against them. What the hell do I have to do to get that man out of my head?

Another knock sounds on my door and I shake my head, disregarding it. If I don't answer it, I won't hurt anyone. I won't hurt the nurse. Squeezing my eyes shut, I try to remember one of the techniques Thomas taught me. Anger can be controlled. It doesn't have to control me. I control it. There's another knock, and I squeeze my eyes tighter. C'mon, Wran, just relax, I tell myself. You are in fucking control.

"Wran?" I hear through the door. "Open up."

Can't they just leave me the fuck alone? Getting to my feet, I yank the door open. Thomas stands before me in a gray robe and black house shoes. For some reason I was under the impression that he lived somewhere away from Pleasure House. This is the first time I've seen him after dinner hour. He shoves through the door and closes it behind him. He goes over to the small chair beside the bed and sits down. I stay leaning against the wall, away from him. I like him. I don't want to hurt him. I don't want him to think I'm not trying. I fucking am. I'm trying so damn hard not to go off right now.

"Come over here," Thomas demands.

I shake my head. Going to him is not a good idea. He's the therapist. He should be able to tell that I'm barely holding it together.

"Wran, I trust you," he says. "Just breathe. In. Out. In. Out."

Taking in a large gulp, I obey him. This is one of the techniques he told me about. Breathing through the situation. Analyzing what triggered the rage. I exhale again and then repeat the steps. I clench my fists at my sides, but I keep breathing. Thomas nods, encouraging me to continue. When my vision is no longer blurring at the edges and my heart is beating at a normal steady rate, I slide down the door. I haven't had an episode like this since coming here.

"Come here," Thomas says again. When I make no move, he gets up from the chair, wraps his robe more securely around himself, and comes to me. He sits down on the floor and watches me. "What triggered you?"

I shake my head at him. The courage to tell him about the dreams still hasn't come. I don't want people to look at me like a killer. I don't want to admit to being a killer and telling him about the dreams will only make what I did more real.

"No one can help you if you don't talk," he says. "You do want help, right? You do want to be able to go home and be around Roxanna without lashing out so harshly, right?"

I glare up at him at the mention of Rox. "Don't you dare use her against me."

He gulps and nods. "That was a bit much, but it did get you to say something. Now, tell me what happened."

I stare at the man. He's really trying to help me, and I know if I don't fully open up, being here is fuckin pointless. How do I tell anyone I killed someone? How can anyone look at me and not see an evil being? How can Rox not see that when she looks at me? Hell, I'm pretty sure the nun on the first day saw it. I'm evil. I'm despicable. I'm going to rot in hell for what I did.

As I stare at Thomas. I feel a tear escape my eye and I bat it away. No. I'm not some weak pansy. My pops told me men don't do this. I am a man. I can control myself. I can control these dreams. I can . . . fuck!

Thomas stares back at me, and there's no judgment there. None at all. Suddenly, my barrier breaks and tears roll down my cheeks. I fucking hate it. Men don't cry. I slam my head into the door again as I fist the carpet.

"I k–killed someone," I tell him. I'm not sure he heard me 'cause he doesn't move. He just nods like every one of his patients admits to something like this.

"James Raine," he states like it is nothing at all. "I know. I do watch the news."

I shake my head at him, sneering. "Did you not hear me? I. Killed. Someone!"

"Did you not hear me?" he questions. "I know, Wran."

"I've hated him for as long as I can remember, but then his daughter came into my life, and I hated myself for caring about any part of that man. Including Rox."

"You love his daughter."

I nod.

"What triggered you tonight?"

I turn my head and eye him. "I've been having night-mares about him. But you already know that."

His brows knit together. "I prescribed you medication for the sleeping. Has your nurse not been delivering it to you?"

"I don't take them," I tell him honestly. "I know what drugs and alcohol can do to people. I don't want to depend on drugs to fix me."

"I understand that, Wran, but sometimes we need help to cope."

"I don't need fucking pills, Doc. I just need Rox, but she didn't answer my call."

Thomas shifts on the floor so that his back is against the wall next to me. "You know depending on her to fix you is not healthy either?"

"I don't," I defend myself. I had to live three years without Rox, and I was just fine. I don't expect her to be able to fix me. I just expect her to be with me. To love me. She's the only person besides Josh that gives a damn about me, and I don't want to lose that.

"From the way you talk and describe her, you both have some codependency issues that need to be resolved. I'm not the right person to help with that; it's not my specialty. But as far as the dreams, have you considered that you feel guilty?"

"Guilty? For killing James Raine?" I stare wide-eyed at the doc. "What makes you think I'm guilty? He was hurting Rox and my daughter! I would happily kill him again."

"Wran, if you can't be honest with me, be honest with yourself. A person that feels no guilt wouldn't be having night terrors that remind them of the situation."

I turn away from him and shove my hands in my hair. Even as he says it, I know he's right. I'm not a killer. I'm not a murderer. Yet I did kill someone. I took a life even though I vowed that would be something I would never do. Even during my stint in the army, I never killed anyone. I didn't see much action, but I still didn't harm anyone the way I planned to hurt James Raine.

My head drops and more tears roll down my cheeks. "I don't understand how Roxy can love me when I'm such a monster. And the fact that she can look at me and not see a monster . . . I hate myself. I hate myself for letting James get under my skin for twelve years. I hate how I treated Rox for twelve years. And it makes me so angry."

I wipe at the tears and blink at my own confession. I can't believe I just admitted that. I have never admitted that. Not even to myself. I don't hate James Raine. I hate myself for letting his actions turn me into this man.

"Good."

I whirl around to face Thomas. "How the hell is that good?"

He smiles at me. "Over the last two weeks, you've told me about your mom, Josh, Rox, and your father. You've even talked about James Raine a little. But you have never talked about yourself. You haven't said one thing about how you perceive yourself. It's good that you just admitted that. Now I know the true cause of your anger problems and we all can find a way to help you cope better. It's not easy being honest with yourself about something like that, Wran. If it was, I would be out of a job."

I shake my head and look over at my crumpled phone. "Telling you that just makes me sound like a pathetic fuck-er."

Thomas pats me on the shoulder. "No. Admitting that makes you human."

CHAPTER 15

ROX

Cade sits me down on a bench in the lobby and then grabs hold of my foot. I pull it from him and wince at the slight pain. I don't know why he's been making a fuss over me. It really is no big deal. It's not like it's broken. He didn't need to drive me all the way to Arlington for this. It was a waste of time. All I want is to go home.

"I'm fine, Cade," I mumble to him. "Can we please just go back to Kingston? I'm tired, and I have to be ready for tomorrow."

He nods. "Yeah, we'll go home after your foot is checked."

Cade takes my foot again, and I watch as he rubs circles on my sole. If I'm honest, it feels good. I've never had someone give me a massage before. Sighing, I sit back against the cool wall and look around the emergency room. The last time I

was in this hospital, I was giving birth to Harley and crying my eyes out as Lynn took her away.

"I'm gonna go get you signed in. Will you be okay for a minute?" he asks as he sets my foot down on the white tile floor.

I arch a brow at him. There is nothing wrong with me. "I'm not fine china, Cade. I won't break."

"You're the finest of china to me."

He walks off and I glance at the couple down from me in the actual waiting room fussing over a baby in a blue car seat. I frown. I never got to do that. I never got to fuss over Harley when she got sick for the first time. I wasn't there for her like the couple down there is for their kid. And after tonight, I probably won't ever be allowed to be there for my Harley. Someone tried to run me over tonight. Someone wanted me dead. I can't possibly bring Harley into this life. Not when people want me gone.

The baby in the blue car seat starts to cry and the woman leans down and smiles at him. She dangles her keys above the baby and the cries soon become giggles. I smile at them just as the woman pulls the child from the seat and glances my way. She watches me for a second and then smiles. Cade comes back and sits down beside me with a clipboard in his hand. He begins filling out the form and I can't help but question how he knows my information.

"Do you have insurance?" Cade pulls his attention from the paper and looks at me. "And what's your social?"

"You know I can fill that out myself?" I wiggle my fingers at him. "My hands are working fine."

Cade grins at me. "I see that, but that doesn't mean I can't do this. That's what I'm here for—to do whatever you need."

I frown at him. He doesn't need to do that. "Cade—"

"Don't," he cuts me off. "I don't need you telling me why I shouldn't. I already know."

With a frown, I tell him my insurance information and social security number. I know I shouldn't give that out to just anyone, but I trust Cade with my life. I turn away from him and look at the woman again. She's looking between me and Cade while she feeds the baby. She smiles and then hands the child over to the man. She gets up from her seat and heads this way. I bite down on my lip as she takes a seat on the empty bench across from us. Cade tenses immediately and looks up at the woman. She gives him a gentle grin and looks at me.

"You two look adorable. I wish I could get that bloke to rub my feet like your gentleman did." She looks to the man in the waiting room, who's now taking an interest in us as well.

"Umm. . . thanks?" It comes out like a question, but I don't truly know what to say about that. "I'm sure your husband does other things you enjoy."

She nods. "He's amazing. I couldn't help but notice that you were looking at us. Are you pregnant?"

My face heats at her question and I look away from her. Cade chuckles next to me. I elbow him in his side. This is so not funny.

"I don't think Rox would give me a child even if I paid her for one," Cade jokes. "She just hurt her ankle, ma'am."

I peek at her from under my lashes.

"I'm so sorry for assuming," she tells me. "You just had that look in your eyes that so many new moms get."

I shake my head at her. "Don't apologize. I shouldn't have been watching you. I'm sorry. It was probably weird."

"Nonsense. I'm Alice." She scoots forward on the bench and reaches a hand out to me.

I lean forward, being careful not to put too much weight on my foot. "Roxy."

She smiles. "You know, you look just like a girl I saw on the news a few weeks ago. She had blue hair though."

My face heats again. Gah! Is everyone going to recognize me now? Deciding to be truthful, I look Alice straight in the eyes. "I sort of have a thing for changing my hair."

Cade grunts and mutters something about my natural hair color and then gets up. I watch as he walks over to the desk and gives the nurse the clipboard.

"Oh Lord," the woman exclaims. "It's you. I'm terribly sorry about what happened. So you do have a child?"

I nod. I glance over at the baby in the man's arms. "I was just thinking that I never got to fuss over her like you guys were doing. I'm sorry for staring."

The baby starts crying again and the woman glances over to her family. She rises. "I should be getting back to him before he gets too cranky. I hope your ankle is all right."

"Thank you."

Cade comes back just as Alice leaves. He immediately takes hold of my injured foot again and starts rubbing it. I lean my head on his shoulder and close my eyes, enjoying the massage. He leans his head against mine and exhales. His hand doesn't leave my foot, and for the life of me I can't bring myself to pull it away from him. I know I should. I know allowing him to do stuff like this is leading him on. I don't care though. I've never had someone show me this much attention—even if the attention isn't needed. I'm sure there is nothing wrong with my foot. I just jabbed it on a rock or something. I'll be okay in the morning and after soaking it in warm water.

"Why did you run away from the party tonight?" Cade pulls his head away from mine and glances down at me.

I don't look at him. He knows very well why I left that party. Oh crap! I left the party without informing Raven where I was going. God, I hope she doesn't freak out. Lowering my foot from Cade's lap, I turn to him full on. How do I tell my best friend that I didn't like seeing him with the redhead without him getting his hopes up?

I shake my head and then run my fingers through my hair. "I'm just not into parties."

"Don't lie to me. You used to love parties." He cracks his knuckles one at a time and then looks past me to the couple in the waiting room. "At least you did when we were younger."

"I was a different person back then."

He grins and pulls my hand away from my hair, stopping me from toying with it. "I know, but I see that girl in you. A year ago you wouldn't have even step foot at the lake."

I try to think back to the girl I used to be. Free. Lively. I was the girl I thought Wran wanted. He had only gone out with girls that were outgoing and loved to party. Girls that knew what they wanted and weren't afraid to take it. I wasn't that type of girl, yet that's who I wanted him to see me as. I wanted to be the girl he brought home, even though I was living with him. I knew he cared about me in a way that wasn't like how he saw those girls, but that's all I wanted to be seen as. One of those girls. Free. Careless. Not a burden.

"Cade, I never liked parties. I liked Wran and he wasn't interested in the artsy girls. Not once did he bring home someone like me, so I changed. That's the girl you saw in middle school."

He shakes his head. "No, I saw all of you. I see all of you. He might have been the reason for your change, but can you tell me that you didn't like acting your age for one night?"

I bite down on my lip and look away from him. I did like it. I liked dressing up and going out with people. The party itself might not be my scene, but everything else was pretty great. I shouldn't have liked it. Before I can give him an answer and embarrass myself, a nurse in green scrubs comes out and calls my name. Cade hops up from the seat and scoops me up into his arms.

"Cade, put me down!" I exclaim.

He shakes his head. "What type of man would I be if I let my lady walk around with a bruised ankle?"

"I'm not your lady."

He lifts a brow at me but says nothing more. He walks us over to the nurse, and she looks between us before her eyes land on me. She takes me in and then Cade sets me down, holding me to him. My feet barely graze the cold tile floor.

"Sorry about that," I apologize for all the ruckus.

"He's better than most boys his age. Please follow me, Miss Raine, and we'll take your blood pressure and gets some vitals."

I nod and Cade practically carries me after the nurse. She checks my weight and Cade has to release me—to my liking. Not so much to his. He doesn't move far though. I roll my eyes and the nurse laughs a little. I see nothing funny about this. Cade shouldn't be acting like this. He shouldn't be acting like we are more. He shouldn't be touching me and making jokes about me giving him a kid. He shouldn't have even brought me to this hospital. I don't want to be here.

Once the nurse is done checking my vitals, she leaves me in a small section of the room that's partitioned off with thin blue curtains. Alone with Cade. I wish she would have told him he couldn't be back here, but that probably wouldn't have made him go away. And I probably wouldn't have had the courage to tell the nurse to send him away if she had asked.

Ugh!

Cade sits down on the chair in front of me and checks something on his phone. When he's done with it, he puts it away and drops his elbows to his knees, leaning forward.

"I know why you left the party," he says so low that I hardly hear him. His eyes flick up to me. "I made you jealous."

My cheeks heat and I shake my head. "That's absurd. You shouldn't give yourself that much credit."

He rises from the chair and takes the few steps to the bed I'm sitting on. He places his palms facedown on either side of my hips. His thumbs skim the sides of my thighs and I squirm against his touch. I bite down on the inside of my cheek and turn my body into lead. I will not let him do this. Not right now. Not ever. Cade really needs to accept that Wran and I are endgame. Wran and I are meant to be.

"Don't do that!" he scolds me. "Don't pretend that I have no effect on you. I saw it at school this morning. I saw it at the party. I made you jealous, and the only reason for you to get jealous of Courtney is if you have feelings for me that you don't want to admit."

Courtney? So that's the redhead's name.

I bite down tighter on my cheek. I do not care. "I never said I didn't care about you, Cade. You're my best friend."

"No. I'm more. We're more than that." He takes my hand from my lap and kisses the palm of it. I try to pull it away from him, but he doesn't let it go. "You're trying too hard not to care, but I see it. Is it that bad to care about me as more than a friend?"

"I'm with Wran," I tell him. "I love Wran. Please, stop this."

He shakes his head. "No. I'm done pretending not to see how I affect you. I'm done letting you pretend we are friends. It doesn't help you or me."

I shake my head at him.

He takes hold of my face to stop me from shaking it. His eyes move from mine and go down.

"Don't."

"I know you love Belmont. I'm not stupid. I'm not whatever you think about in your head. I know what you feel for me might not be a fraction of what you feel for him right now, but you will never know if you don't give us a chance."

"There is no chance."

"Belmont is away for another two weeks, Rox. You guys are broken up. You said that. Give me those two weeks. You wouldn't have had a crush on me if you didn't like me."

What the hell do I say to that?

I can't exactly deny that I had a crush on him. He asked me out, for Christ's sake, and I told him yes before Wran came back in the picture. Cade runs a thumb underneath my eye, and I pull away from him.

"Don't cry," he mumbles to me, and leans his forehead against mine. "Don't cry."

"I love him, Cade. I love him so much. I don't want to cheat on him. I don't want to hurt you either."

"You could never hurt me. Just give us a chance. At the end of the two weeks, if you still have yourself convinced that you don't love me, I won't say another word about an us. Belmont will never have to know."

"Unless I choose you, that is."

Cade's lips come up in a smile. "You said that wouldn't happen. If you're so sure, then we have nothing to worry about."

Except his heart getting broken.

I search Cade's eyes for a second before letting out a deep breath. I do love Cade. I don't know what type of love it is. It's not as strong as what I have with Wran, but he's right. I had a crush on him for a reason. Not to mention he's the one that has been here for me. He's the one that came to get me when Wran couldn't control himself. He's the one that gave me a place to stay when Wran made me want to run away. Cade has been nothing but here for me. Yeah, I didn't care for the lunchroom situation, but as he said, I wouldn't have cared if I didn't sense something more than friendship toward him.

It's wrong though. I shouldn't feel anything toward him. Doesn't that make me a bad person? Doesn't that make me exactly what Claire has been calling me? A whore? A slut? I shouldn't care for two guys. I do, though. Oh god, I'm going to hell.

I close my eyes and take in a deep breath.

No one is going to punish me. I'm allowed to care about people.

Wrapping my arms around Cade's neck, I finger the blond hair that's curling at the nape of his head. I give him a nod, telling him that I will try. I will give him two weeks. It's the least I can do after all the things he's done for me. Cade's blue eyes widen and then darken. He pulls my head closer to his and crushes his lips to mine. For the first time ever, I don't fight it. I don't pull away from him. I kiss him back. I'm allowed to kiss someone other than Wran. I'm allowed to like someone other than Wran. He was with other girls. He was with other girls with me in the next room. I can give Cade two weeks. I can.

Cade pulls me closer to the edge of the bed and deepens the kiss. My stomach flutters and then I wrap my legs around him, kissing him back with just as much ferocity. A throat clears behind Cade and he jerks away from me. My face heats up and I glance past him to see a woman in a white lab coat and a brown dress and boots smiling at us. Cade rubs the back of his neck and takes a seat in the chair farthest from me.

"Well, I can always come back when you two are done." The doctor sounds amused as she walks over to me.

I shake my head at her, face still probably red from the embarrassment. I can't believe I just did that. I can't believe I just kissed Cade, and in the same hospital as I gave birth to Harley. "We're done."

"Oh, don't be embarrassed. I was a teenager once upon a time. I understand hormones."

I turn to Cade but he's looking at his phone. Turning back to the doctor, I give her a halfhearted if not downright awkward smile and shrug. I just made out with Cade in a freaking hospital. And he doesn't even have the balls to look the doctor in the eyes as she laughs at me.

I groan and the doctor laughs. "So, you hurt your foot, Miss Raine?"

I nod. "I–I was running and jabbed it on something. It's not that bad."

"All righty, let's get it looked at, then."

Cade sits me down on the bed and moves a strand of hair from my face. He gets up, but I take hold of his hand. I don't want him to leave. I scoot over on the bed, making sure to be easy on my ankle. I told him it wasn't broken or sprained. It was just a bruised muscle. Doctor said the swelling should go down overnight, but that I should be easy on it. It will still be tender to the touch. But as long as I'm not on it for too long, it should be just fine.

Climbing into the bed, Cade lies on his side and faces me. "You were quiet on the way home."

"I was just thinking. That's all," I tell him. And it's true. A lot has happened tonight. A lot of overwhelming things.

I almost got run over by a mystery SUV. I told Cade that I would give him a chance. "Tonight was a lot."

He nods and frowns. "The truck or . . ."

Cade's voice trails off and I know he's eager to ask me about the hospital. We didn't say much after the kiss. I didn't know what to say. He asked me for a proper chance while Wran is away. I haven't told him Wran wants me to come visit him at Pleasure House. Cade doesn't even know that Wran is at Pleasure House. I didn't think that was something Wran would have wanted shared.

"I promised you two weeks. I can do that, but I was speaking about everything. Cade, someone wanted to kill me. Someone that wasn't my father. I'm scared."

He moves in closer to me and pulls me to his chest. "I know. I wish I could tell you not to be, but I can't. Someone wants you dead, which means we're going to have to be careful. I wish you would report it."

"I'll tell Josh in the morning. He's going to be mad."

"Yeah, I know. He's a Belmont too."

I elbow him in the stomach. "If we're going to give us a try, then you have to stop talking about them like that. They are my family."

Cade groans, but nods. "I know. Why did you say yes, Rox?"

I don't have to ask him what he's speaking of. I already know. He wants to know why now. Why, after all his advances, have I finally given in? With a sigh, I run a hand up his arm. "Because you were right. I was jealous. I didn't like seeing you with that girl. I know it's wrong of me, but I didn't like it. I think I deserve to know why that bothered me so much."

"You love me," he tells me.

"It could just be hormones."

He smirks at me and tilts his head forward. "That only means you're sexually attracted to me. I'm more than willing to help you with those pesky desires."

My face heats and I shove him back. He laughs at me. "I never said I wasn't attracted to you."

He stops laughing. "I know. You said you loved Belmont. I can handle that. I'm going to make you fall in love with me in two weeks."

I stare at him, but I don't say anything. I don't know if two weeks is enough time for anyone to fall in love with anyone. "Do you think two weeks is going to erase twelve years?"

"Of course not." He shakes his head. "I don't want to erase him from your life. I want you to realize there's more to the world than Belmont. He might be your savior, but that doesn't mean you owe him your love."

My brow furrows at him. "I don't feel that way—"

"Yes, you do," he cuts me off. "But that's okay. I'm going to show you what true love is. I have you for two weeks."

Before I can protest his words, he crushes his mouth against mine. The kiss ends all too soon, and then Cade's off the bed and at the door to my room. Sitting up, I glare at him. He shrugs.

"Get some sleep. It's late and you have a date with Harley in the morning."

He walks out the door and closes it behind him. I fall back on the bed and stare up at the ceiling. My hand goes to my mouth and I grin to myself. I kissed Cade. I kissed Cade two times tonight without pulling away. The only person's kiss that I've enjoyed has been Wran. After my father, I didn't think I could enjoy a simple kiss, and after Wran left me, I didn't think I wanted to enjoy another's lips against mine. But Cade . . .

Wow!

CHAPTER 16

ROX

Josh paces back and forth in front of Cade and me on the couch. He's seething. The moment I told him about the black SUV, I thought he was going to start foaming at the mouth like a rabid dog. He's been pacing ever since he came over here this morning. I told Cade I would inform Josh, and I did. Although I figured he would go easy on me since we have to go see Harley today; I was wrong.

"Did you see anyone?" he asks me again. Josh has asked me that same question four times since I told him what happened last night.

I shake my head. "I already told you that."

"No. I mean before the party. You said you saw the SUV outside of this house and at the school. Did you notice anything else, Roxanna?"

"No."

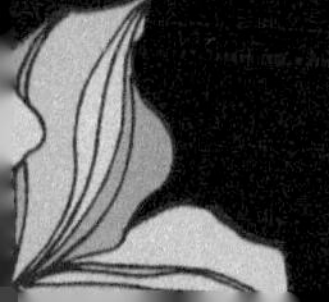

Josh marches over to the wall and leans his head against it. A second later his fist slams into it and I jump a little on the couch. I have never seen Josh respond like that. He comes back over to me and lets out a deep breath.

"You shouldn't have even been at a damn party!" he yells down at me. "What the hell were you thinking, Roxanna? And on a Friday night, of all nights?"

I look away from him and down at my lap. I know it was stupid to go to a party. "I–I just wanted—"

"Wanted what? To lose Harley forever? One drink and that's exactly what would have happened. Hell, you didn't even have to have a drink! What if someone spilled a drink on you? You would still smell like fucking booze!"

"Dude, chill!" Cade yells at him in my defense.

My head drops and I don't say anything. Josh is right. I was stupid. I don't have the luxury of acting like everyone else. I accepted that a long time ago.

"Don't!" Josh warns Cade. "You of all people know what she has to lose, and yet you still invited her to that party. I blame you for this."

"She's eighteen." Cade gets up from the couch. "She has every right to act that age. She has every right to have some fun sometimes. If I thought for one minute that going to a party would harm her or Harley, I wouldn't have suggested it. I care about them just as much as you do."

"Really?" Josh takes a step toward Cade, and I finally get up. I put myself in between them. Josh glares at Cade over my shoulder. "If you care about her so much, why didn't you notice the damn SUV in front of your house? Why did you let her walk off from a party in the middle of nowhere?"

Cade doesn't answer. None of this is his fault.

"Stop yelling at him. This isn't his fault."

"You're right." Josh glares down at me, and I back away from him and into Cade. Cade wraps a protective arm around my waist. Josh looks down at it, but I don't shrug Cade away. Not this time.

"It's both your fault." Josh continues, but he only addresses me. "You know how you should act. You know what you can and cannot do. I understand the lure, Rox, but you can't."

I simply nod at him. I do know, and I made a mistake. Silent tears roll down my cheeks as I look at the floor. This is all my fault. If I would have just told him last night about my suspicions, that SUV wouldn't have gotten near me. I would have been ordered to go home, and everything would be just fine. Cade turns me around in his hold and tilts my face up to his. His face hardens when he sees the tears. Wiping at them, he pulls me close to him. I hide my face in the same black polo he was wearing last night and dry my tears.

When I have myself under control, I pull away from Cade and face Josh. "Let's go get Harley, and then you can continue to degrade my character afterward."

"I'm not degrading your character." Josh lets out a sigh and sinks down on the cushion. "For the life of me, I can't understand what was going through your head last night. I don't know why you wouldn't tell me about the vehicle. You literally texted me last night, Roxanna."

"You said you were out, and I didn't want to disturb you."

"Don't you know by now that you and Wran are my only concerns in life? I would give up everything else to be there for you guys."

Yeah, I know.

That doesn't mean I like it.

"If it makes it any better, I felt like an imposter at that party. It was nowhere near how I remember parties to be."

Cade runs his hands up my arms, and I can feel how tense his body is behind me. I hate this so much. "I'm sorry."

Bending my head back, I peer up at Cade. "For what?"

"I should have known a party wouldn't have been your scene."

Shrugging, I dismiss his statement. We've already talked about me and my views on parties. He couldn't have known. "Stop apologizing for that. I wanted a piece of normalcy for one night."

As badly as I hate to admit it, it's true. After finding some people that truly wanted to hang out with me for me, I didn't want to let them down by rejecting their invitation. Didn't really matter though; I ended up abandoning them at the party anyways. They're probably never going to talk to me again after last night. Not to mention I didn't even inform them of my whereabouts.

I turn back to Josh. His eyes move from me to Cade and back again. "What's going on here?"

I shake my head at him. He doesn't need to know anything. "Nothing!"

"Ouch," Cade murmurs.

"We're just friends, Josh. You know I love Wran."

He rises from the couch and points to Cade's arm still around me. I step out of Cade's hold.

"I know we don't really talk like we used to, Rox, but I am here for you. I shouldn't have gone off on you about last night, but I am here for you too." His eyes move between Cade and me. "You can love more than one person at a time. Wran won't like it, but you can. You can figure out what you want without him."

I blink at his words and then shake my head. No. I don't want him to think that. I don't want him to see me as . . . as a slut. Even if being with both Cade and Wran was acceptable, we live in Kingston. We would be run out of town. I would be run out of town. No. I can admit to myself and Cade that I might have some feelings for him, but no one else needs to know. No one else needs to know that I've decided to be a harlot for two weeks. It's just two weeks. Two weeks and no one will have to know.

"You already know how Cade feels about me," I tell Josh. "He's just being overly protective after last night. I'm with Wran. I love Wran."

Cade's whole body stills behind me and I turn around to look at him. He takes a step away from me and then another. I take one in his direction but he holds up a hand to stop my approach. Crap! I shouldn't have said that.

He looks at Josh and then forces himself to relax. "We're nothing. Just friends. F-R-I-E-N-D-S. Nothing more. Never anything more."

He steps off and I watch him go. I bite down on my lip and then turn to Josh. He tilts his head at me, eyebrows drawing together. "Go after him."

"But—"

"Roxanna, no buts. Go after your friend. We'll talk in the car."

I nod and sprint in the direction Cade went. He's sitting at the dining table with his phone out, some social media app open. I take the seat next to him and place a hand on his arm. He knocks my arm away.

"Cade, please." My voice comes out like a whine. "I'm sorry."

"I thought you would give me a fair two weeks." He fakes a laugh. "Should have known you wouldn't."

"That's not fair. I just don't want anyone to know."

"Then how is that fair? How would I take you out?"

"I thought we agreed Wran wouldn't have to know. You taking me out would assure he would know."

He shakes his head and lowers it to the wooden table. "I guess I wasn't thinking last night. We would never work."

Exhaling, I place my hand to the side of his face and pull it toward me. I get up from the chair and step closer to him. "I still want to try."

His brow quirks. "Really?"

I nod. "Yeah."

He scoots back in the chair, the legs scraping against the wooden floor. Cade pulls me down on his lap and I flinch when he presses into me. I've never felt another guy this close to me before. Bringing my face closer to his, Cade kisses me gently. It's not like the thirsty, heady kiss he gave me last night. This one is sweet. He releases my lips and smiles at me.

"How's your foot?" He peeks down at the cutesy pink ballet flats I have on, that are completely at odds with the dark skinny jeans and band tee. I don't even know the band.

"It's fine. I can walk on it."

"You were also screaming again last night."

I thought since my father was dead, the dreams would go away. They haven't. I'm still having nightmares about what happened and the things that are still coming forth in my memory. They're not as bad as they were before, but when you almost get run over by a black SUV with blacked-out windows, the nightmares are sure to surface.

"I'm fine. I swear."

"Mhmm." Cade frowns at me. "You haven't talked about them or any of the memories. I'm here if you need to discuss them."

I roll my eyes and laugh at him. "Cade, seriously, I'm fine. They're just dreams. My father is dead. You guys saved me when you both . . . did what you did. I have nothing to be upset about or scared of." Except the black SUV.

He rises and sets me on the floor. "Okay. Go see your daughter. I'll be here when you get back."

"Okay."

Walking out of the dining room, I spot Josh standing in the foyer next to the door. He gives me a once-over before going out. I follow him, making sure not to put much pressure on my ankle. It's a lot better compared to last night, but it still aches a little.

When we're in the car and on the road, Josh glances over at me. "So, do you want to tell me what's going on with him?"

"No." The word comes out sharp and clipped. In no universe do I want to talk about that situation with Josh. Or anyone for that matter.

We don't say anything the rest of the ride to Arlington.

"Poshy!" Harley jumps up from the toy blocks and runs straight into Josh's open arms as we step foot in the overly colorful waiting room. Lynn rises from her chair and comes over to me. She hands me Harley's bag with all her necessities. Josh tosses Harley up and she giggles.

"Hey, there's my little rug rat," Josh coos at her, and turns away from Lynn without a word. I watch him walk back down the hall with my daughter and disappear out the double doors before I turn back to Lynn.

"Where are you taking her today?" she questions me.

"Josh wants to take her to the zoo. It's warmer out and she loves the lions."

Lynn nods. "Have a good day."

I force a smile at my social worker and leave her standing in the waiting room. By the time I reach the car, Josh has Harley strapped in her seat and is waiting patiently behind the driver's wheel. Sliding inside, I place Harley's bag on the floor and then glance back at her. She's drinking from her sippy cup and paying me no mind.

"How's the ankle?" Josh asks as he pulls away from the glass building.

"I don't think Lynn noticed anything. It hurts though."

"Maybe that will be a reminder to call me next time."

I roll my eyes at Josh's comment and lean back in the seat.

"Bennett is supposed to meet us at the zoo. He wants to talk to you more about that night."

Right. That night. Gah! My memories have been coming back, but for the life of me, I can't remember what happened that night. Glancing back at Harley, I bite down on my lip. I have to remember. I'm not losing my baby. And I'm sure not letting Lynn think she can just have Harley without a fight.

"What do you remember from that night?" I ask Josh.

He comes to a stop at a light and looks over at me. He rubs his jaw but then shakes his head. "Honestly, what I remember does us no good. You were completely out of it when I made it to the bar. The bartender said that you had showed up there high already and someone had bought you a drink."

"But I was fifteen and obviously pregnant. Why didn't anyone care?"

"Rox, I don't know what to tell you. Much of that night made no sense. I have theories, but those aren't going to get us Harley."

"You never told me your theories."

Josh looks over at me. "You were a handful during that time. I didn't want to add more onto our plate."

"I lost my daughter and I didn't remember why, Josh. I wanted to die. You had no clue what was going on in my head. The only reason I didn't try anything was because of her. She needed me."

Josh doesn't say anything to that. He already knows how bad things got. Josh's phone starts buzzing and he retrieves it from his pocket, tossing it to me. I look down at the message on the screen only to see my guidance counselor's name flash across the screen. Looking from the message and then up at Josh, I tap the message and read it in full.

Tasha: Thank you for last night. I had a good time. Maybe you can finish what you started tonight? You left your handcuffs.

I gasp and drop the phone. Josh arches a brow at me and I pick up the phone from the floor. Handcuffs? I turn to Josh as he takes the exit for the zoo. When did he start seeing Miss Flannigan?

"Who was that?" Josh's eyes go back to the road.

"Umm . . ." My cheeks heat up. "Miss Flannigan. You left your handcuffs."

I stare at him, waiting for some sort of reaction. He doesn't react at all. I can't picture Josh using cuffs on anyone, and I sure can't picture my straitlaced guidance counselor getting handcuffed. Or maybe Josh . . . I shake my head. Nope, I don't want to even think about him in that way. A shiver runs up my spine. Gross.

"You and Miss Flannigan, huh?" I ask him.

"It was just a few dates. Don't go jumping to conclusions," he says and turns into the zoo's parking lot.

Dropping the subject, I turn around in my seat to Harley. She always goes to sleep as soon as she gets into this car. And it's always hard to get her to calm down when we wake her up. Hopefully it won't be nearly as hard today. She really does love the zoo and the lions.

Josh pulls into a vacant spot and turns the car off. He takes his phone from me and starts typing out a message. I peek over at it but can't see who he's texting. A couple of minutes later, his phone pings.

"Bennett is waiting inside by the ticket booth."

I look back at Harley. "Is her stroller in the trunk? She's not going to want to walk."

He peeks over the seat at her. A small grin spreads across his face. "Can't handle your own daughter?"

"Do you want to carry her all over the zoo after waking her up?"

His grin falls. Of course he doesn't, but he would. I know he would. I swear Josh cares about her like she's his own. "It's in the back. I made sure to have it this morning."

Josh presses a button and the trunk opens. He gets out of the car and walks around to the back. He pulls out the huge pink and black stroller. He bought it as soon as he found out that Harley was going to be a girl. Before I got her taken away. With a sigh, I get out of the car and go around to Harley. I undo the belt keeping her in place and take her out. She stares a little but immediately calms when I lay her head against my shoulder. Josh slams the trunk and then moves to us. He takes Harley from my arms and gently sits her down in the chair. Her head falls to the side, but she remains asleep. That's a first.

"Think she'll sleep the entire time?" Josh asks and strolls over to the zoo's entrance.

I give him a pointed look. "It's Harley. When has she ever slept the entire time?"

"Point taken."

Josh pays for two adult tickets and we walk inside the gates. As Josh said, Bennett is waiting just inside. Instead of the casual look he donned the last time I saw him, he's in black slacks and a yellow button-down that seems to make his skin glow even more than it already does. He also has on a black tie and some nice shoes. He must have something to do after this.

We come to a stop in front of him, and he bends down to peer at Harley. He frowns and rises to us. "You guys didn't have to put the child to sleep."

"Oh, trust me, it's better that she's asleep or we wouldn't get anything discussed," Josh tells him.

"So?" I urge him. We don't really have time for all the idle talk. I want to know what he has to say.

He walks off and down the paved passageway. The sign at the beginning of it states aquatic exhibit. I suppose it is a good thing that Harley is asleep. She doesn't do well around water and fish. I don't know why. As far as I know, she shouldn't have a reason to fear them. Then again, Lynn could be keeping something that happened to her from me. Lynn isn't required to tell me anything that happens to Harley while in her care. I don't like it, but I can't change it. It's something I've learned to accept.

The stone pathway turns into metal flooring and the open sky vanishes, cloaking us in darkness, the only light coming from the tanks around us. Bennett comes to a stop in front of a tank with multicolored fish and take a seat on a bench.

"Have you remembered anything helpful from that night, Roxanna?" Bennett asks, never taking his eyes off the fish.

I shake my head. "No. I honestly do not know what happened that night. I don't even know how I got to a bar in Arlington."

"I figured as much," he says, and finally turns away from the glass. "I've managed to pull your file concerning this incident. There's not much to it, since you were a minor when it all happened, and details of that night are slight. I've contacted a friend about you, and I would like you to see him this week."

"What type of friend?" Josh asks and take a seat on the bench as well. He pulls out a small blanket from a slot on the stroller and lays it across Harley. She attempts to roll over in the seat, but the belt keeps her restrained in place. She opens her eyes a little and look around at us. She rubs her eyes and then closes them again.

"He's a therapist that specializes in trauma victims. He helps recover memories lost. I'm hoping he can help you with this. Anything at this point is helpful."

"I have school, but I can meet him afterward. What day?"

"Tuesday?"

I nod my head. Tuesday is actually a great day. I have nothing going on that day. Unless homework counts, but that can always wait.

"I can't make that day," Josh tells Bennett. "I have a meeting I must attend."

"That's okay. Cade can take me. It's no big deal."

Josh narrow his eyes at me. "Cade? Really?"

I roll my eyes at him. There's really no reason why Cade can't take me. I probably shouldn't have volunteered him without asking, but I'm pretty sure he's free. Unless he has football practice. Crap. Pulling out my phone, I shoot him a quick message to verify he's free. A minute later he sends me back a thumbs-up emoji and I laugh at it. He could have just said yeah. I hate emojis. They can mean so many different things.

"He's free."

"All right then. I'll forward you the address and time when I get home. He's very interested in your case."

"So, I have a case?" I know I've asked this before, but it seems so unreal.

"If we can get you to remember something, anything, then yes. Anything can send me and my team down a path. From what you both have stated, there seems to be more than one person behind this. If we can just get a crumb . . ."

"We understand," Josh says, and gets up from the steel bench. Just then, a high-pitched cry sounds and I glance in the direction of the noise. A little boy in jeans and a T-shirt is fighting a man. The man is dragging him by his arm out of the exhibit. I turn to Harley, making sure the noise didn't wake her, but unfortunately it did. She's lying in her stroller with wide eyes, staring at Bennett. I glance at him and frown. He leans forward and grins at her. He tickles her stomach through the blanket. Harley giggles and reaches for the man.

"Do you have kids?" I ask him, trying to understand why she seems to like him. Harley isn't the type of child that takes well to people, but she seems to have taken to Bennett.

I don't know if I like that or not. Especially since she hasn't even taken to me yet, and I'm her mother.

"No. I'm not very good with kids," he answers and gets up from the bench. He goes over to the tank. "Odd, considering most kids like me."

Harley sits up in her stroller, her eyes following him to the tank. The moment a fish swims into her line of view, she screams. Josh instantly takes hold of her stroller and wheels her out of the aquatic area. Josh doesn't come to a stop until we're as far away from the sea creatures as possible and Harley has stopped crying. When he does come to a halt, I drop down in front of Harley and unbuckle her. She reaches for me and I take her with ease, rocking her a little as she buries her tiny head into my shoulders.

"It's okay, sweetie. No more fishy." I look around at all the food vendors and spot the pink and blue cotton candy stand that's always here whenever we come. Going over to it, I take one and pay for it.

Harley's head snaps up as soon as she notices her favorite treat. "Candy!" she squeals and reaches for the little bag.

Opening it, I give her a piece. She stuffs it in her mouth. I know the moment it dissolves; her big coco eyes go wide with glee. It's always cute to see that. Setting her down on the ground, I give her the bag. I know it's bad practice to give her candy this early in the morning, but she doesn't get candy often. Lynn hardly ever gives her any.

Taking hold of her hand, I turn back toward Josh and Bennett. They are deep in conversation about something. As I go over to them, Josh stops mid-sentence and reaches down for Harley. She stuffs another piece of cotton candy into her mouth before wrapping her arms around Josh's neck.

"Poshy! I want cats!" She points in the direction of the lion pen. I have no clue how she can remember the way to the lions but she can't pronounce Josh. It's still so mind-boggling, all the things she knows and all the things she doesn't.

"All right. We'll go see the lions," he tells her. She smiles and untwines her arms from around him to eat more of the candy.

"I suppose I'll let you both get on with your day," Bennett announces. He looks over Josh's shoulder at me. "Roxanna, don't forget to check your messages later for the information about the appointment, and do please contact me if you remember something before Tuesday."

I give him a slight nod even though I know it's a long shot for me to remember anything about that night. I was drugged. If my memories haven't surfaced after almost three years, I doubt they will emerge in three days.

"You could always stay and enjoy the zoo with us," Josh offers. "You bought a ticket. Might as well."

His face scrunches up in disgust as if the mere thought of spending time with us is out of the question. "That's all right. I've never been much of a zoo fan. Don't know how y'all can stand the smell."

"Zoo. Stay." Harley turns in Josh's arms and glares at Bennett. She has a pout on her face that's more cute than insulting. "Stay."

Bennett's nose twitches and he takes a step closer to Harley and Josh. He bends a little so that he's face to face with my daughter. She places a hand on his cheek, her other hand holding onto the plastic bag of candy.

"I can't stay. I have somewhere else to be," he tells her.

She shakes her head. "Stay."

Josh shifts Harley to his other side. "He can't stay."

Her bottom lip quivers and I take her from Josh. She immediately reaches back to him.

"Stay. Stay. Stay!" she cries.

Bennett's brows go up and he straightens up. His eyes flash back and forth between us all.

"Okay," he coos at Harley. "I'll stay."

She smiles and reaches for him. Bennett takes a small, almost unnoticeable step away from her, but I notice it. Apparently so does Josh; he turns away from his friend and sets Harley down in her stroller. She doesn't make a sound and continues eating her candy. Josh turns toward the lion pen and walks off.

"Sorry about that. You might want to leave before she notices you're not walking with them."

He shakes his head. "That's okay. I'll stay for a bit."

"I thought you had somewhere to be." I gesture to his outfit. Slacks and a nice shirt are nowhere near appropriate attire for the zoo.

He looks down at his clothes. "Oh. It was just a lunch date with someone. I didn't want to go if I'm honest. You women can be so—" He catches himself and shakes his head. "I don't mind spending a few hours appeasing the little troll."

I tilt my head to the side, trying to figure this man out. He obviously doesn't like kids—he stated as much—but he's giving in to Harley. I know she can be hard to decline, but I'm her mother. It's supposed to be like that for me. He has no such reason to stay.

"Why are you looking at me like that?" he asks me.

"Why are you staying?"

"She's hard to say no to. I think it's those bubbly eyes."

I bite down on my lip and consider his words. I have no reason to think he means anything else, but after my father kidnapped her, I don't want to take any chances. He's new. I don't really know him. He could easily get one over on me. I don't want Harley in any more danger than she has already suffered.

"I promise you I mean her no harm, Roxanna. Josh would skin me alive. If you don't want me here, that's all you have to say. I understand."

I let out a sigh and shake my head at him. If Josh trusts him, I trust him. Besides, he's helping me with an impossible case. If I can't trust him, then this arrangement won't work. "I guess we have some lions to go see."

He gives me a soft smile and walks off in the direction of the lion pen.

Please, please, don't let me regret this.

CHAPTER 17

WRAN

I take a seat on the lawn as everyone else makes their way over to our little semicircle group session. Since I broke down in front of Thomas last Friday, things have been better. I haven't felt as . . . explosive. Who knew that was all it took for me to loosen up? I had two private sessions over the weekend where he prescribed me a different medication. I don't know why he is giving me meds when he knows how I get about the little white pills. Nothing is going to change my mind about that. I'm just content to have that shit off my chest. Someone knows I killed James Raine. Someone knows I would do it again if I have to. Even if it makes me feel like a piece of rotting meat for doing so.

Josh called me Saturday evening and told me he and Rox will be coming for a visit on Wednesday. I suppose that's one thing I'm looking forward to, especially since he wouldn't tell me anything about Rox and why she's not answering her damn phone. Now that I'm thinking about it, he didn't say one word about Rox the entire hour we talked. That's usually the only thing we have to talk about.

"Hey man!"

I pull myself from my thoughts as Steven takes a seat on the grass next to me. Everyone else follows him and sits as well. Thomas takes the chair that's at the center of the circle and looks at each one of us.

"Hey," I return his greeting as I lean back on my elbows. "Heard you were sent to solitary over the weekend."

He shrugs. "Me? I heard you had that pretty little nurse of yours running scared."

I let out a rough laugh and run a hand through my hair. Yeah, that wasn't my finest moment. I should really apologize to the woman. She was only doing her job. She didn't need a fucker like me scaring her. Although you would think she would be used to it, working in a place like this. Surely the anger management patients aren't as bad as the people in the other wards.

"Just a little misunderstanding," I tell him. "I wasn't in a good mood."

Thomas clears his throat and all the commotion around us comes to a stop. "I hope your Monday started off great."

The group lets out a collective groan, and Thomas chuckles. He asks the same question every day and every day everyone does the same thing: mumble and groan and disregards everything Thomas has to say. It's horrible. I wouldn't want to be in his shoes. The people here have a ton of problems—problems that make what I'm going through seem like child's play. It seems stupid of me to partake in these sessions when they have issues that could potentially land them in prison. I hit Rox once. Once was enough, but at least I'm not beating kids and setting people's cars on fire.

"Would anyone like to share anything today?" Thomas addresses us all.

No one responds.

Thomas's eyes flicker throughout the crowd and then they land on me. "How about you, Mr. Belmont? You had a grave breakthrough this past weekend."

I narrow my eyes at him, but he only grins. His eyes peer into me like a laser and I want to punch him for even suggesting that I let these people in on what the hell I'm going through. Steven elbows me in my side and I scowl at him. He's been trying to get me to open up for quite some time, hounding me whenever he can. I glance around the crowd to see everyone looking at me expectantly. They have all shared more than enough; I guess it's only fair that they expect me to as well. Although I doubt any of these fuckers really care. Scratch that, I'm sure Steven cares more than he should.

Gulping, I stand and meet each of their eyes. Some of them smirk and I wish I could wipe those smirks off their faces. Fuck. Why did I stand up?

I scratch the back of my neck and clear my throat. I give them a small, awkward-as-all-fuck wave. "Hey. I'm Wran, which you know. So, umm, I have no clue what the fuck to say."

Someone snickers and Thomas cut his eyes at them before addressing me standing like an idiot in the circle. "How are you doing this morning?"

"Like I could use some coffee," I tell him, and although it's not what he wants to hear, it's the truth.

"Did you have another nightmare last night?"

My body goes rigid at his question. My eyes drift around the group to see how they are reacting. None of them seem to particularly care. Guess nightmares aren't worth caring about.

"Something like that," I tell him. "I talked to my brother. He's always a nightmare."

"What did you two talk about?"

I shift on my feet and let out a long breath. Here goes nothing, I guess. Thomas isn't going to drop this. "Just random stuff. We talked about my girlfriend, Rox. She hasn't been answering any of my calls. Not since I asked her to come here. Josh was acting weird, though, and didn't really want to discuss her."

"Your girlfriend knows you're here?" someone asks.

My eyes meet the new kid that showed up last week. I nod. "Yeah. I'm working on not keeping secrets from her. I've done plenty of that in the past."

"You're stupid. No girl wants a guy with issues. She's probably out screwing someone else."

My hands clench at my sides as I peer at the punk. His eyes flick down to my balled fists and he smirks. The little fucker wouldn't be smirking if my fist met his face. I don't move though. I don't say anything. A small, very small, part of me has wondered the same thing. Rox is living with Cade. He has a damn crush on her. If I was him, I would be trying to get with Rox any chance I could. And now she's not even answering my calls. Something is wrong. Something is not adding up. Rox would have never gone this long without answering. I mean, we are talking about the same girl that sent me nearly a hundred voicemails after I fled to the military.

"How does the idea of her being with someone else make you feel, Wran?"

I turn back to Thomas, the sneer very evident on my face by now, probably. "Like I want to fuck someone up."

I drop back down to my seat on the lawn before he can ask me any more questions. If that rich prick so much as touched my girl, he's going to be buried alongside her father. And if she so much as lets him . . . fuck! I need to call her. I need to talk to her. Rox would never do that to me. I know she wouldn't. I didn't raise her to be like that. She's loyal. Completely and utterly loyal to me. She wouldn't hurt me like that.

Right?

Thomas doesn't ask me any more questions for the rest of the session. When it's finally over, I jump up without listening to whatever closing words Thomas spurts out and march to the lobby. The nun that was here on my first day is standing at the counter with a Bible in her hand, reading. She looks up at me and closes her book as I come to a stop in front of her.

"Mr. Belmont, how may I help you?" She takes a step back and smiles.

I don't smile. I still don't like this woman. "I need to use the phone."

She bends down and grabs the ancient rotary phone that I've been using since I broke my cellphone. The first time I used this thing, Thomas had to show me how to work it. Seriously, spinning the wheel for every number is a waste of time. This place really needs to jump into modern times.

"Thanks." I dial Rox's number as fast as I can on this contraption. When the phone starts to ring, I inhale. Pick up, pick up. The ring cuts off and I hear breathing on the line.

"H–hello?" Rox's voice comes out shaky and low.

I pull the phone away from me and look at it. Why is she answering like that? Bringing the phone back to my ear, I finally speak. "Rox?"

She lets out a long breath. "Wran? Why aren't you calling me on your phone?"

"Why did you answer the phone like that?"

"No reason," she says all too fast.

My grip on the phone tightens. "Don't lie to me. What's going on?"

"Nothing. I just thought you were someone else. How are you?"

"Been better. Why haven't you been answering your phone? I've been calling you for days."

"I–I do have school and work and Harley," she lies to me. She only stutters when she's lying or nervous.

"Are you still at Cade's place?" I lean against the counter.

The nun takes a seat and looks at me before opening her Bible again.

"Of course. Where else would I be?"

"The apartment. You know, where you live. With me. Not Cade."

"Look, I–I have to g-go. You called in between classes."

"Rox—"

The line goes dead and I pull the phone away from my ear and stare at it. She just hung up on me. She didn't even give me time to fucking talk. I slam the phone down and take a step back. What the fuck is going on with her?

"Mr. Belmont?" The nun calls me, and I look up at her. "I forgot to mention that you received a letter while in your morning session."

She hands me a small white envelope with my name and temporary address on it. It doesn't have a return address. Forcing a smile on my face, I nod at the woman. As much as the nun grates on my nerves, she's not the one that just hung up on me. Rox will be getting an earful the next time we talk. She can't do crap like that. I don't care if she is in between classes. That means she has at least five minutes to hear me out.

I walk back to my room, eyeing the envelope in my hand. No one but my brother and Rox knows I'm here at Pleasure House. And neither one of them would send me a letter. Pushing the door to my room open, I open the letter. Inside is a small piece of folded paper, yellow in color. A sticky note. Why in the world would someone send me a sticky note? Unfolding it, I suck in a deep breath. My eyes scan the sentence.

Just because James Raine is dead doesn't mean she's safe.

I ball the paper up in my hand and drop it to the floor. Grabbing the door handle, I stomp back out to the lobby. The nun looks up and her eyes go wide. She gets up from the chair and backs away from the counter. I round it and yank the phone back up. I start to dial Josh's number, but miss a number and have to start over. When I finally get the number in, it rings once before it's answered.

"Josh?" I yell into the phone. "Get me out of this fucking place."

"Woah, Wran what's going on?" he asks me. "I thought you were doing good."

"What's wrong? What's fucking wrong? What the hell is going on there? Is Rox okay?"

I hear a door shut on the other end of the phone before my brother says anything. He must have been around people. "What makes you think something is wrong here?"

The woman eases her way back into her seat. She never takes her eyes off me. I glower at her. I swear people here don't understand the concept of privacy. "A little space, please. This is private."

She bows her head and then scurries away. She probably wanted to do that anyways.

"Wran?"

"It doesn't matter. Just get your ass here and check me out."

"No."

"No? What the hell do you mean 'no'? My girl needs me!"

"We can take care of her. You need to stay and finish your program."

"I swear to God if you don't come get me, I will fucking hitch back to Kingston," I yell at him through the phone.

"Rox is fine, Wran. There was an accident, but I'm handling it."

I slam the phone down on the retriever. Fuck this shit! How dare he try to keep me away from her. How dare he keep me in this nuthouse when my girl needs me. A hand comes down on my shoulder and I whirl around. I don't think before I swing. I keep swinging until someone grabs me and tackles me to the floor. My head slams into the tiles and ringing sounds behind me. I glance over my shoulder to see two guys in white scrubs holding me. I look up at the phone ringing and then back down at the floor where Steven sits. He's counting and holding his nose. He looks up at me, a grimace on his face. His nose is bleeding and crooked. Fuck. I broke his nose.

"I'm sorry, man. I didn't mean to do that."

Steven gets to his feet, towering over me. "Go fuck your-self."

He stalks away and the two guys behind me drag me up. I pull away from them and fix my shirt. The phone rings again, but I ignore it. One of the nurses reaches for me, but I shrug backward. No way am I going with them.

"You can come with us, or we can force you to. The choice is yours," one of them says.

I laugh at them. Yeah, no way am I going into solitary. Not for this.

"I'm checking myself out," I tell them.

"That's not an option, Wran," Thomas' voice comes from behind me and I turn around to see him standing with Steven and the nun. "What happened?"

"Nothing you can help me with, Doc. Now, if you will, sign my release forms and let me go."

Thomas shakes his head. "No. You signed up for this program. The program states that you will not be released until the four weeks are up."

"You're not stopping me from leaving. It'll be a cold day in hell before I stay here instead of going to her."

Turning, I stomp pass the two men in white suits and head out the door. They can't keep me here. I'm in sound fucking mind. I have every right to check myself out of this place, signature or no signature on a piece of paper. I hear the door open behind me and I turn to see the nurses rush-ing toward me. My feet are running before I even know it, and then I'm tackled once more onto the ground. I shove at the guy, but then someone else grabs me. I peer behind me to see Steven holding my arms. I attempt to yank myself free, but not even I can fight off three guys that have me pinned to the ground. Thomas comes up behind the two nurses with a syringe. He bends down and jabs the needle into the arm that Steven has restrained.

Steven releases my arms and I swing at him. They are heavy, like a ten-pound bag of clay or something. I try to rise, but the world around me sways and I fall back on the ground. What the fuck did Thomas give me? I try to rise again, but black spots dance in my vision and bile rises in my throat. Someone drags me up, but I can't open my eyes. They, too, feel like lead is holding them shut.

"Take him to solitary," is the last thing I hear before going completely out of it.

CHAPTER 18

ROX

The bell jolts me upright in my chair and I slam my knee against the underside of my desk. I glance around the room to see if anyone noticed me sleeping, but nope; they saw nothing. No one is even paying me a lick of attention—just stuffing books in bags and shuffling out the room. Turning my attention to the board up front, I glance over the equations on it and groan. Great. Just great. I actually needed to be awake for this class. I needed to know this for the test on Friday. My eyes move from the numbers that make little sense to my teacher, glaring my way with his arms crossed.

"Roxanna, please stay," he announces over the sound of rushing students.

I grab my book and stuff it inside my backpack along with my empty notebook with drool on it. I have never really had a problem with my classes, but it's been getting harder

and harder to concentrate this semester. The one semester where my attention needs to be at its peak, and I'm faltering.

Rising from the desk, I toss my bag on my back and make my way to the front of the room. I stop shy of my teacher's desk and wait for him to chastise me for sleeping in his class. When he doesn't say anything, I bring my eyes up to meet his gaze.

He comes to the front of his desk and leans against it, studying me like one of those equations on the board. "Are you okay?"

My face scrunches up at his question. He has never before wanted to know how I was. Most of the teachers in this school haven't cared. Most of them look the other way when anything happens. And the ones that do seem to care don't have the nerve to say anything to us. They would rather let us battle it out like teenagers. If only I was a regular teenager.

"I'm fine," I finally answer him, and look over at the door.

"You fell asleep in my class, and since your . . . your father was released, many of your teachers noticed that your grades have been falling."

"My grades are fine. I have a B average." I make sure my grades stay above a C. That's one of the conditions tossed on me when I lost Harley: if my grades dropped below a certain point, my privileges would be taken away. Sure, I was doing better than my current average before everything, but at least it's still better than half the students in this class.

"While that is good, you were a top student. You were an honor student. And now you're sleeping in class."

"I'm fine. Okay? I promise you I'm fine. I just didn't get much sleep last night." True.

I didn't sleep a wink at all. My mind was too occupied with conjuring up nightmares of getting run over by a faceless person in a black SUV. Except it wasn't a nightmare. Not at all.

"I'm sorry to hear that, but I really can't have you sleeping in my class. Maybe you should speak with the counselor."

Shaking my head, I back away from him and walk backward to the door. "I'm fine. I have to go to lunch."

I dart out of the room and down the hall toward my locker before he can say anything else on the matter. No way am I talking to Miss Flannigan. Opening my locker, red rose petals fall to the tile flooring, along with a piece of paper. I glance down the hall in both directions to make sure no one is around. Bending down, I retrieve the piece of paper and open it. Written in terrible blocky letters is a note from Cade.

Meet me in the library. Study room 3.

- C

I shake my head at the rose petals. He didn't think when he put those in my locker. How am I supposed to clean this mess up? Shoving my backpack inside, I slam the door and look down at the mess. Maybe a janitor will clean it up before anyone sees this. Rolling my eyes to myself, I head down the hall to the library. No one is present—not even the librarian. Then again, it is lunchtime. Unlike most schools that split lunch periods between the older and younger students, Kingston High does no such thing. There's not a whole bunch of us, so there's not really a need to split us up. There are literally only like fifty students in my year.

Walking to the back of the library, I locate study room three. The inside curtains are closed, blocking whatever Cade has planned. I push open the door and come to a complete stop. Splattered across the ceiling is a field of stars and asteroids. I turn my head to get a better view of the scene. Gas clouds of greens and blues make the stars glow even brighter. I take a step forward to see more and walk straight into the table. I rub my thigh without pulling my eyes away from the imagery. How in the world did Cade put this on the ceiling?

"You like?" Cade's voice comes from behind me and I turn around to see him in the corner, holding a bouquet of roses. He steps to me and hands the flowers over. "I thought you might like that."

I take the flowers. "What is this?"

"I thought I could take you to lunch." He points behind me and I glance over my shoulder to see what he's referring to. At the end of the table sit two trays with a bag from Aunt May's. "It's nothing fancy, but I didn't have time to go to Arlington for something else."

"You didn't have to do this. I can eat cafeteria food like everyone else."

Cade takes another step in my direction and takes the flowers from my hold. He lays them on the table behind us. "That would be a shitty lunch date."

"Date?"

"That's the kind of things boyfriends do."

I frown at him. "But you're not my—"

"For two weeks I am, remember? And for these two weeks, I'm going to treat you like you should be treated."

I gulp. I didn't think agreeing to give him a chance would result in him thinking we were going to date. I sort of figured we would just do what we've been doing: Hanging out at his house. Watching movies when I don't work. I look down the table at the bag from the diner. I didn't expect him to go out of his way to get me lunch. I did tell him I would try though.

Pointing at the ceiling, I grin. "How did you do that?"

Cade points to the projector in the corner of the room. Ahh, of course it's a projection. Taking my hand, Cade pulls me around the table to the food at the end. He pulls out containers and set them on the trays, followed by packets of plastic utensils and napkins. I sit down in the chair and open one of the containers. The smell of fries loaded with cheese, bacon, and jalapenos blooms and encompasses the room. It's one of my favorites at Aunt May's.

"How did you know I liked these?" I ask Cade as I open one of the plastic forks.

"It's the only thing you order when we're at the diner together."

My brows shoot up. I didn't think he noticed that. No one really notices what I eat. Wran knows my breakfast preference, but that's only because I cooked all the time and I only cooked myself pancakes and bacon. He had no choice but to learn what I liked. Josh still doesn't know.

"I didn't know you paid that much attention to me."

"I know everything about you, Roxanna. Well, maybe not everything."

"Yeah, because that wouldn't be creepy at all." I laugh and take a bite of the fries. "Thank you."

"Don't thank me. Just enjoy it."

I smile at him but then frown. This is only for two weeks. Two weeks and then we're going to go back to being friends. Just friends. I hope he realizes that. None of this is going to change how I feel about Wran. Even though Wran is going to hate me when he finds out about this. Cade isn't going to give up that easy when this all comes to an end. I know that. It's not who he is. He's a fighter. A winner. I highly doubt he has ever been told no before me. Maybe that's why he's so consumed with me. He wasn't when we were younger. Sure, I remember the little touches and nice words, but we were five. It couldn't have been anything.

Putting my fork down, I turn to Cade. "Why are you being so extra?"

He sets his burger down and looks at me—like really looks at me. His eyes search my face and I blush. He scoots his chair over so that he's directly in front of me. One of his hands runs up my arm and keeps moving up until he's cradling one of my cheeks. Leaning forward, he gives me a peck on my mouth. I pull away before he can turn a simple peck into something more. I just ate greasy fries with peppers. My breath doesn't smell the best.

"I'm making up for twelve years. I would have been like this with you if things never happened the way they did."

"You couldn't even hold my hand back then, Caden. You were too afraid of my brother."

"I would have grown out of it. I would have gotten older and made you mine. Our progression didn't happen like that, and I lost twelve years. Those twelve years were hell. I bought an observatory just so I could go there and remember you."

"Caden . . ."

"Don't say it. Don't diminish my love for you. If we were older when you ran away, I would have scoured the world until I found you. I would have never stopped searching. It took me some time and some begging, but I did find you again. We are together again, and if two weeks is all you're willing to give me to prove that we are the ones that are meant to be together, then I'm going to treat you like I should have treated you when we were five. I'm not going to be afraid."

I stare at him with wide eyes, crimson tinting my normally pale cheeks, not speaking. Wow. Wran has most definitely never said anything like that to me. I have no idea what to say to something like that.

Cades slides to the edge of his chair, bringing us mere centimeters apart. He takes hold of either side of my face, his thumbs rubbing circles against my cheeks. I nibble on my bottom lip as his fingers run across my face.

"Tell me you care," he begs. "You don't have to love me, but I need you to care."

I nod. I care. I care more than I should about this boy. I get up and climb into his lap, and the chair rolls back a little as I throw my arms around his neck. Cade wraps his arms around my waist and pulls me flush against his chest. He nuzzles his nose into the side of my neck, peppering it with sweet kisses. A squeal leaves me, and I pull back to look at him. He has a grin on his face.

"I like when you make those cute little noises," he admits.

I groan and bury my face in the polo he's wearing today. I so should not be reacting to him.

"I love you." His words come out just as confident as he is, and I blush. It's not the first time he's said them to me, but it's the first time he's said them while we're chest to chest, in a small study room, his hands on me. The first time he's said them while not trying to debunk Wran or get a rise out of me about him.

I turn my head to the side and look up at him. His sparkling blue eyes assure me that I don't have to say it, even though I can tell he wants me to. I wish I could repeat those words back, but I can't. They would be a lie, and I don't want to lie to him. I don't want to hurt Cade. He means too much to me. He deserves more than me.

"We should finish our lunch," I mumble into his neck.

"I have a better idea." Cade rises from the chair and drops his hands so he's holding me up. He walks down the table, away from the food, and sets me on the edge of it. Taking my face in his hands, he presses his mouth firmly against mine. Without thinking, I open to him and return the kiss. I wrap my arms around his neck, letting the cool strands of his silky blond hair slide between my fingers. As I shift on the table, Cade stiffens, his jaw tightening and his hands turning stagnant against my skin. I break the kiss and look at him, searching his eyes for a reason for the sudden tenseness.

"Please don't stop," he mumbles, and I can feel his breath against my mouth.

Licking my lips, I shake my head. "I wasn't. I wanted you closer."

Cade's bright eyes darken at my confession and he reclaims my mouth with a hunger unlike anything I've ever felt before. His hands drop from my face and move down my sides. Once they reach my hips, he pulls me forward so that my core is against him. Warmth spreads throughout me and I jerk back with a gasp. Cade's eyes fly open and he searches my face. My gaze drops from him and to the carpeted flooring. Taking hold of my chin in one hand, Cade pulls my face back up to meet his. He doesn't kiss me again—just watches me. His free hand roams up my thigh until he reaches the hem of the thin sweater I'm wearing today. I try to pull my face from his hold but he keeps me in place. He shakes his head and his hand moves past the barrier of my sweater. I gasp aloud when his rough hand grazes the side of my stomach.

I shift again on the table. "Cade . . ."

My thought falls short as his fingers move upward, his other hand still holding my face so he can watch me. I close my eyes and moan. I should not be moaning from a guy touching me. From Cade touching me.

"Open those gorgeous eyes," he tells me, voice deep and sounding so not like the guy I befriended at the beginning of the semester.

I obey him.

"You should tell me to stop. We're at school," he says as he reclaims my mouth, his tongue passing through my lips.

"You should . . ."

His fingers move to the edge of my bralette.

"You need . . ."

"Yes?"

He cups my breast and I let out a loud moan, eyes rolling back at the heady sensations going through me. My sounds are probably too loud for us to be in the school's library, but I don't care. This feels . . . wow. "Don't. Stop."

Cade drops my face and presses me back against the narrow table. My eyes open for a second and stars fill my vision. I'm not sure if it's from the projection on the ceiling or Cade's hands roaming my body. All I know is this is good.

How have I not done this with anyone since my first time? The table shakes beneath me and I open my eyes to see Cade hovering above me. On the table. He's way too big to be on this table.

"I wish I could make love to you right here," he says as he lowers his mouth to my neck. Before I know it, he's pulling my sweater off. I cross my arms over my chest. "I wouldn't do that here. Not with you on a table. You're worth more than that."

His lips never leave my skin.

Arching into him, I shake my head. I don't care where. Just as long as he doesn't stop touching me like that. "I don't care."

His hands stop moving and he leans up. "I do."

I'm just about to pull him back down by the collar of his polo when the bell rings. I shoot upright on the table, nearly knocking Cade off. I grip hold of his arms to keep him in place. I scan the table for my sweater, but don't see it. He must have thrown it on the floor. Glancing down to where our lunch is mostly untouched, I let out a string of giggles.

"Guess lunch was a bust, huh? So much for your lunch date," I tell him as he climbs off the table.

He bends down and picks up my sweater. He hands it to me and I pull it on. "I don't know about that. I enjoyed this date."

Cade steps in between my legs and brushes my hair back. He leans in for another kiss, but I push him away, shaking my head.

"We have to get to class, Casanova."

He pulls me off the table. "You ruin all the fun. We could always skip. Don't you have a study hall?"

"Yes, but I sort of fell asleep in calculus. I need to review the chapter I missed."

"All right."

Cade moves around the table to our discarded lunch and gathers the containers into the paper bag. He moves over to the projector and turns it off, and then comes back to me. Taking hold of my hand, he leads me to the door and pushes open one of the drapes. A growl leaves him and he shoves the drapes closed again. I step in front of the door and turn to Cade. His jaw is tightly clenched and he's staring at the drapes as if they are a viper ready to strike. Turning to the door, I grab the edge of the drapes. Cade yanks my hand away and shoves me behind him.

"Cade, what's going on?" I ask him, easing back around to his front. "Why don't you want me to go out that door?"

His face softens and he forces his eyes away from the drapes covering the door. "If I asked you to stay in here and not look past those curtains, would you?"

I cross my arms and shake my head.

"Of course you wouldn't. What if I asked nicely?"

My arms drop to my sides. I look past him and at the door. "You're freaking me out. What's going on?"

Cade shakes his head and exhales. "Nothing. Just don't freak out, okay? And don't read too much into it."

At my nod, he takes hold of the drapes. Before he shoves them back, he lets out another breath. My eyes widen when I see the glass doors. "Disgusting slut" is scrawled across it in red. I take a step away from the door, trembling. How . . . Who . . . ohmygod!

I step back and sink into a chair. This isn't happening. Someone knows what we were doing. And not just someone. Claire. That's the same shade that was on my locker.

Squatting down in front of me, Cade takes my shaking hands in his. "Stop staring at that door. It'll be all right. It's just stupid people being stupid. Besides, you're not that. I know it. You know it. Ignore it."

Ignore it? He's not the one being called a . . . a slut. He's not the one that will look bad. Everyone here already knows about Harley and Wran. And now I–I just let Cade . . . ohmygod, I let Cade touch me in a way that he shouldn't have touched me. I kissed him back. I wanted him. I wanted him so bad. I shouldn't have. I shouldn't have wanted anyone's hands on me. Ohmygod, I'm a slut.

Cade drops my hands and takes hold of my jaw, pulling my face and eyes away from the cruel words on the door. "Stop it! I can practically hear your thoughts and I won't stand for it. You are not a slut. You are not a whore. You are not any of the things that are going through your mind." His thumb brushes against my cheek. "You are loyal and honest and kind, and any person that can't see that is ignorant."

Honest?

Loyal?

Ha!

If I was so honest and loyal, I wouldn't have gotten myself into this situation. I would have told him no when he asked for two weeks. I would be on the phone right now with Wran: The guy that gave me a home. The father of my child. The love of my life. I wouldn't be kissing Cade. I'm not loyal. Not anymore. I'm just a . . . a slut. I'm what Claire and everyone else think me to be.

Cade rises from his crouched position and tugs me up with him. "Come on. Let's get out of here."

I nod, and he pulls me out of the room and away from the words.

CHAPTER 19

ROX

I didn't go to school today. After what happened yesterday, I couldn't. Call me a coward all you want, but I have no intention of seeing Claire. I know she wrote that on the door. It might make me a bit judgmental to automatically assume it was her, seeing as the whole school knows about things I wish they didn't, but I'm not an idiot. Here I assumed Claire and I were on okay-ish terms. We'll never be like we were in middle school, but I thought she had at least ceased fire on me. Guess not. Guess seeing me with Cade after I swore up and down that I had no romantic interest in him broke girl code again. Needless to say, I didn't want to bury myself alongside my father. Not today of all days. Not when I could possibly be getting some answers as to what happened three years ago.

Cade lets out a sigh and I glance up from my lunch and look at him.

"You really need to eat. You haven't since yesterday."

I stare at the noodles before me and shake my head. As hungry as I am, I don't want to eat. The appointment Bennett set up with his friend is today. I don't want to stuff my face with this lo mein only to throw it up if what I remember in this session is not so friendly. I don't know if whatever this therapist is going to do will even help me, but I'm trying to be positive. I need to be positive. If I can't recall any detail of that night, then my chances of getting Harley are none. And that's not something I'm willing to accept. I won't accept losing her.

Cade motions to the veggie lo mein he ordered for me. Picking up a forkful, I shove the noodles into my mouth with reluctance. I chew and chew and chew until it slides down my throat and settles in my stomach like a rock. I set the fork down and glare across the booth at Cade.

"Happy?" I ask him.

He shakes his head. "I'll be happy when you tell me what's wrong. I can't fix anything if you stay inside your head."

I roll my eyes at him. He can't fix anything anyway. He can't go back in time to change the way I reacted to Wran leaving. He can't keep the students at school from calling me names. He can't handle the person in the blacked-out SUV. He can't help me. And that's something I know he hates. I hate that he believes he's useless. I guess he's handling his emotions better than Wran. If Wran was here, I'm sure he would be pounding on something or someone right now. Then again, if his treatment is working, I suppose he wouldn't.

"Cade, I'm fine." I take another bite of my food to show him just how fine I am. "I'm just nervous about meeting with this doctor today. It's weird having someone poking around in my brain."

Cade relaxes back in the booth, crossing his arms over his chest and taking up half his side. He's supposed to be at school right now. He had no reason to skip with me, but he did. I told him this morning that all he had to do was drop me off at the appointment. I really need to get a car. He had other ideas. He saw today as a chance to spend more one-on-one time with me. Before coming to this restaurant, we went to the spring carnival going on at the Arlington fairgrounds. The carnival is nowhere as big as the county fair, but the fairgrounds is the only open space to have such a thing in the city. He won me a pink stuffed unicorn.

Cade leans forward, resting his elbows on the table. The candle flickers across his face and gives him a warm glow. "What are you hoping to remember?"

I glance around the small, downlit space and shrug my shoulders. "I don't know. A face. Anything. Bennett said any small thing could help my case."

"You never talk about that time. Those three years."

I shrug my shoulders again and the few bites of the lo mein start to churn in my stomach. There's not really anything to talk about. I went to school, work, and visited Harley. Nothing happened. I was invisible. I wanted to be invisible. Sometimes I wish I still were. I cried a lot during that time. That's something I'll never forget. I think I cried more then than I ever did when I was a kid living under my father's thumb.

"There's not really anything to talk about," I tell him. "I was miserable."

Through the candlelight, I see his lips dip. "Are you miserable now?"

I stare at Cade, his blue eyes burning into my violet ones. I'm not exactly miserable, per se. He makes things better. The idea of getting Harley makes things better. But I'm still the same girl that lost all her options in life. There's only so much I will ever be able to do. Things that people like him take for granted, I will never get to experience. For the most part, I think I have made peace with that. I would give up everything for Harley. I would do everything over again just to see my daughter smile. Okay, maybe not everything.

Just as I am about to tell Cade that there are different forms of misery and pain, the waitress comes to a stop in front of our booth. She looks at my uneaten bowl, but then her eyes go straight to Cade. She smiles at him and pulls out the receipt. She writes something on it and hands it to him. I frown at her. What the heck makes her think that I'm not paying for this meal? Cade looks at the piece of paper and then hands her a fifty. He tells her to keep the change and she walks away beaming like he just made her day.

"Can I see that?" I ask him, holding out my hand.

He places the receipt into my hand and I frown at it. Our meal, a meal I hardly ate, is only twenty-four dollars. He gave her an almost thirty-dollar tip. No wonder she walked away like this was the best day ever. My eyes then move to the number written on the bottom of the paper. Of course she gave him her number.

"She gave you her number," I mumble at him.

He shrugs and sits back again. "You jealous?"

I shake my head at him. "No."

"Good. You shouldn't be. You should never be jealous of any girl. I only want you."

"I wish you wouldn't say things like that." I motion between us. "This ends in less than two weeks."

He smirks at me as if he knows something that I don't. Getting up from the booth, he holds out a hand to me. "Let's get you to your appointment."

Without hesitation, I place my small hand in his and he pulls me up from the booth. He holds my hand the whole drive to the therapist's office. When we finally come to a stop outside the building, he cuts the engine and turns to me.

"I have football practice, but I let Coach know that I have to pick up you. Just text me when your appointment is over, and I'll make it back here is fast as I can," he tells me.

I nod. "Okay."

"Don't be nervous. You're finally going to get some answers."

My face scrunches up at his statement. "I think that's worth being nervous about."

"What exactly is this doctor going to be doing again?"

"Umm . . . well, he's a therapist that specializes in hypnosis. Apparently it's supposed to help with memory recovery. I just hope I can be hypnotized. It seems surreal, but I will give it a try. I'll give anything a try at this point."

Cade makes a face but doesn't say a word. Like I said, it sounds too good to be true. If all I had to do was let someone hypnotize me to get some answers, I would have done it ages ago. But I promised Bennett and Josh that I would come to this with an open mind. And I promised myself that anything is better than nothing.

I look at the time on the dash and inhale. Well, here goes nothing.

Turning away from Cade, I open the door and get out of the truck. He gives me one more reassuring smile before pulling off. I watch as he leaves the parking lot before turning to the huge building and walking up the steps. I come to an immediate stop once inside the building. It has a clean and sharp interior. Stainless silver elevators. Black, sleek chairs in pairs of two with small tables line the wall at different intervals. Each table as an assortment of flowers on it. The walls are adorned with abstract black, white, and gray canvases above each little sitting area. This isn't what I expect when I think about office buildings.

Someone taps me on the shoulder, and I turn around to see a very radiant Bennett standing before me. He smiles down at me and then takes in the ground floor of this building as well.

"I didn't know you would be here," I tell him. He didn't mention that in his message. Just told me to be here at two, the floor number, and the office number. I don't even know the doctor's name.

"I wanted to be here in case you do remember something. That way I'm getting the information as soon as possible and it's fresh in your mind. That is if me being here is okay with you."

I nod at him. It's probably a good thing for him to get the information firsthand. I'm not exactly sure what's going to happen at this session, but like he said, anything is better than nothing. And he did recommend this doctor. I can only believe he set this up because he's heard or seen the results firsthand.

Bennett gestures to one of the elevators and I go over to it, pressing the up button. We travel to the seventh floor in silence and down the hall to the room labeled 1706. He knocks on the door and a moment later it opens. A lanky man with graying hair at the temples opens the door. He has a thick beard that is peppered with gray hair and cool gray eyes that make me relax right away. He's wearing jeans with a button-down sky-blue shirt, a gray sports jacket, and a quirky gray bowtie with a tiny bowtie print on it. I didn't even think men wore bowties anymore.

The man looks at me and then holds out a hand to me. "You must be Miss Raine. I'm Dr. Dickens."

"Like Charles Dickens?" The words leave my lips before I can stop them, and I look away from the man and at the gray carpeted floor.

He chuckles. "Well, yeah, but only if I was a hundred and fifty years old and could write."

I peek up at him from underneath long lashes and see the humor on his face. He gestures for us to come inside and we do. Dr. Dickens closes the door behind him, and I take a seat on the black leather sectional against the back wall. Bennett takes the chair against the window.

Dr. Dickens goes over to the huge wooden desk that is taking up most of this ten-by-ten room. He leans forward, his elbows propped up on the desk, and looks me over. I glance away from his inquisitive eyes and at Bennett. I'm not sure how this is supposed to go. Does he just put me in a trance? Do I need to say something? Is there a magic word? This isn't really my thing. Yeah, I had to see a therapist when Harley was first taken, as required, but we didn't really talk. She would just sit at her desk and look at me. Occasionally she would ask a question and I would answer, but she always started the session. Dr. Dickens watching me is just weird.

"Sooo," he drags out. "You're here to try to recover memories from three years ago. Care to tell me what happened three years ago that would cause such memory loss?"

My eyes go from the doctor over to Bennett. I thought he already provided that information. "Umm, I thought Bennett told you already."

"He did. But it's always best to hear it from the patient."

I suppose . . .

Biting down on the inside of my cheek, I nod. It's not like everyone doesn't already know what happened to me. The invasive local news made sure people had no questions about anything related to me and Wran and Aspen and my father. I'm sure they dug up stuff from my past that even I am unaware of.

"I got pregnant when I was fifteen, and the father left me. End of story."

"Care to tell me how that made you feel?" he asks and sits back in his oversized black leather chair that looks more like a La–Z–Boy recliner than an actual office chair.

"Furious. Lonely. Lost. I'm pretty sure any negative emotion would describe that situation."

Dr. Dickens glances over to Bennett, and he gives the doctor a nod. Dickens gets up from his chair and walks over to a cabinet and pulls out what looks to be a tripod and some bulky device. Grabbing the back of his leather chair, he pulls it around the desk and settles it in front of me. He sets up the tripod and whatever that device is before taking his seat not even two feet from me.

"Are you aware of what hypnosis therapy is?" he asks me, and I shake my head. "Well, it's a type of therapy used to help the mind focus and become more susceptible to things."

"So you're going to put me to sleep and hope I remember something?"

He brings his hands together, a clap sounding through-out the small room. "Yes, that's exactly what I'm going to do. I'll be talking you through stuff, you'll be able to hear and answer, but you will be unconscious. Does this sound like something you are comfortable with?"

"I don't think I have a choice. I need to remember," I tell him. "I just hope it works."

"I've done this on hundreds of people, and while the results vary, each one of them has recovered some sort of memory."

I nod, reminding myself that anything is better than nothing. I'm trying; that is all that matters. Dr. Dickens turns in his oversized chair and flips on a switch on the side of the device he set up. A blinding light comes on and I flinch away from the brightness. Okay, so this man is trying to make me go blind.

He chuckles. "I never get tired of watching people react to this light. It is brighter than most, but it is necessary for this kind of procedure."

I'll take his word on it. Blinking, I look to the side of the light and straight at him. He gets up from the chair and flips off the main light in the room.

"Can you pull those curtains?" he asks Bennett and sits back down.

The room goes completely dark, the only light coming from the device. As bright as it is, I can only see the light. I can't make out anything else in the room. Not Bennett. Not Dr. Dickens, and he's right in front of me.

"Okay, so I need you to look at the light," he says, and I turn to the bright light. "Now, while looking directly into the light, I need you to count backward from fifty, blinking as you do."

I nod and start counting back. By the time I make it down to forty, black dots are speckling my vision and I'm tempted to turn away from the light. I don't. I want this to work, and if I have to blind myself to get some answers, I will do exactly that.

"Picture the last thing you were doing on that day before everything went black. Keep your eyes on the light and keep blinking as you do so."

I obey and think back to that night. Flashes of Josh's dark hair flood my vision as he looks over my shoulder at the homework I'm doing. His woodsy, musky aftershave invades my senses as he sets my sleep pills on the small island along with a brown bag from Aunt May's. I take the meds and give him a deadpan look. I remember him scolding me, telling me I need to force myself to sleep. That the baby needs me to sleep.

More black dots cover my vision and I blink more, trying to clear it.

"How do you feel?"

I blink again and yawn, but I don't answer him.

"Roxanna."

My name is the last thing I hear the doctor say before the black dots completely encompass my vision and the light vanishes. Everything vanishes.

Laughter rings out and I jerk around. Everything around me is hazy, and I wipe at my vision to try to clear it up. It doesn't clear. Everything looks as if I'm wearing a pair of dark tinted sunglasses: dark, gray, dull. I hear the laughter again and I turn around. There are a ton of people around, but I can't make out any of their faces. I take a step forward and my head floods, nausea creeping up and making my feet wobbly. I reach out and my hands land on something hard and warm.

"Whoa there, li'l lady."

I blink at the obviously masculine tone, hardy yet taunt-ing.

"You don't look like you belong here."

I bring my hand up to my head and squint up at the guy, my vision clearing enough to make out tan skin and a bald head. "Where am I?"

"A place girls like you shouldn't be, but I'm guessing you're used to being places you don't belong."

I turn away from him and look around, even though I can make out nothing but blurs and lights. The smell of stale beer slams into me and I clutch my protruding stomach. I think I'm going to barf. A hand comes down on my bicep and starts pulling me. I yank my arm away and stumble a little on my feet. The man chuckles and I let out a growl that comes out sounding more like a whimper.

"How did I get here?" I manage to ask through the nausea.

"You showed up with your friend about an hour ago. You seemed pretty out of it then. She should still be around here. I saw her a few moments ago."

"She?"

The guy takes hold of my arm again and starts pulling me through the crowd. My shoulders slam into people as we make our way to wherever he's leading me. I do the best I can to shield my stomach. I can't harm my baby. It's a little difficult with him manhandling me, but not too many people make contact with that part of me. The guy comes to a stop and releases my hand. Narrowing my eyes at him again, I can see him sitting down. He takes hold of my waist and pulls me down on him. His strong scent—some cheap cologne masquerading as something more expensive— slams into me. Wran used to use a cheap cologne that smelled similar until I threw it out and bought him something that was more pleasing.

"Yeah, you came in with some chick with blond hair and red lips about an hour ago. You were messed up. Don't know how you got in though. You look twelve."

"I'm not." I defend my age.

"Clearly." His hand grazes the side of my stomach and I stiffen in his lap. "Let me go get you another drink."

"I can't drink," I tell him.

He chuckles and lifts me up. "Your friend gave you something when you first got here."

The nameless man walks away from me and I sit back down in the seat. I rub my hands over my temples, trying to ward off a headache and clear my vision. How the hell did I get to a bar? Clacking heels come to a stop in front of me and a sickly sweet smell surrounds me. Someone sits down opposite me, giggling. I turn around in the booth and squint at the unwanted guest. I can make out long blond hair but not much else.

"Aren't you happy you came with me?" she says, and I know that voice.

"I don't feel so good," I confess.

"You don't? That means you're getting sober. Here, drink this." Something hits my hand and I groan.

"I'm pregnant. I can't drink that."

"Yeah, you can. Didn't I already tell you that?" She giggles. "I'm gonna go have some fun. See you later, Roxy."

I frown at the way she says my name. I hear her heels clack away just as a sharp pain shoots up my spine.

"Roxanna? Roxanna, wake up."

Someone shakes me and I fly my eyes. Light floods my vision and I stare into Bennett's hazel eyes. His face relaxes and he exhales, sitting back on the floor.

"What happened?" I ask, blinking against the bright-ness.

Dr. Dickens gets up and turns on the room's overhead light and comes back to me. "Roxanna, do you remember talking?"

I shake my head. The last thing I remember is that stupid light shining in my face and thinking about Josh telling me to get some sleep.

Turning to Bennett, I arch a brow at him. "Did . . . did I say anything helpful?"

He nods and looks up at the doctor from his position on the floor. "You kept mumbling a name. Claire. Who is Claire?"

Claire?

I suck in a deep breath as giggles ring out in my head. Giggles and clicking heels and blond hair and some guy I don't know. I shake my head at Bennett. No. I must have remembered it wrong. There's no way Claire would have taken me to a bar. Not then. That would mean she . . . she knew I was pregnant before the news broke everything. Claire's a lot of things, but she wouldn't do something like that. She wouldn't give me alcohol.

"Miss Raine, what are you thinking?" Dickens asks me, his eyes searching my face.

"D–did I say anything else?"

"Something about Wran wearing cheap cologne."

I bite down on the inside of my cheek. Claire's a bully, but she's not a criminal. She didn't drug me . . .

"I think I should go."

I rise from the sofa, wrapping my arms around myself. Bennett gets up from the floor as well and places a hand against my shoulder. I flinch away from him. I don't want anyone touching me. Not now. I need to get away from here. To think. I need to confront Claire. I need more answers.

"Roxanna, I need to know what you saw. I need something to look into," Bennett says in a soft voice.

As much as I know he needs that, I need to confront Claire first. I don't want to involve any of my classmates unless I have to and telling him who she is will put a target on her before I even have answers.

"Can I call you tomorrow and talk about this? I just . . . I need to think."

Bennett's hand drops from my arm and he nods.

"Thank you," I tell Dr. Dickens and bolt from the room.

CHAPTER 20

WRAN

Being stuck in isolation for four days fucking sucks. That type of punishment should be illegal. If this place is supposed to foster positive thoughts and reduce anger, then the isolation unit doesn't seem to live up to this place's agenda. Four days I was stuck in my head, thinking about Rox and her father and my father and every damn thing. No TV. No windows. No nothing. Just white walls and a ticking clock and a very uncomfortable bed with thin sheets. I wasn't even let out for meals. Someone delivered those to me through a small slit in the door. It's been hell. At least now I'm out of there. I'm pretty sure the only reason Thomas cut my visitation to insanity short is because Josh and Rox are supposed to visit today. The idea of seeing Rox after nearly three weeks is the only thing that kept me sane. I finally get to see my girl.

Sitting on one of the steps outside Pleasure House, I glance down the road leading up to the entrance. Rox and Josh were supposed to be here twenty minutes ago. When they weren't here on time, I came out here to wait. I'm not sweating it though. They'll show. Josh promised they would show. Besides, it's the middle of the week; traffic getting here is probably unbelievable. I know when my brother dropped me off, it was crazy. The only way they wouldn't show is if something happened.

The letter I received last Friday comes to the forefront of my mind. Surely everything is okay. Josh or Cade or someone would have informed me if Rox was in trouble. Then again, I can see that fucker Cade trying to play the hero just to win my girl over. Yeah, like that would ever happen. Rox would be better off protecting herself if he's all she has to lean on.

The door behind me opens and I glance back to see Thomas walk out. He has a clipboard in his hands. Pushing the glasses he only wears in our sessions up the bridge of his nose, he points down the road. I turn to see Josh's beat-down car entering the gate. Standing, I can't help the grin that spreads across my face. Rox is here. I finally get to see her after forever of not hearing her.

"You look to be in a good mood today," Thomas says as we wait for my visitors together.

I could lie and tell him that it's nothing, but at this point I don't want to. "Yeah. I get to see my girl. I can apologize again."

"I have to admit, I'm a bit curious to meet Roxanna. I feel like I know her well enough. Now a face to the name would help."

"You'll like her," I tell him as I continue watching Josh's car. There's nothing not to like about Rox.

As the car gets closer, though, I frown and straighten my posture. Thomas notices the immediate change in me and shifts his clipboard to his other arm. The car comes to a stop and I frown at the empty passenger seat. I look at the back seat, but it's empty as well. My hands ball into fists, but I quickly unclench them. There has to be an explanation for this. She assured me she would be here. And if I know my Rox, she isn't going to say something and then do the opposite. Something is wrong. I knew something was fucking wrong last Friday.

Josh cuts the engine to the car and gets out. He walks around to me, his eyes not meeting mine. Yup, something is definitely wrong. Josh goes straight to his friend and they bump shoulders. I shake my head at the gesture and scoff. He has never been that friendly with anyone. Sure, he had a few friends in high school, but hell, I haven't seen Josh socialize with anyone other than Rox and me since my school days.

"Where's Rox?" I ask him before he has a chance to start up a conversation with Thomas to keep from telling me. He does that a lot.

He turns around and runs a hand through his growing hair. "She couldn't make it."

"Why? What's wrong?" I ask.

"I don't know. I went to pick her up this morning and she said she had something to do that was important."

"Is Harley okay?" She's the only thing that could be more pressing than Rox's fucking word. "Please tell me she is fine."

Josh pops his knuckles and nods. "As far as I'm aware, Harley is perfect. We took her to the zoo on Saturday."

The zoo? My brother took my daughter to the zoo without me. They couldn't have waited until I was done with this program to take her to the zoo? He's already been around for all her baby firsts—first walk, first word, first run—and he couldn't even wait to take her to the zoo when I was around.

"How about we go inside?" Thomas speaks up. "There's breakfast available and then we'll have our session."

I give him a jerky nod and walk past Josh into the building. I close my eyes and inhale, trying to calm my nerves. So what if Rox isn't here? So what if they went to the zoo without me? I'll have plenty of time to spend with my Harley once I'm out of here. I'll get a lawyer and fight for my child. I will be the one taking her to her first day of school and standing on the porch with a shotgun for her first date. Not Josh.

Exhaling, I let it all go and turn around to my brother. "They have the best pancakes here. Don't tell Rox I said that."

Josh arches a brow at my sudden change. "I do like pancakes, but I don't think anyone's pancakes are better than Rox's."

I turn to Thomas. "What time is the session again?"

He looks down at his clipboard. "You have an hour for breakfast. Be at my office by eleven."

I tilt my head in acknowledgment, my hair flopping over into my eyes. I shove it back and head toward the dining hall. Josh and I gather a tray full of food and find an empty table in the back by a window that overlooks a fountain. He sits down and immediately starts in on the pancakes he grabbed. My eyes are on the empty chair next to him. Rox should be here.

"Have you spoken to Thomas before today?" I lean back in my chair and shove my food to the center of the table. I'm not even hungry.

Josh sets his fork down and copies my gesture. "Yeah. We've kept in touch during your entire stay."

"So you know what happened on Friday."

He nods. "I don't understand why after two weeks you go ballistic. Thomas said you were doing excellent."

I mentally laugh at the way we're talking about my progress in the program like I'm some kindergarten kid that was getting gold stars only to forget my alphabet and stop receiving them.

"Are you sure Rox is okay?" I ask him after a moment of silence.

Josh takes a sip of his black coffee—something else we have in common—before answering. "Yeah. Why do you think she's not?"

I contemplate telling him about the note I received. The last time one of us got a note and didn't mention it, my daughter was kidnapped. Rox nearly died. And I . . . I killed someone. There's no way in hell I want to go through that again. At the same time, I don't understand why anyone would send me a letter when I'm basically out of everyone's reach and can't talk even if I wanted to. That could all be a ploy to get me to say or do something I might regret. Hell, I already have. I ended up in fuckin' isolation because of that note.

Sighing, I decide to tell him the truth. It can't hurt anything, and he needs to be prepared if someone goes after Rox and Harley again. "I got sent to isolation because I took out my anger on another patient." I glance around and lower my voice. "I didn't mean to, but I received a letter Friday about Rox. I wanted to check myself out, but they wouldn't let me and I sorta lost it."

Josh straightens in his chair, his body becoming stiff. He frowns. "That's why you wanted me to come get you?"

"Yeah." I nod.

Josh curses under his breath and slams his fist down on the table. "What did it say?"

"That just because James was dead didn't mean Rox was safe. You would have known that if you hadn't blown me the fuck off when I called."

"Fuck!" Josh hisses, and I glance around. A guy a few tables across from us is watching, and I flip him the bird. He averts his attention right away.

Once my brother's breathing is back to normal, he props his arms up on the table, breakfast forgotten. "We haven't received any notes, but someone tried to run Rox over while she was at a party with Cade."

Rox went to a party? With Cade? For some reason I can't picture this version of my lost girl going to parties. Sure, she went to them before Harley, but now she just seems focused on other things. And with Cade, no less . . .

"You didn't think informing me of something like that was important? Why didn't you call?"

"Because we have no clue who did it. All we know is that it was a black SUV. I have been keeping an eye out for any black vehicles coming and going from Kingston."

I guess that will have to do until he finds out who tried to run her over. I don't like it. I don't like being here when my girl clearly needs me to be with her. There's nothing I can do though. I signed that damn contract. I'm stuck here for the time being. With a groan, I stab my breakfast with the fork and take a bite.

We finish our food without another word. There's not much either of us can say that will change the events that have already happened. Hopefully, Josh and Cade—yes, that fucker Cade—can keep my girl safe. Dumping what we didn't eat into the trash, I make my way with Josh down the hall and to Thomas's office. His door is closed, and I look at the clock down the hall on the wall. We still have a little bit of time until my session.

I don't really know what to talk about with my brother. I had this whole confession planned out for Rox, but she's not here. I had a plan to make her understand that I am truly sorry for the way I reacted to everything. A plan to convince her that my love for her is greater than the hate I have for her father. For the past. For myself. I can't believe she isn't here. It was just a few days ago that she told me she would be here.

The door to Thomas's office opens and the new guy steps out. He looks at me and then Josh before stomping down the hall. Thomas moves aside and motions for us to come inside. I go in and take my usual seat. Josh takes the chair beside me, his back straight as a board while I'm all slumped down. I straighten a little just so I don't seem completely at odds with him.

"How was breakfast?" Thomas asks, more to Josh than me.

My brother looks over at me. "Not better than Rox's pancakes."

Thomas chuckles once and then sits back in his chair. "I imagine not, but it grows on you."

"So," Josh begins, "how exactly do these sessions begin?"

"Like any other session," Thomas says to Josh, and to me he says, "How has your morning been so far?"

I scoff at his question. He knows exactly how my morning is. I just got out of isolation. The one person I've been excited to see isn't here, and now I have to talk to him with my brother. Sure, I thought I could do it with Rox in the room, but I don't really want to give Josh another reason to see me as the troublemaker he had to send away for having feelings for a minor. I'm sure that's how he'll always see me. Talking about my emotions isn't going to change years of him believing poorly of me. In that regard, he's just like our pops. Only he doesn't spend his time degrading me and calling me boy.

I shrug. "Same ole, same ole."

"You got out of isolation. How did that feel?"

"Do I really need to answer that question? Can't we get on to the reason for this whole group session?"

Thomas sits back in his chair. "Please, tell me what you think this session is supposed to consist of. I've noticed that Rox isn't here, and I know how important it was for her to be here. Tell me what you're feeling."

"You're the fucking doc. You should be telling me."

My words come out harsher than I intend them to be. But really? I'm starting to think this whole visitation session was a load of bull.

"Rox couldn't be here," Josh tells Thomas, and leans forward, resting his elbows on his knees. "I'm not sure what happened, but she had an appointment yesterday and it didn't go well."

"An appointment?" I sit up straighter at that. "What type of appointment? Is she okay?"

Josh turns to me, his expression serious. "We've been seeing a lawyer. He set Rox up with an appointment with a therapist to try to recall some of her lost memories of that night. I wasn't there, but Bennett, the lawyer, called and told me she rushed out in a panic."

I blink at his words once, then twice. Lawyer? Why the fuck is she seeing a lawyer without me? The only reason she would have for seeing one is if something is wrong with Harley. But that doesn't make sense either. She wouldn't need a therapist for that.

"I'm confused," I confess.

Exhaling, Josh shoves hair from his face. "Let us not talk about that. We are here for you right now. I just wanted to let you know why she isn't here."

I shoot up from the chair, hands balled into fists and my limbs shaking. Like hell we're moving on from this. He can't just state something like that and not give me answers.

"Wran?" Thomas cuts in before I can say something I might regret.

I inhale and exhale and then take my seat again.

"How about we come back to that topic when you are calmer? It's clear that Rox is a sensitive topic. Discussing something else might be best for now."

"Whatever," I huff out and slump back in the chair.

He turns to Josh. "You've had to spend much of your life caring for your brother and Roxanna. I can only imagine how you feel."

"I had to give up a lot, but I would do it all over again if I had to. He's my brother." Josh doesn't even look in my direction as he says this. Says it like taking care of me because our pops was too much of a waste of space to pull his head out of his ass to do what he should have been doing didn't ruin his life.

I scoff and shake my head at that. Surely he would do something different. There's a ton I would change. Actually, I would change everything.

"You have something to say to that?" Thomas asks me.

I shake my head.

"It's not like you to hold your tongue," Josh states. "Surely this place hasn't changed you that much."

My jaw tics at his assessment of me. "You know what? Fuck you! This session was a mistake. I only agreed to it because I wanted to see Rox. She isn't here, you might as well leave."

"Sorry, that was a bit harsh of me. I didn't mean any-thing by that," Josh tells me.

Sure he didn't.

He doesn't say things he doesn't mean. That's where we both differ.

"I really would like to know how you are, Wran," he tells me. "I wouldn't have suggested this place or Thomas if I didn't care."

I slump back and sigh. Great. Now I'm the fucking bad guy. I know he cares. Too much. But I don't like thinking that he would be better off without me and Rox. It would mean that I ruined his life. Much like I ruined Rox. I might have been the bastard that saved her, but she could be so much more if she had never met me.

Thomas shifts in his chair. "Care to tell us what you are thinking, Wran?"

I glance between him and my brother and then settle on Josh. "You wouldn't change anything?"

He shakes his head. "I like to think that life is destiny. Each thing that happens to us happens for a reason. If I hadn't taken care of you, we would have ended up in the system. Someone would have reported Dad. If not for that, you wouldn't have met Rox, and while I still believe you two are toxic for each other, I wouldn't have my niece if it wouldn't have happened. That little girl means the world to me. So, no. I wouldn't change a thing."

I stare at him for a long time. Guess I can see it that way.

"Sometimes I believe that everyone's life would be better without me in it," I confess to him.

Josh turns in his chair and faces me. "Why the hell would you think that? Yeah, you could clean up your act, but no one's life—not mine or Rox's or even Dad's—would be better off without you."

I shrug. I can't help what I feel. Rox wouldn't have a kid. Josh wouldn't be stuck in Kingston being a cop. And Pops, well, he would probably be the same.

"Listen to me." Josh pulls me out of my head. "Without you, Rox would probably be dead. Without you, there would be no Harley. Without you, I wouldn't have someone to make sure I keep myself in control. You being here, alive and in our lives, helps us more than you will ever know."

I frown at his words. Rox would probably be dead. I don't like to think that would be the case. She was in Kingston. If anything, that town is full of people that care. Nosy people. But I believe someone would have taken in my Rox if they found her.

"I suppose . . ."

I don't finish that statement.

The rest of the session goes by without any conflict. Thomas asks questions and I answer them. Josh commentates whenever he needs to, or to reassures me of things. I can't say that it is a bad session. I learn that Josh is dating some teacher at Rox's school and that he's serious about her. Thomas has a field day with that. Apparently the girl was some geek back in school that everyone made fun of. Josh said she looks nothing like she used to. I can understand that. It's always the ones we look over that turn out to be the ones we care about the most.

CHAPTER 21

ROX

Biting my lip and tapping my pencil on the desk, I watch the clock above the classroom's door. It's almost lunch and I haven't had any time before now to confront Claire. She needs to explain. For the most part, I think I know what she's going to say. Or not say. I just can't believe Claire would stoop that low. Sure, she's a bully. This, though, was not some stupid high school prank. Harley could have died. I could have died. Taking me to that bar was just plain vindictive, and it is high time I stop being so passive when it comes to Claire Wentworth.

I pull my eyes away from the clock and look at the board. That's where my attention should be, especially after Mr. Stevenson pulled me aside the other day to talk about my declining grades. At this point, I don't care to learn calculus anymore. Math isn't going to get me the answers I need

right now. And math is most certainly not going to get my daughter back.

The bell rings and I leap from my seat.

Mr. Stevenson turns around and narrows his eyes at me, his hand dropping from the whiteboard. "You don't leave until I dismiss you."

I glance at the clock and then at all my peers still seated. A few of them in the row next to me arch a brow at me. Yeah, I know. I should be used to Mr. Stevenson holding us a little after class. It's not the first time, and it's not going to be the last. I just really need to get going. Claire has gym this period, and if I want to get to her before she leaves the locker room, then I need to get going.

My teacher points to my desk and I gulp. He's really going to think something is wrong with me. First my slipping grades and now I'm rushing to leave the class. I could say it has something to do with Harley. Surely he wouldn't keep me from going to her. Not now that the whole town knows of her existence. My teacher sets his dry-erase marker down and glares at me. I will never use Harley like that. Claire will have to wait a few more minutes. Nodding, I step back and take my chair once more. He stares at me for a minute before turning back to the board and finishing the equation. He explains it and then proceeds to tell the class our homework. Once he's done, five minutes after the class ended, he dismisses us, and I race out of the room before he has a chance to ask me to stay. I really don't have time to explain to him why I am in a rush.

Without stopping by my locker, I weave myself through the throng of bodies lining the hall until I reach the girls' locker room. The door swings open and a girl I don't know walks out. She stops in her tracks, jumping a little as if startled. She gives me a once-over when she realizes it's me and snickers. The girl steps out of the doorway and another girl joins her. The second one, who I do recognize—Shelia from eighth grade—gives me the exact same reaction. People have been giving me that look since the news broke about Harley. Mainly the girls, but I don't care. Really, I don't. At the end of the day, most girls are catty.

They prance away with a bit too much pep in their step. Shelia manages a quick look over her shoulder at me and giggles again. I clearly hear the word whore leave one of their mouths, and I stiffen a little. Their words shouldn't bother me. I know that, but whoever said words can never hurt you lied through their teeth. Words hurt. Words leave way more scars than sticks and stones. Or in my case, fists and belts and tubs of boiling water.

Shaking off that word, I push inside the locker room. My nose scrunches as the stench of sweat mixed with flowery perfume encompasses me. The sound of running water invades my ears. Shower. Someone's taking a shower. I roll my eyes at myself. Of course someone is taking a shower. This is the locker room. Making my way toward the sound, I step over wet towels and clothes. Someone should really tell these girls that leaving wet towels in a lump on the floor creates mold. That's probably part of the smell. I don't remember this locker room smelling like this when I took gym my freshman year. Then again, I was hardly in this locker room. Wran would take me home to shower and dress.

The water cuts off and I stop walking. My initial reaction is to step back, hide and not make a commotion, but I force myself to stay put. I have every right to be in the locker room. I go to school here as well. And besides, the only way I'm going to get answers is if I demand them. That doesn't include bolting like I just stole the last cookie from the cookie jar.

A tall, slim girl with shoulder-length dirty blond hair comes to a stop in front of me, and for some reason I'm relieved it's not Claire. It's only Janet. She may be one of Claire's entourage, but at least she's not the queen bee herself. Ugh! What is wrong with me? I'm not scared of Claire. She can't say anything that I don't already know, and she's not going to hurt me. Not in the traditional sense anyway. I have no reason to be this worked up about confronting her.

Janet tightens the towel around her chest and narrows her eyes at me. "What are you doing in here? Shouldn't you be auditioning for Teen Mom somewhere?"

Original. Very original. It's not like I haven't heard that a million times in the last month. "I'm looking for Claire. I need to talk to her."

"I'm pretty sure she doesn't want to talk to you," Janet retorts, and walks around me. I turn around and follow her.

If anyone knows where Claire would be right now, it will be Janet.

"Look, I need to speak with her. It's important."

"I can give her a message," Janet says without giving me another glance like I mean that little. "Can't be anything that important."

"Never mind." I roll my eyes and step back, away from her and right into someone else. I turn around and the fiery blonde is standing there with the third member of her group.

"Why are you looking for me?" Claire asks, hands on her hips.

"Have you been in here this entire time?" I ask her.

She nods. "My locker is one over. You would have noticed me if you would have walked a little farther. What do you want?"

My eyes drift back to Janet as she fixes her bra, and then over to Teri. "Do you mind if we talk in private?"

"Yes. I'm perfectly comfortable around my girls. They will never stab me in the back. Twice."

I shift on my feet and ignore that jab. If Claire wants to see the things I did that way, then that's her choice. I explained myself, and I will not have guilt consume me over it. No matter what I would have done, she would have wound up hating me for it.

Straightening to my full height, which is nothing compared to Claire's model form, I give it to her straight. Nothing I say will hurt me. Only her. "You drugged me."

Claire's eyes widen. "What?"

"You. Drugged. Me." I pronounce each word so I don't have to repeat myself again. In all honesty, I don't know if Claire really did drug me. I didn't see that. Or remember that. Or however you explain what happened yesterday. She encouraged me, a very pregnant me, to drink when I was already out of it. There's no telling what else she did.

Claire looks over my shoulder and my eyes follow hers to the other two girls. "Get out."

Teri's brows jump, and she turns to face Claire. "What? You're really sending us away?" She points to me. "Just because this boyfriend-stealing slut asks so? C'mon, Claire!"

"Leave, or the whole school will know about your little obsession by the end of lunch period," Claire snaps. I have never heard her actually yell at one of her friends before, and it's scary.

The girl pales and nods. She takes a hesitant step away and then another until she is rushing away from Claire and out of the locker room. Janet follows her without questioning Claire, and before I know it, we're alone. I'm alone with Claire in a smelly locker room, and my future depends on what she's about to say. My hands shake at my sides, and I rub them up and down my legs to stop them.

"Now, you might want to be very careful with what you say next." Claire's words come out like a threat, but I know for a fact that Claire won't hurt me. It's not her style. Spending all middle school as one of her "friends," I learned that. She likes to have other people do her dirty work. Can't have words getting back to Daddy that his perfect daughter is not doing as she's been told.

"The night that Harley was born, you were with me. You pretended that you didn't know I was pregnant." I glower up at her. "How could you? I understand hating me for your family situation, but drugging me? Really, Claire?"

She jabs her finger into my shoulder. "I did not drug you. Don't you dare accuse me of that again."

Grabbing her finger, I shove it away from me. "I clearly remember us now at a bar!"

"That doesn't mean I drugged you. I'm not an idiot!"

"Then what was I doing with you? And why don't I remember anything from that night?"

Claire turns on her pointy shoes and saunters away from me. I follow her. She comes to a stop at a locker a row over and pulls out a quilted black purse with double Cs on it. She slams her locker and looks at me, ice in her glower and hands fisting her designer purse. She steps to me, her nice shoes tip-to-tip with my fifteen-dollar ones. I don't drop my eyes from her intimidating form though. I know she knows something about that night. And even if she wasn't the one that drugged me, she was at a bar with me. She encouraged me to drink. She has a part in me losing Harley, whether she believes so or not. It's partially her fault.

"We are not friends. I don't have to tell you anything," she informs me as if it's something I don't already know.

"I've known that for a long time."

She rolls her eyes at me and then looks past my shoulder. I turn around to see what has caught her attention, but there's nothing there. I turn back to her. Claire's leaning against the lockers, her arms wrapped across her chest.

"Why do you care now? It's been almost three years."

I lean against the locker across from her, so we're facing each other head-on. "Because I need to know what happened that night. It's important."

"Does it have something to do with Harley?"

I stiffen at my daughter's name on her tongue. Claire doesn't have the right to utter my child's name. Not now. Not ever. "You don't deserve that information. Just tell me what happened that night and then we can both get out of this stinking locker room."

"Fine!" Claire hisses. "I'm only telling you this because I'm not as vindictive as you think. And I didn't drug you."

I shrug and wait for her to continue.

She huffs and sits down on the bench between us. I don't sit. "I lied to my father that night about my whereabouts. I was supposed to be at my mom's place, but I went to a college party on your side of the tracks instead. Do you remember Travis? The senior I had a huge crush on in eighth grade?"

I shake my head. "You had a huge crush on every guy with a pretty smile, Claire."

"I did not! I had a crush on two guys. Two! Wran and Travis."

I roll my eyes at that. Sure. "What's your point?"

"On my way to Travis's place, I passed by your apartment. You were sitting on the stairs reading that ridiculous Peter Pan book. It had been the first time you had been seen in like forever. And you were pregnant. Very pregnant. I stopped to make fun of you. To call you fat. But you were crying. I walked up the stairs and you were mumbling something like a crazy person. At first I thought you were reading the book, but then you said that you didn't want to have her without your Peter Pan. It didn't take long to figure out you were talking about Wran."

"Why would I even talk to you at that point?" Her story's makes no sense at all.

"You were pretty out of it already. You didn't seem drugged. More sleepy and depressed and lost. It was hard to see you like that. I figured bringing you to a party would cheer you up. I don't know why I cared a fuck about you, but I did. And you liked going to parties with me before." Claire looks away from me and starts twirling hair around her pointy faux fingernail. "We sorta got separated at the party. I wanted to find Travis and I didn't want you anywhere near the guy I liked. The whole school knew you were the hottest girl in town, and even with you being preggers, I thought Travis might still find you hot. Guys like that stuff, right? When I found Travis an hour later, I found you too. You were drinking something clear and I thought it was water. It didn't smell like alcohol, but you were acting weird. You were doing a line off the coffee table and that wasn't a side of you I had ever seen before."

I straighten off the locker, shaking my head. "You're lying. I would never do that! I don't do drugs!"

"Calm down!" Claire stomps her foot. "Geez, Roxy. I never said you were a druggie. I said you were doing a line of coke and acting weird. I pulled you away from that shit before you could even get half of it down. You were wobbly on your feet and completely out of it. Your eyes were glazed over, and I was starting to freak out. Travis and some of his college pals just kept laughing and I didn't know what to do. I asked Travis what you were drinking, and he told me water. Your drink didn't smell of alcohol, so I took him at his word. Then he laughed and said that he might've added something extra in it but that you seemed like the kind of girl that didn't care and pointed at your stomach. I got us out of there and took us to a friend's house in Arlington. I couldn't go home. My parents would have been pissed and I couldn't take you to Josh. He's the fucking sheriff. My friend said that she was going to some bar and that it would be okay for us to tag along. I didn't think anything more would happen, Roxy. But you didn't seem to be getting better. Your movements were wrong, and you were completely out of it. You were dancing with some man and he was touching you and you didn't seem to care. I gave you a soda and fries. I thought it would help. But you refused to eat. I tried two more times, but you believed you couldn't drink a freaking pop. I went to the bathroom, and when I came back five minutes later, you were out of it—passed out on the dance floor, and people were calling the police. I couldn't stay there.

My dad would have skinned me alive. I gave the bartender Josh's number and told him to call him. I fled. I didn't know what happened to you or the baby. But when you came back to school sophomore year, you didn't say anything. You just kept to yourself, and I didn't want to talk to you. One night hadn't changed the fact that I hated you."

I take in a deep breath and move to the bench beside her. I drop my head in my hands. "What happened to Travis?"

"He moved out of state and graduated the following spring. I never saw him again after that night. And I'm sorta glad about that. I lost interest after what he said about you. And I didn't want to look like a fool. I already felt like one."

Turning my head to look at Claire, I frown—mostly to myself. "I'm sorry. That I accused you of drugging me."

Claire shrugs. "Why all of a sudden do you care about that night?"

"I've always cared. I just didn't think it mattered."

"You know, I am sorry about Harley. My intention that night was never for you to lose her. You just seemed so depressed—and while that should have made me thrilled, gave me something to taunt you with, it just didn't remind me of the Roxy I had known. That was the first time I had seen you so weak. Even now you're not the Roxy I knew, but you aren't fragile either. You're somewhere in between. It's easy to make fun of this version of you. You don't fight back."

"Yeah, well, I'm tired of not fighting back." I lift my head and cross my legs at the ankles. "Why did you write that on the study room's door the other day?"

"Are you accusing me of something else after I just told you what you wanted to know?" Claire's voice comes out shrill, and I nod. "I didn't write anything on a study room door. I don't even go in the library, if you recall. That old lady creeps me out and she doesn't like my shoes."

My face drops at that. I forgot about Claire's aversion to the library. The one and only time she went there, at least that I know of, she was chased out of the room by the librarian with a fly swatter. Her heels were making too much noise and the librarian kept giving her the evil eye. After the hundredth time of Claire getting up, the woman was fed up with the clack, clack, clacking of Claire's shoes. Still, that doesn't mean Claire didn't write that word on the door. The library was empty. And it was written in the same shade of lipstick that she is wearing right now.

"It was written in your lipstick. You know, the same color you are wearing now and the same color you used earlier this month to mar my locker."

Claire huffs and gives me a pointed look. "I didn't write anything on any door. Plenty of girls wear this exact same shade. You used to when you actually wore makeup. I have no reason right now to taunt you. I have my own problems. I think our friend Ari stated it best: I have ninety-nine problems and you ain't one."

"Not even Cade?" I question her.

She stands from the bench and glares down at me. Her olive complexion goes bright red. "If Cade wants you, he can fucking have you. You're just going to break his heart anyways."

I stand and raise a brow at her.

She shakes her head at me before I can say a word. "Don't pretend, Roxy. We both know that you are in love with Belmont. I don't know why you are stringing Cade along, and at this point I don't care, but don't give me that look when you know I'm speaking the truth."

"I would never hurt him. He's my best friend."

"That might be on your end, but I see the look in his eyes. It's way more than friendship to him. You shouldn't mess with people's emotions like that. I know that's hypocritical coming from me, but I thought you were better than the rest of Kingston. Not to mention, Wran did the same thing to you in middle school and you didn't like being on the receiving end."

"And if I actually care for Cade?"

"Do you?" She purses her lips and taps her heels against the locker room floor. "Can you honestly tell me that you love Cade the way you love Wran? I don't think you do. You don't look at him the way you looked at Wran. And I was around for a lot of the way you looked at Wran, just so you remember."

I glance away from her. Claire's a lot of things, but right now she's right. I don't love Cade. Not like that. At least I don't think I do. He's my friend, and I would do just about anything for him. I am doing anything for him. He wanted a chance, and I'm giving him that. I know more than anyone that liking whatever is going on with Cade while knowing it will go nowhere is wrong. I know that makes me a sick individual. I know it makes me a . . . what everyone seems to think I am.

"That's my point, Roxy."

I lift my head to look at her.

She shifts her bag on her shoulder. "Now, if you will excuse me, I do have real friends to see before lunch is over."

Claire turns on her heels and she clacks her way out of the locker room. I sit back down on the bench and stare at the gray lockers across from me. Maybe she's right. No, I know she's right. I shouldn't be torturing Cade with this façade. He thinks he truly has a chance with me. That's the only reason he even suggested this whole thing. I know otherwise. And it is wrong of me to stay. To pretend. Even if I like the way he makes me feel.

Exhaling, I set my backpack on the bench and pull out my phone. I told Bennett I would give him a call today, and now that I have some answers, I guess I should let him know what I know. It probably won't help. I believe courts call this hearsay. It's not coming from my memory; it's coming from Claire, and for all I know it could be false. It didn't sound made-up, which I'm hoping it's not. It's a lead, and a lead I need.

"Hello?" Bennett's deep, rich voice comes in over the phone and I inhale.

"Bennett? It's Roxanna. I think we should talk."

CHAPTER 22

ROX

After hanging up with Bennett, I make my way out of the girls' locker room and down to my locker. I come to a stop short of it when I see a dark-haired girl dressed in all black and combat boots standing near it. Raven. I haven't seen her since the party last Friday night. I didn't even try to find her after I ran off while they were doing their set. Crap. I probably should have made that a priority, considering they did take me under their wings and befriend me. Yeah, I probably ruined that budding friendship.

Turning on the soles of her shoes, she looks me up and down and crosses her arms over her chest, head tilted and eyes so thin and sharp they could cut. I take the remaining steps to her and give her a smile, hoping that will defuse any anger she might have at the situation. Who am I kidding? A smile isn't going to change that I ditched them after they

so graciously gave me a place. And not only did I ditch them, but I also went right back to Cade.

"Hi." I mentally roll my eyes. Is hi really the best I can do?

"So you are alive?" she clips. "You could have fooled me."

"I'm so sorry." My eyes drop from her, and I bite the inside of my cheek.

"You left us!" Raven yells, her sugary voice dripping with venom. "We searched for you for hours. Hours, Roxanna! We had to find out from someone that you left with Cade. Do you know how humiliating that was?"

"I'm sorry," I mumble without raising my eyes to her. I should have informed them about Friday as soon as Monday came around. Scratch that; she gave me her number. I should have called. Anything would have been better than not letting them know I was okay. Especially after the whole Aspen accident that the local news so gracefully aired for everyone to see. I would be worried to if someone that had gone through that went freaking missing. While they were with me, on top of that. "I wasn't thinking."

"You weren't thinking? That's your excuse? After everything the news said about you, we were freaked out. Sorry isn't good enough!"

I flinch at the venom in her words. She's right. I know she's right, but I don't know what else to say to her. I made a mistake. But in my defense, I was getting chased down by an SUV. And a lot has happened since Friday. My mind hasn't really had the chance to focus on the people that were being nice to me the week prior. Still, it's no excuse.

"Were you just humoring me on Friday? Making fun of the geeky band girl? Did you and Cade have a good laugh at our expense?"

I raise my head to her finally. "Cade's not like that. I'm not like that. My disappearance had nothing to do with any of that. I'm sorry, okay, but don't act like you know me—or Cade, for that matter. He would never make fun of someone."

"Ha! You don't know your boyfriend. He's co-captain of the football and baseball team. They're all like that," she says all like Wran says them, and I don't like it. I thought Raven was better than this. Sure, I don't really know her, and I shouldn't expect anyone to be any certain way, not after the life I've lived, but I didn't take her for being this hostile. This judgmental. She wasn't with me at that table on Friday.

"Look, I said I'm sorry. If that's not good enough, then oh well. That's on you. Go yell at someone else because I really don't want to hear it." I step around her and open my locker. I shove my books inside. I don't turn around as I hear her combat boots clomping down the hall.

I close my locker door and lean my head against the cool metal. I can't believe I just told her that. I can't believe I basically shooed her away. The one person other than Cade that has taken the initiative to even include me in something. I am the worst person alive. At least right now. I could have been a bit more understanding to Raven. She did look for me. Not many people would do that at a party. I'll have to apologize to her better later. Hopefully she won't be upset too much longer.

A throat clears behind me and I lift my head from the metal, turning around to see if maybe Raven came back. It's not Raven I come face-to-face with though. Instead, Tasha, my counselor, is standing in front of me in a long floral midi dress and boots. She brushes a strand of hair behind her ear and tilts her head in acknowledgment of me.

"Do you mind if we talk?" She gets straight to the point. I'm not actually sure what we have to talk about—not that I really want to talk to her. All she's done this year is chastise me for not applying to art school and then overreact when she first saw Harley.

And if that isn't bad enough, she's now dating Josh. I don't think I can face her without thinking about her in bed with him. With his handcuffs involved. That's just weird.

"I'm headed to the cafeteria. Someone is waiting on me," I tell her.

It's not true, but she doesn't need to know that. Cade would normally be waiting, but he has a tour at some university today. He flew out last night and won't be back until late tonight. I had to drive his car to school.

"It won't take long, I promise."

Glancing up and down the halls, I nod. What's the worst that can happen while talking to Ms. Flannigan?

Patting me on the shoulder, she turns and heads in the opposite direction of the cafeteria. I follow her down the hall until we reach the main offices at the front of the school. We enter and the secretary squeals, slamming her laptop closed. I grin at the red-faced, flustered woman, but Tasha doesn't seem bothered by the woman's reaction to us showing up here.

Tasha motions to her office, and I head inside. She closes the door behind her, and I take a seat in the soft leather chair directly in front of the white desk. I really hope she isn't calling me in here to discuss the news or me attending art school again. Sitting, Tasha stares at me, her eyes wide and sparkling. She clasps her hands together and grins. I glance around the room so I don't have to see her. She's acting odd.

"Sooo." I still don't give her my attention as I examine the multiple certificates on her wall. "Why am I here?"

"You graduate in two months' time," she says. "That must be exciting for you."

I turn away from the awards and search her face. She must be kidding. Exciting isn't the word I would use to describe me graduating from high school. Terrifying, maybe. Stressed, for sure. The only thing I have to look forward to is working at a diner for the rest of my life and taking care of my child. While I would do anything for Harley, I never saw myself working at a diner before she was born. That was never my dream. And now I can't really do anything about it. I can't go to art school, no matter what this woman thinks. Lynn has made that crystal clear. And I can't leave this town. The only hope I have right now is that Bennett will be able to get custody back for me. Maybe then I will have some options.

"I'm aware," I tell her. "I'm still not applying to any art schools or universities."

Her grin falls just a tiny bit, but she quickly regains her posture. "This isn't about that. Knowing about Harley, I understand your decision a little bit better. Although there are still options if you change your mind. I could help you—"

"No." I cut her off before she can get started on her whole spiel. I don't want to know what options there are out there. Not when I don't even know if I will be getting Harley back. If my lawyer can't get me custody, then I'm stuck here. And from the information Claire gave me, here is all I have to look forward to. I know living in Kingston isn't all bad. Josh is here. Granted, I'm still not sure how to feel about him after what I learned he did. But he was there for Wran and Cade when they needed him. And he's always here for me when I need him. On top of that, Wran is here. I don't know if I could ever leave him. Not fully. And there's Aunt May. I have people here that care about me. People who, for the most part, have kept me safe and out of the system. I have a family here.

"Okay then." Ms. Flannigan's tone is lower than before, causing me to regret not letting her finish her statements. "As I was saying, you graduate in two months. The top students in the graduating class are required to present a speech. I'm happy to inform you that you are one of the top students. And not just one of the top students. You are the top student. Valedictorian. Congratulations."

"What?" I shriek, eyes wide. I shake my head at her. She's wrong. I'm not valedictorian. Not after this semester. My grades have been falling since the end of February. There's no way I could have the highest grades out of my class. "You have to be wrong. Mr. Stevenson said my grades have been on a decline. And I know it's not just my calculus class."

"Yes, I admit, your grades have slipped a little, but not enough for you to lose your spot at top of the class. You would have to fall below 2.5 this semester for that to happen, and I don't see that being the case."

I shake my head at her again. Me? Valedictorian? Sure, that's what I've been working toward since I gave birth to Harley. My grades staying above a certain point was a requirement placed on me, but I know for a fact that my grades before Harley weren't the best. They weren't the worst, but still . . . there must be a mistake somewhere.

"Roxanna, this is a good thing. You should be proud of yourself," Tasha tells me, but I'm still trying to wrap my mind around the whole thing. I actually did it. I actually made valedictorian. And yet I will still be stuck inside Kingston's city limits. "Are you okay?"

Tasha pulls a tissue from the box and hands it to me. I swat at my face and nod. Yeah, I'm great. So, so great. Lots of people want to be the top in the class. Lots of people can't.

I am. I just accomplished one of my many goals. The only goal I will ever be able to accomplish. I'm excellent. "When do you need the speech?"

"Three weeks before the end of the semester. We have to go over and approve it."

I nod again and rise. "Okay."

"Ms. Raine?" Tasha calls, and I stiffen at the use of my actual surname. Not many people call me that. Not many people even use it. Just Lynn, and even she uses it on rare occasions. For the most part, I hear "Raine" in conjunction with my father. James Raine. Hardly ever Roxanna Raine. Not from teachers. Not from friends. And not from Aunt May. No one wants to be tied to a murderer, and that's all my surname does: tie me to my father. I buried him. I don't want to be tied to that man any longer.

"Please don't call me that." I glance down at my counselor. "It's just Rox or Roxanna or Roxy. Don't link me to that man."

She stands and clasps her hands in front of her. "I see. You know you don't have to be ashamed of what happened to you. What he did."

I shake my head at her. No, she doesn't see. I'm not ashamed of what happened to me. I'm not the only person with a father like mine. There are thousands of kids that wish they could escape their situation. Thousands of kids that don't have the courage to run away like I did. No, I'm not ashamed that my father hurt me. My guilt goes deeper than that. Way deeper.

"I'm going to go get lunch before the bell rings," I tell Tasha, and turn away from her, not really wanting to admit to anything that's going on in my head.

My father is dead. Gone. And I only wish it could have been by my hands.

Walking out of the office and down the hall toward the cafeteria, I hear my phone go off. I stop and pull it from my pocket. Cade's name flashes across my screen, and I answer. He's supposed to be on a tour with some fancy football team's school. He shouldn't be calling me right now. I'm pretty sure his future is more important than talking to me about whatever.

"Why are you calling? That's disrespectful," I answer the phone.

Cade laughs and I hear static in the background. "You would say something like that. So, how are you feeling?"

"What do you mean? I'm fine."

"Just fine? Shouldn't you be more than just fine? You're valedictorian."

"How do you know that?" My voice comes out a bit too high, drawing the attention of someone. They give me one look and keep on their way. "Hold up; let me get outside."

"Okay."

I reverse my steps and head toward the front doors of the building. As I push through them, a gust of wind blows into my face and I shiver. As much as I dislike summer, I'm ready for it. The weather here has been crazy. One day it's warm. One day it's like it's going to snow. Spring sucks. At least it's not raining today.

I go around to student parking and get inside of the white car Cade let me drive to school. He wouldn't let me drive the truck, but that's understandable. He loves that truck the way Wran loves his car. Guys. They are so predictable.

"Okay, talk," I say into the phone. He shouldn't know about that. I wasn't going to mention valedictorian to anyone. Not when there's a possibility that I won't have that honor by the end of the year.

"Ms. Flannigan called me into the office Monday and told me. She wanted me to do an introductory speech for you."

"Huh." Guess it's not a mistake. "Why would she want you to give that speech?"

Someone says something in Cade's background and he's silent for a moment. I hear him tell whoever, the tour guide or coach probably, that he's liking it so far. I guess he would like a school like that. One far, far from here. A school where he can truly be who he's meant to be and not this small-town quarterback.

"Are you listening to me?" Cade's voice cuts through my mental rant.

"Huh? Oh yeah," I lie.

"Really? What did I just say?"

"Umm . . . something about why you are giving a speech."

"I said that I'm giving the speech because I'm the only person the school officials ever see you with. They wanted someone that knows you to introduce you."

I roll my eyes at that. Do we really need an introduction speech just for me? Everyone knows me. I'm the artsy-fartsy girl that got knocked up by her savior and then lost the child. At least that's all they really care about. It's not like anyone is going to want to hear about me as a person anyways. Not these students.

"Oh."

"So how do you feel?"

I slump back against the car seat. "Like it's all a joke. Like at any moment, Tasha is going to tell me they made a mistake. Cade, I don't want to be valedictorian."

"Yes, you do." There's shuffling in the back. "I've seen the way you study. And don't forget, I was watching you way before we ever started talking again. I know you want this. I know how much stuff like this means to you. Just like I know you're scared because you don't believe you deserve it. Well, you do, Roxy. You deserve valedictorian and so much more. If I could give you the world, I would hand it to you on a gold platter."

"Cade," I moan out at him. "I don't deserve it. What am I going to do with that honor? Someone that can actually make something of their life deserves it. I'm stuck here. It will do me no good. I'm not getting a scholarship to some school thousands of miles away. I'm not going to become a doctor or a lawyer or anything like that. I'm a waitress. And

I'm okay with being a waitress. I accepted that a long time ago but handing me something like that . . . it's cruel and mean. I can't use it."

"Only you think that. You worked for it. Besides, only you are stopping yourself from going away to that art school. Only you think you can't be a lawyer or a doctor or an astronomer. I'm pretty sure Belmont would agree with that. Roxanna, you have choices. Even if you do or don't get custody of Harley, you have choices. Being valedictorian is an honor, even if you are just a waitress planning on going to community college."

I hear the bell ring in the background, and I sigh into the phone. "But someone else could use it better."

"Someone else didn't work for it." There's more talking on Cade's end of the phone. He replies to whoever said something before giving me his attention again. "Look, you deserve this. We can talk more about it when I get back in town, but I have to go right now. They want to show me the gym."

I roll my eyes at that. "All right. See you tonight."

"Hey wait!" he rushes before I cut the call.

"Yeah?"

"I love you."

"Cade," I groan again, and he ends the call before I have time to tell him to stop saying that. I stare at the phone in my hand before I remember hearing the bell. I only have study hall, but I want to finish a painting in the art room before the end of the day. Putting my earphones in my ears, I turn on the playlist that I like to paint to and get out of the car.

I'm barely a foot away from the car when someone pulls on the back of my shirt. I twirl around only to come face to face with someone bulky and big in a black mask that covers half of their face. They have stubble, but that's the only thing I notice before I whirl around and run. I don't get far. They slam into me and we go crashing down to the gravel parking lot. My earbuds are yanked out and I roll over to kick at the masked stranger. The man laughs and grabs my leg. He reaches behind him and pulls something from his back pocket. When his hand comes back in front of me, I still at the sight of a gun. He's pointing a gun at me.

I shake my head at the person.

"You make one more move and you won't be able to move again."

I gasp at that. "W–what do you want?"

He cocks his head to the side. Lowering the gun, he grabs my arm and pulls me up from the ground with him. I look around for anyone but stop when I see the blacked–out SUV down the street. I should have seen that when I came out of the school. Stupid, stupid, Rox.

He turns me around, not answering the question. I glance at the steps that lead up to the school. All I would need is to get inside those glass doors. Get inside, and I'll be safe. I can call Josh and . . . and . . . and tell him what? That I was stupid and not paying attention to my surroundings?

"Walk and walk slowly. We don't need to draw any attention," he hisses in my ear.

"That mask isn't helping your agenda," I hiss back.

I hear the gun cock and I take a step. "If you run, I shoot, Roxanna."

He knows my name? I shake my head. Of course whoever this is knows me. Why else would he be after me?

I take another step and then another until I'm right beside the steps of the school. I glance over my shoulder at the man, his thunderous eyes almost black, and he glares back at me. I look away from him, and before I know it, I'm running up the steps to the school. He won't pull that trigger. We're in a school's parking lot. He wouldn't be able to get away in time before someone heard.

Right as my hand touches the door, I hear a low pop and a burst of pain spreads throughout my shoulder. My hand drops from the door just as the man pulls me back. I struggle in his hold, but he just continues pulling me away from the school's entrance.

A cry leaves me when he jerks me hard around the steps and then flattens me against his broad chest. "Smith and Wesson Model 17 does the job quite nicely."

That is the last thing he says before shoving a cloth over my nose and mouth.

CHAPTER 23

ROX

"Come on! You're going to be late!" I yell at Wran.

He arches a brow at me in the mirror and smirks. "You're more excited about this than I am. It's just a school dance. One, I might add, you talked me into going."

"It's prom, Wran! You can't miss prom. I want to know everything."

He turns around and leans against the sink. I frown at his choice of attire but don't mention it again. He's the only guy I know—not that he or Josh let me hang with many—that would wear a T-shirt and Chucks to prom. Prom!

I cross my arms over my chest and glare up at him. I'm not going to say a word. Nope! I'll let his date do that. Date. He's going on a date. I suppose I can't be too upset about that; I told him to go. He didn't even want to go to prom, but there was no way he was going to miss it. Sure, it's just his *junior prom, but it's still prom. I won't get to go to one for another four years. Besides, even with the T-shirt, jacket, and Chucks, he still looks good. Too good. Gah! I shouldn't be thinking he looks that good. He's like my brother. It's so wrong.*

Wran pulls my arms from around my chest and pulls me to his side. "Do I look okay?"

I elbow him in the side and glare up at him. "Nope. You look sloppy."

He laughs and fingers some loose strands of my hair. "I really don't know why you insisted on me going. I don't even like Tiffany."

"You had her here last week," I remind him. He must like her enough to have her here. To have her here and in his room. With the door locked.

Wran glances down at me for a long second. "You know that doesn't count."

"It counted enough a week ago."

"You and your little smart fuckin' mouth."

I giggle at him and step away from his side. Just as I do so, a tightness in my lower stomach has me cringing. My stomach has been weird all day. It's not hurting, per se. It just feels wrong. I mentioned it to Josh when he came to pick me up from school today, but he just told me to stop eating gummy worms. I haven't even had any gummy worms to-day. Although now that I think of it, I should probably take the bag I do have out of my backpack before they melt and become one big giant glob.

"You okay?" Wran straightens and pushes up the sleeves of his suit jacket. "You look nauseous."

"I'm fine," I tell him. He's so not using my stomach to get out of prom. I want pictures of him smiling and having fun. Even if he is there with another girl.

He bows down so that he's closer to my height and lifts my chin. "Are you sure? You've been looking a bit paler than normal."

I nod. "Yeah, you just finish getting dressed. I'm going to go make you a smoothie before you leave."

"You don't have to do that."

I ignore his words. He always has a protein smoothie after working out. If he didn't miss a workout, I'm not going to miss making him his smoothie. It's us. And something Tiffany can't do behind a locked door. "You always have one around this time."

"You know there's going to be food and drinks at this stupid dance, right?"

I swat a hand at him and leave so he can finish getting dressed. I can make a smoothie if I want to. Going into the kitchen, I stop short when I see Josh standing there in his cop uniform. He's eating a sandwich and looking at something on his phone. Usually, I'm never inside the main house, so I don't really see him in here. But since it's prom and Wran obviously needs help, I'm here.

Josh looks up from his phone and arches a brow at me. "Homework done?"

Nope! "Of course. You know I always do my work."

He tilts his head to the side. "Show me."

"Josh."

"Roxanna." He says my name like a father scolding a petulant child, and I don't like it. He knows my homework isn't done.

"Fine, it's not done, but Claire is coming over after Wran leaves for the dance and we're going to work on it together."

"It's almost seven o'clock. What have you been doing all day?"

I roll my eyes at his question. I've been stalking Wran. Okay, not stalking since he really doesn't care if I hang around, but that's more important than doing civics homework. "I'll get it done. I promise. I just wanted to make sure Wran looked decent for the dance. You know he can't dress himself."

A small grin graces Josh's lips but he quickly wipes it away. "Make sure you do your homework and that you're in bed before ten o'clock."

Fat chance. I won't be going to bed until after Wran comes home, and hopefully he won't be bringing Tiffany inside with him. I give Josh a nod and step inside the kitchen, heading toward the fridge. I swear these guys would starve if it wasn't for me going to the store every week to shop. I pull out the spinach, celery, and apples Wran likes in his drink, along with the disgusting protein powder he consumes. I don't know why he needs that stuff. Protein builds muscle. He already has them. He doesn't need more, or he'll look like some crazy bodybuilder guy on steroids.

"So Wran is going to prom? When did that happen?" Josh asks as he maneuvers his way out of the kitchen. "Last I heard, he wouldn't be caught dead at some school function."

"Monday. I talked him into going. I want to know what to expect when it's time for me to go to prom."

"You always could change his mind about things." His words come out in a mumble, but I still hear them. Lately Josh has been saying stuff like that, and I don't understand. I don't get why all of a sudden the things I do and say are wrong.

Ignoring him, I put all the ingredients in the blender and turn it on. My stomach swims at the sight of the smoothie, and I step away from the machine. I clutch my stomach and groan. This shouldn't be happening. I didn't eat anything bad today. I would remember.

"Stomach still upset?" Josh asks me and presses the button on the blender to turn it off.

I nod. "It'll be okay."

Just as I say that the sudden urge to pee wooshes over me and I turn to head back to the bathroom. Wran is coming out as I round the corner, and I have to stop and look at him for a second. He actually makes a T-shirt look good. It's not formal, but no one looking at him can't say he isn't suited up nicely. I mean, this is nice for Wran. His normal day consists of ripped jeans and a black shirt. Sometimes they have bleach spots on them that he somehow makes look okayish, and other times he doesn't even shower. This is definitely an upgrade.

"Your smoothie is on the kitchen counter. Excuse me." I push around him and head into the bathroom. Rushing over to the toilet, I slide my leggings down. A heart-breaking scream leaves me as I stare at blood all over my white underwear. I drop down to the toilet and scream again. Ohmygod. Ohmygod. Ohmygod! The door to the bathroom slams open and the brothers stands there, looking around as if someone might be in here besides me. I bring my knees up to my chest and hold them. What is happening to me?

"Why you screaming?" Wran asks, looking around the small bathroom again.

I shake my head at him and look at Josh. Josh takes the hint and backs away from the door. Wran closes it behind him and comes over to me. He drops to the floor in front, and I'm hoping he can't see all the blood. I don't want him to see me like this.

"What's wrong, Rox?" Wran urges me.

I shake my head at him.

"Come on. Talk to me," he says and pulls my arms from around my knees. He pulls me up from the toilet, but then stops. His eyes aren't on mine. Instead he's looking at the leggings I was doing my best to shield. "Umm . . ."

"I'm dying," I cry when he doesn't elaborate more. "There's so much blood."

"No!" he shouts a little too loud. "You're not dying. This is . . . um . . . you . . . fuck. Let me go get Josh. He can explain this shit better."

"No!"

"Rox." Wran groans into his hands. "I'm pretty sure he can handle this better than I can."

"What's wrong with me?" I sit back down on the toilet.

"Nothing. I swear. This is normal. You're perfectly normal," he tries to calm me. "But, um, I'm going to need to run to the store for a moment. Stay in here and lock the door." He pulls a large wad of tissue from the roll and shoves it at me. "Here. Put this in your underwear until I get back."

I look from him to the tissue in my hands. "Why?"

"To soak up some blood. I'll be back in like five minutes and then I'll try to explain that." He gestures down to my leggings without looking down. Before I have time to say anything, he scrams from the bathroom like lightning. I glance down at my unwearable underwear and grimace. Inhaling, I shove the paper in my pants and pull them up. Wiggling, I go over to the door and lock it like he said. Surely I'm okay if he's rushing to the store. Maybe this is normal. I mean I know he said this is normal, but that was a ton of blood. I don't know anyone that bleeds like that.

Grabbing some more tissue, I place a big blob of it on the tile floor and sit. Maybe that will keep it from transferring. I look over at the door and sigh. He said he'll be right back. I place my forehead on my knees and wait. There's a knock on the door and I stiffen. I don't move from my spot. I don't want to talk to anyone but Wran. And I most certainly don't want to talk to Josh.

"Roxy?" Josh calls.

"Go away!" I shout at the door.

"Are you okay?"

My eyes stay trained on the door before I say a word. Wran said I was fine. I believe him with all my being. "Yes. Go away!"

"Okay."

I hear his boots walking away, but I still don't relax. I won't relax until Wran gets back here and tells me what's going on. My body shouldn't be doing this.

I stay crouched on the floor for what seems like forever when there's another knock on the door.

"Lost girl, it's me."

The sound of Wran's voice has me getting up from the floor. I take a chance and look down at the tissue. There's blood on it too, but in splotches. Like it was just a transfer. I go over to the door and open it. Wran barges in and closes the door behind him. He has a brown paper bag in his hands. He sets it on the sink and then looks at me. "How do you feel?"

"Like I'm going to punch the next person that asks me that."

"Okay, moody. That's good."

"Moody?"

"Nothing," he mumbles and pushes past me and over to the tub. He turns on the water and adds in my favorite bubble bath. "Come here."

I go over to him and take a seat on the toilet beside the bath. "I'm going to be okay?"

"Yeah." He turns to me and sits down on the floor. "You know, sometimes I forget that you are getting older."

"Really?"

He nods. "Yeah. And then other times, it's fucking obvious."

He leans forward and brushes my hair back behind my ear.

"Is that a bad thing? Me getting older?"

"Yes and no."

"I don't understand. Everyone gets older, Wran. It's part of life."

"There are lots of things that are a part of life." He points to my stomach. "That being one of them. Girls, um, start their periods when they get old enough to have babies."

"Babies? I don't want to have a baby. I'm too young."

"Have you had your health class yet?"

"I have it next semester. Josh forgot to sign the permission slip before school started."

"Fucking Josh," Wran curses under his breath. "This would be so much easier if you had health class. All girls get this. It's normal."

"Then why does my stomach hurt?"

His eyes widen a bit and his brows knit together. "Um, cramps. Girls get cramps when they have their . . . this. Look, I'm going to take you to Aunt May, and she will explain this to you tomorrow. As for right now, take a bath and put on one of those." He points to the brown paper bag. "Just stick it to a pair of underwear."

I nod, not really understanding. I'll have to do some research when I go back out to the cellar. Or maybe call Claire. She always knows everything.

"When you're done, meet me in the cellar. We'll watch movies for the rest of the night."

I shake my head at him. No. He has prom. He can't stand up Tiffany. That's just cruel. "We can't. You have a date. You can't stand her up. That's mean."

"Have you not figured out that you are the only girl that matter to me?" he tells me and pulls me off the toilet. "You're becoming a woman tonight. I won't leave you alone."

"A woman?"

He nods. "Yeah. And a woman needs her guy to slave for her during her time of need. That's me."

I grin at him. "Slave?"

"Don't let that get to your head. Come tomorrow, everything's going back to normal. You only get nice Wran for one night. Now, get in the tub."

I laugh at him and do as he says. If one night is all I get with him being like this, then I'm perfectly happy with that.

"Wran!" I lurch awake and groan at the pressure in my shoulder.

"Not quite, darling," someone says, and shoves me back down. A whimper escapes me and I turn my head to see who just said that. A man in a black mask that covers half of his face comes into focus and then everything from the school parking lot blasts to the forefront of my mind. I try to move away from him, but he digs his hand into my shoulder. I scream out in utter agony while white spots dance in my vision. I slump back down.

"Behave and this will end faster," he hisses.

"You s–shot me," I stutter out, my voice quivering from the memory and the pain in my shoulder.

"I told you not to run."

"You tried to kill me. Why wouldn't I run?"

He lets out a throaty laugh and it seems to vibrate off the walls. I glance around the dark space. Windows so deeply tinted I can hardly see through them meet my eyes. The black SUV. He dragged me to the black SUV. Oh god. I'm going to die.

"If I wanted to kill you, I very well could have. That little stunt by the lake was only to let you know I was watching."

I turn away from the window and look at him as well as I can. "What do you want with me?"

"Me, personally? Nothing. You're just an annoying teenager. Although watching you with that one fellow was interesting." His eyes dip from mine and they travel over my body. His stare on my body, even though it's covered, freaks me out. "I don't really see the appeal."

"Let me go. Please," I whimper, and his eyes shoot back to mine. "If I mean nothing to you, just let me go. I won't report you."

He chuckles again. "Report me. To your little sheriff. That idiot is the most incompetent fool I have ever seen with his sorta power. He's a joke. This whole assignment has been a joke."

"Then let me go."

He shakes his head and grabs my face, forcing it back down and away from him. "No can do. Already been paid. And I don't believe in fucking over my clients. Now shut up and be still."

Before I can say more, his fingers press into my shoulder. My eyes widen as a hot pain blazes throughout my entire upper half. His fingers dig in more and I claw at his pant-covered legs, digging my own fingers into him. He shushes me, but I can't stop the weeping. It hurts. God, it hurts. After a minute, the pressure of his fingers starts to ease. He drops something beside my head, but I refuse to look at it.

"There. It's out, but this part is going to be much more painful."

"Please no," I whimper.

"Sorry, darling, but I can't have you bleeding everywhere. Hold your breath."

I do as he says, but the moment I feel the pain of a thousand needles being poured over my wound, I scream a blood-curdling scream. My head grows light, the pain increasing by the second, and then everything just stops.

CHAPTER 24

WRAN

One more week. That's all I have left. You would think I would be ready to leave Pleasure House, but after Rox stood me up and then didn't even have the nerve to call me, I'm suddenly not looking forward to having to go back to Kingston to see her. I mean hell, it's Friday—two days past the time I was supposed to see her—and I haven't heard a word. On top of that, Josh isn't answering his damn phone either. I thought we at least worked through our issues in that little session. Guess not.

I walk into the dining hall and take a tray, packing on today's breakfast special. As I make my way over to my regular seat in the back by the window overlooking the garden, Steven walks in front of me and stops.

He gives me a grin, and I arch a brow at him. He very well knows that I'm not a morning person. I'm generally more pleasant after a couple mugs of coffee. Well, at least that's what this place calls it. It's more like sludge if you ask me. While most of the food is good, that is not. I miss Rox's coffee.

"Why don't you come eat with the gang?" he asks.

I step aside him and continue over to my table. "Not really in the mood."

"This has something to do with your little lady standing you up, man?"

"She didn't stand me up." She so fucking did. "She just had school shit."

"Well you still have all of us. Come eat with us."

"This is not the morning to be around me. I'll stay here."

"Come on, dude." He bumps me in the shoulder and my hands tighten around my tray. "It'll be fun and get your mind off of being stood up."

"She didn't—"

"Yeah, yeah." He grabs my tray and starts walking out of the cafeteria. I stare after him. Fucker really has a death wish this morning. He knows I don't like being bothered this early. Everyone here has put that together. I have no clue why he needs to badger me today. My stomach growls, and I stare after him. If I don't go, then my stomach is shit out of luck. We only get one tray for each meal. We can pack that one tray with as much as we can eat, but one tray, nevertheless. And he took mine. With a growl, I follow him out of the dining hall.

I come to a stop when I see Thomas and everyone from our little therapy group standing around a cake with grins on their faces.

"Happy birthday!" they all yell, and I immediately reverse my steps. Nope. I can't handle this today. How the hell did they even figure out it was my birthday? I'm pretty sure that's not something Thomas can do—go through my file and tell everyone. Fuck nah, this isn't happening. I'm out of here.

Someone grabs my arm and I shove them away.

"Wran." Thomas says my name with a warning.

"What the fuck?" I point behind him at the cake and decorations and shit.

"You mentioned you don't really care to celebrate your birthday yesterday in our session."

"And that gave you the right to put together a lame-ass party?" I ask him.

He shrugs his shoulders. I run my hand through my growing hair and turn to leave. Thomas grabs hold of my arm again and I shake him off again. I don't want to be here. He knows damn well why I don't celebrate my birthday. Stomping back to my room, stomach and breakfast forgotten, I slam the door and lurch onto the slim twin bed. He should have known better.

A party isn't going to make me forget that my mom died in my arms. A party isn't going to change that the one person I want to see more than anyone right now is probably at another party with some rich prick. I shake my head and shove Rox out of my mind. Fuck her. She can have Cade. She can live in that big fancy house on their side of the tracks all she wants. I don't care. I don't need her or Thomas or Josh or anybody. I just need me and me alone. That's the only person anyone can truly count on in life: themselves. Everyone else dies or leaves.

With a sigh, I sit up on my bed and stare out the window at the green pastures. I've been here nearly a month and I still can't seem to control myself. Maybe this was a complete and utter fail. I couldn't even handle a party. A party Thomas and Steven probably worked all night to put together. Damn. I'm such a fucking prick.

Getting up from the bed, I make my way out of the room and back down to the common area. Everyone's still there. Steven looks up from where he's perched on the bench and a shit-eating grin spreads across his face. I wish I could slap it off. Thomas turns around with a proud smile on his face and comes over to me. He slaps me on the shoulder before pulling me all the way inside the common room.

"I knew you would be back," he says so only I can hear.

"Really?" I ask him. I had no intention of coming back. For all intents and purposes, I would have been perfectly fine in my room for the rest of the day. Okay, maybe not the rest of the day. My stomach would have had me up in search of something to eat sooner or later.

"Yeah. You're not as bad as you want people to believe."

Ha! If that's not the understatement of the year. "I'm probably worse," I mutter under my breath.

Thomas shakes his head just as Steven brings me my tray. I take a strip of bacon off the tray and stuff it into my mouth. God, that tastes good. I sink down onto the bench next to the new kid, whose name keeps escaping my memory, and pluck another piece off my tray. The kid beside me groans in disgust, but I don't give a damn. Thomas comes over and takes a seat next to me.

"So we have a whole day planned," Thomas tells me. "I thought we could take a trip into the city."

I nearly choke on the bacon lodged in my throat. Did the fucker just say city? I've seen nothing but foliage for miles. If there's a city, it must be filled with horses and hay. There wasn't even a city when Josh brought me up here. At least not that I saw. Then again, I was out of it. Half of the drive, I slept.

"City?" I ask him.

"You wouldn't have seen it on your way up here. We have to bypass Pleasure House to get to it, but I think going out today, seeing how you handle the real world, would be a great test to my program. If you can go a day without getting upset at a civilian, I call it a success."

"You do realize that's impossible?" I ask.

Thomas grins.

"All right then! Let's get a move on it," Steven shouts. "I got some shopping to do."

Grabbing the sausage links from the tray, I shove the remainder of it at Steven. If they want to use my birthday as a field test, then I guess there's nothing I can really do about it. Anything is better than sitting in this place, waiting on a call that's probably never going to come anyways.

By the time we make it back to Pleasure House, it's dark out. I hop off the bus and stare up at the night sky and all the stars. Today went well. I even got to do a little shopping. Apparently Josh approved this little field trip on Wednesday when we discussed my birthday. He left some extra change with Thomas. Rox didn't call, but that's okay. I knew she wouldn't. She hasn't cared much about anything since coming back from Aspen. Or rather she just hasn't cared about me. I know I deserve her coldness, but she was the only one I expected to even remember I was born today.

Someone taps me on the shoulder and I turn my head to see Tevin, the new kid, staring up at the stars with me. "You're not about to spit some bull about all the kings of the past slumming it up there are you?"

I shove the kid away. I hate to say I even know what he's referring to, but when you practically raise a toddler, you get used to all the Disney references.

"Seriously though, why are you looking at the sky?" he asks.

Glancing away from the stars, I shake my head. I have no fuckin' clue why I'm looking at them. She's not. And the only reason I even have the slightest interest in them is because of my lost girl.

"I don't know. Something must be wrong with me."

"If there wasn't, you wouldn't be here."

"Fucker."

He laughs and walks past me into the building. I give the night sky one last look-over before I head inside the building as well.

As soon as I step foot into the lobby, the nun that can't stand me rises from her chair behind the check-in desk. She beckons me over and hands me a manila envelope.

"What's this?" I ask her. I wasn't expecting any mail today, and I'm sure Josh would've just given me something the other day when he was here.

She shrugs and sits back down, taking hold of her Bible again. I head down the hall to my room and open the envelope. The first thing that comes out is a small black flip phone that looks like it belongs in the early 2000s. I flip it over, arching a brow at the thing. Opening it, I scroll through the numbers only to find one number programmed into it without a name associated with it. I pull out the remaining items in the envelope. My breath leaves my body as I stare back and forth between photos. Photos of Rox. Photos of Rox unconscious. Photos of Rox unconscious in the back of a vehicle.

The photos fall from my hands, and I grip the tiny phone until a popping has me lessening my hold. Someone is going to pay if she's hurt. Releasing my grip on the phone,

I toss it onto my bed and turn the envelope over. There is no return address, just my name in black curly writing. Okay, so this came from a freaking woman. No man writes like this. I reach inside the envelope again to see if I missed anything. Nope, there's nothing else inside. So a phone and photos. Doesn't make any sense. Why would anyone send those to me? While I'm in here? Not like I can do anything. Whatever this lady wants, she would have been better off getting in touch with Josh or that rich prick Cade.

A buzzing goes off, and I glance over my shoulder to where the phone lies on the bed. I arch a brow at the thing. That's weird and disturbing as all hell. I turn and drop down on the bed, eyeing the phone. Picking it up, I open it. There's a message on the screen. I tap it and notice a stream of messages that has been coming in every half hour since early day. At least that makes this less creepy. I know someone isn't staking this place out for me. Still, whoever this is has Rox. Or wants Rox. Those photos could be fake.

I read through all the messages. Threats demanding I call now.

There is no way in hell I'm giving this lunatic my time. Rising from the bed, I head over to the window and stare up at the night sky. What if they do have Rox? I can't let her get hurt again. Fuck!

Stomping back over to the bed, I slump down on it and yank the phone up again. Flipping it open, I navigate to the messages and read them again. Calling would only be playing into this sicko's game. And after Aspen, I don't want to play any more games. I don't want any more blood on my hands. I just want to finish my stint here and go back home. I want to get my daughter out of state services and build a white picket fence for her and Rox. I don't want to do this shit again. I don't want these damn games.

Forgetting the phone, I get up from the bed and head out of the room. If anyone knows what to do, it's Josh. He said he's been looking out for black vehicles in Kingston. Maybe he has already handled this situation. Maybe there is nothing to truly freak out about. Surely he wouldn't let anything happen to Rox while he's in town and he knows shit is going down.

I go up to the nun's station and she sets her book down. "How may I help you, Mr. Belmont?"

"I need to call Josh," I tell her, getting straight to the point. I don't have time now to deal with a hypocritical nun.

"Are you aware it's after hours?" She points to the clock on the wall beside her.

I lean over the desk and look at the clock. Crap. Maybe I can persuade her.

"Please, it's important. It won't take long and it's only five minutes after." I do my best to give her one of those smiles that I know the ladies like. "I'll even be willing to go to Sunday mass with you if you let me."

She narrows her eyes and cross her arms. "The Lord would expel you from the premises."

"Please. I really need to talk to my brother. You know I wouldn't be here asking if it wasn't important."

The woman looks me over, her eyes flickering across my distressed face. She sighs and reaches down to the landline. Thank God or whoever is up there. There was no way in hell I was using the phone that sicko sent.

Mouthing a thanks to the woman, I quickly dial my brother's phone. It rings and rings and rings. When it goes to voicemail, I slam the phone down on the retriever, which earns me a sidelong glance from the nun. I smile and pick up the phone again. He can't very well ignore me two times in a row. It rings, and I hold my breath. Come on, Josh, pick up. On about the fifth ring, the line cuts.

"What?" Josh screams into the phone.

I bite down on the inside of my mouth to keep from yelling back at him. "Is Rox okay?"

The line is quiet for a long time, and I don't like it. Josh not wanting to answer means something is definitely wrong with my lost girl.

"Why do you ask?" he questions me.

"I don't have time for games, bro. Just answer the question."

"She . . . we don't know," he admits.

"What the fuck do you mean you don't know?" I scream, and the nun glares up at me. I mouth sorry to her and turn around. "How do you not know if she's not okay?"

"She's missing, Wran. The last person that saw her was Claire."

"Claire? Why the hell was she with Claire?" I shout again and wince at the rage in my own voice. Today was going so well. I was doing good. "Josh, you have to find her."

"How did you know something was wrong?" he questions me.

I pull the phone from my ear and stare at it. Do I really want to tell him about the burner phone and the photos? I shake my head at myself. Of course. Someone keeping secrets the last time is how we ended up in Aspen. Secrets are how I ended up doing something that I can't get out of my mind. We don't need secrets now. Not when Rox is tied up in the back of a vehicle.

I bring the phone back to my ear and exhale. "I got a package today," I whisper into the phone so the nun can't hear. "I got a package a few minutes ago with a burner phone inside and some photos. Pictures of Rox, Josh."

"Was there a note?" His voice picks up, urgent. "Anything so we can find her?"

I shake my head even though he can't see me. "No. Just the phone and the photos. Whoever sent it wants me to call them. They have been leaving messages all day. I'm guessing they tracked the package."

"Have you called them?"

"No. I don't really want to."

"We have no clues. None. All we know is that she was taken from school. We found Cade's car with the door open."

"Fuck. You said you were keeping an eye out," I whisper-shout into the phone.

"I was!" he shouts back at me. "The deputy on duty fell asleep. I suspended him."

"Can you do that?"

"I don't give a damn right now, Wran. Our girl is missing!"

I grin into the phone. "You do realize you just referred to Rox as 'our girl.' Means you don't dislike her as much as you want her to think."

"Shut up, smartass." Josh inhales and then exhales a couple of times. "Call whatever number is in that phone."

"What?" I exclaim. Nope! I ain't calling that damn number. Is he trying to get me committed to somewhere other than an anger management facility? "Josh, I'm not calling that number."

"Do you want Rox back?"

"Don't use her against me."

"I'm not. I'm asking you a question. That phone is our only lead. Whoever took her did a great job at covering their tracks. There was nothing. Nothing, Wran. No fingerprints. No hair. Nothing. No one even saw or heard anything. If calling that number is going to get me a lead, then fucking call it. We'll deal with your issues later."

"Oh and what exactly do I say? 'Hey, you have my girlfriend. Give her back'?"

"I see you're still calling her your girlfriend," he mutters.

"Is there a reason I shouldn't?" I ask him, dead serious. If he knows something concerning my relationship with Rox, I want to know before I get back home and walk in on surprises. I can't picture Rox not being there waiting for me. She is the one that told me to get help, and all of this has been for her. She wouldn't walk away from us. Not after all these years. I believe that completely. The girl is loyal to a fault. "You know what? Don't answer that. Rox wouldn't leave me."

"Right." Josh says it way too quickly for my liking. "Go call that number so we can get our girl back."

"Can't I just give you the number and you call it, Sheriff?"

"It was sent to you. Apparently whoever it is wants to talk to you directly. So no, you can't, brother."

I let out a groan and turn around to see the nun leaning against the desk, eyes on me and her book long forgotten. "Do we need to call the police?"

I slam the phone against the retriever. Nosy-ass nun. "Nope!"

"Someone's missing?"

"Yeah, you if you don't mind your own business." I stalk away from the lady and back down the hall to my room, regretting my threat as soon as I leave. The woman did nothing wrong, but the last thing we need is other people's involvement. I run my hand through my hair. I can't believe I have to talk to some sicko. Hasn't Josh learned that me and sick fuckers don't go hand in hand? I always end up doing things I regret.

Marching into my room and over to the bed, I grab the phone from where I tossed it. I open it and look at the number again. I still don't understand why anyone would want to talk to me, of all people. I can't do anything from inside Pleasure House. I can barely breathe. I stare at the phone for a long time before sighing. Here goes nothing.

CHAPTER 25

ROX

I jump awake and wince at the tenderness in my shoulder. With a groan, I roll over on the bed and touch where the aching resides. There's a bandage there. My eyes snap open as I realize I'm on a bed and not the cold metal floor of a van. I sit up straight, dots dancing in my vision as the room comes into focus. Glancing around, I take in the all-white interior and the windowless walls. There's hardly any furniture, and the room looks like it should have padded walls. There's a movement to my left and my eyes snap to the figure. Her back is to me. I blink at the long blond hair and slender figure. That hair looks so familiar.

Yawning, I sit up straighter and the woman slowly turns around. My eyes widen at the sight of her and I let out a gasp. It can't be. I shake my head and blink a few times. The woman doesn't disappear. She grins and runs her pointy-nailed fingers along the back of a tan dog.

"Mom?" I choke out and lick my lips. "But you died. I–I saw—"

She grins again, and I try to remember exactly what I saw as a child. I know there was an accident. My dad said she died in a plane crash, but then I had that memory of her death in the car accident. Maybe she didn't die. Maybe I'm remembering it wrong. No. I can't be. I shake my head. Dad was cruel to me because of her death. He said I looked like her. I remember that. I remember everything he did to me because I looked like her. I reminded him of her.

"How?"

The woman laughs again as she makes her way over to the bed. She sits at the very edge, as far away from me as possible and still stroking the dog. "It's funny watching you try to put the pieces together."

"I don't understand," I utter. "This makes no sense."

"It makes perfect sense, dear. What do you remember of your mother?"

My mother? "You're my mother." I rub my palms against my eyes and blink at her again.

"Answer the question, Roxanna."

"Y–you were, um, nice. You gave me gifts all the time. Um, I don't know what you want me to say."

"Do you remember how much I loved your brother more? Do you remember how much I yanked your hair when I combed it? Do you remember how I never wanted you to call me mother?"

I shake my head. "I . . . what?"

Falling back against the bed, I wince at the pain that shoots across my upper back. My mother never did those things. Did she? Am I remembering her wrong? Oh god.

The woman barks out a laugh. "You are really trying to remember what your mother was like. I heard you had lost your memory, but when I saw you with Caden, I didn't believe it. You clearly have some memories."

I shake my head again. This woman can't be my mother. I know my mother, and her voice never sounded like nails on a chalkboard. She never sounded so . . . so cold. "Who are you?"

Her eyes light up and she sets the dog down on the bed. Grinning, she brings her hands together and claps three times. "Ding, ding, ding! A point goes to you. That, my dear, is the ultimate question. Who am I? Who are you? Who are we really?"

I sit up again and stare at her. Huh?

The dog gets up, waddles across the bed, and jumps down. I watch it walk over to the side wall and it sits. My eyes go back to the woman when she shifts again on the mattress. I jump a little at the close proximity. She reaches out and touches my hair, running the strands through her fingers like they're made of silk or something.

"You look nice as a blonde."

I shift back on the bed and do my best to get away from her and her creepy grin. "Um, thanks. So who are you?"

She shoos my question away with a bat of her hand. "I'm your mom, silly."

The woman gets up from the bed and goes over to the dog. She picks it up and looks down on the floor. There's a stain tinting the white carpet. She points a sharp finger at the dog. "Bad doggy!"

I look over at the door and then back at her. This woman is nuts. Surely I can get to that door before she can pull her attention away from the pee stain on the floor. Easing out of the bed, I do my best to not make a sound. When my feet hit the plush white carpet, I'm lucky for it. The floors don't squeak or anything. I give the woman another quick glance, but she's still too occupied with disciplining the dog. Poor dog. If it has to deal with her crazy on a daily basis, I feel sorry for it. It's clear the woman has a few loose screws. I make my way over to the door and turn the knob. It squeaks and I cringe. I don't even have to turn around to know that the woman heard that. Instead I yank the door open, ready to make a run for it.

The chance doesn't come as a tall brooding man in all black turns toward me. I'm guessing it's the man that shot me.

"Yeah, you didn't think it was going to be that easy, did you?" I risk looking over my shoulder at the mom imposter. She's cradling the dog in her arms again, like a baby. "Back on the bed, missy."

I turn around and look at the brute in front of me. He takes a menacing step forward and I shrink back. This man shot me on school grounds. I don't want to know what he would do to me here and with her orders. Slowly stepping away from him, I go back over to the bed and take a seat.

The woman points to the man. "I've instructed him to shoot to kill this time around. If you try to run, he will kill you. So unless you want to visit dear daddy, you will stay put, young lady. It would be a shame to kill such a beautiful representation."

I glance between the two of them and nod. At least this time around, I don't have to worry about Harley getting harmed. I can deal with me being here. I can figure something out. This lady doesn't sound all too bright, so that only leaves her muscle man. Looking him over again, I try to notice any weaknesses he may have—hurt ankle, weak leg, something. He stands stiff as a board. Giving nothing away. He's going to be a problem, but until I can distract the impersonator, I can't do anything.

Scooting over on the bed, I let out a breath. "So who are you really? You can't be my mother."

"Why can't I be?" She sits back down on the bed, this time on the opposite side of me and at the foot. "I mean, we could be twins, don't you think?"

"I know what I saw. She's dead." I state it plain and simple. My mom is dead. This woman may look like her, but she is not her. "So who are you?"

She giggles. "That's a funny story. Do I want to tell it before boyfriend one calls or after?"

"Boyfriend one?" I ask her, not sure what she means.

She looks back at the man standing in the doorway and he speaks. "Wran Belmont. Son of Taylor Belmont. Younger brother of Josh Belmont. Ex-military. Twenty-three. Currently a resident of the Pleasure House Institution."

I arch a brow at the man's facts. Okay, so they have been doing their homework on me. They know my family and friends. They know way too much for my liking.

"Wait, did you say call?" My head snaps back to the woman.

She nods. "I know my package arrived at Pleasure House, and if he doesn't respond to my messages, then I will soon come up with a more creative way of getting his attention."

"What messages? What do you want with Wran?"

"Oh I don't want anything to do with him. Everything I want has to do with you!" She points a sharp nail in my direction. "Playing with him is just for fun."

"Fun?"

She nods. "You see, I was getting bored of leaving you messages. You kept thinking it was that one girl, and she's boring as a field of sunflowers. So I turned to Wran. I was going to go after Caden, but that would have been way too easy. I want to see Wran squirm."

My eyes widen at her admission. She's the one that left the message on the library door. And I accused Claire. Ugh! Now I have to apologize to Claire. I don't want to do that. Claire might not have written the word on the library study room's door, but she has still done plenty of other things. But I can't fault her for this. It would be wrong.

"You know what?" the lady asks with way too much glee in her voice. "I think I will tell you who I am. It's quite funny. Funny and sad. Funny and heartbreaking. Just funny actually."

I scoot back until my back is resting against the headboard. "Okay. Then who are you?"

"I'm your mom, silly."

I internally groan. Not this again. I know she's not my mom. Just because you wear someone's face doesn't make it so. "I thought we decided against that fact."

"No, I'm being serious. I am your mother. Well, your biological mother. We do have the same eyes, after all. Do you know how rare it is for people to have violet eyes? Less than one percent of the population. We're special like that."

For the first time, I take in her features. All her features. Sure enough, she has the same purple eyes that I thought were unique to me and my mom. That doesn't mean anything. She could be wearing contacts.

"You could be really good at impersonating people."

"I wish. My life would have been so much easier," she exclaims and pets the dog again. It whimpers and wags its tail. "I am your mother. You see, there once were two little girls that belonged to a farmer. They met this boy that belonged to a lawyer. They grew up and he chose one, but not the right one. That made sister one very angry. One day she saw her opening. The boy that had turned into a man was not so happy anymore. The sister he chose was not a match, as he originally thought. So he had an affair with sister one. For a few months he was happy. Apparently nothing keeps him happy long though. He left when sister two gave birth to his son. Nine months after that, a surprise was left on his door and sister two wasn't happy anymore. That surprise was you, my dear. I gave you to him as a memory. But that only angered the man and he had me committed. But at least I made the sister regret him."

I stare at her, eyes wide. What. The. Actual. Fuck? This woman is my mother? I shake my head at her and her story. No. There is no way my mother had a sister and I didn't know. There's no way my father cheated on my mother. He was many things, but I know he loved my mom. He only did those things to me because of her. You don't hurt your child the way he hurt me if you're not grieving a loved one.

This woman is lying.

Plain and simple.

"I can see you are having problems believing my story."

"It's all lies."

"Unfortunately it's not. I loved James Raine and he chose my twin sister. They were not a match. I could have made him happy—truly happy—if he would have given me half the chance. You know, you met me once. James and my sister came to visit me at the hospital, and you were with them. Two, I believe. And my sister was holding you like you were her own. They wanted me to see you. They wanted me to know you were taken care of. I didn't care. James is a good man. The best man. Of course he would take care of his daughter."

Humph! "That man was a monster and crazy. Just. Like. You. If your story is true, then yeah, you two would have been a match made in hell."

"Aw!" She claps her hands together again. "That is the nicest thing you could have said. See? We're already bond-ing."

Bonding? "Is that what you want? To bond?"

Her giggle turns into a cackle. "Don't be silly. I wouldn't go through all this trouble to bond with a daughter I never really wanted. You have something I want."

"No I don't."

"Yes you do, dear."

"What could I possibly have that you would want?"

She looks over at the bulky man. "Care to explain?"

He gives her a curt nod. "Your father made sure to keep offshore accounts. When he was murdered, everything went to you."

I shake my head. "No, he didn't leave me anything."

"Well, technically no, he didn't. But your name was put on the offshore accounts. You are the only one with access to all the money he left behind."

I look between the two of them. "You want his money? Fine, you can have it. I want nothing that belongs to James Raine."

"Yeah, well, it's not just that, dear." Her sugary voice pulls my eyes away from her muscle man. "I thought once my sister was out of the picture, James would see that we belonged together. I thought I would get the life I always deserved. I thought I would finally be the one in the big house with the chauffeured car and nice things. But no, even after she died in that wreck, James still chose someone else. You. You stole the life I should have had."

I look at the muscle man. "Is she for real?" He doesn't respond. I turn back to the woman. "You wanted to get tortured and beaten? That's the life you wanted? You're crazy."

"He did that because he loved you. You were a naughty girl. If you would have behaved, you would have been rewarded."

My brows dip at the words leaving her lips. I shake my head at her. "No! You are truly stupid if you believe any of the words coming out of your mouth. James Raine was a monster." Flashes of my nightmares—memories—skirt through my mind. I can practically feel his hands on my flesh now, and I hold back a barf. "I'm glad he's dead. I only wish I could have ended that bastard myself. You know, when we buried him, I threw a yellow rose on his grave. That's how relieved I was."

I glance away from the woman. That's the only thing I regret—not killing my father myself. And if I had to go back, I wouldn't hesitate to let Wran kill him again. The day he was put in the ground was the happiest day of my life. I was free. I was saved. Nothing is going to change that.

"Tsk. Tsk. Tsk." My so-called mother chastises me. "Little girls shouldn't have such vile mouths. I think it's time you went back to sleep, dear."

From the corner of my eye, I see her muscle take a step forward. I shake my head, but he keeps coming. I roll over on the bed and wince when I land on my shoulder. A rough hand comes down on my ankle, and I put as much force as I can muster into a kick. My foot lands upside his jaw and a pleasing crack sounds around the room. He rubs his jaw for a second before a grin spreads across his face. His teeth are bloody and his eyes are piercing. I gulp at his wicked grin.

My mother moves from the foot of the bed and grabs something off the man. When her hands come back into view, she holds a small handheld gun. She points sit at me and I freeze. I know she said if I run, she would shoot, but I didn't really think she meant it. Not after confessing to wanting money to which only I have access. Kind of defeats the purpose of me being here.

"You," she yells at the man. "Stop playing games and put her out. She can't go very far."

The man looks over his shoulder at her and then back at me. He swipes his hand across his mouth, blood smearing into his beard. "I was going to make it painless, but now I think you need to taste the sweetness of blood too."

I don't get a second chance to run. I see the man's fist coming my way and then nothing.

CHAPTER 26

WRAN

I stare at the man bound to a cross in one of the stainless glass windows and sigh. He's supposed to be the world's savior and yet here we are in this mess. He isn't saving Rox. He isn't saving anyone. I bite down on my cheek and shake my head. Why the fuck—my eyes snap to the lynched man again—did I even come here? It's not like I'm all that holy anyways.

With a groan, I let my head fall into my hands, my hair flopping over. When I get out of here, I'm going to have to get a haircut. I shove it back just as someone clears their throat. My head whirls around to find the nosy nun from earlier. Sans her Bible.

She gestures to the empty spot next to me on the pew. "May I sit?"

I shrug and she does. This is more her domain than mine, so I can't really tell her no. She looks over to the window that held my attention a few moments ago.

"I've never seen you in the chapel before," she says, her eyes moving from the stainless glass scenery and back to me. "You want to talk?"

"I thought you believed I was the devil's spawn," I lash out at her.

"This is a church, Mr. Belmont. You may not respect me, but please respect our God."

I scoff at that. Our God? My God wouldn't let all this shit happen to a girl that doesn't deserve it. He wouldn't let an innocent child go through what Rox went through. And he wouldn't have felt the need to make me suffer along with her.

"I figured you were a nonbeliever," the nun mutters. "But you did choose here to come after you got off the phone with your brother."

Resting my elbow on my knee, I glare at her and throw all my respect out the window. How dare she question my beliefs? Just because I'm not dressing in a potato sack and reading from some book all day every day doesn't mean a thing. "One, I never said I didn't believe. Maybe I believe only to hate him. And two, why the hell are you in my business?"

"I see." She rises. "I'll be going. I'll pray that whatever has you troubled, you'll get answers. Just know that if you don't talk to Him, He won't talk back."

My glower lowers and my muscles loosen up. I look back over to the depiction of Christ. I shake my head. Nope, I'm not talking to some picture. Getting up, I smile at the woman. "Look, I'm sorry. I have nothing against you or this place. And I don't mean to act like an ass all the time, I just—"

"Don't know who you are," she cuts me off.

"What?" My brows scrunch together, not understanding her statement.

"I see it all the time, Wran."

I shake my head at her. "That's not it. I know exactly who I am." I'm Wran fuckin' Belmont.

"If that's the case, why are you here? In my experience, people only come to a chapel when they need help figuring that part out."

I lean against the side of the pew. What the hell? She obviously wants to talk. "My girlfriend is in trouble and I have no clue what to do. Josh wants me to confront the person, and I don't think it's a good idea. I don't want to have more bad deeds on my conscience. I've done so much wrong and one mistake can't be undone. If I listen to Josh, it'll happen again."

"May I ask what you did to develop so much guilt?"

I narrow my eyes at the woman. "You're a nun, right? You can't judge people, correct?"

"Everyone judges everyone, Mr. Belmont. Just like you judged me when you first walked into Pleasure House."

I don't point out that I judged her only after she made the fucking cross sign after seeing me and not knowing my story.

"If it makes it any better, my judgment doesn't truly matter. No one's does; only the big man's does."

I do my best not to roll my eyes at the woman. "I killed someone. He had kidnapped my daughter and was hurting my Rox. I–I wanted him to suffer. And I had planned on him suffering. But . . ."

My words trail off. I don't know exactly how to express how I feel. I killed someone. It was planned. But I never expected that I would ever take someone else's life. And now I can't shake it. If I call the number on that phone, I might do it again. If whoever sent that package truly has my Rox, I know I will flip out. Thomas might think this place is helping me, but it isn't helping that much. And I don't want to be a murderer. I don't want to be Rox's father. Because as much as I loathe the man, the words he spoke to me right before I shot that gun are true: I am exactly like him. And sooner or later, Rox is going to figure that out. I'll be left alone, and everything that matters to me will be gone. I can handle a lot a shit, but I can't handle Rox leaving me. I can't handle never getting to see Harley grow up. And I most certainly can't handle my own daughter knowing I'm a killer.

I don't want to be a murderer.

I want to be the savior.

And that's something I will never be.

Not truly.

The burner phone in my pocket goes off, and I stiffen. Guess whoever sent this thing was tired of waiting on me to make up my mind.

The woman in front of me takes a step back. "I'll let you take care of that."

She turns and walks back up the aisle and the phone rings again. I yank it from my pocket and flip it open. I stare at the number on the screen, letting the device vibrate in my hold another time before pressing the little green answer key.

"Who the fuck is this?" I seethe into the phone.

"Aw, boyfriend number one," a feminine voice says with glee. "You don't disappoint, Wran Belmont."

"Don't make me ask again."

"Ooh, you just sent shivers up my spine. I see why she likes you. She must get her taste in gentlemen from me."

I pull the phone from my ear and look at it. Is this woman flirting with me? After sending pictures of Rox tied up? I glance back over my shoulder at the glass window before shaking my head. Nah, she can't be. I walk out of the church and out of the building. I give the stars one look before sitting down on the cool concrete steps. There's a giggle on the other end of the line and I can't help the frown that creases my face. Her laugh sounds familiar. Too familiar.

"Who are you?" I ask into the phone, a little calmer now. Getting riled up isn't going to help with this woman. I think she likes it.

"You know, Roxanna asked that exact same question," she chirps, and I hate it.

"I don't care who you are. What do you want?"

She giggles again. "You're going to give a woman a complex if you keep talking to her like that. I want what all women want: a nice house with a white picket fence, two point five kids, a loving husband, and a dog. Oh, and financial security. I suppose I have some of that. Although the child is very disappointing, and I could do without the other one point five."

Huh? "I'm afraid I'm not following you. What do you want from me?"

There's a bark on her end and then she shushes something. I can hear a tapping and hushed whispers. There's shuffling in the background and then a door closes. Okay, so she's working with someone. That's good to know.

"I want you to do something for me," she chirps. "Complete the mission and your dear Roxanna will be returned unharmed."

I let out an unintentional laugh. She must think I'm an idiot. That sounds too easy. Too simple. Which means there's more to it than that. And I'm pretty sure she won't be returning Rox. The fact that she went after Rox in the first place instead of coming straight for me is evidence of that. Josh said that Rox mentioned the vehicle had been following her. You don't follow someone for that long if you want something from someone else.

Instead of voicing my disbelief, I say, "You know where I'm at. What makes you think I can do anything for you? I'm under lock and key."

"I know, but what's the point in doing all of this if I can't make it somewhat entertaining? Boyfriend number two wouldn't have been nearly as fun to mess with. Besides, something tells me the infamous Wran Belmont can do anything."

Boyfriend number two? "What the fuck are you rambling about?"

The door behind me opens and Thomas steps out, a bottle of water in one hand and a few pills in the other. I suppose when my nurse saw I wasn't in my room, she went to him. He sits down on the steps beside me and hands me the water. I don't take the phone from my ear. If anything else happens in that background, I want to know.

"Who's there with you?" she asks in an almost sing-song voice.

I ignore her and take the bottle of water from Thomas. I don't make a move to take the pills. If I'm going to have to deal with this lady, I don't want any medication interfering with my thinking. He gestures for me to take the meds. I shake my head. Nope, still not touching that stuff.

Thomas frowns and withdraws his hand. He glances at the phone that I shouldn't have. "You need to come inside. It's after curfew and they can't lock up without you being in."

"I wouldn't do that if I were you," the lady tells me in response to Thomas.

I ignore her again. "Just let me finish this call. It's important."

"Are you talking to Roxanna?" he probes. For all intents and purposes, I haven't disobeyed the rules of Pleasure House. I'm always in my room when I'm supposed to be, and I go to every session. Even all the group ones. For me to blatantly disobey the rules, I would have to be talking to Rox.

And I let him believe that. "Yeah. Got this phone while out. I needed to talk to her. Josh gave me some unsettling news earlier."

"Is she okay? Is Harley all right?" Thomas asks loud enough for the lady to hear. The concern in his voice is real, though, and I can't bring myself to be pissed that he mentioned my daughter's name for this psycho to hear.

I clench my jaw to keep myself levelheaded, praying to the bastard that created us that the woman didn't hear my child's name. The last thing I need is someone else trying to kidnap her again just to get to me. Hell, this woman having Rox is enough. I can somewhat handle that. Barely, but somewhat. I haven't blown my shit yet.

When the lady doesn't ask about Harley, I let out a sigh. "I'll be inside in a second. Please, Thomas."

His shoulders fall but he nods. Getting up, he looks out over the wide expanse of greenery cloaked in nightfall. I follow his gaze to the long road that leads up to this place. For what it's worth, being out here is peaceful. It's beautiful.

A slice of Neverland amongst the chaos of man. Rox would love it out here where the stars are so potent.

"You have five minutes." Thomas cuts into my thoughts. "If you aren't inside in five minutes, the guards will come get you."

I nod and watch as Thomas goes back into the building. When he's out of sight, I turn my attention back to the woman on the phone. He gave me five minutes. That should be plenty of time to get answers out of her.

"That was interesting," she coos.

"Shut the fuck up," I tell her. "What you need from me?"

She laughs, and this time it's not the giggle that makes her sound almost whimsical. It sounds maniacal, and for some reason I can't place where I know that laugh. It's familiar. Both laughs. I've heard them before, but I can't for the life of me put it together. This woman has to be someone I know.

"I can't very well tell you what I need if you want me to shut up."

I roll my eyes at the phone and throw my head back. I hate difficult people. She knows exactly what I meant. At least James fuckin' Raine came out and told us what he wanted. Sure, he played his little game, but he was honest. I cringe; fuck, this woman actually has me seeing some decent part in that man.

I run a hand through my hair and exhale. "I'll do whatever it is you want. Just let Rox go."

"Umm, no. That doesn't work for me. You're going to do what I want anyways."

"Which is?" I ask again.

"My dear James left Roxanna something that I really quite need. You need to get it for me."

"Again, under lock and key. How do you expect me to get anything?"

"Not my problem. I will send you a message with what you need to know. You have until noon tomorrow to get me what I want. And to make sure you follow through, I will be sending you little snippets of motivation. Starting right now."

Before I can ask her about her crazy talk, the phone beeps against my ear. I pull it away and see an envelope icon indicating a message. I tap it and nearly drop the phone at the sight of Rox on a bed with a man holding a gun to her head. She's already unconscious, and there's a bruise across her face. Her nose appears broken and her right eye is swollen. I bite down hard on the inside of my cheek just seeing what they've already done to her. She doesn't deserve this shit. I don't even want to think about what they'll do to her if I don't comply.

My hold on the phone become unbearable. I pull it back to my ear. "If you touch her again—"

"I think it's my time to tell you to shut up, boyfriend number one. I will do with her what I please. I mean, I do have that right, after all. She is my offspring."

I suck in a huge breath and the woman giggles. Her laugh slams into me with a weight I didn't know a laugh was capable of. That's why I know that fucking laugh. Rox has that same exact one. Or at least she did. She doesn't giggle much now like before. But I don't understand. Her mom died. Her whole family is dead now. This woman shouldn't have Rox's giggle and laugh.

"How is this possible? You should be dead."

The woman on the other end of the line lets out a frustrated sigh. "I'm not going into the story again. I'm sure she will tell you if she survives this."

"If you're her mom, why the fuck are you doing this?"

"Simple. Because I want to and I was bored. It's always fun messing with someone else's life."

I stand up from the cool steps, rage bubbling in my veins. "You're fucking psycho."

"I've been told that. I don't care. Just get me what I want."

"You still haven't told me!" I yell into the phone.

"Bye bye for now."

The line goes dead.

I stare at the phone with clenched teeth. What. The. Fuck? How am I supposed to get this psycho something when I'm stuck in this place? My hand tightens around the phone as the blood in my veins picks up speed. This woman really has Rox. She had a gun to Rox's head.

She.

Hurt.

My.

Rox.

Turning on the balls of my feet, I rush back inside and over to the check-in station. The nosy nun, Helena, that's usually here is nowhere to be seen. No problem. She wouldn't have stopped me anyway. I pull the phone up and immediately dial Josh's number. He answers after two rings, but I can't even bring myself to say anything. I sway on my feet for a second, my heart about to jump out of my chest. I take the rolling seat and slump down, bringing the retriever with me.

"Wran?" Josh asks. "What's going on, brother?"

I don't say anything. I can't.

I can't believe this shit is happening again. Maybe I should have stayed away. Maybe coming back for her has put her on every lunatic's radar. The three years I was away, shit like this wasn't happening. She was safe. She was safe without me bulldozing myself into her life. Maybe Josh was right all along. Maybe Rox and I are wrong for each other. We must be if the moment I come home, stuff like this starts happening.

"Wran, you're scaring me." Josh's voice comes out rushed. "Did you call?"

I nod and laugh. "She didn't give me time. She called me."

"She?" Josh asks.

"I thought Rox's mom was dead."

"Hold up; I'm going to put you on speaker so Cade can hear better."

"You're with him?" I mumble.

"Yeah," Cade answers. "And Rox's mother is dead. I was in the crash with them."

"Come get me now."

"No," my brother says. "Just tell us what needs to be done. We'll handle it."

They'll handle it? They let her get fucking taken! "Come get me!"

"I can get our girl back," Cade speaks when my brother refuses to acknowledge my scream. "I will, I promise."

I lean forward in the chair and rest my forehead against the table. My breathing comes out in rushed puffs, and I can't help the fire sliding up my spine. I breathe in once and exhale. I do that over and over again, but it's not working. I lift my head and my sight sets on a ceramic jar with pens and pencils. I grab it and throw it across the hall. It smashes against the wall, a deafening shatter sounding throughout the lobby.

"Wran! Calm the fuck down before you get put back in isolation," Josh scolds me. "How are we supposed to get Rox back if we have no communication with whoever you talked to? Think for once in your life. We need you sane!"

I run my hand through my hair. He doesn't get it. He's never loved someone with his whole heart only to see them hurt when he showed up. He's never been forced to sit on the sidelines like he's making me do now. They can't protect her like I can. They can't save her. I can; that's who I am to her. Her savior. I've been playing that role my entire life and if I'm not the one going after her . . . If Cade goes after her . . .

I'm going to lose her.

"Please, Josh. Come get me. I need to see that she's okay."

"No," he tells me again. "You've been doing amazing. And for the first time in a long time, you had fun. Thomas called. You laughed and hung out with people. You have a few days left and I'm not going to let you leave early for this. Cade and I can handle it."

I shake my head at his words. They can't. They can't. They fucking can't!

"I'll lose her."

"If you believe that, then you don't deserve her," Cade says into the phone. "She loves you. We both know that. And if you don't know you getting better and staying safe is what she would want, then you are an idiot, Belmont."

I know he's right. That is what Rox would want. She would want to deal with this on her own. She would want for none of us to come playing hero. But there's no way I'm telling that rich prick that I agree with him.

"Did she tell you what she wanted?" Josh asks.

"Yeah. Apparently James left something for Rox and she wants it. She said she'll text me with the details."

"When she does, forward the message to me."

"You really aren't coming?"

"If I thought you being here would help, I would. But after Aspen . . ." He trails off. "I lost my father to alcohol. I'm not losing my brother to the turmoil that can be prevented. I'm sorry."

When Josh puts it like that, I can't bring myself to object. I was—am—a complete mess after Aspen. "Fine. I'll send you everything. Just please get her back."

"You have my word, little brother."

CHAPTER 27

CADE

A chime sounds throughout the house and I'm grateful for the distraction. Josh has been on my case since we lost Rox a few days ago. I can't blame him. I promised him I would look out for her, and then the moment I leave her alone, she gets taken. If I would have known leaving her side for a mere second would result in this, I wouldn't have gone on that tour.

Standing, I walk out of the sitting room and head down the hall to the foyer. The doorbell chimes again just as I make it to the door. I don't know who would be visiting at this hour; someone for my father maybe. He tends to have plenty of late-night visitors. At least he's out of the country for the time being and I don't have to hear him and his latest Kingston conquest.

I open the door and freeze at the sight of a shivering Claire. She steps inside the foyer without me inviting her in and rubs her hands up and down her bare arms. She's been blowing up my phone for days, but my mind is nowhere on prom. Quite frankly, I don't even want to go at this point. Claire was simply my backup option when Rox kept rejecting me.

"Claire, I'm a bit—"

"Have you found her?" Claire cuts me off and silences me with her question.

And here I assumed she wanted to bug me about prom. I shake my head in response, still baffled by the fact that she cares enough to brace the cold rain. I know Claire isn't as bad as she makes herself out to be. She's a nice person when she lets people in, but she and Rox have been on the outs for a while. I didn't think she would care one way or the other about Rox getting kidnapped.

"Well, do you know anything?" she asks, her frustrated voice rising an octave.

A brisk wind blows inside, and I shut the door. Claire might not be my favorite person, but I don't want her to get sick. She's already wet. And dripping all over my foyer. "Why do you care all of a sudden?"

Claire narrows her eyes at me and places her hands firmly on her hips. "Just answer the question and I'll be on my way."

"We contacted Wran. He's supposed to be sending some info to Josh. That's all I know. Now, you answer my question. I thought you two have that whole frenemy thing going on."

"One," she pokes me in the chest with a fake nail, "learn the meaning of frenemy if you're going to use it. It's beneath you to use words you don't understand, Cade. Two, I just need to know she's okay. I was the last person she was with, and I don't want to be implicated in her kidnapping. And three, when did you and Wran become such great friends? I thought you two wanted the same girl. I wouldn't trust anything that came from a Belmont. Wran probably kidnapped her himself. He's twisted like that."

"Don't insult me in my own house. I don't trust anything Wran Belmont says. I'm going to get Rox back."

"Fine. Just make sure she's okay."

I give Claire a nod and do my best to hide the smirk forming on my face. I know her too well to believe she came here just so she wouldn't be implicated in a kidnapping. She's a great actress, after all. Her fronts are near perfect. I know she cares about Rox even if she lies to herself and everyone else. Rox was the only real friend she ever had.

Claire turns back toward the door and shivers. She winds her arms around herself again as if bracing for the damp outdoors. With a sigh, I pull off my leather jacket and hand it over to her. She takes it and slides it over her bare arms. I would offer her a ride home, but I don't want to miss any news. I don't want Josh leaving without me if Wran sends notice. I've let Rox down one too many times already. And if I'm going to have a chance at changing her mind about her feelings, I need to be the one that's there. I need to show her that I can be just as heroic as Belmont. He saved her from her father, but I will save her from whatever threat is looming now.

I won't let Belmont manipulate her into going back to him. Not after knowing what her requited kisses are like.

"Thanks," Claire mumbles and opens the door. "Please keep me updated."

"Wait," I call after her.

Claire stops and glances over her shoulder at me.

"You know, you can admit that you miss Roxy."

She scoffs. "That is never going to happen."

Shutting the door behind her, I go back to the sitting room. Josh is staring at his phone as if confused by something. I go over to him and snatch the phone from his hold. He jerks out of his stupor and takes it back before I have a chance to take in what has him at a loss. I honestly don't think I've ever seen the older Belmont look so distraught. He always seems to have his life together.

"Did Wran send you the information?" I ask him.

He nods but says nothing.

"Then why are we still lounging in my living room? Let's go get our girl."

I take a step back, ready to bolt out the door. He has what we need to get Rox and he's just standing there. Josh seizes my arm and I shrug him away. We are squandering time. Anything could be happening to her. Anything . . .

"Stop!" Josh shouts at me. "We can't."

I freeze at his tone. The older Belmont hardly ever loses his cool. Not that I've seen, anyways. "What do you mean?"

Josh shoves his phone in my face, and I take in the info on the screen. My chest contracts as I get why he stopped me.

"That's information to an offshore account in Rox's name. Whoever sent my brother this is trying to set Rox up. A wire transfer that large is going to be reported to the IRS and Rox is going to look like . . . Hell, I don't even know, but this doesn't look good."

I drop down on the sofa. What he's saying is true. That's a crap ton of money being requested, even by my standards. And if the woman has the account information, this can only be a setup. She doesn't really need us. That doesn't make any sense either. No matter who makes the transfer, it's in Rox's name. It'll look like her doing and she'll be incriminated regardless.

"I have an idea. It's crazy and it may backfire—"

"No way." I'm not going to let anything backfire on Rox.

"It's not really your choice, Cade."

I frown at him, knowing he's right. The only reason he's even here at all is because I neglected to take care of Rox like I told him I would. She was alone at school when I knew someone was after her. Josh is being kind by letting me tag along on his search. He's also trying to keep me from doing something "utterly stupid and immature." His words, not mine. I would have found a way to get Rox back. With or without the Belmonts. Besides, I'm sure I have more resources in my front pocket than both brothers have in their entire closet. Well, my father does, but I'm sure his people would be happy to work for me as well.

"What's your idea?" I finally ask him.

"You have a trust fund, right?"

I nod. Of course I have a trust fund. I don't have access to it, but I do have one. "Why do you want to know?"

"How much is in it?"

I narrow my eyes at him and shrug my shoulders. "I don't have access to it. I get control of it on my twenty-first birthday, but it'll most likely be enough to set me for life." Or nothing at all, depending on my father's mood.

"Would you be willing to gamble your future?"

"Yes." I don't have to think about it. I would gamble a thousand times over if that meant getting Rox to safety. Most people would think me crazy for doing such a thing, especially for a girl that doesn't love me the way I love her, but I don't care. It's Rox. I have faith she will come to see what's best for her. She has to.

Josh arches a brow at me. "You sure?"

I give him a pointed stare. "I said yes, didn't I? Don't question it."

Josh crosses his arms and studies me for a moment, then exhale. He runs his hand through his hair. I don't know why he's acting as if this wasn't his idea. He asked me.

"You know, this isn't going to make Rox love you the way she loves my brother." He states it as if I'm unaware of Rox's feelings for Belmont. People's feelings change all the time. Hers have changed.

"I'm well aware. Are you aware that she's not in love with him?" Not like he is with her. I admit, I didn't think Wran Belmont could truly love her until an hour ago on the phone. He was convincing. All too convincing. For the most part, I thought he viewed Rox as a possession. He saved her so now she belongs to him. Not once did I believe his words. They didn't sound genuine, and I've watched for a few years on the sidelines as she stopped believing in much of anything. I supposed that was me seeing what I wanted, but I know for a fact that Rox does not love him that way. Not now. She may believe she does, but she doesn't. She wouldn't have agreed to be with me for two weeks if she did. I should feel bad about that—making her realize there's more to life than him—but I don't. He doesn't deserve her.

"Yeah, I know. But that's something Roxanna must figure out for herself. Hell, for all we know, we might be reading her wrong. She could very well be in love with him. We just don't want her to be. It's better for them both," Josh says and takes a seat on the sofa.

I frown at his words. I don't like the idea that I could be off base with her. And if I am, she's going to do everything in her power to push me away. I can already see it. Rox always does what she thinks is best for everyone else.

Getting back on topic, I take a chair next to Josh. "Now is not the time to discuss this. We have to get our girl back. So what's the plan?"

CHAPTER 28

ROX

3 years ago

I wrap my arms around my protruding stomach, shaking my head as someone walks toward me. All I can make out is their outline dressed in blue. I put my hand up to stop them from coming any farther. They're going to hurt my baby. I must protect my baby. Nausea comes at me again in waves, and I lean over the edge of the bed. Nothing comes up. When did I get in the bed? I drop my hand and shake my head.

"I thought she was unconscious," someone says.

My brows scrunch in confusion. Unconscious? Are they talking about me? I'm not unconscious.

"She was when she was brought in. She just woke up."

I don't recognize either voice.

"We'll have to sedate her to get to the baby."

Sedate? "No! You can't have my baby!" *I shout at them and sway on the bed. I squint, trying to make out the features of the man that just said that, but everything is hazy. Someone rushes over to my side and puts a hand on my arm. I go to shove them away when a cramp in my lower stomach stops me short. My hand grips my stomach and the cramp turns into a blazing pain.* "Ahh!"

"Are you—"

An actual scream leaves my lips as the muscles in my lower back and stomach feel like they're being twisted. I rise from the bed a little but hands lower me back down. I shake my head as tears start to stream down my cheeks. This can't be happening. It's not time. I need more time. Wran isn't here. I'm not ready. I can't do this without him.

"Please calm down, miss." *The person beside me runs her hands up and down my arms.* "Take in deep breaths."

I shake my head and shove the hands away from me. How about she takes in freaking deep breaths?

Another round of pain zips through me. My nails claw into the bed as I cry out and hunch forward. This time something does come up, and it burns.

"It's okay, sweetie. It's going to be okay," *she coos, and I want to tell her to bite her own head off. She's not the one suffering here.*

The person in the blue comes closer. He places a hand on my arm and eases me backward. I shake my head ferociously at him. I don't want to lie down. I want Wran. "She's burning up. Was the epidural administered?"

"We didn't think it would be safe for the baby. Her alcohol level was too high, and she had other narcotics in her system. We didn't want to risk harming the baby."

Black dots blur my vision even more as I twist and bite into the pillow, my tears soaking through the thin fabric. I don't know why anyone would choose this. It hurts. It hurts so so bad. I hate Wran. I absolutely hate him. This is all his fault.

"Miss Raine, we need you to turn back over before you hurt yourself and the baby."

"Leave me alone!" I shout at them.

"Go get her brother." The doctor speaks to the lady. "Maybe he can calm her down."

I swipe my hand across my mouth and take in a deep breath. That's what they told me to do in that stupid yoga class Josh made me go to. I suck in a breath. And then another and another. It doesn't stop the pain. More dots blur my vision, and the last thing I hear is my name being called over and over before the blackness completely encompasses me.

Beep, beep, beep.

My eyes flutter open for a second and white walls flood my vision.

Beep, beep, beep.

I glance over at the heart monitor machine and my brows dip in confusion. I follow the wire of the IV to my forearm.

Beep, beep, beep.

A low humming pulls my attention away from the needle attached to my arm, and I glance over to see Josh sitting in a lumpy green chair holding something wrapped in a yellow blanket. The same yellow blanket he bought when he found out I had more than a stomach bug. He's smiling and his eyes are sparkly. There are also bags under them like he hasn't slept in days. Josh turns a little and I inhale at the sight of dark hair peeking from beneath the yellow blanket.

Beep, beep, beep, beep, beep, beep.

That's my . . . my baby. I had my baby. And Josh is holding her first.

Josh's head swings over to me when the heart monitor starts going haywire. He's holding my baby before me. Josh gets up and gently carries her over to a plastic-looking bed. My eyes track him the entire way. I shake my head when he lays her down. He should be bringing her to me. I want to see her. She's mine. I want to see her. He tucks a loose piece of fabric around her and then comes over to me. He sits on the edge of the bed, his eyes flickering over my face.

"Oh Roxanna. You're awake." He says it as if I've been out for a while.

My eyes flick from his concerned face to the plastic bassinet. I open my mouth to ask for her, but words won't leave my lips. My mouth feels like it's been stuffed with cotton for decades. Josh looks over at my baby and stands. He goes over, retrieves her, and then brings her back. He tilts her a little so I can see her, and I can't help the water that swells in my eyes. She looks just like Wran. She has his chocolate eyes.

I rise on the bed and moisten my lips. I reach out for her and Josh hesitates for a moment. He glances from the pink-cheeked baby to me and back again. When he decides it's okay, he places the baby in my arms. For some reason I expect her to cry or something. Babies are supposed to cry. Instead, her wide eyes just look at me. She does nothing else—not that I'm expecting her to; she's a newborn. The tears I've been holding back spill over as I take in her curly black hair and tiny body.

This is my baby.

This is my daughter.

I glance away from her and to Josh. "Wh-what happened?"

I don't know how I manage to speak through the dryness, but I do. I need to know what happened. I should not have given birth to her. It's too early.

Josh's brows draw together. "What do you mean?"

"How d-did I get h-here?"

Josh's eyes widen for a second, his eyes moving over my face. "You passed out last night. I got a call from a bartender in Arlington. I was informed that there were narcotics and alcohol in your system when we got here."

I shake my head at him. There's no way. I would never . . . "N–no. There must be some mistake. I–I was at home last night. You were there."

"Rox, I left the apartment around seven. Is that the last thing you remember?"

Beep, beep, beep, beep, beep, beep.

My breathing picks up, and I can practically hear my blood pumping in my veins. I glance from him to the baby in my arms. No, he's lying. There must be some other explanation. I don't do drugs. I've never done drugs. He knows this. I wouldn't hurt my baby. I wouldn't. I shake my head at him again.

The door to my hospital room opens and a woman in blue scrubs comes in, with two people trailing behind her. I look from the nurse to a man dressed in a white coat to a woman in a blazer and back again.

Josh stands from the bed. "What's going on?"

The nurse comes over to me and smiles. I don't return her gesture. "Do you have a name for her?"

I stare down into the eyes of my child and nod. "H–Harley."

"I need to check her vitals and then yours. Is that okay?"

I nod. The nurse's brows draw together and she bites down on her lip. She glances from me to the baby.

"Y'all checked the baby's vitals earlier this morning," *Josh speaks just as I'm about to hand Harley over.*

I pull my baby back to my chest, not understanding why they would need to check vitals again.

"Is s-something wrong with my b-baby?" I ask no one in particular.

The nurse shakes her head and peeks over her shoulder at the doctor and the random woman. "No, of course not. You have a healthy baby girl. This is just customary for premature newborns."

My eyes search the woman's face and then I nod again. Josh eases back down beside me as I hand Harley over to the nurse. She smiles but the smile is tight. She turns around and gently hands my baby over to the woman in the blazer. I rise on the bed, looking between the three adults.

Josh jumps to his feet. "What the hell is going on?"

"Mr. Belmont, please lower your voice or we'll have you escorted out." The doctor finally speaks as he takes a step forward, holding a clipboard in his hand. He comes shoulder to shoulder with the nurse, a frown marring his face. "Miss Raine, when you came in last night, there were toxins in your system. By law, we are required to report such things."

Beep, beep, beep, beep, beep, beep.

I shake my head at them. "I don't understand. Give me my baby."

The woman holding my child steps forward and I blink up at her. She shifts Harley, and for the first time I notice a bag in her arms. A big bag. A bag that would hold baby stuff.

"I'm sorry, Miss Raine, but I am taking Harley into state custody."

I lurch forward on the bed. "No!"

"*Like hell!*" *Josh screams.*

"*Mr. Belmont,*" *the doctor chastises again.*

I yank the IV from my arm and get up from the bed. I sway a little and step toward the woman with my baby. The doctor and the nurse act immediately, grabbing hold of me and trying to shove me back down on the bed.

"*Let her go,*" *Josh says, but no one listens to him.*

The woman eases over toward the door with my baby and I shove out of their hold. I stumble forward, my hospital gown falling open. I don't even care that everyone in this room can see my backside. I struggle to get to my feet, and just as I do, a sharp pain rips through my lower stomach. I wince and move my hand down to my stomach. My hand comes back bloody.

"*Shit,*" *I hear Josh hiss, but my attention is solely on the woman in the blazer.*

"*Give me my baby!*" *I cry out.*

The woman has the nerve to look regretful as she moves closer to the door. "*I truly am sorry, Miss Raine.*"

She steps out the door and I go to take another step for her. I stumble forward, but someone catches me. I shove at the person, trying to get out that door, but their hold on me is unrelenting. I glance up to see Josh's boyish face.

"*My baby,*" *I cry, and point to the door.* "*I want my baby.*"

"*Shh.*" *He rubs a hand over my head.* "*Don't worry. We're getting Harley back.*"

"*She took my baby,*" *I cry into his shirt.*

Josh rubs my back and lets me cry.

CHAPTER 29

ROX

Present

My eyes fly open and just as I'm about to let out a scream, someone's hand clamps over my mouth. I wince at the pressure on my face, then turn my head to see Cade kneeling on the floor beside the bed. I glance away from him and around the room. There's no sign of my whacko bio-mother or her hulking bodyguard.

Cade slowly removes his hand from my mouth.

"What's going on?"

"We're getting you out of here," he tells me.

We're? "Wran's here?"

Cade frowns at the mention of Wran's name and shakes his head. "Belmont's still at Pleasure House."

My heart crashes at his confession. Wran isn't here. He isn't coming for me. Just like he didn't come back three years ago. I am an idiot. Of course he isn't coming to get me. He's stuck in Pleasure House—and even if he could, why would he? I basically told him I didn't want to see him until he got help with his problems. And on top of that, I've been messing around with Cade. God, I wouldn't even come back for me.

Cade grabs my chin and gently brings my face over to his. He shakes his head. "Don't, Rox. Don't you even let those thoughts in your pretty little head. I'm the last person that should be telling you this, but Belmont loves you. I hate admitting it, but he does. If he could have been here, he would have. He argued with Josh, but you know Josh."

His thumb caresses my chin as he says this, and even though I know it's true, I can't help thinking that if Wran really, really wanted to be here, he would be. He's Wran Belmont, after all. Nothing keeps him from what he wants. He's a badass and he's not afraid to use it when he needs it. He's not here because he doesn't want to be here.

Biting down on my bottom lip, I stare into Cade's stormy blue eyes. "You came for me."

"I'll always come for you. Now can you stand? We really need to get out of here or the whole plan is going to fall apart."

I nod. "Plan?"

Cade's eyes flick to me and then over to the door. "Just know that this place is about to be swarming with FBI agents in about twenty minutes."

What?

I jerk upright on the bed, wincing as I do so. My hand goes to my shoulder where the hulky douche shot me. I can't believe they called the freaking FBI! How do you even get in touch with the FBI?

Cade's eyes widen as the comforter my bio-mom must have placed over me falls away. "What the hell happened?"

His voice rises and my eyes snap down to the shirt I've been wearing since I was brought here. It's dyed with dried blood that spans almost the entire shirt. I pull the comforter back over me as if that's going to help Cade unsee all the blood that has been lost. I shake my head at his wondering eyes. I don't want to explain this. I don't want him looking at me like I'm some damsel. I'm not. I was shot. I've been through worse. Much, much worse.

Rolling my eyes at his expression, I drop the comforter and get to my feet. There's a tiny sting in my shoulder from the shift, but it's bearable. "Where are we going, and where is Josh?"

Cade literally has to force his eyes away from the blood-soaked shirt. "He's out front with your . . . um, that woman. According to some blueprints Josh obtained, there should be a door off the kitchen that leads out. While he's handling them, I'm getting you out."

I shake my head at him. "It's too risky. You shouldn't have come."

"I shouldn't have come, but it would have been okay for Belmont to come?" His brows dip in confusion.

I bite my lip, not knowing how to explain this to him. He's the golden quarterback with a future ahead of him. He doesn't need to be tied up in something like this. He should be off planning for life after graduation. Selecting a dorm room at whatever prestigious college he plans on playing for. He shouldn't be breaking into a fortress to get me. He shouldn't be planning coups with the FBI. He shouldn't come running for me. I can't be saved. And he can't be my savior.

"You are you, and Wran is Wran. This is something he would do. The consequences aren't as high for him."

"Don't fool yourself into thinking that," is all Cade says as he rounds the bed and goes over to the door.

I follow him, not sure what to think right now. He opens the door a smidge and looks out. When he's sure it's clear, Cade takes my hand and pulls me out of the room and down a long hall. My eyes widen at all the photos lining the walls. They are photos of me, James, and Mom. Shaking it off, I take in the images. I'm a kid in all of them. They are from before I ran away. One photo captures my breath and I stop. Cade backtracks the few steps he took and stands beside me. In the photo, I'm wearing a white and yellow dress, standing at James's side. I'm six in the photo. I know because I remember that day like the day I first met Wran. It's the day I ran. James and I had gone to some event for his company. He dressed me in that dress after cutting me out of my jeans and T-shirt.

Jeans are for messy little boys, not beautiful girls meant for pleasing. How many times do I have to tell you dresses only? Princesses wear dresses.

After forcing the dress on me, we went to the party. I wasn't allowed to talk to any of the other kids that were there. James told me to smile and stay quiet. He was drinking the entire night and when I thought it was okay for me to speak, I spoke to the only kid at my table. He was a boy about my age with curly red hair. I don't remember his name, but he said my dress was pretty. He offered me his chocolate chip cookie, and I spent the rest of the party thinking James didn't notice me talking. And not just talking but speaking to a boy. I was wrong. James was well aware that I had disobeyed him, and he took it out on Ms. Wells. He waited until I felt safe in my room, stomach full of warm milk and Ms. Wells grilled cheese sandwich, before he reared his ugly head. That night I lost my nanny, my friend, and the only life I had known.

Cade tugs my hand and pulls my mind from the past. He turns so that he's facing me. I look away from the photo and up at him. One of his hands travels up my arm until he's cradling my face in his hand.

"That's the ugliest dress I have ever seen," he whispers to me, and I smile.

"Why do you say that?"

"You hate dresses. You have for as long as I've known you."

"I don't hate them; I just don't like to be forced into wearing them."

In all honesty, none of the dresses James bought me were horrendous. They all made me look like some expensive porcelain doll when all I wanted was to play outdoors with other kids. If he hadn't forced me into them, I probably would have loved them. My real mom always gave me pretty ones. She gave me the one in the photo.

Cade's thumb caresses my cheek, and my face heats under his lingering stare. He tilts his head forward just as a furious scream sounds from somewhere in this house. I jump away from him, not even realizing how close we are. There's a loud bang, and I can hear the faint clickety-clack of shoes.

Heels.

She's coming back.

And if she's coming back, so is her bodyguard.

Cade seizes my hand and literally drags me down the hall. "Come on, Rox. We have to go."

I don't hesitate in following orders. There's no way I'm getting caught by that man. She told him to kill me if I tried to run. I don't know how many days have passed since she told him that, but I highly doubt he wouldn't shoot to kill.

As the rapid clicking starts to get closer and louder, my heart starts to speed up. My breath comes out in short pants, and I can't help the meltdown I know is about to occur. They can't find me. I must get out of here. I must get Cade out of here. He has way too much to live for. He has a future that I want him to live. And maybe, just maybe, I can live it through him. It won't happen unless we get out of here.

Cade comes to a complete stop and I collide into his back. I wince at the pain that ricochets up me from the collision. Grabbing my hand, Cade pulls me to a door and rushes us both inside. He closes it as silently as possible. The room falls into complete darkness and it takes a moment for my eyes to adjust. When they do, I peer around the tiny closet and nearly scream when I come face to face with a bride of Chucky doll. Cade's hand comes down hard on my mouth, turning what would have been a scream into a smothered squeak.

Shh, he mouths.

My eyes flick from him to the doll and back to him. When he's certain I'm not going to freak out over the doll, he drops his hand. I'm just about to ask him why we're in a coat closet when I hear the stomping of heavy feet bypass the closet. I push further back into the closet until my back hits the wall. Not long after the stomping, the clickety-clack follows. They stop in front of the door, or at least they sound like it.

"She's not in the room," the man says.

"Ugh! Find her now and kill whoever gets in your way!" my bio-mother yells at the man.

"What about him?"

Him?

Josh?

"Put him in the room, dimwit. That little spawn of mine cares way too much about him; my little dolly will come looking for him. Of that, I'm sure."

I shake my head at that. No. She can't have Josh; she just can't! I need him. Harley needs him. Even Wran needs him.

Turning to me, Cade grabs hold of my shoulders. "Don't start freaking out. He will be okay."

"We have to get him."

"No."

"But—"

"Rox, no!" he yells at me in a whisper. "Josh can handle himself. My job is to get you out. The FBI will be here shortly. That woman is not going to harm him anymore in that time. She wants you, not him."

I shake my head at him. I don't care who is coming. Josh has been a brother to me since I was six. He took care of me. Hell, he even got Wran off for murder somehow. He's the only man that my child knows. I'm not leaving here without him. "Cade, he's my family. I can't just leave him."

"I would never ask you to. I'm asking that you trust in the plan. Josh knew it wouldn't be easy getting you out. So did I."

I let out a sigh. "What's the plan? I need to know before I agree to anything."

"Don't you trust me?"

"Of course!" My voice comes out a little too high. "But this is Josh."

Cade runs his hand over his face and then lets out a frustrated huff. "I'm guessing your father embezzled money and put it in offshore accounts under your name. That's what she wants—the money. Josh has a friend that has a friend that knows how to get in touch with the FBI. We deposited a large sum of money into the account to make it look like embezzlement and then withdrew it."

"A large sum?"

"My trust funds. Josh's friend knows the sum of it."

"Will you get it back?"

"Yeah."

"Okay."

"Okay?" he asks. "You'll let me do this? You'll let me get you out of here?"

I nod but say nothing. If he wants to play hero for twenty minutes, I'll let him. I don't think this plan is going to work, but he does. I'm not going to shatter his hope. Logic is no matter to crazy people like my . . . my egg supplier and sperm donor.

Cade's mouth comes down on mine hard and he pulls me closer to him. His hand intertwines with my hair, and I kiss him back. He pulls back just as fast and grins at me. "Thank you. I will protect you this time. I promise."

This time?

I arch a brow at him, not sure if he can truly see it in this dark closet. When hasn't he been by my side? He's been here since the beginning of this year. Sure, we had a rough start, but Cade has been protecting me, whether he knows it or not, since I finally let him in. He's been my support, my friend, my lifeline. Without him, I probably would have done some extremely stupid stuff.

Cade turns away from me and cracks the door a little. The light shining through the crack allows me to take in his stiff stance. Without looking back at me, he grabs hold of my hand and pushes out of the door. He looks back at me one time, a finger placed against his lips to make sure I stay quiet. I nod, and he rushes us down the hall.

We round a corner and come to a stop in what I guess is supposed to be a formal living room. There are two white sofas facing each other and a marble coffee table with gold legs in the center. The carpet is plush and pink. A fireplace with gray brick tile lines the back wall. The focal point. However, there's no artwork. Just more photos of me. Framed photos of me. All recent. There's one of me from the day I buried James. In a black dress with a smile on my face. There's one of me and Wran. One of me and Cade at the mall. We're laughing in the photo and he's looking at me as if I'm his whole world. He's carrying my bags. And then there are some more artistic ones. One of me sleeping, up close and personal. A shiver runs up my spine at the thought of them that close to me.

I turn around and gasp. Cade turns around and his eyes find what I'm looking at. There are pictures of us. Big pictures on canvases. Of us in not so friendly positions. Of us in the library. Of us the night Cade brought me home from the hospital. Of Cade carrying me out of the woods by the lake.

Shaking my head, I take a step back. And then another one and another one until the backs of my legs bump against something. I look down at the side table housing a candle and a few books. This can't be real. They haven't just been watching me; they've been documenting me. Taking pictures of me that shouldn't exist. This is too much. They have gone way too far.

I rub my hands up and down my arms as I take in all the photos one more time. The hair on my skin rises, and it's like something is crawling just beneath the surface. I start scratching my arms, red welts forming. First my dad kidnaps Harley, and now this. I shake my head.

I can't.

I can't.

"I can't!"

"Rox!" Cade chastises me. "Shh, we don't need to draw attention to us."

The room starts to spin, all the images of my infidelity reeling in my vision. This is it. I laugh out loud. A horrid, dreadful chuckle. This is my punishment. Dad always said that little girls that disobey would be punished to the nth degree. That no punishment would be great enough. This is mine. Wran is never going to forgive me.

Cade steps into my line of vision, blocking out the photos of us in compromising positions. He grabs my hands to stop me from scratching, and when I try to yank them away, he pulls them to his chest.

"Baby, please stop. They're just photos." His voice is soft. Too soft. Like he knows this is my breaking point as well. "Look at me, Roxanna."

I shake my head.

He drops my hands and the next thing I know, he's pulling my head up. His hand is tight against my chin. For some reason I like it, and I don't know why. Freaking awesome! I'm going crazy now too. I guess it's not such a stretch, considering who my parents are. I'm going to be just as crazy as them.

"Rox, there is nothing on these walls that you should be ashamed of."

"Easy for you to say," I mumble while trying to pull my chin away from him. Cade doesn't let me go.

"I see a beautiful, strong, smart girl in those photos. I see a girl that is learning what life is truly about. So someone caught us making out. So what? Everyone does it. There's nothing about these images I'm ashamed of."

"If Wran—" I start.

"Fuck Belmont!" Cade cuts me off. "How many girls has he been with? How many have you been forced to witness over the years? He can't say anything about you kissing someone else."

My hands move up his forearms and I exhale. "I don't want him to hate me."

Cade brings his forehead down to mine. His mouth grazes the top of my right cheek. "He won't ever know. Not if you don't want him to. I promise."

Rising on my toes, I tilt my head back and allow my lips to gently graze his. "We should probably find that exit."

"Yeah." But he doesn't let me go.

I pull away from him and he lets out a sigh. Taking my hand in his again, we turn around and head out of the living room. We make a right turn to backtrack our steps and come to a stop. Standing with her arms across her chest and a grin on her red lips is my bio-mom. She's wearing a lace dress and nude pumps. That's not what she was wearing when her bodyguard knocked me out. My eyes move from her to him. He's still in his all black, but at least now I can see his face. If it wasn't for the fact that he shot me, kidnapped me, and then punched me, I would consider him handsome. He looks like one of those runway models you see on the cover of GQ. All sharp angles and smoldering eyes. Green eyes. His hair is blond like Cade's, but more of a dirty blond. Why someone that looks like him would need to be a hired hand, I will never understand.

Cade steps in front of me, guarding me against the maddening pair. A chuckle leaves the woman's lips and it makes me squirm. Man, I hate her voice.

"Well, well." She takes a step forward and Cade steps back, pushing me with him. "I see you found my gallery."

"Stay where you are!" Cade yells at her.

"Boyfriend number two needs to stay quiet. This is between me and my daughter."

"I'm not your daughter," I say over Cade's shoulder. "Where is Josh?"

"He's safe. For now. But he won't be for long unless you give me my money. All of it. I know it's not in the account. And that bag couldn't hold nearly what I requested. Where's the rest of it, Caden?"

"Let us go," he demands.

She points down the hall. "Your exit is down the hall and to the left. I love a game of cat and mouse. How about I give you a head start? If you can get to the door, you live. If we catch you, you die."

"How would you get your money then?" he questions her.

"Oh, only you would die. I'll still have my darling girl, and let's not forget about boyfriend number one." She giggles, and I bury my face in the back of Cade's shirt.

"Just surrender," I mumble into him. "Leave."

He turns his head to look over his shoulder. "Never again."

"One, two," the woman sings. "I'd be running if I were you."

Cade takes a step back, and then another one. He doesn't drop my hand as he takes off into a sprint. From behind us I can clearly hear the overly sweet chuckling of that woman. Then it stops. Everything stops as a shot ring out, followed by a heart-shattering scream.

CHAPTER 30

ROX

My whole world stops as a bloodcurdling scream leaves Cade and he plummets to the cold stone floor. He brings his knee up to his chest and cradles it. My legs give away and I scurry across the small distance to him. He cries out again.

"Cade!" I gasp. "Ohmygod, ohmygod, ohmygod!"

"Go," he hisses through pants.

I shake my head at him. "No. I will never leave you."

"You two are sickening."

I whirl on my knees to see my whacko bio-mom and the guard. She gestures to us and the giant man takes a step in our direction, a gun in his hand. He raises it and points it to where Cade lies in the fetal position, holding his knee.

"No, please!" I beg, staring up at the man with as much pleading in my gaze as I can muster. He can't do this. Some part of this man must see this as wrong. We've done nothing. Cade has done nothing.

"Please," I beg again.

I watch as the side of his mouth tilts up and his hand flexes around the gun. Ohmygod, he's going to kill us. Moving closer to Cade, I try to shield his body. If anyone must die today, it will be me. I won't let Cade suffer because he cares too much about me.

"Wait!" yells the psycho behind the giant, gun wielding man. "Let's make this interesting."

The woman's puppet lowers the gun, and he sneers at us. That man is way too trigger–happy if the woman telling him to stand down has him in a tizzy. I glance away from Cade for a moment as she steps forward, a Cheshire cat smile on her flawless face. Evil people shouldn't resemble angels.

"I won't let Wilden here kill boyfriend number two if you answer one question," she utters in her overly musical voice.

I roll my eyes at her sugary tone, knowing there is nothing sweet about this woman. She is the devil incarnate, and for the life of me I can't figure out how I came from not one but two lunatics. "Fine."

She grins and whirls around like me answering one stupid question for Cade's life is so monumental. A question for a life? Easiest choice ever. Besides, there is nothing she can ask that she doesn't probably already know. Not if that gallery gave anything away.

The woman bounces on the balls of her feet and claps. I can't help but picture her as one of those overly enthusiastic anime girls that everyone thinks are total ditzes. "All righty then." Her gaze flicks to Cade, who's still cradling his injured knee. "I know you love both of the boys in your life. Hard not to. They are yummy snacks. But which one of them means the most to you? Which one would you choose if they made you?"

I stare at her for a long time. Why in the world would she care about something like that? It has nothing to do with the money or her. My eyes go back to Cade. He's watching me, wincing every few seconds, as if waiting for me to answer as well. Of course he wants to know the answer too. The last two weeks have been nothing if him not trying to convince me that he's the better man. And I suppose he is. But choose? How can I choose between the man that's been here my entire life and the one that makes me feel like I'm not utterly ruined and hopeless? And as much as I hate to admit it, I need them both. I'm not supposed to be that lost little girl anymore. So much has happened to me, and I thought I had moved on from that. But a part of me is always going to be that girl. I don't feel like that with them. I feel powerful. Wanted. Even desired.

"You don't have to," Cade tells me, his eyes searching my face.

"Yes, yes I do, or you die." I can't let Wilden pull that trigger. Not again.

I turn back to the woman and inhale. "I love Cade. He's my best friend. You know that. Your gallery wall tells you that."

She shakes her head. "Nah-uh, child of mine. I want an honest answer. If boyfriend number one was here, Wran, and they were both facing down the barrel, who would you beg to save?"

"That's not what you asked," I snarl at her.

"I also didn't ask who you loved. Any idiot can tell you care for them both. It's almost like James and the two sisters all over again. Except he made the wrong choice."

"You can't ask me that."

"Oh, but I am. And tick tock, Roxanna. Your time is running out. Tick tock, tick tock, tick tock."

"I . . . I . . ." I struggle to answer the question. This is so not a fair question. I glance down at Cade, not sure how to answer this. I love him; I do. This isn't fair. My two weeks aren't up. Who's to say I won't feel stronger later? She can't ask me this. Cade's eyes never leave mine as he waits for a response as well.

"Tick tock," she sings again.

I drop Cade's questioning stare as Wilden raises the gun and points it at Cade again. I shake my head at him, begging. He smiles at my pleas and I gulp. The gleam in his eyes is all too alarming. He wants to do this. He wants to kill.

"Tick tock!"

"Wran!" I blurt and clamp a hand over my mouth. I can't believe I said that. I close my eyes and exhale before turning around to see Cade's face. It's stony and tense. His usual spirited azure eyes are hard and distant, like he himself can't believe I just blurted out Wran's name when his life is on the line. "I'm so, so sorry. I didn't—"

"Doesn't matter. I already knew," he cuts me off. My heart cracks wide open at the jarring pain his words send through me.

The woman giggles at our exchange, and I quite literally snarl at her. I don't get a chance to do or say more as a loud crash sounds, causing everyone to flinch. Glancing over my shoulder, I scrunch my nose at the god-awful smell drifting from down the hall. Just then I remember Cade telling me about their backup. This must be it.

"Well don't just stand there!" my bio-mom shrieks. "Go check it out!"

"Are you sure you can handle her?" Wilden gives me a point-blank look.

I smile up at him as if I'm innocent. The woman stomps her feet at him and shoves him away. He takes that as his cue and jets past me and Cade. Looking from Cade—who is just lying there with hooded eyes now—to the woman, I get to my feet. Her head snaps in my direction. Now that her muscle is gone, she's easy pickings. I haven't seen any type of weapon on her. Not unless overly priced heels count.

She crosses her arms and glares at me as if that's going to scare me. If she knows me so well, she should know that she should have kept her muscle man. She just hurt my friend. She has Josh. Her time is up.

I take a step in her direction as the smell worsens and the atmosphere fogs up. There's a cough from behind me and I look down at Cade. His eyes are closed now. I have to get him out of here. Get that wound looked at.

"I wonder if he's going to stick around now." My eyes shoot from Cade and narrow at her. "You did just say you wouldn't have saved him if boyfriend number one was here."

"You bitch," I hiss at her and take another step in her direction.

"Nuh-uh." She steps back and pulls something from her pocket. She holds a tiny pink gun in her hand and aims it at me. "You didn't really think I wouldn't have protection. I don't like getting these well-manicured nails dirty, but I will if forced. This whole situation could have been—"

A choking cough cuts her off from a rant. I take my opportunity and charge at her. The pistol flies from her hold and lands somewhere on the floor. I shove the lunatic into the wall, and she cackles. I don't know what about this is funny, but I guess when you are this crazy you must find things funny to keep you sane. She grabs hold of my hair and yanks hard. I don't make a sound. She won't get the pleasure of knowing that freaking hurt.

I shove her back again and bring my hand up to her face. Hard. The slap rings out, and the side of her face lands with a crack against the wall. She doesn't move for a moment, but I'm not stupid enough to think that will stop her. When she turns her head back to me, there's a grin on her lips. I don't like it. I take a cautious step away from her crazy, and that makes her grin spread. Before I know it, her heeled foot comes up and I'm lying flat on the floor. A sharp pain zips across my back and I hiss.

She's on me in a second. A hand comes across my face and copper fills my mouth. Her other hand pushes into my shoulder.

"This could have been easy," she says, her fake nails coming for my face again. I ball up and try to shield myself from her claws. "All I wanted was what I deserved, and you gone. Is that too much to ask? I did suffer giving you birth."

The sound of a gunshot stops the woman from hitting me again. She searches over her shoulder for the tyrant, but with the hazy gas, it's nearly impossible to see that far down the hall. I don't wait for her to notice her mistake. Instead, I flip us over and grab her head. Her eyes widen a little too late and I slam her skull down into the stone floor. She laughs, and I gouge at her eyes, repeating the process. The laughing continues. I don't understand it. She should be out cold.

"I'm h–harder than I l–look." She grins, and I flinch at the blood covering her teeth. "You c–can't finish me. You can't hurt M–mommy."

The word mommy has me tightening my hold on her head. I slam it down again into the flooring. Then again and again and again. The woman's eyes roll back, and I inhale at the blood by her head. I yank my hands away from her and look at them. Red paints my fingertips and my eyes widen in horror. I just . . . did I . . . I wrench back and watch the woman. Her chest rises a little and I exhale. I didn't. I should have. This woman is not my mother. Scurrying away from the unconscious form, I get to my feet. I peer down the hall to the room I was once in and then at Cade. He's out cold too. And there is blood pooling around his leg. I start to bend down next to him when I hear footsteps. My body goes still as I wait to see who's coming. I really should probably run, but I don't want to leave Cade here if it's that Wilden guy. Squinting, I notice the outline of three figures, arms raised, dressed in dark colors. I exhale and rush forward.

The man in front lowers his arms and catches hold of me. He tries saying something to me, but I don't hear it. I don't want to hear it. I just want them to get Cade some help. I point to the boy on the floor, and the man in front of me signals for the two behind him to go forward. They do and I turn to watch them. When they start to pick Cade up, I inhale and go into a coughing fit. The man who tried saying something to me pats me on the back, but I bat his hand away and sprint down the hall toward where Josh is located. Cade's safe; he's in good hands. Now I need to see Josh.

Making it to the room, I push open the door. I come to a stop when I see Josh sitting on the floor with his hands and feet bound. He's conscious, but hardly. There's a duffel bag beside him. That must be the money. I go over to him, dropping to my knees, and tap his shoulder. His eyes flutter open and he rolls his head. His hair flops over and I notice a cut above his right eye. I gently touch it and he winces.

"Sorry," I mutter, and start pulling at the knots on his wrists. "Your FBI guys are here."

"Roxanna." He utters my name, and I forget the bindings on his wrists. I stare at him, taking in his shaggy black hair and his boyish face. I could have lost him today. Josh could have died coming for me. The only brother I've truly known. He rushed in here without a solid plan, 'cause let's face it, his plan was crap and ill thought out. But he came. Josh came for me.

I throw my arms around his neck and he lets out a humph. Silent tears roll down my cheeks, and I don't even try to stop them. I don't care if he hates me for the Wran thing. I don't care if he doesn't see me as a sister. He's my family. He's always been my family, and I've been horrible to him since Wran told me what he did. He could have died today, and I never even told him I was sorry for what I said to him. I never told him that I was thankful for all he's done for me. And for Harley.

"I'm so, so sorry." I weep into his shoulder.

I hear his breath catch, but he doesn't say anything to that. A knock on the door has me peeking over my shoulder. The air isn't as foggy in this room as it was in the hall. I can clearly see a tall man with brown eyes standing in the doorway. He assesses the situation before walking in, his eyes falling on the duffel bag beside us. He removes the gas mask covering his face and offers a gentle smile.

"We need to get a move on it and get y'all checked over," he says in a heavy Southern drawl.

"I'm fine," I tell him. My back is only aching a little, and I really don't want to go back to the hospital. Wilden patched me up good enough. I point at Josh. "But he has a cut on his eye. I'm not sure if that's his only injury."

The man nods and stoops down beside us. He pulls out what looks to be a boxcutter and takes Josh's bound hands into one hand. He easily cuts through the rope and then goes to work on the ones around Josh's ankles. When Josh is completely unbound, he shakes out his hands. The man helps him to his feet, but Josh pulls away from him.

"Just a headache." Josh finally says something, and I sigh in relief. "Thanks for coming, Phoenix."

"Phoenix?" I ask the combat-suit-wearing man.

"Ms. Raine." He tilts his head at me and then at the duffel bag. "Grab that. We'll be needing it."

I nod and pick up the bag.

"Now let's get you checked out," he says.

"I told you I was fine."

"It's customary."

Only my dressing needed to be changed when I was observed. Josh had a mild concussion. But we've been sitting in the Arlington Hospital's waiting room for seven hours now, waiting on them to finish doing surgery on Cade's knee. They told us he would be able to leave two hours ago, but they didn't give me any information about his knee. I'm not family, so I'm not privy to it. They didn't seem to care about that when Kingston's quarterback was asking a crap-ton of questions when he brought me in.

The door to the hospital slides open and a familiar blonde prances inside dressed in skintight jeans, heels, and a crop top. I get up from my seat and go over to where Claire stands at the nurse's station.

"Hi," I greet her. Gah, hi sounds so lame.

"Roxy," Claire states in her usual saucy tone. "Good to see you're not dead."

I roll my eyes at her. "I, um, want to apologize to you."

"Don't bother. We both know you're a bitch and won't mean it."

"Actually, I do mean it. I'm sorry for thinking the worst of you. You didn't deserve that."

She looks at me full on, her eyes softening. "And I'm sorry for writing that shit on your locker. I knew it would hurt you. And I'm sorry for all this." She gestures around the hospital. "You don't deserve the hand you've been dealt."

I hold out a hand to her, making a peace offering. "Friends?"

She knocks my hand away. "Never again."

I burst into laughter and then Claire joins me. The nurse shushes us as the buzz to the double doors leading to the back sounds. I turn around, hoping that Cade is finally coming out. When the doors open and I see his face, I exhale. He's in a wheelchair and he's got crutches lying across his legs. From the knee down, his right leg is in a cast. Cade tilts his head back and says something to the nurse. The man wheeling him nods and tows him over in our direction.

"You ready to go?" Claire asks, pushing me aside so she can stand before Cade.

He nods, not sparing me a glance.

"Go?" I ask them. "Go where?"

"I'm taking him home," Claire states.

"No, Josh and I are taking him home," I tell her.

"No, you're not," Cade finally says.

I look down at him. My brows draw together in confusion. "I don't understand."

"It's simple. I called Claire. She's taking me home."

"Why?" My voice comes out sounding too whiny, but I don't care. Why would he call her?

"Because I don't want to sit with you and Belmont's brother for an hour after getting my knee blown out for you, only for you to choose another man! That's why, Rox."

I bite down on my bottom lip as tears well in my eyes. I don't shed them. I simply nod and step away from the wheelchair. I deserve that and so much more from him. I knew Cade would be the one hurt after the two weeks. I knew I would choose Wran, yet I still went along with everything for selfish reasons.

"You're welcome to come back to the house. I just need time," Cade tells me, and wheels himself over toward the doors.

Claire doesn't make a move to go after him. She just stares at me for a long time before giving her attention to the male nurse. He hands her a prescription and some other forms. She grabs a pen from the nurse's station and signs them.

"All righty then. He has physical therapy every Wednesday. Make sure he's there. He'll probably resist at first, so be prepared for that." The nurse says this to neither one of us in particular. "The antibiotic should be given once a day, and the cyclobenzaprine is for muscle spasms he might have. It will also act as a pain reliever. The cyclobenzaprine will make him drowsy, so be cautious when giving it to him. The naproxen is also a pain reliever that works well when combined with the other. He can take those twice a day. I recommend in the morning and the evening. With meals. Got all that?"

Claire nods. "Yeah, I got it taken care of."

The nurse walks off and I turn to see Cade watching both Claire and me. I take a step in his direction, but Claire grabs my arm to stop me. I knock it off. She has no right to keep me from going over to him. I honestly don't even know why she's the person he would call when he has a whole football and baseball team at his call.

"Give him time," Claire whispers at me. "He'll come around."

"How much time?"

"Rox, he just lost his entire future. No school is going to let him play football with his injury. No scholarships. No pro ball. He put it all on the line for you, and in the end you choose the guy that literally hurts you. You're going to have to give him as much time as he needs to come to terms with that decision."

I nod but stay quiet. She's right. For the first time in forever, Claire is right, and I can't even argue against her. I blurted out Wran's name when my best friend needed me to say his. I deserve his ire. Claire walks away and I watch her wheel him out of the hospital. When they turn from my vision, the tears I've been holding back finally fall.

I'm going to make this up to him.

Even if it's the last thing I do.

CHAPTER 31

WRAN

A knock on my door has my eyes snapping over to look at the clock on the wall. Ten o'clock. Check-out time. Going over to the door, I open it to see my nurse standing there with a grin on her face. Everyone here is probably ready for me to leave. I haven't made anyone's job easy, but oh well. I got what I needed out of this little adventure. At least I hope I did. Thomas seems to think I did well. Honestly, I don't feel any different. Not after my freak-out when Josh refused to come get me.

"Good morning, Mr. Belmont. Your brother is here to pick you up," she tells me.

"Thanks." I step out of the room, close the door behind me, and walk down the hall alongside the nurse.

"Dr. Thomas wanted me to ask if you would like the prescription for the dreams?"

I frown down at the petite woman. She, more than anyone, should know that I don't like taking drugs.

"I'll take that as a no, but if you want my opinion, I believe they will do you some good."

I scoff at her analysis. Sure, they probably would help, but that doesn't mean I'm going to start popping drugs just so my mind won't think of things. Next thing I know, I'll be doing something more than sleep pills. That's not happening. Not on my watch. I have Rox, and a daughter that's going to need me lucid. I'm not going to risk it.

"Tell Thomas I appreciate it, but I don't think they are for me. Besides, I haven't dreamed about James since Thomas threw me in isolation. Maybe that should be part of his program."

The nurse giggles and I arch a brow at her. This woman hasn't shown me one emotion other than fear since I walked through the door of Pleasure House and now she's giggling at something I said. Hell, she must be really ready for me to leave this place.

"I don't think that would make this institution all that pleasant," she replies and comes to a stop in front of Josh at the lobby desk.

The crazy nun that's always manning it looks up from her crossword puzzle and hands a clipboard to me. I sign it right away and hand it back over, turning my attention to Josh. There's a bandage above his eye, and I grin at him. Serves him right for leaving me in this place when my girl needed me.

I gesture to the bandage. "I take it you handled everything."

He nods. "Only have to meet with Phoenix to conclude the account. Rox won't be implicated."

That's good. Still wish I had been there, but at least this mess is over. Rox is safe. "All right. Take me to my girl. I think it's time we had a face-to-face talk."

Josh sighs and runs a hand through his hair. "You know, she's still staying at Cade's place."

"Don't care. I'm getting her back today. It won't be easy, bro, and she'll probably make me grovel like a damn fool, but I don't give a fuck. You just keep your nose out of it this time. We're both adults."

Josh arches a brow at my statement, and I ignore it.

Relenting, he says, "Okay."

He turns away from me and heads out the door. I give the crazy nun a smile, a real smile, and follow after my brother. The drive back to Kingston is too quiet. Neither of us talks. There're a million things I want to ask about—mainly how they made that nutcase suffer—but that's probably the least important thing I want to know.

When we pull up outside Cade's fancy house, all the feelings I had about them come rushing back. He can give her a two-story house with pillars and columns and shit. Any car she wants. He can do so much more for her than I ever will. What if she would rather be with one of them? What if she doesn't want to come home with me?

"What are you waiting for?" Josh asks me when I don't make a move to get out of his crappy car.

"What has she been like with him while I was gone? You insinuated at our group session that she was possibly with him."

Josh shakes his head. "I don't even know what to tell you. Pretty sure whatever they were doing is over."

"What do you mean?" I look back up the drive at the house. "I can't picture that fucker ever letting her go after getting his claws in her."

My brother slumps back in his seat, head resting against the headrest. "He lost."

"He was always going to lose," I breathe.

"Yeah, well, he wasn't so sure about that, and neither was I. The entire time she was here, she had this radiance about her. She glowed. She was the happiest I've ever seen her, but when she had to pick, she chose you."

I inhale at that, pondering what that means. She chose me. She chose me even though he makes her happy. Something in my chest constricts. I lean forward and set my elbows on my knees. If I don't make her "glow," then what good am I to her? If Josh hasn't seen her that happy before, maybe she chose wrong. Maybe, and that's a big fucking maybe, she should be with the rich prick.

"You don't think she has ever been happy with me?" I ask Josh.

"I think the timing has never been right."

I glance back at the door and pause when I see that it's open now. Rox is standing at the door with Cade beside her in a wheelchair. He glares in my direction and gone is the preppy pretty boy that had no care in the world. His expression is hard and cold and very unlike the boy that's been hanging around Rox.

Pulling my gaze away from him, I turn to Josh. "What happened to that fucker?"

"There are always casualties in war."

"Meaning?"

"I'll let Rox explain if she's up for it. Now get out of my car. I have a meeting with Phoenix."

For once I do what he says and get out. I'm Wran Belmont. I should have no qualms about confronting my girl. Getting my girl back. Yet my brother's words keep repeating in my head. She's been happy. She's been radiant. She's been glowing. Those are all the things I want her to be. Yet she wasn't with me. I know that's my fault, and I'm man enough to admit that I have messed up in a major way, but hell . . . Rox and I are cut from the same cloth. We are one and the same. We have to be in order for us to work so well. And for some reason, we do. We mesh, and that's never going to change.

I take a step forward and she holds up a hand to halt me mid-step. Cade shifts his glare from me to her. He says something with a scowl on his face and Rox's face dips. She bites down on her lip and says something back to him. My jaw clenches at the look gracing my Rox's face. Whatever that fucker said to her couldn't have been good if she looks like someone just killed her puppy. Hell, her face fell so fast you would think someone told her all the stars had died.

Opening the door, Rox steps outside. She walks over to me and I scan her. Fuck, how is it possible for her to have gotten even more beautiful in a month? She comes to a stop in front of me, biting her lip. Her eyes don't reach mine. Instead they stay solely focused on the ground. I glance down to see just how interesting our shoes are.

"Hi," she says, but she doesn't look up.

"Hey, yourself," I greet her as well. Honestly, this is awkward as hell. Especially since she won't look at me. I glance behind her to see Cade still watching our exchange. His arms are crossed and there's a smirk on his pretty-boy face. Someone should really tell that fucker that smirking doesn't work when you look like a pimply twelve-year-old and have yet to grow facial hair.

"It's really good to see you, Rox. I've missed you," I tell her, trying to break the awkward tension between us.

She shifts on her feet and it takes her a minute before she raises her head and looks at me. Her eyes are glassy with unshed tears, and I don't know what to think about that. I take a step in her direction, attempting to close the distance between us, but she raises a hand to stop me. She moves away from me. I don't expect the ache in my chest at the sight of her moving away from me.

"Why are you here?" she asks me.

"I was released today."

"No, why are you here?" She gestures around us. "At Cade's place?"

"You're here, Roxanna."

A tear slides down her cheek, and I reach out to wipe it away.

"You shouldn't be here. What? You thought I'd come rushing back just because you completed a program?"

Her words cut something deep in me. No, I didn't think she would just forgive me. I hit her for fuck sake. I knew I would have to grovel, but I didn't expect her harsh words. Words that don't sound like Rox.

"I know that program doesn't change me, but I'm trying. I'm here because you are the most important person in my life. You told me to get help, and I did. What has changed?"

She looks over her shoulder at Cade, and her body trembles. My eyes narrow at her posture before turning on that fucker. What the hell did he do to her?

Rox turns back to me. "I love Cade."

She says it so low that I almost miss it. I nod at her admission. I know she loves him. That's fine. She can love whoever she wants. "I can deal with him. I know I can't be the only person in your life, and you are allowed to care about other people. Even one of them."

More tears roll down her face. "Don't be understanding."

"Why?"

She shakes her head at me, blond strands flying every-where.

Taking hold of her hand, I pull her over to me and wrap an arm around her waist. Her head falls against my chest, and her small frame starts really shaking in my hold. It doesn't take me long to realize she's full-on weeping.

"Talk to me," I urge her. "Please, you're killing me."

She lifts her head and looks at me, those gorgeous pur-ple eyes dark and sad. "We can't be together."

My body tenses at her words. Yeah, I knew there was a huge chance she would tell me that, especially after she iced me out, but I still had hope that her love for me would win out over her hurt.

"I don't accept that," I mumble in her hair. "You haven't given me a reason to accept that."

She pulls away from me and wipes at her tears. "Isn't me not wanting this anymore reason enough?"

"Nope. Don't forget I know you. I raised you."

Her head drops and she starts biting her lip again. Her hands go up and she fingers the longer strands of her hair that have grown in the month I've been away.

"I slept with Cade," she mutters.

My hands clench at my sides and my body goes rigid. She's lying. I know for a fact she is. She only bites her lip and plays with her hair when she's nervous and lying. Twelve years have taught me that much. Why she's telling me this, I don't know.

Unclenching my hands, I exhale, and she glances up at me. "I don't care. We'll move past it."

She watches me for a long time, not saying anything. The tears stop flowing, and for the first time since she came out that door, there's a sparkle in her amethyst eyes. She takes a tiny step in my direction. A jarring noise, like a whistle, sounds, and Rox jumps back. The spark in her eyes dies and her head lowers. I stare back at the door. Cade's still there. He has a shit-eating grin on his face as he lowers what seems to be a metal whistle. He doesn't even attempt to hide it. Fucker.

"Just go home, Wran," Rox says. "I'm staying here with Cade."

"Like hell!"

"If you don't leave, I will make it so you never get to see H-Harley again."

I glare down at this version of my lost girl. "You would use our daughter against me for that fucker?"

"I-I—"

"You don't have to say a thing, Roxanna." I cut her off before she can give some lame lie as to why she has to. "I'm out of here, but don't you think for one second that this is over. Because we are far from over, baby."

I don't give her a chance to say anything to that. I turn and walk away from the fancy fucking house and the sad lost girl. That prick has really done a number on my girl, and he's going to pay for that. I don't care what I have to do, she will be coming back to me. We will be a family. And I will be the one laughing in Cade's fucking face.

This isn't over.

Acknowledgments

To my Family: Thank you for all the support. Thank you for taking my calls after crazy long days and letting me vent about a scene I'd written. I couldn't write such emotional, angsty, and downright problematic stories without you putting up with me. I love you all.

To Amy: You are the best. You always go above and beyond for me, especially for this book. I know life has been taxing this year, but you never failed me. You rock!

To the Bloggers and Bookstagrammers: Thank you all for participating and helping me spread the word about this series. I couldn't do it alone. Your passion for books, not just mine, is truly something to behold. You all are freaking fantastic!

To the readers: Thank you, thank you, thank you! I can't possibly thank you enough. I love you all. Nothing would be possible with passionate readers like yourselves. And if you are new to me, thank you for giving me, Rox, and

Wran a chance. I promise it means just as much to them as it does to me.

ALSO BY

T. Marie Alexander

Kingston City Limits Series (Completed)

The Lost and the Scarred (Book 1)
The Saved and the Sorry (Book 2)
The Worthy and the Willful (Book 3)

Better Than Revenge Duet

Nothing Sweeter

Standalones

Revelation

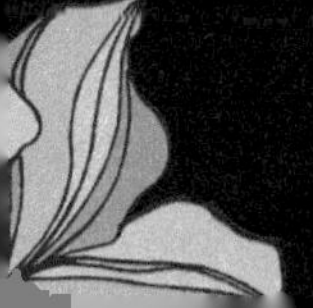

Follow T. Marie at:
Facebook: @authortmariealexander
Tiktok: @authortmariealexander
Instagram: @authortmariealexander

You can even check out my website:
www.tmariealexander.com